I dozed and fell into a half dream. Carleton was in that dream, with his wife beside him. She was laughing at me for my simplicity. They both were. Then Ellen was there. "We did not kill your husband, mistress. T'were not us."

A voice, rather shrill and strident, broke into my dreams. "I have heard of you. You have a fine son, I believe." Suddenly Carleton brought something he had been holding behind his back and placed it over his face. It was a mask, evil, horrible and frightening. I screamed and woke myself up. I had had a bad dream but the memory of it would not be dismissed. It stayed in my mind like a sleeping snake waiting to uncoil and strike. . . .

PHILIPPA CARR

Lament
for a
Lost Lover

FAWCETT CREST • NEW YORK

LAMENT FOR A LOST LOVER

THIS BOOK CONTAINS THE COMPLETE TEXT OF THE
ORIGINAL HARDCOVER EDITION.

Published by Fawcett Crest Books, a unit of CBS Publications,
the Consumer Publishing Division of CBS Inc., by arrangement
with G.P. Putnam's Sons.

ISBN: 0-449-23657-9

Alternate Selection of the Literary Guild
Selection of the Doubleday Book Club

Printed in the United States of America

10 9 8 7 6 5 4 3 2 1

THE FAMILY TREE

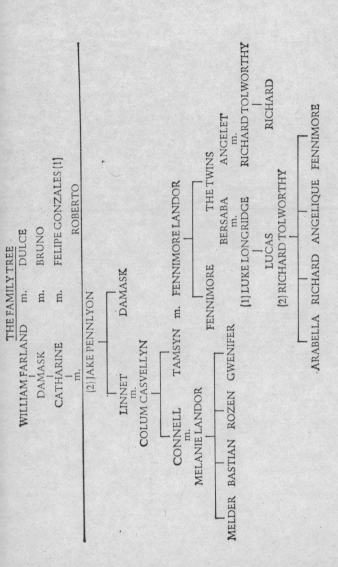

Contents

THE EXILES

THE RESTORATION

Lament
for a
Lost Lover

THE EXILES

Strolling Players at Congrève

Although I did not realize it at the time, the day Harriet Main came into our household was one of the most significant of my life. That Harriet was a woman to be reckoned with, that she had an outstanding and very forceful personality, was obvious from the first, and that she should take on the post of governess—though briefly—was altogether incongruous, for governesses are usually subdued in manner, eager to please and so much aware of the precarious nature of their employment that they suffer acute apprehension, which they cannot help betraying to those who are in a position to take advantage of it.

Of course the times were extraordinary and since the Great Rebellion had brought about such change in England, everything, as people about us constantly said, was topsy-turvy. Here we were, exiles from our native land, living on the hospitality of any foreign friends who would help us; and although it was a comfort to remember that the King of England shared our exile, that did not help us materially.

Being seventeen in this year 1658 and having fled with my parents when I was ten years old, I should be accustomed to the life by this time—and I suppose I was; but vivid memories lingered with me and I liked to talk to my brothers and sister of the old days, which made me appear wise and knowledgeable in their eyes.

There was so much talk of that past and so much speculation as to when it would return that it was constantly in our minds, and as no one ever expressed a doubt that it would, even the little ones were ready to hear the same stories of past splendours in the Old Country over and over again, for in recording them one was not only talking of the past but of the future.

Bersaba Tolworthy, my mother, was a woman of strong character. She was in her late thirties but looked like a much younger woman. She was not exactly beautiful but she had a vitality which attracted people. My father adored her. She represented something to him and so did I, for of all the children I was his favourite.

My mother kept a journal. She told me that her mother, whom I remembered, for we had stayed with her in Cornwall before we fled from England, had presented her and her sister Angelet with journals on their seventeenth birthdays and told them that it was a tradition in the family that the women should keep account of what happened to them and that these were preserved together in a locked box. She hoped I would carry on the custom, and the idea appealed to me. Particularly as there were journals going right back to my great-great-great-grandmother Damask Farland who had lived at the time of Henry VIII.

"These journals cover not only the lives of your ancestors but tell you something about the events which were of importance to our country," said my mother. "They will make you understand why your ancestors acted in the way they did."

Because there was something rather odd about my birth and she thought I should understand the position better if I knew exactly how it happened, she gave me her journals to read when I was sixteen.

She said: "You are like me, Arabella. You have grown up quickly. You know that you have not the same father

13

as Lucas, but share him with the little ones. That could be puzzling and I would not have you think that you did not belong to your father. Read the journals and you will understand how it came about."

So I read of my maternal ancestors, of gentle Dulce, Linnet and Tamsyn, of wild Catharine and my mother Bersaba, and as I progressed I realized why my mother had given me these diaries. It was because she thought there was something of Catharine and herself in me. Had I been like the others and her own sister, my Aunt Angelet who was now dead and whose life was so entwined with that of my mother, she might have hesitated.

So I learned of the stormy love of my mother and father, which they secretly consummated while he was married to Angelet, and of how because I was about to be born, my mother had married Luke Longridge and from that marriage came my half brother, Lucas, who was less than two years my junior. Luke Longridge had been killed at Marston Moor, and Angelet had died when her baby was born, but it was years after when my father and mother found each other. By that time the Royalist cause for which my soldier father had been fighting was lost, Charles I beheaded and Charles II had made a desperate and unsuccessful attempt to gain the throne. He had escaped from England, and my father and mother with Lucas and me joined the exiles in France.

Since then they had had three children, Richard named after my father, so always called Dick to distinguish them; Angelique, named with my mother's twin sister in mind although she had been Angelet, and Fenn—Fennimore—after my mother's father and brother.

That was our family living the strange lives of exiles in a strange land, every day waiting to hear from England that the people were tired of Puritan rule and wanted the King back; when he went, we as staunch Royalists would go with him.

My mother used to say: "A plague on the wars. I could be for the side which would let the other live in peace." I knew from her diary that she had been married to a Roundhead as well as a Cavalier, and that Lucas must remind her sometimes of his father. But the love of

14

her life was my father—and she was his—and I knew she would be on his side whichever that was. When they were together in our company—and that was not often, for he was a great general and must follow the King to be ready if ever it was decided to make a bid for the throne —their feeling for each other was obvious.

I said to Lucas: "When I marry I want my husband to be like our father is with our mother."

Lucas did not answer. He did not know that we had not the same father. He couldn't remember his own, and he was called Lucas Tolworthy, though he had been born Longridge as I suppose I had. He hated the thought of my marrying, and when he was a little boy he used to say *he* was going to marry me. I had bullied him, for I was of a dominating nature. Lucas used to say that the little ones were more afraid of me than of our parents.

I liked everything to be orderly and that meant done the way I wanted it, and because we were left a good deal alone—for when my father went away my mother accompanied him whenever possible—it did mean that I fancied myself as the head of the family. Being the eldest I slipped naturally into the role, for although I was less than two years older than Lucas, there was a big gap between Lucas and me and the little ones.

I could remember so well the time when we had left for France . . . and before it too, for I was after all ten years old. I have vague pictures of Far Flamstead and the terror I sensed in the house when we were waiting for the soldiers to come. I can remember hiding from them and catching the fear of the grown-ups, which I only half believed was real; then I remember a new baby and my Aunt Angelet going to Heaven (as I was told) and how we went traveling interminably it seemed to Trystan Priory, which is clear in my memory even though it was seven years since I left it. My cozy grandmother, my kindly grandfather, my Uncle Fenn . . . it is there forever in my memory. I can remember second cousin Bastian riding over from Castle Paling and always trying to be alone with my mother. Then suddenly it all changed. My father came. I had never seen him before. He was tall and grand and could have been frightening, but he did not frighten me.

My mother has said: "When you're frightened just stand and look right in the face of what frightens you and you will very likely find there is nothing to fear after all."

So I looked this man straight in the face and what my mother said was true, for I discovered that he had a very special love for me and that my existence made him very happy.

I did not want to leave Trystan and my grandparents and they were very sad to see us go, I knew, although they tried to hide it. Then we were at sea on a little boat and that was not very pleasant.

But at last we arrived in France and there were people to meet us. I remember being wrapped in a cloak and riding with someone on a horse through the darkness to Château Congrève . . . and there I had been ever since.

Château Congrève! It sounds rather grand, but in fact it is scarcely worthy of the name of Château. It is more like a large rambling farmhouse than a castle. It does have pepper-pot-shaped towers at the four corners of the building and there is a flat roof and ramparts. The rooms are lofty, the walls thick stone, and it is very cold in winter. There are pasturelands surrounding it, worked by the Lambard family who live in a hutlike dwelling nearby and supply us with our meat, bread, butter, milk and vegetables.

Château Congrève was lent to us by a friend of my father with two women servants and one man to look after us. It was refuge for our family until, as we said, England returned to sanity. We had to be grateful for it, my mother told Lucas and me, for beggars cannot be choosers, and in view of the fact that we were exiles from our country and had only been able to bring with us very few of our worldly possessions, beggars were exactly what we were.

It was not a bad place to grow up in. Lucas and I became very interested in the pigs in their styes, and the goats tethered in the field and the chickens who claimed the courtyards as their territory. The Lambards—father, mother, three stalwart sons and a daughter—were kind to us. They loved the little ones and made much of them.

Our mother stayed at the *château* when her children were born and those had been good times, but I knew that she was constantly uneasy because she was wondering what was happening to our father. He was in the King's entourage, and where that might be none could be sure, for Charles wandered about the continent seeking hospitality where he could find it, always hoping that he would receive the necessary help which would enable him to regain his throne. As one of his greatest generals, our father could not be far away, and as soon as she could safely leave a new baby, our mother left us to be with him.

She had explained it to me who must in turn explain it to the others. "Here in Château Congrève you are safe and well. But your father must be near the King, and who knows where the King will be from one day to another? Arabella, your father needs me, but because you are here I can feel happy to leave the children in your care."

Of course that delighted me. She knew my nature well because it was like her own must have been when she had been my age. I liked to feel that they were dependent on me. I would take care of everything, I promised her, until that happy day when the King regained his throne and we all went back to England.

So we lived our quiet lives in Château Congrève, where we had an English governess who had come to France before the Great Rebellion to teach a French family. She was very glad to come to us, and although we could not pay her well at the time, on that great day, which none of us ever believed would fail to come, she was to have her reward. Miss Black was middle-aged, tall, thin and learned, the daughter of a clergyman who told us often how glad she was to have left England before its shame, and she used to vow that she would never go back until the Monarchy was restored. She suited us well. She taught us reading, writing, arithmetic, Latin and Greek. French we spoke easily. She also taught us deportment, good manners and English country dancing.

My mother was delighted with her and said that we could count ourselves fortunate to be blessed with Miss Black. Lucas and I used to call her the "Blessing" behind her back. We wouldn't have dared do so to her face, for we were extremely in awe of her.

17

There were long, dreamy summer days. Whenever I hear the cackle of a hen or sniff the pungent odour of goats and pigs, I am transported right back to those days at Congrève which I now realize were some of the most peaceful I was ever to know. I used to think sometimes that they would go on forever and ever and we should all grow old waiting for the King to regain his throne.

The sun seemed always to shine and the days never seemed long enough and I was always supreme. I led the games, which were usually playacting because that was what *I* preferred. I was Cleopatra, Boadicea and Queen Elizabeth, nor was I averse to changing my sex if the leading character did not belong to my own. Poor Lucas protested now and then, but as I was always the one who decided what games we should play, I demanded the major role. I can remember Dick and Angie wailing: "Oh, I am tired of being a slave." Poor little things—they were so much younger than Lucas and I were that we considered it was a privilege for them to be allowed to enter our games at all.

The great adventure was evading the earnest Miss Black, who had a trick of turning any adventure into a lesson, which did not please any of us. Our existence was one long attempt to avoid her. Yet we were fond of her in a way; she was part of our lives; she constantly told us that everything that was unpleasant was for our own good, and I could imitate her precise manner in such a way that sent the others nearly hysterical with laughter.

It was really due to Miss Black that I began to fancy myself as an actress. That must have been particularly hard for my family to endure, for I would learn passages from Shakespeare by heart and inflict my histrionics on my long-suffering brothers and sister.

We forgot during the long summer days that we were exiles. We were pirates, courtiers, soldiers, participating in glorious adventures, and I, delighting in my superior years, ordered their lives.

"You should sometimes stand aside and let Lucas take the lead," Miss Black used to say, but I never took her advice.

So the years passed; now and then my parents would

be with us. They were times of rejoicing. But then they would go away, very often out of France, for the King was in Cologne most of the time and where he was they must be.

Sometimes during their brief stays at Congrève I used to listen to their talk over the dinner table when Lucas and I were allowed to join them. There would always be some scheme for taking the King back to his rightful place. The people were tiring of Puritan rule. They were remembering the old days of the Monarchy. "Soon now . . ." they used to say. But still it failed to happen, and life at Château Congrève pursued its pleasant way. We would all be melancholy after our parents had left, then some new game would absorb us and we would forget them and forget about going home. The days of exile were sweet enough, and we were soon back to the old game of outwitting that lovable bogey, Miss Black.

One morning Miss Black did not appear. She was found dead in her bed. She had died during the night of a stroke. And instantly, it was said, so she suffered no pain. She had died as discreetly as she had lived, and she was buried in the cemetery close to the *château,* and every Sunday we would take flowers to her grave. We could not inform her relatives even if she had any, for all we knew was that they were in England and naturally we could do nothing about that.

We talked about her a great deal; we missed her sadly. Not to have to escape from her, not to poke gentle fun at her made a great gap in our lives. Once I caught Lucas crying because she wasn't there anymore, and after accusing him of being a crybaby I found myself weeping with him.

When my parents came to the *château* and heard of the death of Miss Black, they were horrified.

"The little ones must not miss their lessons," said my mother. "We cannot have them growing up ignorant. My dearest Arabella, it is up to you to make sure that this does not happen. You must teach them as Miss Black would have done until we can find another governess, which I fear will not be easy."

I enjoyed my new role, and I was soon flattering myself that the children's education had not suffered as much as my parents feared. I was playing a part and I believed I did it very well.

It was a dark winter's afternoon when the strolling players arrived. The wind had started to howl in from the north, and when it did that it buffeted the walls of the *château* and seemed to creep in through every aperture and discover those which we had not known were there before. In the centre of the hall we had an open fire. The *château* was very primitive and couldn't have changed much since the days when the Normans settled in these parts and built their stone-walled fortresses, of which this was one. I used to imagine the tall blond Vikings clanking into the hall and sitting round this fire telling stories of their wild adventures.

It was afternoon, but so dark because of the snow clouds, when we were startled by a clatter in the courtyard and the sound of horses.

As the *châtelaine* of the castle, very much aware of her position, I summoned Jacques, our only manservant, to discover what was happening.

He looked a little uneasy, and memories far back in my childhood were stirred. I was reminded of the terror at Far Flamstead when we feared the Roundhead soldiers might pay us a call, and if they did we knew they would take our food, our horses, and if our homes were grand they would destroy them because they did not believe that anyone should have fine clothes or luxurious surroundings. They believed that people could only be good if they were uncomfortable.

But then we were not in England, and in any case the war was over and I supposed people now lived peacefully in their homes even in England, and probably enjoyed their comforts in secret if they could manage to.

Jacques came back into the hall. He looked excited.

"It's a party of strolling players," he told me. "They're asking for a night's shelter and they'll do a play for us in return for their supper."

I understood Jacques' excitement and I shared it.

"But of course," I cried. "Tell them they are welcome. Bring them in."

Lucas had come down, and I whispered to him what was happening. "They will play for us!" he whispered. "We shall see a real play!"

There were eight of them—three women and five men. They were heavily wrapped up against the weather, and their leader was a middle-aged man, bearded, thick-set and of medium height.

He took off his hat when he saw me and bowed low. He had laughing eyes which almost disappeared when he smiled.

"A merry good day to you," he said. "Is the master of the house at home . . . or perhaps the mistress?"

"I am the mistress of this house," I replied.

He looked surprised at my youth and accent.

"Then whom have I the honour of addressing?"

"Arabella Tolworthy," I answered. "I am English. My parents are with our King, and I with my brother"—I indicated Lucas—"and other members of the family are staying here until we return to England."

His surprise was over. It was not such an unusual situation.

"My request is that we may have a night's shelter," he explained. "We should have travelled to the nearest town but the weather is too bad. I doubt we should reach it before the snow comes. I and my troupe would pay you well with rich entertainment for a little food and a place to lie down . . . anywhere . . . just shelter from the weather."

"You are welcome," I said. "You must be our guests and we would not ask for payment, but I confess the thought of seeing you play gives us a great deal of pleasure."

He laughed. He had loud, booming laughter.

"Beautiful lady," he cried, "we are going to play before you as we never played before."

The children had heard the arrivals and came running down. Lucas told them that the visitors were players and were going to play for us. Dick leaped high in the air as

21

he always did when excited, and Angie joined him while young Fenn kept asking questions, trying to find out what it was all about.

"Bring everyone in," I cried, taking command of the situation, glowing with pleasure at having been called a beautiful lady and pleased as ever to show my authority as the *châtelaine* of the castle.

They came. They seemed to fill the hall. Their eyes gleamed at the sight of the fire and I bade them to come and warm themselves.

There was a middle-aged woman, who could have been the wife of the leader, and another whom I judged to be in her late twenties . . . and Harriet Main. Three of the men were bordering on middle age and there were two younger ones. One of these appeared to be very handsome, but they were so wrapped up that I saw little of their faces, and when I had brought them to the fire, I said I would go and see what food we could give them.

I went to the kitchen and saw our two maids, Marianne and Jeanne, who had been bequeathed to us with Jacques to look after our needs and were all we had.

When I told them what had happened they were gleeful.

"Players!" cried Marianne, who was older than Jeanne, "Oh, we are in for some fun. How long is it since we had players call here? They usually go only to the big houses and castles."

"The weather has brought them to us," I said. "What can we give them?"

Jeanne and Marianne would put their heads together. I could rest assured, they said, that the eight players would be adequately fed and might they come to see the play?

I readily gave my permission. We would ask the Lambards in to see it too. Our audience would be very small even so.

I went back to the group in the hall. That was the first time I really saw Harriet. She had thrown off her cloak and was stretching her hands out to the fire. Even crouching over the fire as she was I could see that she was tall. Her thick, dark, curling hair released from the hood had sprung out to give a beautiful frame to her pale face. I

22

noticed her eyes immediately. They were dark blue, rather long; mysterious, concealing eyes, I thought them; and their thick, dark eyelashes were immediately noticeable, as were her heavy black brows contrasting with her pale skin. Her lips were richly red, and it was only later that I discovered that she used a lip salve to make them so. Her forehead was higher than is usual and her chin pointed. So many people look alike that you see them once and don't remember them. No one could ever have looked at Harriet Main and forgotten her.

I found I was staring at her; she noticed this and it amused her; I expected she was accustomed to it.

She astonished me by saying: "I'm English." She held out her hand to me. I took it and for a few moments we looked at each other. I felt she was summing me up.

"I have not been long with the troupe," she said, speaking in English. "We are on our way to Paris where we shall play to big audiences . . . but we call at houses on our way and play for our lodging."

"You are welcome," I said. "We have never had a troupe call before. We are all looking forward to seeing you play for us and will do our best to make you comfortable. This is not a grand place as you see. We are exiles and here only until the King returns."

She nodded.

Then she turned to the players and said in rapid French that I was sympathetic and they must all give of their best this night as that was being given to us.

I had decided that as soon as the potage was hot they should eat, so I summoned them to the table and the great steaming dish was brought in. The contents soon disappeared, and while they ate I was able to take stock of our guests, who were all colourful and all spoke in resonant voices, giving great importance to the most trivial comment.

The leader of the troupe and his wife made much of the children, who were overcome with excitement.

Then the snow started to fall, and Monsieur Lamotte, the leader, declared that it was fortunate indeed that they had come upon Castle Plenty in good time. I was apologetic about Castle Plenty, and, as I pointed out to them,

23

we were so unaccustomed to guests that I feared we could not entertain them as we would wish.

How exciting their conversation seemed. They talked of their plays and their parts and the places in which they had played, and it seemed to us all listening that an actor's life must be the most rewarding in the world. Jeanne and Marianne, with Jacques, came and stood in the hall listening to the conversation which seemed to grow more and more sparkling as time progressed. I sent Jacques to tell the Lambards that they must come over to see the play. He came back and told me how excited they were at the prospect.

Harriet was less talkative than the others. I saw her looking around the hall as though judging it—comparing it I suspected with other places in which she had lived. Then I would find her eyes on me, watching me intently.

She was seated next to the very handsome young man —whom they called Jabot. I thought he was a little conceited because he always seemed to demand attention. When Angie went to him and, placing her hands on his knees, looked up in adoration at his face and said: "You *are* pretty," everyone laughed, and Jabot was so delighted that he picked her up and kissed her. Poor little Angie, overcome with shyness, immediately wriggled free and ran out of the hall, but she came back to stand some distance away where she could not take her eyes from Jabot.

"Another admirer for you, my boy," said Madame Lamotte, and everybody laughed.

Fleurette, the other female player, her lips tightening I noticed, said: "We must tell the little one that Jabot is constant to none."

Harriet shrugged her shoulders and replied: "That is a commonplace," then she started to sing in a deep rich voice:

> "Sigh no more ladies,
> Men were deceivers ever . . ."

And everyone laughed.

They sat a long time at the table and I went into consultation with Jeanne and Marianne. We must give them supper after the play, which was to take place at six o'clock, and we must make sure it was a good supper. What could we do?

They were determined to provide the best possible supper in the circumstances. Jacques was already busy bringing their trappings into the hall. The children stared on in wonder at the carpetbags in which tawdry garments could be seen—but they did not seem tawdry to us then. The players had brought an enchantment with them.

They would sleep in the hall, they said. They had rugs and blankets, and they would be off next morning as soon as it was light. They must not be late for their engagement in Paris.

I protested. They must not sleep on the floor. The *château* was not grand by any means, it was little more than a farmhouse, but at least we could put a few rooms at their disposal.

"The warmth of your welcome is like a hot cordial on a cold day," declaimed Monsieur Lamotte.

That was a night to remember. The candles were burning in their sconces and what an entranced audience we were. The tall Lambard sons, usually so vocal, were silent in wonder, and the rest of us shared in their awe. The children sat cross legged on the floor. By good luck there was a dais at the end of the hall and this they had turned into a stage.

The play was *The Merchant of Venice*. Harriet was Portia, and of all the players she was the one from whom I could not take my eyes. She was clad in a gown of blue velvet with something glittering around the waist. Daylight would show the velvet to be rubbed and spotted, the girdle some cheap tinsel stuff, but candlelight hid the imperfections and showed us only that beauty in which we were only too ready to believe.

This was magic. We had never seen real players before. We had dressed up now and then and played our charades, but this seemed to us perfection. Jabot was a handsome Bassanio; Monsieur Lamotte was a wily Shylock

25

with a hump on his back and a pair of scales in his hand. The younger children cried out in horror when he appeared in the court scene, and Angie wept bitterly because she thought he really was going to take his pound of flesh. "Don't let him, don't let him," she sobbed, and I had to console her and tell her to wait and see how Portia was going to make it all come right.

How she declaimed, how she tossed her head. And how incredibly beautiful she was! I shall never forget Harriet as she was that night, and they could never played before a more appreciative audience than we were. We were all so innocent and inexperienced. Jacques watched, his mouth agape, Lucas was in ecstasies and the little ones were amazed that there could be such wonders in the world.

When the last scene had been played and Bassanio united with Portia, the children embraced each other and laughed with joy and I think we all felt a little bemused.

Monsieur Lamotte made a little speech and said he thought we had enjoyed his little play and as for himself he had never played before a more appreciative audience —which I imagine was true.

The maids scurried to the kitchens, and props were cleared away and very soon we were sitting down to a meal such as, I was sure, had rarely been served before in Château Congrève.

There was magic abroad that night. Dick whispered to me that our good fairies had sent the snow so that those wonderful people could come to Congrève. The Lambards stayed to supper and Madame Lambard brought in a great pie full of chicken and pork topped with a gold-brown crust. She had heated it in the oven, she said, and had she known how we were to be honoured, the crust should have been made to represent a stage, for, she confided, she was a dab hand with a bit of pie crust.

Monsieur Lambard brought in a cask of wine. This was an occasion we should never forget.

The children were too excited to be sent to bed and I said that as a special treat they might stay up . . . even Fenn. Though it was true that before long he was fast asleep on Madame Lamotte's lap.

They talked . . . all of them at the same time, for it was clear that they preferred talking to listening, so there were several conversations going on, which annoyed me as I could not bear not to hear *all* that was being said. Monsieur Lamotte, as the head of the group, had taken the place on my right hand and he engaged me in conversation, and he told me of the plays which he had acted in and the towns throughout the country where he had played.

"My ambition is to play before King Louis himself. He is a lover of the theatre, which is what we would expect of one of such talents, eh? What they want is comedy, I believe. We need good comedies. There is enough tragedy in the world, little lady. People want to laugh. Do you agree?"

I was ready to agree with anything he said. I was as bemused as the rest.

Harriet was seated halfway down the table next to Jabot. They were whispering together and she seemed angry. . . . I noticed that Fleurette was watching them. There was some drama going on there. I was very interested in what Monsieur Lamotte was saying but I was intrigued by Harriet. I should have liked to know what she and Jabot were quarrelling about.

I was glad when the conversation became general and they all started talking of their plays and acting little bits for us. Harriet sang—most of them songs we knew from Shakespeare. She sang in French and then in English, and the one I remembered particularly was:

> "What is love? 'tis not hereafter;
> Present mirth hath present laughter;
> What's to come is still unsure:
> In delay there lies no plenty;
> Then come and kiss me, sweet and twenty,
> Youth's a stuff will not endure."

She had a lute, and as she sang she played it so sweetly, and I thought I had never seen anyone as lovely as Harriet was with her black hair falling over her shoulders and her eyes a luminous blue in that pale strange face.

"There should be more singing on stage," said Madame

Lamotte, caressing Fenn's soft blond hair. "The audience likes it."

"You have a beautiful voice," I said, looking straight at Harriet.

She lifted her shoulders. "It passes," she replied.

"What wonderful lives you all must have!" I cried.

They laughed and I could not quite understand the glances which passed between them. I knew later they were a little cynical.

Monsieur Lamotte said: "Aye, it is a grand life . . . I'd take no other. Hard at times. And for the English players now . . . life is a tragedy. What a barbarian this man Cromwell is! There is no longer a theatre in England I understand. God help your poor country, little lady."

"When the King comes back there will be theatres again," I said.

"People will not want the old Globe and the Cockpit," said Harriet. "They will want new playhouses. I wonder if I shall ever see them."

Then the talk became general. More wine was drunk and the candles guttered, and although I did not want the evening to end, my eyelids were pressing down over my eyes as though they refused to stay open any longer. The children were all asleep and Lucas was finding it hard to keep awake.

I told Jeanne that the children should be taken to their beds and they were carried off, Mrs. Lamotte insisting on carrying Fenn.

This broke up the party, and it was Madame Lamotte, back in the hall after kissing Fenn and all the children fondly, a fact of which they were too sleepy to be aware, who announced that they should get some sleep as they had a heavy day's travel ahead of them.

The servants and I took them to the rooms we had assigned to them—the three women were in one and the men in another. I apologized for the scantiness of the accommodation at which Monsieur Lamotte declared, "It is princely, dear lady. Princely."

Then I went to my room, undressed and tried to sleep, which was quite impossible after all the excitement.

I felt depressed because tomorrow they would be gone.

The *château* would settle down to its normal routine which I now knew was intolerably dull. I should never again be able to delight in its simple pleasure as I had before. I wanted to be an actress like Harriet Main. She had stood out among them all.

How magnificently she had played and how I should have loved to see her act the part in English. What we had seen had been a French translation much abridged . . . and losing a great deal in the translation as must be expected. Monsieur Lamotte had said that it was one of the most popular of Shakespeare's plays and that was why it had been translated into French. Perhaps they should have done a French play, but they had played Shakespeare as a compliment to us.

How gracious I thought them! How charming! Of course they were acting all the time, but how pleasant that was!

I went into a reverie then. I imagined that King Charles was restored to his throne, that he opened theatres all over the country and that our parents came to take us back to England. We were at Court and there was a play for the King's entertainment in which I was chosen for the principal role.

It followed on naturally from that wonderful evening.

Then I heard voices. I sat up in bed. They were in the corridor . . . low hissing voices.

I put a wrap about me and, going to the door, opened it slightly.

Two women were standing in the corridor. One of them was Harriet Main, the other Fleurette.

"I'm sick and tired of your jealousy," Harriet was saying.

"Jealousy! I wouldn't be in your shoes. Today's favourite is tomorrow's outcast."

"You should know," retorted Harriet, "having lingered long in the second part."

Fleurette brought up her hand and slapped Harriet's face sharply. I heard the contact distinctly.

"Don't dare lay hands on me," said Harriet, returning the slap.

"You English slut," was the answer, and to my horror she lifted her hand again. I saw Harriet catch her wrist and shake her. Then Fleurette suddenly wrenched herself free and Harriet stepped backwards. Behind her were three stairs. It was a good thing it was not the main staircase. She toppled and fell.

"That'll teach you," hissed Fleurette. "That's what you needed. A fall . . . before Jabot drops you. It'll prepare you for what's to come."

I was half out of the door, ready to go and see if Harriet was hurt, then I realized that I should only cause embarrassment if they knew I had been eavesdropping, so I hung back. I saw Harriet get to her feet and come tottering back up the three stairs.

"Go on," jeered Fleurette. "You're not hurt. You could have a wall fall on you and you'd come bobbing up. I know your kind."

"Then," said Harriet, "you should be careful not to anger me."

Fleurette laughed and went into the room I had prepared for them. A few seconds later Harriet followed.

It was clear that they disliked each other and I fancied the handsome Jabot was the reason. Life might be exciting in the playacting world but it was clearly far from serene.

I was awake early next morning. It had been long before I slept and then only fitfully, and the first thing I thought when I awakened was we must feed the players well before they went out into the cold.

I went to the window. It was no longer snowing and there was only a faint white layer on the ground. I had hoped that they might be snowbound and have to stay with us because the weather was too bad for them to travel. I pictured our having plays every night.

I went to the kitchens. Jacques was already there with Jeanne and Marianne. They were bustling about preparing ale and bread with cold bacon, as determined as I that the actors should be fed well before their departure.

The *château* had taken on a new vitality since they had arrived. Now their voices could be heard—such loud resonant voices; they could not say a good morning without making it sound full of drama, and we were all a little depressed because their stay was coming to its end.

Jeanne set the table in the hall while Marianne hastily stirred up the fire, which had not completely died down during the night.

Monsieur Lamotte descended and came at once to me. He kissed my hand and bowed. "Dear lady, rarely have I spent such a comfortable night."

"I trust you were warm enough."

"The warmth of your welcome wrapped itself around me," he replied, which might have been another way of saying that the bedclothing had not been very adequate, which I could well believe.

Madame Lamotte came down with the three children to whom she was telling the story of one of the plays in the company's repertoire.

She greeted me effusively and declared that all her life she and the entire troupe would remember with pleasure their visit to Château Congrève.

Their eyes widened with delight when they saw the food, and Monsieur Lamotte declared that they would partake of it at once.

"We are ready, loins girded, like the children of Israel. Alas, there is a sadness in our hearts. I know that you would extend your hospitality to us for another night . . . and I will tell you this, dear lady, part of me hoped to see a blizzard blowing that we might be forced to fall once more upon your kindness. Inclination, dear lady. But there is duty. If we do not reach Paris on time, what of those who are waiting to see our play? They are expecting us. We are booked, lady, and every true actor would rather disappoint himself than his public."

I found myself replying in similar vein. I deeply regretted their departure. I should have been happy to entertain them longer, but of course I understood the need for them to move on. They had their work and we were grateful indeed to have been given such a dazzling example of it, which we would never forget. . . .

As they were about to sit at the table Madame Lamotte said: "Where is Harriet?"

I had, of course, noticed her absence, for she was the

31

first one I looked for. Any moment I had been expecting her to descend to the hall.

Madame Lamotte was looking at Fleurette, who shrugged her shoulders.

"I woke her up, just as I was coming down," said Madame Lamotte. "She should be here by now."

I said I would go and tell her that they were ready to eat.

I went to the room which I had assigned to the women and saw Harriet, who was lying on the bed. She looked just as beautiful in the morning as she had in candlelight. Her hair was escaping from a blue ribbon with which she had tied it back and she was in a low-cut bodice and petticoat.

She smiled at me in a way which I felt had some meaning but I was not sure what.

"They are waiting for you," I said.

She shrugged her shoulders. And held up her foot. "I cannot put it to the ground," she said. "I could not walk on it. What am I going to do?"

I went to the bed and gingerly touched the ankle which was faintly swollen. She grimaced as I did so.

"It's sprained," I said.

She nodded.

"But on the other hand you might have broken a bone."

"How do I know?"

"In time you will. Can you stand on it?"

"Yes, but it's agony."

"Madame Lambard has lots of remedies. I could ask her to look at it. But I do know one thing and that is that you should rest it."

"But . . . we have to move on. What is the weather like?"

"Cold but clear. There's no more snow . . . just a thin layer of yesterday's on the ground. Nothing to stop travelling."

"They will have to move on. There's the engagement in Paris." Her lips curved into a smile. "Mistress Tolworthy . . . would you . . . could you possibly be so good as to let me stay here until I can walk properly? Let me explain. I sing and dance on stage . . . as well as act. You see, if I hurt my foot through not taking care now, my career could be ruined."

I felt a sudden wild excitement. The adventure was not over. She was going to stay . . . the member of the troupe who excited me most.

I said quickly: "I should never turn anyone away who needed our help."

She reached out her hand and I went and took it. I held it for a moment, looking into her strange but beautiful face.

"God bless you," she said. "Please let me stay awhile."

"You are welcome," I replied smiling, and my pleasure must have been apparent.

"Now," I said briskly. "I will call Madame Lambard. She may well know what has happened to your foot."

"I slipped on the stairs last night," she said.

Yes, I thought, when you were quarrelling with Fleurette.

"It is most likely to be only a sprain. I will tell Madame Lambard."

I went down to the hall where they were eating quantities of bread and bacon and drinking ale.

I said: "Mistress Main has hurt her ankle. She is unable to walk. I have invited her to stay here until she is able to do so. You need have no fears that we shall not look after her."

There was a deep silence at the table for a few seconds. Fleurette could not hide a secret smile and Jabot kept his eyes on his tankard of ale.

Madame Lamotte rose and said: "I will go and see her."

I went into the kitchen and said to Jeanne and Marianne: "Mistress Harriet Main is going to stay on for a few days until she is fit to rejoin her companions. She has sprained her ankle."

Their faces lit up with pleasure. The kitchen seemed a different place; the fire seemed to glow more brightly.

The adventure was not over then.

The air was sharp and frost glittered on the trees as

we waved them off and stood watching their departure. Slowly, because of the packhorses, they made their way to the road, Monsieur Lamotte leading his troop like a biblical patriarch.

I felt as though I were watching a scene on a stage. This was the end of the first act and I was thankful that it was not the end of the play. Upstairs lay the leading actress, and while she was on stage the drama must continue.

As soon as they had gone I went upstairs. She lay on her bed, the rugs pulled up to her chin, her hair spread around her. She was smiling, almost purring; I thought she had a grace which could only be described as feline.

"So they've gone," she said.

I nodded.

She laughed. "Good luck to them. They'll need it."

"And you?" I asked.

"I have had the good fortune to hurt my ankle here."

"Good fortune. I don't understand."

"Well, it is more comfortable here than on the road. I wonder what shelter they'll find tonight. Not as cozy as this, I'll swear. I've never played before an audience which gave me such rapt attention before."

"Oh, but we know so little here of plays and suchlike."

"That would explain it," she said, and laughed again. "As soon as I saw you," she went on, "I hoped we should be friends."

"I am so pleased. I hope we shall."

"It is so kind of you to let me stay here. I was terrified that I should do my foot some harm. My feet are an important part of my livelihood, you understand."

"But of course. And you will soon recover. I am going to get Madame Lambard to look at your ankle."

"There is no hurry."

"I think there is. She will know if anything is broken and what should be done."

"Wait awhile and talk."

But I was firm. I was going immediately to call Madame Lambard.

Madame Lambard greatly enjoyed doctoring us. She always assumed an air of wisdom, lips pursed, head on one side, trying to talk of things we should not understand. There was a room in the Lambard dwelling which was entirely devoted to the distilling of her herbs . . . a room full of strange odours with a fire and a cauldron perpetually simmering on it and dried herbs hanging from the beams.

When she heard that one of the players had hurt an ankle, had stayed behind and was in need of her help, she was overcome with delight. Of course she would come. She would lose no time. The players had been wonderful. Alas that they could not stay and give them another performance. Even her sons had been excited. They had talked of nothing else since.

She came bustling up to the room in which Harriet lay, exuding a desire to be of service. She prodded the ankle and made Harriet stand on it, at which Harriet cried out in pain.

"Rest it," declared Madame Lambard sagely. "That will heal it. I can find no bones broken. I shall put a poultice on it. My own special one. I'll swear that by tomorrow you will feel the benefit. There is no great swelling. It will be healed, I promise you, very, very soon."

Harriet said she did not know how to thank us all.

"Poor lady," said Madame Lambard. "It must be irksome for you. All your friends gone on . . . and you left here."

Harriet sighed, but I thought I detected a secret smile about her lips that seemed to indicate that she was not as sorry to stay here as might be expected.

"Alkanet," said Madame Lambard mysteriously. "It's in the poultice. It's sometimes known as bugloss. There's viper's bugloss and field bugloss and the healing properties are without doubt. I've known it work wonders."

"I know it well," replied Harriet. "We call it dyer's bugloss. The sap gives a red dye. It's good for colouring the cheeks."

"You . . . use that?" I asked.

"On stage," she replied, her eyes downcast and her mouth, which she did not seem to be able to control, showing some amusement. "We have to look larger than

35

life on stage, otherwise those in the back row would not see us. So we make ourselves as colourful as possible."

"I like hearing about the players," said Madame Lambard. "What a wonderful life you must have."

Again that wry quirk of the lips. I thought for the first time: She is not what she seems.

How we petted her! Marianne and Jeanne made special dishes for her; Jacques enquired for her. Madame Lambard came in three times during the first day to change the poultice; the children peeped in to talk to her and it was difficult to get them away. Lucas clearly adored her, and as for myself I was fascinated too.

She was aware of this. She lay back on her pillows and clearly revelled in her position.

What seemed strange to me was that she did not seem to be very disturbed that the company should have left her behind. I supposed that she was so worldly that she was quite capable of making the journey alone when the time came to join them. I was very innocent.

The next day she told us she still could not put her foot to the ground without suffering great pain, 'although while she rested it, it did not hurt. So we continued to dance attendance on her and treat her like an honoured guest and it did not occur to me that she was deceiving us, but on the third day I made a discovery.

The children had gone riding with Lucas. I had decided at the last minute not to go with them. Jacques was cutting up wood for the Lambards, Marianne and Jeanne were in the kitchen concocting some special dish for Harriet, and I decided that I would go up to see her.

I knocked at the door and there was no answer, so I quietly pushed it open and looked in. The bed was empty though rumpled. Harriet's clothes were there, but where was she?

I could not understand it. A horrible desolation came over me. She had left us. How dull it would all seem now! But how could she have gone without her clothes? No. She was somewhere in the castle. But where? And how could she have left her room when she could only hobble in the utmost pain?

She had tried to walk. She had fallen. She was lying

36

somewhere in pain. I must find her, for she must be here. She could not have left the house without her clothes.

As I stood there, my hand on the door, I heard light, running footsteps and they were coming towards this room.

My heart started to pound as I went into a dark corner of the room and stood very still there, waiting.

Harriet came running in. There was no sign of a hobble. She tripped round the room, pirouetted on her toes, and then looked at herself in the mirror which stood on the table.

She must either have sensed my presence or caught a movement in the mirror, for she spun round as I emerged from the shadows.

I said: "Your ankle is greatly improved."

She opened her eyes very wide. Then she shrugged her shoulders.

"Well," she said, sitting down on the bed and smiling benignly at me, "it was never very bad. Though I did twist it. I slipped on the stairs. Then when it was a little swollen the idea came to me."

I should have been warned that anyone who could show such little concern at being found out in a deception like this must have been in a similar situation before.

She smiled at me appealingly. "I so much wanted to stay," she said.

"You wanted to stay here . . . when . . ."

"It's comfortable," she said. "More so than some dirty old inn, some poor lodging, not enough food because we can't pay for it . . . Oh, much better than that."

"But your Paris engagement . . . ?"

"Our *hopes* of a Paris engagement. Do you think they would want us . . . a poor company of strolling players . . . in Paris!"

"But Monsieur Lamotte said . . ."

"Monsieur Lamotte has his dreams. Don't we all? And it is nice to think they are realities. It's a trick people have . . . particularly actors."

"Are you telling me that you pretended to hurt your ankle so that you could stay here?"

"I did hurt my ankle and when I woke up warm in my bed . . . your bed shall we say . . . I thought: I wish

37

I could stay here . . . for a little while. I wish I could talk to the interesting Arabella and become her friend, and be loved from afar by the adorable Lucas and bask in the admiration of the delectable babies . . ."

"You are talking like Monsieur Lamotte."

"That's because I am . . . or was . . . one of his players."

"Are you going to join them now that you have discovered that you can walk quite painlessly?"

"It depends on you."

"On me!"

"Certainly. If you decide to turn me out I shall join them. I shall tell them that the rest I have had and the ministrations of the good Madame Lambard have cured me. But I shall only do that if you turn me away."

"Are you suggesting that you should *stay* here?"

"I have been thinking of it. Young Master Dick has been telling me of a very estimable lady who has, alas, gone to her Maker—Miss Black whose name is spoken with awe. She was the governess and it is a great misfortune that they are now without that one so necessary to their future."

"I have been teaching them. Lucas has helped me."

"That is admirable, but you have your duties about the *château*. Lucas is too young and has scarcely finished his own schooling. You need a governess. If you decided to engage me I should do my utmost to give satisfaction."

"A governess? But you are an actress."

"I could teach them literature. I am well versed in that. . . . I know the plays of England and France by heart . . . or some of them. I could teach them to sing . . . to dance . . . to carry themselves as they should. I could really supply a finish to their education."

"Do you really mean that you *want* to stay here in this quiet, dull, old *château!*"

"Where there is good fire to warm myself, good food to fill myself and a certain companionship which I feel could become important to me." She was looking at me earnestly, almost pleadingly. "Well, Arabella, I see you are the one who makes decisions here. What is your answer?"

I said: "You know I would never turn anyone away who needed shelter."

Her smile was dazzling. I felt I wanted to keep looking at her as well as listening to her. Of course I wanted her to stay. Of course I was delighted that she had suggested it, even though I was a little shocked that she had pretended so convincingly, but then she was an actress.

When I told the children that Mistress Main was to be their new governess, Dick set the young ones leaping high into the air—their special way of conveying approval. Lucas thought it would be good for the children and that our parents would be pleased. I was not so sure of the latter and made up my mind that I should not tell them that Harriet had been a player before she had decided to become a governess—not until they had seen her for themselves that was, and had, as I was sure they would, succumbed to her charm. Jeanne, Marianne and Jacques were pleased to have a new excitement brought into their lives. Madame Lambard could not but approve of one who had so rapidly shown the efficacy of her cures.

And so Harriet Main settled in our household.

It changed at once as I had known it would. Even her clothes were different. She had dresses of brocade and velvet which looked wonderful in candlelight. The children thought her beautiful, which in a strange, exotic way she certainly was. They could not take their eyes from her. Lucas was ready to be her slave, but I was the one she wanted most to impress.

Sometimes she wore her magnificent hair in curls tied back with ribbons, at others she dressed it high and set glittering ornaments in it. The children thought she must be a princess to possess such jewels and I hadn't the heart to tell them that they were the cheapest paste. On her they looked real; she had the power to transform anything she put on.

We were all becoming quite knowledgeable about plays, and lessons often took the form of dramatic acting. She would assign our parts, taking the best for herself— but how could I blame her for that?—and rehearse us, promising us that when we were ready we would perform for the servants and the Lambards.

We were all caught up in the excitement, particularly myself. She said to me once: "You would have done quite well on the stage, Arabella."

She had completely won our hearts, and I was afraid that one day she would grow tired of us and decide to rejoin the company of players, but she showed little sign of doing that and seemed perfectly content with our way of life. She made a habit of coming to my room after the others were in bed and we would talk—or mostly she talked and I listened.

She would always sit near the mirror and now and then glance at her reflection. I had the impression that she was outside the scene, looking in on the play. Sometimes it seemed to amuse her.

One night she said: "You don't know me, Arabella. You are as young as innocence and I am as old as sin."

I was always a little impatient with these theatrical utterances, largely because I felt they impeded the truth and I was anxious to discover the truth about Harriet.

"What nonsense," I said. "I am seventeen years old. Is that so young?"

"It is not necessarily years which determine our age."

"But it is exactly that."

She shook her head. "You are gloriously young at seventeen . . . whereas I at twenty . . ." she hesitated and looked at me mischievously . . . "two," she added. "Twenty-two . . . yes, not a day more, but since I am in a confessing mood tonight, I will whisper to you that I have been twenty-two for more than a year and sometimes I am merely twenty-one."

"You mean you pretend to be younger than you are!"

"Or older. Whichever seems expedient. I am an adventuress, Arabella. Adventurers are made by fate. If I had what I wanted from life I shouldn't have had to go out and adventure for it, should I? Then I should have been a high-born lady living quite contentedly. Instead of which I am an adventuress."

"High-born ladies have become exiles, don't forget, so perhaps they have to adventure a little in these times."

"It's true. The Roundheads have made schemers of us all. However, I always wanted to be an actress. My father was an actor."

"That explains your talents," I cried.

"A strolling player," she mused. "They used to come through the villages and stay where business was good. It must have been very good in Middle Chartley, for they stayed long enough there for him to seduce my mother, and this seduction resulted in the birth of one destined to become the finest jewel in the world of the theatre. Your own Harriet Main."

The tone of her voice changed. She was a wonderful actress. She could make me see the strolling player, the simple country maiden, who was enchanted by his performance on the stage and equally so it seemed by that other performance under hedges and in the fields of Middle Chartley.

"It was August," said Harriet, "for I am a May baby. Little did that simple country maiden realize what would happen when she dallied in the cornfields with her lover. He was very good looking—she told me afterwards, for I never saw him, nor did she after they left, for she did not know then that besides planting the seeds of love in her heart he had planted something else in another part of her anatomy."

Her conversation grew racy and there were times when I was unsure of what she meant, but I gradually learned; she certainly was educating us all—myself no less than the others.

"In those days," she went on, "there were no women players. Their parts were played by boys, which was trying for strolling players if they wanted women. No wonder they looked to the village maidens to supply their needs. Sometimes they played in big houses . . . castles, mansions. That was what they looked for, but they did very well on the village greens, because there was little that appealed to country folk so much as fairs and strolling players. So he played his romantic roles, Benedict, Romeo, Bassanio . . . He was one of the leading players and took these roles on account of his good looks. It was a busy life for him—always on the move, learning new parts, search-

41

ing for girls and persuading them to supply his needs. Oh, yes, he was very handsome. My mother said he was, and I don't think she ever really regretted what happened.

"The players moved on and he promised to come back for her. She waited but he never came. She used to make up all sorts of reasons why he hadn't come back. She thought he had been killed in a brawl, for he was a great fighter and, she said, would pick a quarrel as easily as wink his eyes if anyone upset him. But she had her own burden to bear. A child whose father had disappeared. It was a great crime in the eyes of those who had never had the inclination or opportunity to be other than virtuous. Of course some girls would have gone to the river—there was one conveniently close to Middle Chartley—but my mother was not the sort for it. She had always had a great zest for life and she believed there was something good round the corner. She refused to see the dark side, and even when it was presented to her, black as soot, she'd swear she could see the light round the corner. 'Only a matter of waiting,' she used to say. 'It'll sort itself out.' But of course my existence soon become apparent, and there were scenes of recrimination in the cottage on the village green. All the maidens who had succeeded in not getting caught, as they called it, were deeply shocked by my mother who had; they had to show their horror to prove their own innocence, you understand. She lived through that time, she told me after, because she was always hoping that he would come back. I was born and my mother worked hard in the fields and I was a constant reproof to her; all the local men thought that being no longer a virgin she was there to provide sport for them. She learned how to fight, for she was determined, as she said, to wait for my father.

"I was five years old when we went to the Hall. Squire Travers Main had taken a fancy to her when he was riding by with the hounds. In fact so taken with her was he that he decided that my mother was more interesting prey than the fox. I was with her at the time and he stopped, so she told me, to compliment her on the pretty child . . . myself. He was a kindly man with a wife who had had a hunting accident a year or so before and was an invalid. He was no lecher. He had the occasional mistress, which was understandable with a wife in such a condition. However, the outcome was that my mother was invited to the Hall to be a housekeeper or serve in some way . . . in the beginning undefined, and she went on condition that I went with her.

"Our fortunes changed that day. My mother was companion and lady's maid to her ladyship, who was also rather taken with her, and from this it was a short step into the Squire's bed. There were no children, and both the Squire and Lady Travers Main took an interest in me.

"I was taught to read and write, at which, my dear Arabella, I made great progress. By this time I had decided I would be a lady. I had had a taste of cottage life. I had been informed by village hobbledehoys that I was a bastard, and I found the taste bitter. It was different at the Hall. The Squire and his lady never called me bastard; indeed their attitude towards me suggested that far from being not on an equal footing with the village children, I was superior to them; and they were determined to make me more so.

"My mother's position grew more and more secure. Lady Travers Main relied on her. So did the Squire. He did not entertain very much, nor was he entertained; I think at that time everyone was becoming anxious, wondering what would happen in this conflict between the King and Parliament. It didn't occur to any of them I was sure that there would be victory for the Roundheads. They all believed the army would soon deal with them.

"The Squire was too old for the army. We were far from any big town and it seemed to take months for news to reach us. We went on in the old way. They were so fond of me that they had a governess to teach me, and my mother was like the *châtelaine* giving orders. Her ladyship didn't seem to mind. She realized that the Squire must have his woman, and she preferred it to be my mother rather than anyone else. It was a comfortable, cozy atmosphere I grew up in."

"You were lucky."

"Now I'm not one to believe all that much in luck. You make your own luck. That's how I see it. My mother kept herself to herself . . . until the Squire came. Then she

43

was faithful to him . . . although she was pestered. She had something. Some women do." She smiled when she said that, implying to me that she was also the owner of this desirable something. "But she never strayed and the Squire was grateful."

"You took your name from him."

"Well, it seemed wise. When I was about fifteen the Squire had a riding accident. My mother nursed him but within a year he was dead. Her ladyship was failing too. My mother was growing a little worried because she could see that life was going to change and the easy days might well be over. For a year or two it went on. The servants resented my mother a little because the Squire was no longer there to give her position in the house some standing, you might say. Who was she? they began to ask each other. Why was she better than they were? They remembered that she had produced me out of wedlock and I heard that word bastard again.

"When her ladyship died, a cousin came to the Hall. He saw how my mother ran the place, and as I told you she had that something which appealed to men. I think he was ready to step not only into the Squire's shoes but into his bed. My mother didn't like him. He was not like the Squire. We had to think quickly. But nothing offered itself then. It was when the cousin cast his eyes on me that my mother said we were leaving.

"So we took with us a fair amount of baggage which we had collected over the years, for the Squire had given us both rather extravagant presents from time to time—as had her ladyship, so we were not penniless. The war was over. Oliver Cromwell was our Lord Protector and all the theatres were closed and there was no more merrymaking to be enjoyed. It was a dreary prospect. We had no idea where we should go. My mother thought we might get a little house somewhere and perhaps live frugally on what we had managed to save.

"A few days after we had left we went to an inn and there was a company of strolling players—no, it was not what you are thinking. My father was *not* among them, but when my mother mentioned him they knew of him. He had done well in the old days, they said. He had played

44

before the Court and the Queen had complimented him. She was particularly fond of playacting. But now the King had lost his head and the Queen was in France and so was her son the new King. There would be no life for actors until the new King was restored to his throne, they said. And they secretly drank to the downfall of the Protector, which was a daring thing to do. But they had plans. They were going to find their way to France because there the theatre flourished. The French loved the theatre. There actors could live like lords. There was no hope for England while the Puritans ruled.

"They stayed a few days, and strangely enough my mother became enamoured of one of the leaders of the troupe, and he of her. As for myself . . ." She smiled secretively. Then she said: "But what am I saying? I am talking too much."

"I find it very interesting."

Her eyes were veiled. "My tongue runs away with me. You understand little of these ways of life."

"But I should learn, should I not? You have become our governess. It is your place to teach us. And, Harriet, there is so much I have to learn."

"That is true," she said, and she fell silent for a while; and shortly afterwards she bade me a rather abrupt good night.

For some days she seemed rather reticent and I guessed she was wondering if she had told me too much.

What excitement there was when we did our little play on the dais in the hall. Our audience were Jeanne, Marianne, Jacques and the Lambard family. It was a short drama in which Harriet played the lead, of course; Lucas was her lover and I was the villainess who sought to poison Harriet. The children had parts, and even young Fenn came in and brought a letter, saying, "This is for you," which for some reason unknown to the rest of us sent him into transports of mirth which he found it impossible to control. When I drank the poison draught which I had prepared for Harriet and fell sinking to the ground, Madame Lambard grew so excited that she cried out: "Though you don't deserve it, Mademoiselle Arabella,

45

what you want is a drop of my agrimony cordial." "She's too far gone for that," said Jeanne. "And it wouldn't be right to save her, her being what she is." Then Fenn burst into tears because he thought I was dead. So the drama threatened to become a farce, and it was fortunate that my sinking to the floor in my death agony was the end.

Afterwards there was the supper just as we had had on the night when the players were with us. Monsieur Lambard brought in some of his wine and Madame Lambard had baked a great pie with a stage worked on it with strips of paste and we were all very merry except Fenn who kept hold of my skirt all the time to reassure himself that I was not dead.

When I think of that night and how simple we all were and how amused Harriet must have been, I look upon it as the end of an era, and I sometimes wished that I could have stayed as I was on that night forever, believing that everyone in the world was good.

Harriet was happy too. She was the centre of our lives at that time. There wasn't one among us who did not realize that the exciting turn our lives had taken was due to her.

The day after the play a rider called at Congrève with letters from my mother. There was one for each of us—even Fenn.

I took mine to my room that I might be alone while I read it.

My dearest daughter,
It is so long since I have seen you. I think of you all constantly. There is change in the air. I have a feeling that before long we are all going to be together. News has come from England that in September Oliver Cromwell died, so he has now been gone for some months. This is going to mean change. Your father thinks that his son can never command the same respect, and that as the people are growing weary of Puritan rule, they may ask the King to return now. If this could come about our lives would be completely changed. This is the best news we have had since the King's father was martyred.
Another piece of news for you, my dear. Lord Evers-

leigh, who is here with us, tells us that his family have taken a house quite near Château Congrève. Your father and I thought it would be pleasant for you to meet them. They will be getting into touch with you and may well ask you to stay with them for a while. Congrève is hardly the place for you to entertain, I know, but if that should be necessary, everyone understands the difficulties in which the times have placed us. If you have an opportunity of visiting them you and Lucas should take it. I know the Lambards, with Marianne, Jeanne and Jacques, would look after the little ones. It would be an opportunity for you to meet people. Your father and I are often worried about your spending day after day in that place. If only things were normal we should be arranging for you to meet young people of your own age and kind. Alas, it is impossible now, but who knows perhaps before long, it will be different. In the meantime it would be interesting for you to meet the Eversleighs. I have been unable to come to see you because so much is going on here. Imagine the excitement after Cromwell's death!

But I hope to see you before long, dear Arabella. In the meantime keep your spirits up. At least you are in safety where you are and you are old enough to remember what it was like in those days at Far Flamstead and even later at Trystan.

Much love to you and always remember that you are ever in my thoughts.

Your devoted mother,
Bersaba Tolworthy.

I could see her as I read the letter. I had admired her fervently from my earliest years. She had always seemed so strong, and my hazy thoughts of those far-off days were dominated by her, the leading spirit who seemed omniscient guiding us all.

Dearest mother! I wondered what she would think of Harriet. She would have understood immediately that she was deceiving us, I was sure. My mother had always been very wise in the ways of the world.

I wrote a letter for the rider to take back when he left the next day.

I hesitated as to what I should say about Harriet and this was an indication of what Harriet's presence in the house had done for me. For I was now thinking of prevaricating, telling half-truths, whereas before I should not have dreamed of withholding anything from my mother.

Yet what if I had told the bald truth! Strolling players came and one of them pretended to hurt her ankle so badly that she could not travel. She stayed behind and is now living here. She teaches us to act and sing and dance.

I believe my mother would have left everything to come and see what it was all about. A strolling player! An actress who had schemed to stay. She would never approve of that.

How could I explain the charm of Harriet, the fascination, the irresistible allure? Yet I must say something. Not to tell her would be quite deceitful; yet to tell her everything that happened would alarm her.

I pondered. It was the first time it had not been completely easy and natural to take up my pen and write to my mother just as I would talk to her if she were here.

At last I wrote:

My dear mother,

I was happy to receive your letter and I shall hope to meet the Eversleighs. I daresay they will call on us first. We are quite able to entertain them here. Marianne and Jeanne are very good and they like people to come here. I expect it is a little dull for them.

Some people called here during the snowy weather because they could not continue with their journey. Of course we gave them shelter and with them was a young woman. She is very talented. She sprained her ankle on our stairs and when the others had to leave, for they had business in Paris, she asked if she could stay behind as she was unable to walk. She is very lively and handsome and comes from England like the rest of us. She saw how we were placed since Miss Black's death and how Lucas and I were trying to teach the children and she offered to stay and help teach them in exchange for bed and board.

I accepted her offer and it has proved very satisfactory. She is very knowledgeable about literature, English and French, and she is teaching them these and how to speak well and sing and dance. The children all adore her. You would laugh to see Fenn. He is very gallant to her and she was very touched when he brought her the first crocus. Angie and Dick rush to sit next to her and you would have been amused had you seen the little play we did a few nights ago. The Lambards and the servants were our audience, and even Fenn had a part. Everyone enjoyed it and the children are still talking of it.

Of course Harriet Main arranged it all and we should never have thought of it—or been able to do it—without her.

I think you will be pleased to hear that she is with us because I know you have been worried since Miss Black died.

It would be wonderful to see you and my father. Oh, if only we could all be together in our own home. It is good to know that you are well and perhaps soon it will come to pass.

Your loving daughter,
Arabella Tolworthy

I read through my letter. I had told no lies. I was sure she would think it was good that we had a kind of governess even if she were not another Miss Black. I couldn't help smiling at the comparison. There could not have been two people less like each other.

I half hoped my mother would return. I should be interested to hear what she thought of Harriet. And at the same time I was afraid that she would . . . which showed, of course, that I had my suspicions about the fascinating creature.

The next day the messenger went off with our letters. I stood at the watch window in one of the towers so that I could see him for as long as possible.

It was a small room, rarely used, with a long narrow slit of a window; the only furniture was an old table and chair. There was a seat cut into the side of the aperture where one could sit while looking out.

As I turned to leave, the door opened and Harriet came in.

"I saw you come up," she said. "I wondered where you were going."

"I was just watching the rider."

"Going away with all those letters you have written to your family."

"We look out for arrivals now and then and hope that they will be our parents. But the messenger with letters is the next best thing."

She nodded.

"He brings and takes," she mused. "And you give them all the news?"

"Some of it."

"You have told them I am here?"

"But of course."

"They'll want me to go."

"Why should they?"

"A player. An actress. They won't like that."

"I didn't tell them that you were an actress."

"What, then?"

"Oh, I said you came with a party of people and because of the snow you had to stay here. You hurt your ankle and stayed on and then said you would help teach the children for a while. That's how it happened, wasn't it?"

"So you didn't tell them everything."

I did not meet her eye. "I told them no lies," I defended myself. "And I said how fond the children are of you and that they are attending to what you teach them and how we did our little play."

She laughed suddenly and threw her arms about me.

"Dear Arabella!" she cried.

I extricated myself with some embarrassment. I felt I was growing a little like her. I was no longer the innocent girl I had been, always so natural with my parents.

"Let's go down," I said. "What a gloomy old place this is. Imagine a man sitting up here all day watching to see who was coming, and giving the alarm if it was an enemy."

"They must have had a lot of enemies to make watching a full-time occupation."

"Oh, he watched for friends as well. And he composed songs while he watched. Watchers were always minstrels so I heard."

"How interesting!" She slipped her arm through mine as we went to the top of the spiral staircase. "Nice of you to

50

give a good account of me," she went on. "You would have aroused their fears had you told them I was an actress who contrived to remain here. Good. Now we shall not have to put a watcher at the tower to look for anxious parents. Sometimes it is helpful to tell a little of the truth when the whole could be disturbing."

We went downstairs.

I was a little uneasy. Yet I knew that I should be very unhappy if my parents had wanted to send her away.

That night she came to my room for another of our talks. I think the letter I had written to my mother made her more sure of me than she had been.

She took her seat near the mirror; her hair hung loose about her shoulders. I thought her very lovely. I could see myself reflected in the mirror. My thick, straight brown hair was also loose, for I had been about to brush it when she knocked at my door. I was very like my mother and I knew she was an attractive woman. I had inherited her vitality, her finely marked brows and deeply set, rather heavy-lidded eyes, but I felt my brown hair and eyes were insipid beside Harriet's vivid colouring, but then, I consoled myself, most people would seem colourless in comparison.

She smiled at me, seeming to read my thoughts. That was disconcerting in Harriet. I often felt she knew what was in my mind.

"Your hair suits you loose like that," she said.

"I was just about to give it a brushing."

"When I disturbed you."

"You know I enjoy talking to you."

"I came to say thank you for your letter to your mother."

"I can't think why you should do that."

"You know very well why I do. I don't want to leave here . . . yet, Arabella."

"You mean you may sometime . . . soon?"

She shook her head. "Well, I suppose *you* wouldn't want to stay here forever."

"We have always believed that someday we should all go back to England. There was a time when we daily expected the summons to come. Then we stopped looking for it, but I suppose it has always been there in our minds."

"You wouldn't want to stay here for the rest of your life."

"What a notion. Of course, I shouldn't."

"If you were in England they would now be looking for a husband for you."

I thought of my mother's letter. Wasn't that just what she had implied?

"I suppose so."

"Lucky little Arabella to be so well cared for."

"You forget I'm caring for myself."

"And you'll be very good at it . . . when you've learned a little more about life. It's been so different for me."

"You told me quite a lot about what had happened to you. Then you stopped. What did you do when you fell in with those strolling players and your mother liked one of them?"

"She liked him so much—I suppose he reminded her of my father—that she married him. I shall never forget the day of her wedding. I have never seen her so happy. Of course she was well content with the Squire and it was a dignified life she had there. Lady of the Manor almost. But she had been brought up very strictly and she had never felt really respectable. Now she did. She had had a strolling player lover who had given her a child; now she had a strolling player husband and that seemed to make it right in her eyes. She always referred to him as Your Father. And I really believe the two merged together in her mind."

"Did she join the company?"

"It wasn't much of a company. By this time theatres were pronounced sinful in England and strolling players, if discovered, would have been thrown into prison. So they planned to go to France. It wouldn't be easy. They were going to do puppet and miming shows . . . because of the language, you see. But they reckoned they could learn that in time. It wasn't a very bright prospect, but what else could they do when there wasn't a hope of playing in England at all? We set out and a few miles off the French coast a terrible storm blew up. Our ship was wrecked; my mother and her new husband were drowned."

"How terrible!"

"At least she had had that supreme happiness. I wonder whether it would have lasted. She had endowed him with all the virtues she had moulded onto my father. It was strange, really. My father disappeared and her husband died before she had time to realize they did not possess them."

"How do you know her husband didn't?"

"I knew by the way he looked at me that he wouldn't be the faithful, loyal creature she had built him up to be."

"So he wanted *you* . . ."

"Of course he wanted me."

"Then why did he marry her?"

"He wanted her as a wife. He wanted to be looked after, cared for by a mature woman. He was eager to take her, and don't forget I went with her."

"What a disgusting creature!"

"Some men are."

"What happened to you then?"

"I was rescued and taken ashore. I was fortunate that the men who rescued me were employed by the local landowner, the Sieur d'Amberville, a gentleman who was, as you have guessed by his title, a power in the district. He lived in a fine old *château* surrounded by vast estates. First I was taken to the cottage in which my rescuers lived and news went round that I had been saved from the sea. Madame d'Amberville came to see me, and realizing that I was somewhat distressed to find myself in such a humble dwelling, to which, I made it clear, I was unaccustomed, she said I should be taken to the *château,* and so I was given a delightful bedroom there and Madame's servants waited on me. When she questioned me, she had the impression that I was the daughter of Squire Travers Main."

"Which you gave her no doubt."

"No doubt. And she realized then why I found a workman's cottage distasteful. I stayed on until I recovered, and then I told her I must go, and when she asked where, I said that I did not know, but I could not encroach any longer on this hospitality of the d'Ambervilles. She was loth to let me go and an idea came to me. There were several young d'Ambervilles . . . six of them from the ages of five to sixteen, and that was not counting the eldest daughter of eighteen and her brother Gervais, the eldest son, who was twenty years of age. So I suggested to her that I should become . . ."

"The governess?" I said.

"How did you guess?"

"Sometimes history has a habit of repeating itself."

"That is often because what happens once makes us resourceful in similar circumstances. It's what is called experience."

"I always knew you were very experienced."

"Indeed I am. I became the governess. I taught the children as I now teach your sister and brothers. I was a great success and I enjoyed my stay with the d'Ambervilles."

"Why did you leave?"

"Because the eldest son, Gervais, fell in love with me. He was very handsome . . . very romantic."

"Did you fall in love with him?"

"I was in love with the title he would have and the lands and the riches. I am being very frank tonight, Arabella. I think I am shocking you a little. Mind you, I liked other things about him besides the worldly possessions which would one day be his. He was gallant, adoring, everything that a lover should be. Hot-blooded and passionate. He had never met anyone like me. He wanted to marry me."

"Why didn't you marry him?"

"We were discovered." She smiled as though amused by the memory. "In *flagrante delicto* . . . almost. By his mother. She was horrified. 'Gervais!' she said. 'I can't believe my eyes.' Then she went out, banging the door loudly. Poor Gervais. He was horrified. It was very embarrassing for a well-brought-up boy."

"And what about you?"

"I knew it had to come to a head, and I thought it was better to have the family's consent to the marriage before it took place. The French are more conventional than we are at home. They might well have cut him off with a few sous. After all there were two other sons and Jean Christophe was rising twelve—one of my most appreciative pupils—so Gervais was not indispensable. Now they knew how far it had gone. From what Maman had seen during her brief glimpse into our love nest it was possible that I might already be enceinte and a little d'Amberville on the way."

"You really mean . . ."

"My dear, sweet, innocent Arabella, isn't that what life is all about? If it were not so, how should we replenish the earth?"

"So you really were in love with Gervais . . . so much that you forgot . . ."

"I forgot nothing. It would have been an excellent match. Gervais appealed to me; he was madly in love with me; and his family had shown me kindness."

"It did not seem the way to repay it."

"What, by making their son happy? He had never known anything like it. He told me so many times."

I tried to understand her. It was difficult. I did know that, if she had been here, my mother would have decided that she must go at once.

"Should you not have waited until after the marriage?"

"Then, my dear Arabella, it would never have happened at all. Think what poor Gervais would have missed."

"I think you are rather flippant about what should be treated seriously."

"Innocent Arabella, flippancy is often used to disguise seriousness. Of course I was serious. I was summoned to the salon. There I was confronted by the elders of the family. There was a long speech about my betraying their trust in me and how they could no longer allow me to stay under their roof."

"What about Gervais?"

"Dear Gervais. He was such an innocent really. He said we would go away together. We would snap our fingers at the family. We would marry and live happily ever after. I told him that he was wonderful and I would love him until I died, but being of a practical nature I was asking myself what we would live on. I knew what hard times could be; Gervais had no notion. I could live by my wits perhaps, but poor Gervais was not endowed very lavishly with those useful assets; and I was appalled by the thought of poverty. When they said he should be cut off, I knew they meant it. After all, when you have several sons, you can dispense with one who displeases you—even if he is the eldest. Besides it serves as a good lesson to the others. Madame d'Amberville had been horrified by what she had witnessed. She implied that she would never be able to look at me again without remembering it.

"While all this was happening a party of strolling players came to the village. The d'Ambervilles, being of a rather religious turn of mind, had not encouraged players. However, they could not prevent their playing in the village. I went to see tham and there I met Jabot. You remember Jabot?"

"Of course I do. I have a confession to make. I heard you and Fleurette quarrelling about him on the stairs."

"So you were eavesdropping." She laughed aloud. "Now, my not so virtuous Arabella, how can you criticize me? So you overheard us, did you?"

"Yes, and I saw you trip down the stairs."

"Good! That added authenticity to my hurt ankle."

"So you went from Gervais to Jabot?"

"What a difference. Jabot was a man of the world. He was quite an actor. A pity he did not have a better chance to show his talents. Perhaps he will one day. He is ambitious, but women will be his downfall. He can't resist them and he likes them in variety."

"He liked you *and* Fleurette."

"Among a thousand others. But he had talents . . . Jules Jabot . . . in many directions. He noticed me at once. I talked to him. I pleaded that I was the maiden in distress. The son of the house had forced his attentions on me and because of this I was asked to leave. Jules Jabot has a romantic streak. He said afterwards I played my part well. I told him, of course, that I came of an acting family and he took me along to Monsieur Lamotte. As a result, when they left I went with them and stayed with them for several months and then one day we came to Château Congrève and you know the rest."

"Why did you want to leave them for us?"

"It was a hard life. I would rather be a successful actress than anything, but not a strolling player. There is little comfort in it. Only those with a love of the profession could do it. Jabot lived on the adulation of the audience. You should have seen him after one of his heroic performances. He strutted like a cockerel. Women will be his downfall. There was always trouble for Jabot about women. He had that something which is irresistible."

"What! Another of them!"

"You mean that I have it?"

"And your mother . . ."

"You may smile, dear Arabella, but one day you may know what I mean. Let me tell you this. You are completely ignorant of the world in which I have lived. It may be that you will always remain so. So many people do."

"Not now we have met," I said soberly.

She looked at me steadily. "I see," she said, "that I have brought some change in your life."

"What happened with you and Jabot? Was he your lover?" She did not answer but looked at me rather mockingly. "So soon after Gervais?"

"It was piquant, because he was so different. I loved Gervais. He was so tender, reverent. Jabot was quite different, certain of success and arrogant. And one an aristocrat and the other a poor strolling player. You see what I mean?"

"There would be a word to describe your conduct, Harriet."

"Come, tell me what it is."

"Wanton."

She laughed aloud this time. "And are you deeply shocked? Would you send me away for fear I contaminate you and your little sister and perhaps your brother?"

"You will leave Lucas alone," I said fiercely.

"He is young enough to be safe. You do not understand me. I am a normal woman, Arabella. I love and I give

57

and I take. That is all. You have seen Jabot. Surely you understand?"

"He was Fleurette's lover too."

"That was before I came. She never forgave me, but if I had not been there, there would have been someone else."

"What I don't understand is that you seem to take it all so lightly."

"That, dear Arabella, is the way to life. Enjoy it while you can, and when that which you enjoyed passes from you, look for something else to take its place."

"It must have been very dull for you at the *château* after these adventures. We had no lovers to offer you."

"You had a certain comfort. I was tired of the road. I knew they were going to fail in Paris. I had had enough of them all . . . even Jabot. I think he was cooling off and I like to be the one who cools off first. You interested me greatly. Do you know, as soon as I saw you I knew we should be friends. I enjoyed my little charade . . . and the way you took it was just what I would have expected of you. Now you have made me respectable for your mother and that has strengthened the bonds between us. You know that, Arabella."

"I wish . . ." I began.

"That I were the sort of young woman you would meet in your normal social round if you were in England? No, you don't. You know I am different. That's why you like me. I could never conform to a pattern. And do you know, Arabella, I have a feeling that you couldn't either."

"I don't know. I feel I don't know very much about myself."

"Never mind. You're learning." She yawned. "And do you know, I fancy there may be some surprises in store for you. Now I will go to my room. Good night, Arabella."

After she had left me I sat thinking of her for a long time.

A few days later a messenger rode over with a letter which was addressed to me.

I sent him to Marianne and Jeanne to be given food and drink and a room to rest in while I read my letter.

It was addressed to Mistress Arabella Tolworthy, and came from Villers Tourron.

Dear Mistress Tolworthy,

I have had the great pleasure of meeting your parents in Cologne and have heard much about you and your family. We have recently arrived at Villers Tourron and, as like yourselves, are in exile awaiting the summons to return, I think it would give us all great pleasure if we met. We have a large house here and although not like home, we can entertain our friends. Your parents have given their permission for you and your brother to visit us and I and my family are hoping that you will do so. My son and daughter are with me at the moment. Edwin, my son, will shortly be joining the King, for as you know there is much activity in that quarter just now and hopes are high. If you would care to accept this invitation, do please give a message to our man. It is a two days' journey by road and there is a comfortable inn on the way where you could spend the night. There is no reason why we should delay and I suggest that you should come in two weeks' time. Do please say yes. Having met your parents and heard so much about you, we are all eager to meet you and your brother.

Matilda Eversleigh.

I was delighted. It would be interesting. I went to find Lucas to tell him about it.

He was in the schoolroom with Harriet. I was glad the children were not there. They would hate our going away, but naturally we could not expect the Eversleighs to invite them.

"Lucas," I cried, "here's an invitation from the Eversleighs."

"The people our mother mentioned. Let me see."

He read the letter, Harriet looking over his shoulder as he did so.

"You want to go?" she asked.

"I think we must. Our parents want us to."

"It should be interesting," said Lucas. "After all, we stay here all the time. It used to be so dull, though we never noticed it much. Only when . . ."

Harriet gave him a dazzling smile.

"We shouldn't be away long, I suppose," finished Lucas.

"Two weeks perhaps," I said.

"What of the children?" asked Harriet.

"In her letter our mother said they would be all right with the servants. And so they should be."

"They'll hate your going," said Harriet.

"For a few days and then they'll be used to it. And think of the excitement for them when we come back."

"I shall miss you," said Harriet wistfully.

I said I would go to my room and write the acceptance of the invitation; and I left Lucas and Harriet together.

The messenger went off with my letter, and as soon as he had gone I began going through my wardrobe. What one wore was not important at Congrève but visiting would be different.

The door opened and Harriet came in.

She looked at the brown dress which lay on my bed. "You can't take that," she said. "It doesn't suit you."

She picked it up firmly and hung it up in the cupboard.

"You have very little to go visiting in, Arabella," she said. "I think we should attempt some refurbishing."

"I daresay they live much the same as we do. They're in exile too."

"They contemplate entertaining so they will surely make some show. Really we shall have to look into our wardrobes. I could lend you something if I wasn't . . ."

She hesitated and I looked at her sharply.

"Coming with you," she added slyly.

"Coming with us. But . . ."

"It will be more fun," she said. "Just think how we will talk of it afterwards. You'll need me there, Arabella."

"But the invitation was for me and my brother."

"How could it be otherwise when they didn't know I was here."

I looked at her steadily. Her eyes were dancing with mockery.

"How can you come, Harriet, when you have not been invited?"

"It's simple. If I had been your sister, they would not have hesitated to ask me."

"But you are not my sister."

"But I am your friend."

"You couldn't just arrive with us. How could I explain your being there?"

"You will explain beforehand. It is so easy. 'Dear Lady Eversleigh, I have a friend who has been staying with me for some time, and I could not really leave her at the *château* while we are away. I answered your invitation in a rush of pleasure because I was so delighted to have it. But now I see that I cannot really leave this friend. It would be most impolite and I know you will understand. She is charming, of excellent family, in fact one of ourselves. Now if it would make no difference to you, it might be that you will extend your invitation to her. . . . If so how delighted we shall all be to come. Do forgive the blunder I have made. It was such a joy to get your invitation that I suppose I answered it without thinking of my responsibilities. . . .' There, what about that."

"I can't do it, Harriet. It would be quite wrong."

"I think it would be quite right. But of course if you would rather I did not come . . ."

"I know it would not be half as much fun without you. But I don't see . . ."

Harriet spent the rest of the afternoon making me see. And the next day Jacques rode over with a note such as she had suggested.

He came back in a few days with a reply.

My dear Mistress Tolworthy,

But of course we shall welcome your friend. She must come and be a member of our party. My son and daughter are very much looking forward to meeting you.

Matilda Eversleigh.

When I showed Harriet the reply she laughed with pleasure.

"What did I tell you?" she demanded. And I must say I was delighted that she was coming with us.

Proposal in a Tomb

Jacques accompanied us. After our arrival he would go back to Congrève, but it had seemed wise to have him with us on the road. We stayed a night at the inn which the Eversleighs had recommended and the following day arrived at Château Tourron.

It was much more grand than Congrève. There were no goats or chickens in sight, and it had an air of graciousness though a little decayed.

Jacques led us into the stables where grooms hurried up to take our horses, evidently having been warned that we were coming.

A servant appeared and took us into the hall where Lady Eversleigh was waiting to greet us.

She was a tall woman, somewhere in her late forties, I guessed, with masses of light fluffy hair and rather babyish blue eyes and fluttering hands. She was clearly pleased to see us and turned first to Harriet.

"I am so delighted you have come," she said. "I so much enjoyed meeting your mother . . ."

Harriet smiled and, lifting her hand slightly, indicated me.

"I am Arabella Tolworthy," I said.

"But, of course. So like your mother. How could I not have seen? My dear, welcome, and this is your friend . . . and your brother. We are so pleased to have you. Was the inn comfortable? We have stayed there and found it good . . . as inns go. Now you must be tired and wish to wash or have some refreshment. We will show you to your rooms first. Have you brought much baggage with you? So difficult travelling. I will have it brought up."

Lucas said we had two saddle horses and they were in the stables.

"One of the men will see to that. Now come with me. I have put you two ladies together. I hope you will not mind. We have not a great deal of room. My son and daughter are so pleased that you have come. They will tell you so themselves. There are some little ones left behind, I believe. Oh, dear, what a pity they are so young!"

In spite of her somewhat inconsequential manner, I thought she was assessing us rather shrewdly and me in particular.

The room I was to share with Harriet was large and contained two beds. There was a carpet on the floorboards, and although it was furnished in a slightly more grand manner, it reminded me very much of the Château Congrève. Lucas was settled close by.

"I hope this will be adequate," said Lady Eversleigh. "How I should love to be back at Eversleigh Court. How different! How spacious! How adequately we used to entertain our guests there." She sighed. "But it will come and you must be feeling the same about your homes . . ."

"We yearn for the day when we can return," said Harriet, and although I looked at her sharply, she went on: "But the news is more hopeful. Perhaps it will not be long before we are making our plans to go home."

"It must be soon. There is great excitement among the King's entourage. My husband is there, you know, for it was there that he met your parents. That dreadful Cromwell . . . dead! And this son. He is not like his father

. . . a fellow of no account, I have heard. That is all to the good, don't you see?"

We replied that we saw absolutely, and she said she would leave us to refresh ourselves and then if we would come down to the salon she would have the utmost pleasure in introducing us to her son and daughter.

When the door shut, Harriet looked at me and laughed.

"At least," said Harriet, "our hostess is not at a loss for a word."

"She is very friendly."

"And seems delighted that we have come. I wonder what the son and daughter are like? I suppose we have been invited to provide them with companions of their own age. Well, it is a little more grand than our own dear *château*. There is a shabbiness though. I suppose it could hardly be expected that the French nobility should hand over their best properties to the exiles."

"You are somewhat critical, considering that but for your coming to Congrève, you might have been living very frugally with your band of players."

"I don't forget it, but that does not prevent my making a reasonable assessment. What shall we wear for our first meeting with the young?"

I looked down at my riding habit. It was not as immaculate as it had been when we set out, naturally, but it had not occurred to me until that moment. "Really," I said, "I have no idea."

"Then you must put your mind to it. First impressions are important. For you your blue muslin with the lace collar, I think. It is fresh, young and innocent looking, as you are, my dear Arabella."

"And for you," I retorted, "brocade or velvet? Silk or satin?"

She grimaced. "It is more necessary for me to make a good impression. I don't carry your credentials, remember."

"As my friend, I think you do."

"Even so, I need an extra fillip. They know that you are the worthy daughter of a worthy general high in the King's favour. All my glory is reflected. I must try to make a little of my own."

"Very well," I replied. "Wear your most elaborate dress, but it will be your manners on which you will be judged."

She laughed, mocking me, and when we dressed she selected one of her simplest gowns. She looked charming in it, I thought, for the blue wool with a peaked bodice set off her slender waist; and with her hair piled high and drawn off her face to show that high forehead, she looked regal.

Lucas was already in the salon when we came down and Lady Eversleigh took Harriet and me by the hand and led us forward.

"Just an intimate gathering tonight," she said. "I thought it better that we get to know each other before the others arrive. Yes, we are having more friends visiting us. That is why I must put you two in the same room, for which I do apologize."

"It is because of my unexpected coming," said Harriet quickly, "so it is for me to apologize."

"Please . . . please we are delighted to have you. I always say the more the merrier. It is merely that not being in our own home we are cramped for space. Now here is my daughter Charlotte and Sir Charles Condey . . . a very dear friend. And where is Edwin?"

"He will be here shortly, Mama," said Charlotte.

Charlotte, I assessed to be in her late twenties. She had a mild face, with light brown hair hanging in rather reluctant curls, which looked as though the slight breeze would unwind them and let her hair return to its natural state which was completely straight. Her mouth was smallish and rather pinched, and there was a fawnlike look about her as though she were poised for flight and would leap off if she should be startled. Her gown suited her; it was of silk and lace and of a deep blue which accentuated the colour of her eyes which were rather large but too prominent for beauty.

She took my hand and smiled at me. Timid, I thought and eager to be friends. I warmed to her.

Sir Charles Condey was bowing. He was, I guessed, about the same age as Charlotte. Of medium height, inclined to be rotund, which made him look shorter than he actually was. Big brown eyes which reminded me of those of a horse, large features generally, pleasant, but rather lacking in vitality, I assessed, but easy to like as long as one did not have to spend too much time with him.

I reprimanded myself for making hasty judgements. My mother had warned me of it. I remember her saying: "People who sum up others on a first meeting are invariably mistaken. You can only really know people after years of living together and then it is amazing what one has to discover."

"I trust you had an easy journey," said Sir Charles.

"We did," I told him. "It was just as Lady Eversleigh said it would be."

He was looking at Harriet. She was smiling. The special smile I had noticed she bestowed even on Lucas. Sir Charles blinked a little as though he were slightly dazzled.

"It was so good of Lady Eversleigh to let me come," she said. "I am staying with Arabella and her family."

"We are glad you did," said Lady Eversleigh. "We shall be a large party, and it is always so much easier to entertain with a crowd."

"Oh, I do agree," said Harriet. "There are so many more things one can do with numbers."

"As soon as Edwin comes we will go in to dinner," went on Lady Eversleigh. "I can't think what is keeping him. He knows we have guests."

"Edwin is never punctual," said Charlotte. "You know that, Mama."

"Many times I have reasoned with him. I have told him that unpunctuality is bad manners just as much as slamming a door in someone's face. The implication is that there is something more interesting to claim the attention and therefore everything else can wait. That is what my husband Lord Eversleigh impressed on me. As a soldier he is naturally the most punctual man alive. I had to mend my ways when I married him. Really one would not believe that Edwin . . . Ah, here he is. Edwin, my dear boy, come and meet our guests."

All her annoyance had faded at the sight of her son, and

I could understand it. I thought Edwin Eversleigh was the most attractive man I had ever seen. He was tall and very slim. He faintly resembled his sister Charlotte, but the likeness had the effect of making her look more insignificant than ever. His hair was the same colour as hers, but it was more abundant and had a faint kink in it which made it manageable. He wore it to his shoulders after the fashion which had prevailed at the time when King Charles had lost his head. His loose-fitting coat of brown velvet was braided and tagged about the waist. His sleeves were slashed to show a very white cambric shirt below. His breeches matched his coat in colour. It was not his clothes, though, which I noticed but the man himself. I imagined he was several years younger than Charlotte; that he was his mother's darling was obvious. The way in which she said: "My son, Edwin," was very revealing.

I find it difficult to describe Edwin as he was at that time because to give an account of the size of his nose and mouth and the colour of his hair and eyes conveys little. It was something within him—a vitality, a charm, a quality which was immediately obvious. When he came into a room something happened. The atmosphere changed. Attention was focussed on him. I knew what Harriet meant when she said that some people had this quality. She had it, of course. I saw that clearly now.

Edwin was looking at me, bowing, smiling. I noticed the way he half closed his eyes when he smiled, how his mouth turned up at one corner more than the other.

"Welcome, Mistress Tolworthy," he said. "We are delighted that you should come."

"And that she has brought her friend, Mistress Harriet Main," added his mother.

He bowed. "I shall be eternally grateful that you allowed me to come," said Harriet.

"You are a little rash, I can see," he said, and I noticed that one eyebrow lifted higher than the other just as his mouth did when he smiled. "If I were you I should reserve a little of that gratitude for a while. Wait until you get to know us."

Everyone laughed.

67

"Oh, Edwin," said Lady Eversleigh, "what a tease you are! He always has been. He says the most outrageous things."

"You should banish me from polite society, Mama," said Edwin.

"Oh, my dear, how dull it would be if we did. Let us go into dinner and all get to know each other."

The hall was rather like the one at Congrève. There was a dais and on this the table had been set because it was such a small party. Only we did not sit in the traditional way facing the main hall, but round the table as would have been done in a small room.

Lady Eversleigh sat at one end of the table with Lucas on her right and Harriet on her left. Edwin was at the other end with me on his right and Charlotte on his left. Sir Charles Condey was between me and Harriet.

"It would be so much more convenient if we had a small dining room," said Lady Eversleigh. "But we have become accustomed to makeshift in the last years."

"Never mind," said Edwin, "we are soon going to be at home."

"Do you really think so?" I asked.

He touched my hand which was lying on the table—only briefly but I felt a thrill of pleasure in the contact. "Certain of it," he said smiling at me.

"Why are you so certain?"

"The signs and portents. Cromwell has kept his iron grip on the nation because he is a man of iron. Richard, his son, fortunately for England, has none of his father's qualities. He has inherited the Protectorate because he is his father's son. Oliver took it with his own strength. There's a world of difference."

"I wonder what is happening at our home," said Lady Eversleigh. "We had such good servants . . . so loyal. They didn't want these Puritan ideas. I wonder if they have been able to keep the place going." She turned to Lucas. "Isn't it wonderful to contemplate going home?"

Lucas said that it was, but that he could remember nothing of his home, although he recalled a little of his grandparents' place in Cornwall.

"We escaped there," I added. "My mother made the long journey across the country with Lucas and me. Our home, Far Flamstead, not far from London, had been attacked by the enemy but not completely destroyed."

"A sad story and too often repeated," said Charles Condey.

Harriet said: "I can remember so well my escape from England. We had warning that the enemy were approaching. My father had already been killed at Naseby and we knew the cause was lost. My mother and I and a few faithful servants hid in the woods while they ravaged our home. I shall never forget the sight of our home in flames."

"My dear!" said Lady Eversleigh.

Everyone was looking at Harriet now but she would not meet my eye.

How beautifully she modulated her voice! She was acting a part and she was a superb actress.

"All those treasures which one has preserved through one's childhood . . . the dolls . . . I had puppet dolls which I made perform for me. They were real to me. I fancied I could hear their screams as the flames consumed them. I was very young, of course . . ."

Silence at the table. How beautiful she was. And never more so than when she was acting a part.

"I remember waking cold, with the dawn just showing in the sky and the smell of acrid smoke in the air. It was quiet. The Roundheads had destroyed our home, changed our lives and gone on."

"By God," said Edwin, "when we get back they shall pay for what they did."

Charlotte put in quietly: "There was violence and cruelty on both sides. When peace comes it will be best to forget this dreadful time."

Charles Condey agreed with her. "If only we can go back to the old gracious life, we'll forget this."

"There has been nearly ten years of it," said Edwin.

"It will be a new start," Charlotte said. Charles Condey looked at her and smiled and I realized they were lovers.

Harriet was determined to maintain the centre of attention.

"We went back to the house . . . our beautiful gracious home which I had known all my life. But there was little left of it. I can remember searching frantically for my puppets. They were gone. All I found was a piece of charred ribbon . . . cherry coloured, which I had put on the dress of one of them. I treasure it to this day."

Oh, Harriet, I thought angrily, how can you! And before me too, who knows that you are lying.

I did meet her gaze then. It challenged me. All right then, betray me. Tell them that I am the bastard of a strolling player and a village girl, that my mother was the mistress of the Squire, and the Roundheads never came near the place where we lived on his bounty. Tell them.

She knew I would not. But I would speak to her when we were alone.

Edwin leaned towards her. "What happened then?"

"Obviously we could not stay in the woods. We walked to the nearest village. We had a few jewels which we had taken with us to the fields. We sold these and lived on the proceeds for a while. In one village we fell in with some strolling players. They were having a bad time and performed in secret, for the Puritans were getting a big hold on the country at that time and, as you know, they were against playacting. The theatres were soon closed but there were still a few players on the road. So we joined them, my mother and I, and do you know for a short time I discovered that I had a talent for acting?"

"That does not surprise me," I said, and she smiled at me again, daring me to expose her.

"I made some puppets. I did my little performance with them and then they let me act with them. I took small parts at first and then bigger ones. But things were getting worse. Although the villagers were pleased to see us, we never knew when one of them would be an informer. It became too dangerous so we came to France. My mother was drowned on the way, for we were wrecked. I was saved and went to the home of some friends of mine. I stayed with them for a while."

"How very interesting," said Lady Eyersleigh. "Who were they?"

Harriet hesitated only for a fraction of a second. She dared not say the d'Ambervilles—if indeed her story concerning them was true. How could one be sure with such an actress?

"The de la Boudons," she said. "You may know them."

Lady Eversleigh shook her head. How could she know a family which existed only in Harriet's imagination.

"Later," continued Harriet, "I went to Arabella and I have been with her some time."

"We must all band together in these times," said Lady Eversleigh. "And how glad I am that you came!"

"It was so kind of you to let me. Arabella and I are such fast friends and I know that she did not like the idea of leaving me behind . . . and nor did I."

"You are very welcome," said Lady Eversleigh. "I am sure you will help to enliven the company."

"Harriet always does. Ever since the strolling players came." This was Lucas. I had forgotten that he would be wondering about her story. So it seemed had she.

She parried that thrust with the utmost ease. "Oh, yes, what a time that was. I was with the de la Boudons when these strolling players came to them. They played for us and I told them about my being with the players and they let me take part. Apparently they were quite pleased with me, and as one of their leading players had deserted them, they asked me if I would help them." She paused then went on: "I will be honest . . ."

How can you, Harriet? I thought. She must have seen the shocked look in my eyes, for she smiled secretively. She was more lovely when she was involved in mischief, and I knew they must all be thinking how enchanting she was.

"The de la Boudons had been very kind to me . . .

71

but life with them was so dull. I asked if they would allow me to go with the players . . . just for an adventure. They understood that the players had brought back memories to me. They were most sympathetic. They were sure that I was a great actress, and when they heard that the company were going to Paris, they were eager for me to join them. So I did, and by great good fortune we came to Congrève. There I hurt my ankle and was forced to stay behind when the players left. I realized, of course, that I was not meant to be a strolling player, and when Arabella and dear Lucas implored me to stay, I agreed."

"We are all very glad that you did," said Edwin. "Otherwise we should have missed the pleasure of knowing you."

"We might well have met when we all return to England."

"Then the pleasure would have been too long delayed."

Harriet became animated. "You remember our play, Arabella . . . Lucas? How like the hall at Congrève this one is. It has the dais . . . it makes a good platform. What fun we had. We must tell them."

"The play we did," said Lucas. "Wasn't it wonderful? It was all due to Harriet, of course. We all took part and the Lambards—the nearby farmers—and the servants were our audience."

"You enjoyed it, did you not, Lucas?" said Harriet. "You were very good in your part."

"I was sorry for Arabella," said Lucas. "She had to die at the end."

"The reward for my ill-spent life," I said.

"Really?" Edwin was smiling at me. "I can't believe that you spent life in any ways but worthily."

"In the part I was the murderess. I prepared the poison draught for Harriet and took it myself."

"It was a French melodrama," Harriet explained.

Lady Eversleigh had grown rather pink. "Wouldn't it be fun if we could do a little play? We have several guests coming and there are people around we could invite to see it. Do you think you could play the same thing again?"

"Are they English, your visitors?" asked Harriet.

"Yes . . . all of them ˙. . . all exiles like ourselves."

"Our melodrama was decidedly French . . . all about love and passion."

"A most interesting subject," said Edwin.

"Very French," insisted Harriet.

Charles said: "Are you suggesting that these are subjects which don't interest the English?"

"No, indeed. Many are interested in them but in secret."

"How amusing," said Edwin.

"Come," Harriet parried, "you know this to be a fact."

"In Puritan England, I daresay?"

"What I am suggesting," said Harriet, "is that we should do a play which is entirely English. Shakespeare, for instance."

"Wouldn't that be rather beyond us?" asked Charlotte.

"I know some abridged versions which make it quite easy to stage."

Charlotte said: "You must have done it in French."

"Er . . . yes, but I could do the translation. What do you say that we form our band of players. . . . All of us will have a part."

"You must not count me in," said Lady Eversleigh. "I have the guests' comfort to think of. We haven't the servants here we had at home."

"Then the rest of us," said Harriet. "That makes a company of six. We can manage. We might get someone else to join us for a walk-on part."

There was no doubt that they were all excited. Conversation was all about the entertainment we should give.

We sat long over the table, and as we left it Lady Eversleigh whispered to me: "How glad I am that you brought your friend."

I was silent when we were in our room that night and it was Harriet who opened the subject as we lay in our beds.

"Stop being so smug and self-righteous," she said.

"I have said nothing," I replied.

"No, but you look like a holy martyr. Don't be so silly."

"Listen, Harriet," I said, "I brought you here. If I went to Lady Eversleigh and told her that you came to us with the strolling players, that you pretended to hurt your ankle so that you could stay and be our governess, what do you think she would say?"

"What a deceitful creature that Arabella Tolworthy is. She has foisted this adventuress on our house and deceived us all."

I couldn't help laughing. It was so like Harriet to turn the tables.

She looked relieved.

"What harm is done?" she asked. "We are going to have a successful house party because of our play. You know how people love that sort of thing. Do you remember the Lambards . . . even the Lambard men? . . . They had never had such an evening's entertainment in their lives."

"But they were simple country folk."

"I tell you everyone loves a play. What did Lady Eversleigh whisper to you as we left the table? Don't bother to tell me. I heard. 'How glad I am that you brought your friend.' " For the moment she was Lady Eversleigh and I laughed again. Of course no harm was done. Of course everyone was going to have a better time because Harriet was with us.

I shrugged my shoulders.

"So now you see reason. I think our play should be *Romeo and Juliet*."

"You *are* ambitious. Isn't that going to be the most difficult one to do?"

"I like a challenge."

"Should you like to be challenged as to the authenticity of the story of your life?"

"Don't carp. We're going to do *Romeo and Juliet*."

"With a cast of six!"

"Not the play in its entirety, of course, and there are others coming. Scenes from it cleverly linked to make a whole. It's possible to do that, you know. It is what is done all the time. I see Edwin as Romeo."

I was silent. I had been trying not to think too much of Edwin, but he kept intruding into my thoughts.

I had never seen or even imagined anyone so attractive. He was so good-looking, so poised; one felt he would be in command of any situation. When he had looked at me and given me that rather crooked smile, I had felt a glow of

74

pleasure. When he had touched my hand, I felt a tremor of excitement. I wanted to be near him, to listen to what he had to say. I knew I was too excited to sleep and this was mainly due to Edwin.

"Do you?" Harriet persisted.

"Do I what?"

"You're not asleep are you? See Edwin as Romeo, I said."

"Oh, yes . . . I suppose so."

"Who else? That Charles Condey? He hasn't half the charm. Or Lucas. He's far too young."

"Romeo wasn't very old, was he?"

"He was an experienced lover. Yes, it will have to be Edwin."

I did not answer and she went on: "What did you think of him?"

"Think of whom?"

"Oh, wake up, Arabella. Edwin, of course."

"Oh, I thought he was very . . . pleasant."

"Pleasant!" She laughed softly. "Yes, I suppose you could say that. I believe he is most attractive in every way. He's the heir to a great title and if they should regain their estates . . . and they should and more also if the King is restored to the throne . . . he will be very rich indeed."

"You have discovered a great deal."

"It slipped out here and there and I pieced it together."

"Ingenious!"

"Not in the least. Just plain reasoning. Charles Condey is not without means either."

"You *have* done your work well."

"I just use my ears and eyes. Mademoiselle Charlotte is enamoured of Condey. I think there may well be an announcement. Remember we were told it was a *family* gathering tonight. Well, that is significant, don't you think?"

"Perhaps."

"Poor Charlotte, she is hardly the world's most attractive woman, is she?"

"How could she be when you have seized that title?"

"How discerning of you."

"Not particularly. I thought it was the message you were conveying at the table and after."

"You are a little sour tonight, Arabella. Why?"

"Perhaps," I replied, "I am tired. I should like to sleep, you know. It has been a long day."

She was silent.

Sour? I thought. Was she right? Was I thinking that I wanted Edwin to like me, to be interested in me; and I wondered if it would be possible for him to notice me very much when there was such a dazzling creature as Harriet about.

The next day everyone talked of nothing but the play. Harriet called a meeting in the morning and we all discussed how we should set about the project.

Oddly enough she had the script with her. "I always take a few with me when I visit, because if people show themselves to be interested, I am ready," she explained. So she had planned this. I saw it clearly now. She had led the conversation that way during dinner; she had come prepared. Sometimes she astonished even me.

But she had certainly fired their enthusiasm. Lady Eversleigh was delighted, for I could see that Harriet had taken the burden of entertaining her guests completely from her shoulders.

Other guests would be arriving over the next few days, and when they did we would put the proposition to them, and if any of them would like to join in, they could do so.

Romeo and Juliet would be difficult, Harriet admitted, but if they could do it, it would be like a touch of home to the exiles, and she was sure it would be more welcome than some light French farce. We should have to work, of course. We should have to learn our lines, but as the play would be very much abridged, that would not be such a great task except for the principals.

She smiled at Edwin. "You must be Romeo," she said, and there was admiration in her gaze.

" 'O Romeo, Romeo! wherefore art thou Romeo?' " he said. "That's all I know of the words."

"Then," I said, "you will have a great task before you."

"We shall have a prompter," soothed Harriet.

76

"I'll be prompter," volunteered Charlotte.

Harriet looked at her coolly. "Perhaps that would be a good idea. Though we do need so many players, there are not many female roles."

"Bess Tredager will revel in it," said Edwin. "She'll like a big part. And then there is John Messenger and James and Ellen Farley. They will relish it."

"Then," said Harriet, turning to Charlotte, "it seems likely that we shall need you just out of sight with the script. It's not a bad idea, as there are so few women's parts in the play. Some of the women may have to take men's roles. That should be amusing. There are only the Ladies Capulet and Montague . . . and the Nurse, of course."

She was looking at me, a trifle maliciously, I thought. It was almost as though she wanted to shut me out.

She had turned to Edwin. "We shall have to work hard together," she said.

"I am sure it will be more like pleasure than work," he replied.

"Are you good at learning?"

"No good at all," he replied cheerfully. "I think you should make me the scene shifter."

"Ah, scenery! We have to devise something. But you are certainly Romeo. The part fits you."

"Then I shall have to rely on Charlotte. And I'm sure you'll give me a tip too when I need it."

"You can be sure I shall do all I can to guide you," replied Harriet.

Lady Eversleigh looked in to say that there were several trunks of clothes in the attics and we might like to go through them to see if we could find something that would be useful. We were all excited at the prospect and immediately trooped up to the attics.

What a hilarious morning that was! There were clothes in trunks which must have been there for years. Shrieks of laughter echoed in the old rafters as we tried on the oddest of garments. Harriet, however, found much there that could be adjusted. There was in particular a little black cap which fitted closely to the head. It was covered in stones which looked like coral and turquoise and had a peak which came halfway down the forehead. I was the first to see it; I seized it and put it on my head.

"It's lovely!" cried Charlotte.

Edwin was smiling at me. "You must wear that," he said. "It suits you."

Harriet had come to me. "Why, it's Juliet's cap," she said. "It's just the thing." She took it from my head and put it on her own. I suppose if it had looked effective on me, it would look doubly so on her. She certainly looked very handsome, for the jewels set off her magnificent colouring.

Charlotte said surprisingly: "It really suits Arabella's colouring better."

Harriet took it off and looked at it. "What a find," she cried. "It *is* Juliet's cap."

We were all late for the midday meal but Lady Eversleigh was delighted. She was a born hostess and she must be thinking that her guests would so appreciate this house party that they would talk about it even when they returned to England.

That afternoon we went for a ride and I found myself side by side with Edwin.

He told me that very soon he would be expected to go to England. They were waiting for the command to leave. It seemed that the time had come to assess the effect of Oliver's death. This was why he was with his family. At the appointed time he would leave for England to, as he put it, "spy out the land."

"Wouldn't it be rather dangerous?" I asked.

"If our mission were discovered . . . perhaps."

"What I remember of it," I said, "there was so much wanton destruction. I can recall how peaceful it seemed when we came to France, because even when we were with my grandparents in Cornwall, there was an uneasiness and we were watching all the time."

"Danger can be exciting," he said. "There is always that, you know."

"Do you find exile dull?"

"The last few days have been far from dull. I am so

78

glad my parents met yours and that this should be the result."

"It is kind of you to say so, and a great adventure for us. We have lived very quietly in Château Congrève."

"I know how it is. My mother has found it most irksome. In the old days she always had the house full of guests. Her desire to get back is an obsession."

"As it must be for so many. Are you among them?"

He was silent for a while. Then he said: "I have always been able to accept what is—perhaps because I don't take life seriously enough. You'll no doubt find me rather frivolous."

"Shall I?"

"Oh, yes. In these days it is better not to take things too much to heart. Life changes. Let us enjoy what we can while we can. That's my motto."

"It's probably a good one. It prevents repining."

"Laugh and be merry, for who knows what the morrow will bring?"

"It must be wonderful to feel like that. You are never greatly concerned about what may happen."

"My father says I should be more serious now that I am a man, but it is difficult to cast off the habit of a lifetime. I have the gift . . . if you can regard it as such . . . of living in the moment, forgetting the past and letting the future take care of itself. At the moment I am completely happy. I can think of nothing more delightful than riding with Mistress Arabella Tolworthy."

"I see you are gallant and determined to flatter me, but as you have already warned me that I must not take you seriously, I shall not do so. I daresay you would be as happy or happier riding through an English country lane with Mistress Jane or Betty."

"At this moment I ask nothing more. Perhaps if I were in an English country lane with Mistress Arabella that could be a more desirable project, but it hadn't occurred to me in my moment of pleasure. If I were at home that would mean that the excitement was over. I have to confess another failing. I enjoy excitement."

"And danger?"

"Therein lies the real excitement."

"I think," I said, "you do not mean all you say."

"I mean it at the moment. Later on perhaps I should mean something else."

"You are a fickle person, perhaps?"

"Fickle in some ways, constant in others. Constant in friendship, I assure you, and I hope, Mistress Arabella, that you and I are going to be friends."

"I hope that too," I answered.

He leaned towards me suddenly and touched my hand. I think I was already half in love with him.

The others caught up with us. I noticed that Harriet was riding with Charles Condey and that he was still a little bemused by her. Charlotte was with them. She did not betray that she had noticed Charles's attitude towards Harriet, but I had already assumed that she was a girl who would not show her feelings.

While I was changing, Harriet came in. I had slipped off my riding habit and put on a loose gown.

"You look pleased with yourself," was Harriet's comment.

"I like it here," I replied. "Don't you?"

"I like it very much."

She rose and looked at herself in the mirror. She took off her riding hat and, shaking out her hair, picked up the Juliet cap which was lying on the table and put it on. She studied her face from all angles.

"What a discovery!" she said.

"It's really rather beautiful."

She nodded, keeping it on her head, still looking at her reflection and smiling almost secretively.

"You and Edwin seemed to get along very well," she said.

"Oh, yes. He is easy to talk to."

"He's very charming. Rather fond of the ladies I should say."

"Perhaps that is why we like him. Naturally we would like those who like us."

"Clever observation," she said with sarcasm. Then she looked at me through half-closed eyes. "It wouldn't surprise me . . ." she began and stopped.

"What wouldn't surprise you?"

"If the meeting had been arranged with a purpose."

"A purpose? What do you mean?"

"Don't assume innocence, Arabella. He is an eligible young man . . . extremely eligible. You are not without some eligibility. Daughter of a general, who is friend and close associate of the King. You see what I mean? Here we are in exile where it is not so easy to mate suitably. Therefore, when an arrangement can be gracefully made, it is."

"You do talk nonsense. I shan't marry for years. Besides . . ."

"Besides what?"

"We should both have to agree, shouldn't we?"

"By the look of you I would say that if the proposition were put to you, you would not be altogether unwilling."

"I scarcely know him . . ."

"And he? I think he would be malleable. He is easygoing. I can't see him putting up a fight against what was so eminently suitable. Oh, Arabella, don't look so cross. Think how lucky you are to have your future so carefully planned."

"This is your usual romancing. I think the lies you have told since you have been in this house have been . . . outrageous. Perhaps I should not have been persuaded to bring you."

"Think of all the fun you would have missed."

"And take that cap off your head. It looks quite ridiculous."

"Wait until I wear it on the great night. I wonder what will have happened by then?"

"That even you cannot prophesy," I replied.

"We shall have to wait and see," she replied, smiling at me.

I lay awake that night, thinking of what she had said. Could it really be true? I had to admit that it was possible. I was seventeen and because of our exile there was very little hope of my meeting someone whom I could marry. I wondered if my parents had discussed my marriage with the Eversleighs. Our mutual standing was such that neither family would be averse to a union, and I supposed it was a great concern to parents as to how they were going to get their children married.

Had Edwin really been chosen for me? I had to admit that, although I should have preferred him to have chosen me romantically, I could not help being excited by the prospect.

I had never in my life seen a young man so handsome, so gallant, so attractive. But then what young men had I seen? The only one I could compare him with was the actor Jabot and of course he was very different from him. I had not liked Jabot in the least and could not understand why Harriet and Fleurette could have been jealous about him. Edwin had everything to make him appeal to a romantic girl, and I was a romantic girl.

What a glorious adventure! I was in love with Edwin and he was the man my parents had chosen for me.

The next day more guests arrived and they were all extremely excited by the prospect of the play. Parts were assigned. Harriet was Juliet and Edwin, Romeo. I was Lady Capulet, which I said was absurd, as I should portray Harriet's mother.

"It will be a test of your powers as an actress," she told me severely.

Charles Condey was Friar Laurence.

"It will suit him," said Harriet with a laugh.

I don't think I had ever seen her so excited. She was at the centre of everything.

Everyone was drawn into the project. The servants were eager to help. One of them was an excellent seamstress and she was working almost the whole of the day making costumes. Harriet was in her element. She sparkled; she grew more beautiful than ever, if that were possible. Everyone referred to her. I called her the Queen of Villers Tourron.

She spent a good deal of time with Edwin—rehearsing, she told us.

"He's quite a good actor," she said. "I am really making a Romeo of him."

She spent a little time with Charles Condey too, schooling him in his part. I was a little worried about Charlotte because she seemed to become more withdrawn than ever.

I remonstrated with Harriet when we were alone.

"I don't think Charlotte is very happy about you and Charles Condey," I said.

"What about us?" she asked.

"You know he is becoming infatuated by you."

She shrugged her shoulders. "Is that my fault?"

"Yes," I answered shortly.

She burst out laughing. "My dear Arabella, it is up to Charlotte, is it not?"

"Charlotte is a girl who would never deliberately set out to attract a man."

"Then it serves her right if she loses him."

"Oh, come, men are not prizes to be won for . . . I was going to say for good conduct . . . but I could hardly call the way you are behaving that, could I?"

"Oh, but they are," she said. "Some people have prizes presented to them when they really don't deserve them. Others have to work for them. Charlotte may lose hers simply because she has made no effort to keep it."

"Are you trying to *win* Charles Condey?"

"You know I always go for the top prizes. He's hardly that."

"Then why not leave him to Charlotte?"

"Perhaps I will."

I was very uneasy, but after our talk I noticed she was less with Charles than before. She said she had to concentrate on her scenes with Romeo.

She was rather upset one afternoon after the midday meal when I came to our room to get a book and I found her there. When I asked if anything was wrong she grimaced and said: "Lady Eversleigh wants to talk to me. I am to go to her room at three o'clock."

"Why?" I asked in alarm.

"That is what I should like to know."

"It's something about the play, I expect."

Harriet shook her head. "I am not sure. She looked very grave, and what was more disconcerting she said little. You know she is usually so loquacious. I wondered

83

why she couldn't say it there and then. But this seems to be a secret."

"You don't think she has discovered you are not what you seemed? Can she know about those atrocious lies?"

"Even if she had she wouldn't want to send me away. The play would collapse without me."

"Conceit!" I said.

"Truth!" she parried. "No, it can't be that. I wonder what it is."

I had rarely seen her so concerned as when she went for her talk with Lady Eversleigh, and when she came back, I was waiting for her in our room. Then she was really angry. Her cheeks were scarlet, her eyes blazing—and she looked magnificent.

"Why, Harriet, what is it?"

She threw herself into a chair and looked at me.

"*You* are to play Juliet," she said.

"What are you talking about?"

"The royal command," she said.

"She sent for you to tell you *that*."

Harriet nodded. "She didn't say so but she thinks I am spending the time with her precious Edwin that he should be spending with you."

"I can't believe it."

"Oh, yes, it's true. She was very friendly, thanking me profusely for coming and working so hard to make her party a success. She appreciated that, she said. But she makes it quite clear that you are to play Juliet so that you can play at love with Edwin-Romeo. That is what is to be. It's an ultimatum. Underneath all that inconsequential femininity, Matilda Eversleigh is a woman of iron. She knows what she wants and she is going to get it.

"I said to her: 'But the part is demanding. It needs a real actress. Arabella is not that. She hasn't the experience . . . the acting ability to play it.' She laughed and said: 'My dear Mistress Main, it is only a game, you know. It will amuse our guests and that is its object. The little mishaps are such fun in games like this. Don't you agree? And Charlotte tells me that Arabella looked quite beautiful in the cap you found in the attic.' Then I thought to myself it's that cat Charlotte who has done this."

"Don't speak so loudly," I warned. "And Charlotte is not in the least like a cat."

"She is. Sly, secretive, ready to scratch."

"Well, you shouldn't have offended her by flirting with Charles Condey."

"Oh, nonsense! How can I help being more attractive than Charlotte? It is no great achievement in any case. Ninety-nine women out of a hundred would be that."

"Well, go on," I prompted. "What else did Lady Eversleigh say? I trust you hid your fury."

"I didn't show by a twitch of my nose or a twist of my lips how furious I was. Or if I did . . . she put it down to my love of the art."

"Your love of yourself more likely. Tell me more."

"She became a little coy. 'Our families,' she said, 'are hopeful that there might be a match between Arabella and Edwin. For a long time my husband has admired General Tolworthy. He is one of the best soldiers in the King's army. The King is very grateful to him.' I nodded and said with sarcasm which was lost on her: 'When we get back to England the King will want to show his gratitude to people like the General.' 'He has promised,' she answered, 'so I think that once we are back . . .' I finished for her: 'His daughter would be an excellent match for your son.' 'That is what Lord Eversleigh thinks,' she replied, 'and so do Arabella's parents. The times make everything so difficult and it is rarely that a happy arrangement can come about. It is for this reason that I should like to see this matter settled.' "

I was shifting uneasily on my chair, feeling embarrassed and a little angry that my affairs should be discussed in this way.

"Then it came," went on Harriet. "The play was *so* romantic. Juliet and Romeo were the great lovers of all time. She thought it would be rather charming for the two who everyone was hoping would want to make a match of it should play the parts together."

"And what did you say to that?"

85

"What could I say? I caught something in her eye. I think Charlotte had been carrying tales. I had an idea that if I refused she would have made it impossible for me to stay here. She is a very ungrateful woman. She has already forgotten that I have prevented her house party's being a tiresome bore. The fact is she doesn't want me to play love scenes with Edwin and she thinks you and he should. It will be a little practice for you."

"Well, I think it's all rather sordid. What are we going to do?"

"You'll have to play Juliet, and the way you'll play it I should think would be deterrent rather than a spur to love."

"There are times," I said, "when you are insufferable. I do believe you think no one is of the least account but yourself."

I was thinking of Edwin then; his tender look, his easy smile, his tall, lean body and his rather sleepy brown eyes. I was in love with Edwin. My parents and his wanted us to marry. How could *I* feel incensed because Harriet had been robbed of her part? I was glad. I would play Juliet. Edwin and I would spend hours rehearsing together. I should be with him all the time. I had been a little bored with Lady Capulet.

I must confess that I admired Harriet. I knew what a blow it was to her. Naturally as the professional actress she had wanted the main part and should have had it. But after her outburst to me, she determined not to show her anger.

She called us all together and explained that some parts would be changed. She herself had too much to do stage-managing so she was not going to play Juliet after all. She thought I could do the part. She herself would take over the Nurse which was a really big role. They would see that this would mean a little change here and there.

I looked at Edwin, wondering if he would mind.

He smiled at me with that lovely tender smile, and taking my hand kissed it as Harriet had taught him to do in the part.

"You will find me lacking," he warned.

"As you will find me."

"I can't believe that."

He pressed my hand warmly. I was so happy. Then I remembered what he had said about accepting what was offered him and reconciling himself to it. But I was sure he was pleased to play the lover with me.

As for myself, I kept thinking of what Lady Eversleigh had said to Harriet. Our parents wanted us to marry. *I* wanted us to marry. Everything now depended on Edwin.

They were enchanted days for me. I was with Edwin a great deal. We learned our words. I knew his off by heart and constantly prompted him. It was not difficult for us to play at lovers, and I began to think that he was in love with me as I was with him.

It seemed strange that the theme of the play was the feud between two families and that the lovers loved and sought to marry in spite of this, while with us it was entirely the opposite. Our parents had put us together that we might fall in love.

And we have! We have! I wanted to sing.

I loved the way he said:

"It is the east, and Juliet is the sun!
Arise, fair sun, and kill the envious moon, . . ."

He added once: "I know what he means by that. The brightness of the day only comes to him when Juliet is there."

"Of course a little while ago he was in love with someone else," I pointed out. "Do you think he would have been true to Juliet if he had married her?"

"I am sure he would," he answered.

"Otherwise," I added, "it would all seem so pointless."

"Life can sometimes be pointless, but let's assume he would have been faithful unto death. Which he was . . . anyway."

"He had scarcely time to be anything else."

Edwin was so ready to laugh. He imbued our rehearsals with a sense of hilarity and I threw myself into it wholeheartedly.

I had never been happy like that at any time in my life.

Because I enjoyed the closeness of Edwin, the touch of his hands, the ardour in his voice when he embraced me, I knew that I wanted him as my husband. Before Harriet had come, I might have been a little ignorant of the relationship between men and women; but since she had come, I had learned much of these things. I had read my mother's journal and she had said when she showed it to me that I was like her, which meant that I would not shrink from the physical aspect of love as some women like my Aunt Angelet had.

I knew that I wanted to make love with Edwin and that I should not lie shrinking in my marriage bed.

I loved the scene in the gallery when Juliet and Romeo are together and morning has come and he must leave her. I savoured the words:

"Wilt thou be gone? It is not yet near day:
It was the nightingale and not the lark, . . ."

And Romeo answers:

"It was the lark, the herald of the morn,
No nightingale: look, love, what envious streaks
Do lace the severing clouds in yonder east:
Night's candles are burnt out, and jocund day
Stands tiptoe on the misty mountain tops.
I must be gone and live, or stay and die."

We did the scene again and again. It was his favourite too, he told me, although he hated leaving me.

"It's only a play," I told him, laughing.

"Sometimes I feel I am not acting at all," he answered. "I can't be, because I am sure I should be the world's worst actor, and I fancy I cut quite a dash as Romeo." Harriet was very critical of us when we rehearsed together. She was trying to make the Nurse the great part in the play now, and I must say she did it superbly. Although she could not look the part. Sometimes I think she did not intend to. She wanted everyone to say she should have taken Juliet.

But rehearsing was great fun and Harriet was superb. Lucas had now become Paris, the husband chosen for Juliet by her parents, and he played it better than I had expected he possibly could.

He told me that he had never enjoyed anything so much as this visit. "And it is all due to Harriet," he added. Then he frowned. "She did not tell of her coming as it really happened." He adored her and did not like to think she had disguised the truth. Then he smiled and added: "Harriet is by nature an actress and I think that she cannot stop herself playing a part."

I could see that Lucas was growing up.

The day before the play was to be performed there was intense excitement throughout the *château*. We should have a considerable audience, for Lady Eversleigh had filled the place to its utmost capacity and because of the play she was inviting all those who were near enough to come. If necessary she said they could sleep on the floor of the great hall. It would not be the first time this had been done.

We had been through our dress rehearsal the previous day and I had thoroughly enjoyed it. I had always amused the children by imitating Miss Black, and I remembered how Dick and Angie had rolled about in mirth. I had been dressed up once and played the part of a robber who had come to the *château* to kidnap us all. I had so frightened the children that they had been nervous for weeks, and I realized I had been foolish, but at the same time I had played my part with conviction. And now I was determined to make a success of Juliet not only because I loved playing to Edwin's Romeo but I wanted to convince Harriet that, although I might not give such a spectacular performance as she would have done, I was a tolerable actress.

Of course Harriet had her own special magic, and I could see that when she was on the stage even in a part such as that of the Nurse, everyone wanted to look at her all the time. She knew her words to perfection; she gave me a rather supercilious glance now and then, and I had the impression that she was almost hoping I should forget my lines. The scenes between the Nurse and Juliet were longer than they had been, for when she was to play the part she had extended them and they were there almost in their entirety. I could feel her eyes on my Juliet cap which she herself had longed to wear. I had the feeling that all the time she was resisting an impulse to snatch it off.

The great day came. Harriet had said that there would be no more rehearsing. What we must do now was to put the play from our minds. We had had the dress rehearsal, which had gone off fairly well; all we could do now was wait for the night.

I laughed at her and said she took it all too seriously. We were not professional players whose livelihood depended on our performance.

I walked in the gardens and Edwin joined me.

He asked me if I were nervous about the play. "It's only a game really," I said. "If we forget our lines everyone will laugh, and it will probably be greater fun than if we play like professionals, which we can't in any case because we are not."

"My mother is hoping to make an announcement tonight," he said.

My heart began to beat faster and I waited expectantly, but he went on:

"She is hoping Charles is going to ask Charlotte to marry him in time for her to come onto the stage when the play is over and tell the company of the betrothal." He frowned. "I am a little anxious," he added.

"Why?"

"Charles has changed. I think poor Charlotte knows this. Have you noticed the difference in her?"

"I thought she seemed a little sad. But then I don't know her very well and she has never seemed lively."

"Charlotte has always been like that . . . the opposite of her brother. She is serious-minded and hides her feelings. But I don't think she is very happy now."

"Does she want to marry Charles or would it be one of those arranged marriages?"

"She wants it fervently, or did, and he seemed eager. But lately it has changed."

I thought: Since we came. It is obvious Charles has

fallen in love with Harriet. Oh, poor Charlotte. She must be wishing she had never set eyes on us.

"Perhaps I'm wrong," said Edwin, and then characteristically, "I'm sure I am. There'll be an announcement tonight, you'll see. After all it's what he came here for."

He took my arm and pressed it. I was very happy then.

"Do you know," he went on, "I fancy that before long I shall have to go away."

"To join your father?"

"No . . . to England."

"That would be dangerous."

"I should not go in my own name. We would cross the Channel in secret and land in some lonely spot and we should be wearing somber clothes so that we looked exactly like everyone else. I am to spy out the land to meet those whom we know to be Royalists, to see what the mood of the people is . . . to pave the way for the King's return."

"When?"

"I am waiting now to hear. Messengers could come any day with a command for me to leave at once."

"Not before the performance tonight!"

He laughed. "Oh, no fear of that. What a tragedy! Do you think the play would be impossible without me?"

"Where should I find another Romeo?"

He turned to me and smiled very tenderly, I thought. "You would find one," he said, "much more worthy than I."

"After all this rehearsing!"

He looked away almost uneasily. "It won't be like that, I'm sure. We shall no doubt be given several weeks' warning. We would have to make ready. It is a matter which will have to be very carefully planned . . . and rehearsed, far more carefully than *Romeo and Juliet*."

"I suppose so."

He took my hand. "Why, you are really concerned."

"I don't like the idea of your being in danger."

He bent towards me and kissed my cheek. "Dear Arabella," he said. "How good and sweet you are. I wish . . ." I waited and he went on: "There is no real

91

danger if we are careful. We shall be in our own country, and after my recent experience as an actor, I shall know how to play a Puritan completely satisfied with the rule of the country, and we shall be going to those whom we know will be our friends. So, there is no need for anxiety."

"Do you really think the people want the King to come back?"

"It is what we have to find out. If they do then he will go, but unless the people are behind him, he hasn't a chance."

"You know him well, do you?"

"As well as most know Charles. The perfect companion, merry, witty, never serious. One can never be sure if he means what he says."

"You mean . . . unreliable."

"Perhaps, but I never knew a man with greater charm."

"Maybe his charm is due to his royalty."

"Not entirely. But that could be part of it. Everyone is prepared to love a king, and if he gives them reason to, well then the love is so much greater. Oh, I am sure we shall be back soon, Arabella. What a day that will be when we set foot on our native soil!"

"I wonder what we shall find."

He touched my cheek lightly and said: "For that we must wait and see."

We talked then of England as we remembered it, and because I was with Edwin it was the gay things I remembered. When I was with him I could share his outlook on life. Everything was pleasant; if it was not, one shut one's eyes to it and refused to acknowledge its existence. It seemed a good way of living.

The play was to be performed at six o'clock and after that there was to be a feast in the dining hall. The audience's seats would be hastily removed and the old trestle tables set up and the food all ready in the kitchen would be brought in. With great ingenuity and with the help of some of the grooms, Harriet had arranged that a portion of the hall at the side of the dais should be curtained off, and there the actors would await the appropriate moment to step nimbly onto the dais and play

92

their parts. Charlotte was to be in the hidden section with a sheaf of papers to prompt those who forgot their lines. I was very conscious of Charlotte. She was trying to be bright and not quite managing it, and she looked mournful in repose. I knew it was because of Charles Condey and I felt guilty because I also knew that his feeling for Charlotte had grown lukewarm since Harriet had bewitched him. I was angry with Harriet. She should be ashamed, for it was clear that she had no deep feelings for Charles Condey.

As the day progressed the tension within the *château* increased and in the early afternoon the actors retired to their rooms to prepare themselves.

At six o'clock we were all assembled. Seats had been set up in the hall and everyone for miles around who could possibly come was present. The servants were there in force, so it was a fairly large audience. We could not complain of them, for there was a hushed silence as the play began and I doubted many of them had ever seen anything like it. Harriet's supervision had meant that to uncritical eyes we were by no means bad, and to see the ancient hall transformed into a theatre was something magical.

My first scene was with Harriet and of course it was her scene. It was only when Edwin and I came face to face that I really felt I was giving my best. I couldn't help thrilling with pleasure when he, seeing me from afar, said I hung upon the cheek of night like a rich jewel on an Ethiop's ear, and I was to remember for a long time after, the thrill of hearing him say of Juliet, "I ne'er saw true beauty till this night."

And so it seemed to me we played for each other. We were the lovers. We met and loved—at least I did— as those two did. Surely, I told myself, he could not have played as he did if he had not cared for me.

I think I did rather well in the mausoleum scene. To see Edwin lying there, poisoned, I understood exactly how Juliet must have felt, and I believe I was really tragic when I snatched his dagger and pretended to plunge it into my heart and fell across him.

It was typical of Edwin that he should propose in

93

such circumstances. "Cheer up," he whispered. "Will you marry me?" I was carried completely back into reality, for I had really been thinking of how heartbroken I would be if he were dead. Edwin was suppressing his laughter and I had difficulty in doing the same.

The final speeches were made. The Duke had commiserated on the follies of enmity and the families had become friends. The play was over.

Everyone applauded wildly. Edwin and I sprang to life and came to stand with the others to take our bow. Harriet, hovering in the centre, took a hand of each of us and we stood there together.

She spoke to the audience and said she hoped they had enjoyed our effort. They must forgive us our faults, but we had done our best, at which Lady Eversleigh replied that she and her guests, she knew, would remember it forever.

Then Edwin stepped forward.

"I have an announcement to make," he said. "It is a new ending to the play. Romeo and Juliet did not die after all. They lived on to marry and be happy ever after." He turned, and taking my hand, brought me to stand beside him. "I have great pleasure in telling you that this night Arabella has promised to become my wife."

There was brief silence and then the applause rang out. Lady Eversleigh came onto the dais; she held out her arms and embraced us both. Then she kissed us solemnly.

"It is the perfect ending," she said.

The feast was prolonged. There was singing and dancing. The guests were very merry. It was nearly midnight when those who could reach their homes left and the others settled down to the accommodation they could find at Villers Tourron.

I had remained in my Juliet costume, and in the room I shared with Harriet I was reluctant to take it off. I felt the magic would somehow end if I did.

Harriet was watching me.

"You will remember this evening for quite a long time, I should imagine," she said.

"I suppose one does remember the day one is betrothed."

"Very dramatic, wasn't it?" she said. "Trust your future husband for that."

"It seemed the right moment."

"Most effective, I grant you."

"You are not pleased, Harriet?"

"Not pleased? What makes you think that? It is an excellent match. As good as any girl could make. If the King does go back to England and the Eversleighs regain their estates and more also, you will have a very rich husband. When did he ask you?"

"When we were in the tomb."

"Not a very appropriate moment, surely."

"It seemed just right," I replied ecstatically.

"You are bemused," she said.

"I am allowed to be happy on such a night, am I not?"

"Don't hope for too much."

"What's the matter with you, Harriet?"

"I'm thinking of your happiness."

"Then rejoice, for I have never been so happy in my life."

She kissed me lightly on the forehead. Then she stood back. "The cap was too tight for you," she said. "It's left a mark."

"That'll soon pass."

I felt rather sorry for Harriet. She had so wanted to be Juliet tonight, and it was a pity, because I knew that for all the flattering compliments I had received, she would have done it so much better than I.

All next day I went about in a state of euphoria. I received congratulations, scarcely listening to them. I was carried off by Lady Eversleigh who kept impressing on me how delighted she was, and she told me that she was sending off a message to her husband and my parents that very day, so that they could share the good news. Would I like to write to Mother and Father and let them see how happy I was?

I wrote to them both.

Dearest Mother and Father,

The most wonderful thing has happened. Edwin Eversleigh has asked me to marry him. I am so happy. Edwin is wonderful, so handsome, so kind and so merry. Everything is a joke with him. He's hardly ever serious. We have had such fun playing *Romeo and Juliet* together— he Romeo, I Juliet. He actually proposed during the death scene. Do write to me soon and tell me that you are as happy about this as I am. I have no time for more, as the messenger is about to leave.

Your loving daughter,
Arabella Tolworthy.

The messenger left with the letters and Matilda Eversleigh kept me with her to talk to me and to tell me how well we should get on together. She was sure that the estates would soon be restored. The family mansion, Eversleigh Court, had not been destroyed by those dreadful Roundheads.

She would not let me go, though I was longing to be with Edwin, and at length when I did get away from her, I heard that Edwin had gone riding with several others it seemed. I went to my room. Harriet's riding clothes were missing so she must have been one of the party.

It was late when they came back. Harriet seemed in very good spirits.

Several of the guests were still staying on, and that night in the great hall the talk was all of the previous night's entertainment and the betrothal announcement at the end of it.

The musicians played and we sang. Harriet enchanted everyone with her singing. Then we danced. Edwin and I led off the dancing together, and people watching us, I heard afterwards, said that they could have believed they were back at home and the trouble was over, the spoilers of our country vanquished and good King Charles upon the throne.

"Did you enjoy your ride today?" I asked.

He hesitated only briefly. Then he shrugged his shoulders. "You were not with us," he said. He said the most delightful things.

"So you missed me."

"That, my dear Arabella, is what I would call an unnecessary question."

"I should just like to know the answer."

"I should miss you whenever you were not with me. I know you were with my mother and how much she wanted to talk to you, so I was self-sacrificing. I shall have you for the rest of our lives."

"I didn't know you were going riding or . . ."

"You would have wanted to come. I knew, so I left you with my mother."

"I didn't hear you all leave. I knew afterwards that Harriet had gone."

"Oh, yes, Harriet," he said.

"Poor Harriet. It was a blow to her not to play Juliet. She would have been perfect."

"Different, yes," he said. "But now we are together, let's think of what's to come."

"I have thought of nothing else."

"When we get back to England . . . that will be the time! Then we can live naturally . . . just as though that ridiculous war never happened. That's what I am waiting for."

"First, though, we have to get there. You have to go away soon."

"That will not be for long. And then I shall come back and ever after we shall be together."

One of the reasons I most enjoyed being with Edwin—apart from the fact that I was deeply in love with him—was that he carried one along on his ever-present optimism so that one believed in it as wholeheartedly as he did.

How happy I was during the days that followed.

Then something disturbing happened.

Charles Condey left. He pleaded urgent business, but I knew the real reason. The night before he left, Harriet told me that he had asked her to marry him.

She watched me closely as she told me this.

"Harriet!" I cried. "Did you say yes?" And even as I spoke I was thinking, Poor Charlotte.

She shook her head slowly.

"Of course," I said. "I knew you didn't love him."

How wise I felt myself to be in my own exalted experience. I was so happy that I wanted everyone to share my happiness, particularly Harriet. I would have felt it to be wonderful if she could have become betrothed at the same time.

"It would not have been suitable," she said.

"But, Harriet . . ."

She turned on me suddenly. "Good enough for me, you are thinking. A strolling player's bastard. Is that it?"

"Harriet, how can you say that!"

"You are to marry the scion of an ancient house. Money and title in due course. Lady Eversleigh! That is well. You are the daughter of a great general. But anything is good enough for me."

"But, Harriet, Charles is of good family. He is young and charming."

"A third son . . . without means."

"Well, the Eversleighs apparently thought him good enough for Charlotte."

She was venomous suddenly. "They were hard put to it to find anyone to take Charlotte. There would have been a big dowry along with her. Once they were back in England . . . Charles Condey would have done very well for himself."

"It shows how noble he was in giving it up. I mean it shows he was really in love."

"Dear Arabella, we are not discussing his feelings, but mine. When I marry it must be someone equal to your gallant bridegroom."

"Harriet, there are times when I don't understand you."

"Which is just as well," she muttered.

Then she was subdued and would say no more, but she had made me uneasy and I could not recapture that first bright flush of happiness.

I noticed too that, though Charlotte tried to be bright, there was a sadness beneath her efforts. My own happiness was clouded. I wanted to show friendliness towards her but it was not easy. Charlotte had encased herself behind a defensive wall.

Two days after Charles had left, when the guests were gradually departing, I went up to the turret to the lookout tower. I was expecting letters from my parents, and from there I could see right out to the horizon.

Perhaps it was too early yet to receive replies, but I wanted to look just in case.

There was a door which led onto a stone parapet and below this was a sheer drop to the ground. I don't know what it was that sent me there at that time. I liked to think it was some instinct, but I thanked God that I went.

Charlotte was there, her hands on the stone parapet. And the horrible realization struck me that she was poised to jump.

"Charlotte!" I called, my voice shrill with terror.

She started and hesitated. I froze with horror, for I thought she was going to throw herself over before I could reach her. "No, Charlotte. *No!*" I cried.

Then to my relief she turned and looked at me.

I have never seen such misery as I saw in her face, and I felt a deep pity that was tinged with remorse because I knew that I was in a way responsible for her unhappiness. It was I who had brought Harriet to Villers Tourron. But for Harriet she would be a happy girl now, betrothed to the man she loved.

I ran to her and caught her arm.

"Oh, Charlotte!" I cried, and she must have seen the depth of my feelings, for they called forth some response in her.

Acting purely on impulse, I put my arms round her and for a few seconds she clung to me. Then she drew quickly away and the habitual coldness had crept over her face.

"I don't know what you think," she began.

I shook my head. "Oh, Charlotte!" I cried. "I understand. I *do* understand."

Her lip trembled slightly. I felt she was going to tell me that she had been admiring the view and ask me why I was behaving so ridiculously. Then her lips tightened and there was contempt in her look . . . contempt for herself. Charlotte was of a nature that would despise hypocrisy. She could not pretend.

"Yes," she said, "I was going to jump over."

"Thank God I came."

"You sound as though you really care."

"Of course I care," I said. "I'm going to be your sister, Charlotte."

"You know why?"

"Yes," I said.

"Charles has gone. He did not love me after all."

"He did perhaps, but he was . . . bemused."

"Why did *she* have to come here?"

"I brought her. If I had known . . ."

"Perhaps it's as well. If he is so easily . . . bemused . . . he might not have been a good husband, do you think?"

"I think he will come back."

"And you think I would take him then?"

"It depends how much you love him. If you loved him enough to do that . . ." I looked towards the parapet . . . "perhaps you would love him enough to take him back."

"You don't understand," she said.

"Come away from there. Let us go somewhere where we can talk."

"What is there to say?"

"It is often helpful to talk to someone. Oh, Charlotte, it will not seem so cruel later on. I am sure of it."

She shook her head and I slipped my arm tentatively through hers. I was waiting to be repulsed, but she accepted the gesture and I fancied was somewhat comforted by it.

She stood still, misery in her eyes.

"He was the first who ever looked at me," she said. "I thought he loved me. But . . . as soon as she came . . ."

"There is something about her," I assured her. "I daresay most men would be attracted . . . temporarily."

"What do you know of her?"

"Please come away from here. Let us go where we can talk."

"Come to my room," she said.

I felt a wave of exultation. I knew I had come just in time and had averted a tragedy. I felt flushed with triumph and sure that I could talk to her, reason with her, turn her away from this dreadful thing she had been about to do.

She took me to her bedroom. It was smaller than the one I shared with Harriet. It had the remains of some grandeur, though like the rest of the *château* it showed signs of shabbiness.

She sat down and looked at me helplessly. "You must think me mad," she said.

"Of course not." How should I have acted if I had found that Edwin loved someone else?

"But it is so weak, isn't it? To find life so intolerable that one is ready to give it up."

"One should consider those left behind," I pointed out. "Think of the effect it would have on your mother, on Edwin . . . and Charles . . . He would never forgive himself."

"You're right," she said. "It's a selfish gesture . . . when there are those who would suffer. It's a sort of revenge, I suppose. One is so hurt one looks about to hurt others . . . or at least one doesn't greatly care if they are hurt."

"I am sure when all these things are considered, you would not take that sort of action. It was something you contemplated on the spur of the moment."

"If it hadn't been for you I should be lying down there on the stones . . . dead."

I shuddered.

"I suppose I should say thank you for saving me from that. I should feel grateful, but I am not sure that I do."

"I don't want you to feel grateful. I only want you not to do it again. If the impulse came to you and if you stopped awhile to consider . . ."

"What it would do to others . . ."

"Yes," I said, "just that."

"I don't want to live, Arabella," she said. "You don't understand. You are lively, attractive, people like you. I am different. I have always been aware of being unattractive."

"But that's nonsense. It is because you retire into yourself and don't try to make friends that you have this feeling."

"Edwin is so good looking, isn't he? I noticed it in the nursery. It was always Edwin people noticed. My parents

101

showed their preference. So did our nurses. Look at my hair . . . straight as a poker. One of our nurses used to try to make it curl. But half an hour after it emerged from the curl papers, it was as though I had never endured the discomfort of them. How I hated those curl papers. They were significant in a way. They meant that all the efforts in the world couldn't make me into a beauty."

"Beauty doesn't depend on curl papers. It comes from something within."

"Now you're talking like the priests."

"Oh, Charlotte, I think you've built up this aura round yourself. You've made up your mind you're not attractive and you tell everybody so. I should be careful. They might believe it."

"It's one thing I have been successful in then, for they do."

"You are wrong."

"I am right . . . proved to be by . . . this." Her voice broke suddenly. "I thought he really cared for *me*. He seemed so sincere . . ."

"He did. I know he did."

"So it seemed. She only had to beckon."

"She is exceptional. It is unfortunate that we came here. Sometimes I wish . . ."

"She is evil." Charlotte was looking at me steadily, and her eyes glowed with prophecy. "She calls herself your friend, but is she? I sensed the evil in her . . . the moment I saw her. I didn't know she would take Charles . . . but I knew she would bring disaster. Why did you bring her here?"

"Oh, Charlotte," I cried, "how sorry I am. How I wish I hadn't."

She softened suddenly and looked at me with real affection. "You must not blame yourself. How could you have known? It is I who must thank you for saving me from that folly."

"We are to be sisters," I said. "I'm glad of that. At least this has brought us together. Let us be friends. That is possible, I know."

"I don't make friends easily. When I was at parties

before we came here, I was always the one in the corner, the one who was only wanted when there was no one else. That seems to be my role in life."

"It is you who make it so."

She laughed bitterly. "You are stuffed with homilies, Arabella. I think you have a lot to learn about people. But I am glad you were there tonight."

"Promise me this," I said. "If you ever think of such a thing again, you will first talk to me."

"I promise you," she said.

Then I rose and went to her. I kissed her cheek. She did not respond but she coloured faintly, and my heart was filled with pity for her.

She said: "It isn't going to be easy, is it? Everyone will know that he has gone. Poor Mama, he was her hope. A third son, not much prospects, but what can we hope for for poor Charlotte?"

"There," I said. "Self-pity! It's not going to be like that in the future, Charlotte."

She looked at me disbelievingly.

"Don't forget," I said. "You promised me."

When I returned to my room I felt shaken. I was glad Harriet was not there. My happiness with Edwin made me understand Charlotte's grief. She must have loved Charles as I did Edwin. It was unbearable . . . Thank God I had been on the spot.

Poor Charlotte! My new sister! I made up my mind I was going to care for her.

I saw very little of Charlotte for the next few days. I had a notion that she was avoiding me. I could understand that. Naturally she would feel embarrassed by what had happened and I would remind her of it. Though when I did see her a warm glance passed between us, and I glowed with pleasure thinking of the good I would bring to Charlotte when I was married to Edwin. I would give parties for her and find a husband who would be so much better than Charles Condey.

Then the letters arrived from Cologne . . . earlier than we had expected. My parents had written:

Our dearest daughter,

Your news fills us with joy. We have been so anxious about you. Everything is so difficult in view of the times we live in. And now this has come about. Lord Eversleigh shares our joy. He is a charming man and there is no one we would rather have as our son-in-law than Edwin.

Lady Eversleigh will tell you the news and this may mean a change of your plans. Rest assured, dear Arabella, that if Edwin and you agree to the suggestion, you have our blessing. She will explain everything to you. Our love, our congratulations on this wonderful thing that has happened. We are assured of your happiness.

Your loving parents,
Richard and Bersaba Tolworthy.

I was a little bewildered by the letter but was not long left in doubt. I had scarcely finished reading it when one of the servants came in to tell me that Edwin was asking that I join him in the salon.

I went down at once. He was standing by the window, and when I came in he hurried towards me and took my hands in his. Then he drew me to him and held me fast.

"Arabella," he said, his face against my hair, "I shall be going away very soon."

"Oh, Edwin," I cried, all the joy in being with him deserting me. "When . . ."

"There are two weeks left to us," he said. "So . . . we are going to be married immediately."

"Edwin!"

I withdrew myself and looked at him.

He smiled brightly, but I fancied there had been a faint cloud on his brow which he hastened to dispel.

"It is what they wish," he said, ". . . my parents . . . and yours. . . ."

"And you, Edwin . . ." I heard myself say in a rather small, frightened voice.

"I? I want it more than anything on earth."

"Then so do I."

He picked me up, and as my feet were swept off the ground he hugged me.

"Come," he said, "let us go and tell my mother."

Matilda Eversleigh's feelings were mixed. She was overjoyed that the marriage was to take place so soon and at the same time apprehensive about Edwin's journey overseas.

"There must be no delay," she said. She knew of a cleric who would marry us and he should be sent for at once. The smaller of the two salons should be transformed into some semblance of a chapel and the ceremony would be a simple one.

I could not believe this was happening. Such a short time before I was in Château Congrève and had never heard of Edwin Eversleigh. Now I was to be married to him. I thought of the children who had been left behind and wondered what they would think when they heard the news.

We should just have a week or so together before Edwin left. I felt life was moving along too fast for me to savour it fully.

But I was happy . . . as I would never have believed I could be. I was deeply, romantically in love, and it seemed fate was determined that nothing should stand in the way of our union and was in fact rushing us madly towards it.

Edwin and I rode together, talked together and made plans for the future. Soon, he said, we were going home, and home was Eversleigh Court. There we should begin our married life, and it must be soon, for they would not be sending him to England if they were not almost certain that the people were ready to rise against Puritan rule and recall the King.

There in Eversleigh Court all would be well with England . . . and with us.

The days flew by and yet there was so much to do in each of them. I was exhausted by bedtime and usually fell fast asleep as soon as my head touched the pillow. I was glad, because I did not wish to talk to Harriet. Since my encounter with Charlotte I had felt aloof from her. I thought she had deliberately set out to attract Charles, with what tragic consequences I knew, because I had helped to avert them.

I woke up one night and was aware that Harriet's bed was empty.

I called her name softly but there was no reply.

I lay there wondering where she was. I could not sleep because I was so uneasy.

It was just before dawn when she crept in.

"Harriet," I said, "where have you been?"

She sat down on her bed and kicked off her shoes. She was wearing her nightgown and a wrap over it.

"I couldn't sleep," she said. "I went down into the gardens and walked a bit."

"At this time of the night!"

"It's not night. It's morning. I feel sleepy now."

"It'll soon be time to get up," I pointed out.

"Then I should get some sleep before it is." She yawned.

"Do you often . . . do that?"

"Oh, often," she said.

She threw off her wrap and pulled the bedclothes up about her.

I waited awhile. Then I said: "Harriet . . ."

There was no answer.

She was either asleep or pretending to be.

The smaller salon had been converted into a chapel and Matilda Eversleigh had indeed found a priest who would marry us.

It was a simple ceremony, but I could not have been more enthralled if it had taken place in Westminster Abbey.

As Edwin took my hand I felt overcome with emotion because he was my husband and I his wife.

I was so happy I wanted to sing a paean of praise to the fate which had brought him here at this time.

Matilda Eversleigh—now my mother-in-law—had determined that the wedding should be celebrated in as grand a manner as was possible in the circumstances, and she had invited everyone within travelling distance. The guests were mostly the people who had been present during the house party, and during the feast which followed the ceremony, there were inevitably references to Romeo and Juliet.

I was like one intoxicated. I was unable to savour my happiness because I could not really believe it was happening.

The future seemed perfect. I was married to the man with whom I was passionately in love; my family approved absolutely and their only regret was that they could not be present; my new family had received me warmly. Matilda purred with pleasure every time she looked at me. I had had a warm letter of affection from her husband; and with even Charlotte (who, I must confess, had retired into her shell and had become as aloof as she had been when we first met), I had managed to form a special relationship.

In such a mood I retired with Edwin to my bridal chamber.

As I prepared for bed I thought of what I had read in my mother's journal of the differences between her and her sister, Angelet. My mother warm and passionate, her sister frigid, fearful of this side of marriage. I knew that I should resemble my mother in this respect. And I was right.

How I loved Edwin. How kind and tender he was! And how happy I was to love and be loved. I had never imagined such happiness as I experienced during that week of marriage.

It was true that over us hung the threat of separation. The fact that he would soon have to leave was the very reason for a hasty marriage, but Edwin's nature being what it was, he did not look beyond the day or even the hour, and he carried me along with him.

I did not see so much of Harriet during those days. Naturally I no longer shared her room, and when I did look in to the one we had occupied, she was rarely there. Of course we met at meals but then there were others there. I felt there was a subtle change in her. I had never seen her anxious before, and I could not imagine her so, for she had always seemed to have a blind faith in her future, but there was a shade of something in her expression when caught unaware that made me a little uneasy.

I determined to talk to her, and as we left the table one day, I whispered to her that I must do this. She nodded and we went up to the room we had shared.

"Harriet," I said, "are you worried?"

She hesitated. "No," she said at length. "I confess, though, that I am wondering what I should do next. Here are you facing a lifetime of married bliss . . ." Her lips curled in a way that sent shivers of alarm through me because it implied that she did not believe in that blissful lifetime. "And I . . . where do I come in?"

"You could have married Charles Condey."

"How can you, secure in your love match, suggest that I should take something less?"

"I'm sorry, Harriet."

She lifted her shoulders. "It's no fault of yours. You happened to get born into the right family, a matter for which you can neither be blamed nor praised. Let's be serious. I have been wondering what I shall do now. Life has changed, hasn't it? We are no longer at dear, old Château Congrève where I should use my talents in the schoolroom."

"I shall be going back to Congrève with Lucas when Edwin goes away. There are so many things to arrange there."

"And when Edwin returns?"

"Naturally I shall be with my husband. I shall have to look after the little ones too. We haven't discussed it in detail. Edwin will have to join the King and his father and wait there for whatever is going to happen. I shall go to Congrève to look after the little ones and you will come with me, Harriet."

"It's very simple really, is it not?" she said.

"Of course. You will stay with us . . ." My voice trailed off. The time would come when Edwin would take me to my new home. The family home. Matilda Eversleigh would be there and perhaps Charlotte. I knew that neither of them would want Harriet in their home.

Harriet was watching me, reading my thoughts.

"For a while," I said briskly, "nothing will have changed much. As soon as Edwin goes I shall return to Congrève, and you and Lucas will come with me. Then we shall see."

She nodded. I saw her smile secretly as she turned away.

The Dangerous Mission

They were days of ecstasy and fear. As the time grew near for Edwin's departure I was beset by anxieties.

Wasn't he going into danger?

"Danger!" cried Edwin. "What danger could there be? I'm going to England . . . our home."

"A Royalist in Puritan England!"

"I tell you I'll ape the Puritan to perfection. I have to get my hair cut. Shall you love me just the same with a Roundhead crop?"

"Just the same," I assured him.

"My dear, faithful Arabella. There's nothing to be afraid of. We shall just drop into Eversleigh. . . . It's a Roundhead stronghold now. My cousin is there. It's a joke, I believe. All the gilded treasures packed away very carefully and kept out of sight. He's changed his name to Humility. Humility Eversleigh. The name itself is a joke. He knows it. That's why he's chosen it. Humility is the last thing you can accuse my Cousin Carleton of. I wonder how he's making out. He'll have to be as good an actor as I am to deceive them. He must be, because he seems to be managing it—and without the benefit of my grounding as Romeo."

"You are a natural Romeo, Edwin."

"Oh, come, my darling, are you detracting from my triumph?"

How I clung to him! I loved him so much. I loved the nonchalance with which he undertook this mission. Nothing could ruffle my husband. I fancied he would emerge from any situation his lovable, handsome, laughing self.

We used to walk in the gardens while he told me of the project. "You won't recognize me as a Puritan," he declared. "Oh, Arabella, you won't fall out of love with me, will you? Promise me?"

I promised that nothing could ever make me do that.

"Cropped head, black hat unadorned by a single feather, plain dark jacket and breeches. I might be allowed a white collar and cuffs . . . very, very plain. I shall have to compose my features and try to be solemn."

"That will be your most difficult task."

"I fear so." He forced his face into a lugubrious expression that was so comical it set me rocking with laughter in which he joined.

"Tell me about Cousin Carleton."

"Cousin Carleton is one of those characters called larger than life. He is large in all ways. He stands several inches over six feet and he has an oversize personality to go with it. He only has to speak for everyone to stand to attention. I believe he would have put the fear of God into Oliver Cromwell himself. As for Oliver's poor little son . . . I don't think he will stand a chance against Carleton. That's one of the reasons I think we shall soon be returning to England."

"Tell me about him seriously."

"We were brought up together. He is ten years older than I, and for ten years he believed he was heir to the title and lands. In our family these things only go to the family if there is no male heir, however remote. Unfair to your sex, my love, but Eversleigh law. My father's younger brother, James, married and had a son, Carleton. It was a long time before my parents were fruitful. Then they produced a girl who died two days after her birth. In due course Charlotte appeared. By this time it seemed certain that Carleton would be the heir. He expected it. He came to Eversleigh and at ten years of age acted like the master of all. Then I appeared. What consternation in the opposing camp! What rejoicing in ours! Uncle James bowed to the inevitable and shortly afterwards was thrown from his horse and died, defeated. His wife, Aunt Mary, survived him for two or three years, then she died quietly in her bed of a cold which turned to a congestion of the lungs. Carleton accepted his fate, continued to lord it over us all and stayed on at Eversleigh. He took an interest in me. Made me ride bareback, run, swim, fence, in the hope of bringing me to his standards, and naturally even he had to fail in that impossible task. So you see he really brought me up."

"He did not resent you?"

"Not *me!* I think he would have liked to own everything in due course. But he has a share in the estates and he seemed to look upon me as something of a weakling who would always need his guidance."

"A weakling . . . you!"

"Well, my dearest, Carleton finds everyone a weakling when compared with himself."

"I think he sounds rather objectionable."

"Some people find him so. He's a bit of a cynic. Perhaps life has made him so. He's witty and worldly. . . . I wonder how he's managing now. He's Royalist from the crown of his head to his toes, and how he's playing the Puritan I can't imagine."

"Why did he stay in England?"

"He refused to leave. 'This is my home and here I stay,' he said. It was his belief that someone should be there. If not, how should we know when the country was ripe for the King's return? So he stayed. I think the role appeals to him. Ever since the King escaped he has been acting as King's spy at Eversleigh . . . and not only there. He goes about the country sounding people. He could raise an army if the need arose, but of course we all hope for a peaceful return. We don't want another civil war. I don't think the people would have it anyway. The last was disastrous enough. Oh, Carleton has done good work. I doubt not the

111

King will wish to reward him. Carleton is just the kind who will appeal to His Majesty."

"As you will, too."

"I haven't Carleton's quick wit, his worldliness. He is just the kind of man the King likes to have around him."

"I believe the King is known to have a fondness for the society of women."

"Discreetly put, dearest."

"And your cousin?"

"It is yet another interest Carleton would share with the King."

"He has no wife, then?"

"Yes, he married. There are no children, which has been a trial to him."

"And what does she think of this . . . interest in the opposite sex?"

"She understands it perfectly because she shares it."

"It doesn't sound a very desirable marriage."

"It works. He goes his way. She goes hers."

"Oh, Edwin, how unhappy I should be if we became like that."

"There is one thing I can promise you, Arabella. We never shall."

I took his face in my hands and kissed it.

"It would be too much to expect that everyone could be as happy as we are," I said solemnly.

He agreed.

How the days flew past! I wanted to catch them and hold them to prevent their escape, for the passing of each one brought our separation nearer.

Sometimes Edwin disappeared for hours. Once or twice he returned in the early morning.

"There are so many preparations to be made, sweetheart," he said. "You know I hate to be away from you."

Then we made love passionately, and I implored him to get his work done speedily and come back to me.

Inevitably there came the day when he must go.

His hair had been cropped and he was dressed in his sombre clothes. Some might scarcely have recognized him, but he could never lose that merry expression which was so essentially his, that implication that life was something of a joke and not to be taken seriously.

I said good-bye to him and watched him ride off with Tom, his man, who was to share the adventure with him. Then I went to our bedroom to be by myself for a while.

As I shut the door I was aware that I was not alone in the room. Harriet rose from a chair.

"So he has gone," she said.

I felt my lips trembling.

"Poor deserted bride!" she mocked. "But there is no reason why you should remain so."

"What do you mean?" I demanded.

"I think you have disappointed him, Arabella."

I stared at her in astonishment.

"Just think what an ardent bride would do. Don't look so amazed. She would go with him, wouldn't she?"

"Go with him?"

"Why not? For better or worse and all that. In England or France . . . in peace or war . . . in safety or danger . . ."

"Stop it, Harriet."

She shrugged her shoulders. "You have led too sheltered a life. But I can see that you enjoy marriage. You all but purr. You really have been helping yourself to the cream. I knew how it would be. Well, what are you going to do now? Sit like the lady in the tower, chastity belt securely fastened to await her lord's return?"

"Please don't joke about this, Harriet. I am not in the frame of mind to accept it."

"Joke! I'm serious. You know what a good wife would do."

"What?"

"Follow her husband."

"You mean . . ."

"Exactly what I say. Why should you not? I think it may be what he expects."

"Follow him . . . I should never catch up with him."

"Oh, yes, we shall. He is reaching the coast in three days' time. There he will have to wait for the tide. If we left after dark tonight . . . when they are all in bed . . ."

"*We!*"

"You don't imagine I should let you go alone, do you?"

"It's madness."

She shook her head. "Madness not to. How do you know what will happen to him? A newly married man needs a wife to comfort him. Having tasted the honey-dew of connubial bliss, he will need it and look for it. If you are not there . . ."

"Stop it, Harriet."

"Think about it," she said. "There is till tonight. I shall come with you, for I would not allow you to go alone."

She rose and went to the door. There she paused to look back at me. Her smile was sly, secretive. She looked as though she could probe my innermost thoughts and was doing so.

When she was gone, I was bewildered, but in my mind I was preparing myself. Was it a wild scheme? Perhaps, but the more I thought of it, the more I knew that now it had been suggested to me, I was going to do it.

In a day or so's time we should be together.

How excited Harriet was. I could see this was the sort of exploit which appealed to her. How right she had been when she had said she must adventure!

We spent the rest of that day together, making plans. The two of us would leave as soon as the household had retired. We would ride through the night and by morning we should reach the inn where Edwin had stayed.

She knew which one it would be. She had heard him mention it, she said. L'Ananas in the village of Marlon.

"The sooner we join up with them the better. It is not exactly *comme il faut* for two women to be riding about the countryside together."

She had thought at first of dressing up as a man. That appealed to the actress in her, but even she could not quite succeed in such a role. "As for you," she said, "everything about you suggests you are of the feminine gender."

114

I was in a fever of excitement. I wrote two notes, one to my mother-in-law and one to Lucas. I was sure, I said, that I should soon be back . . . with Edwin. As for Lucas, he must return to Congrève—which he was going to do in any case—and look after the little ones.

"Oh, Harriet," I cried as we rode along, "how glad I am that we did this! I wonder what Edwin will say?"

"He'll laugh at you," she answered. "He'll say, 'Could you not do without me for a few weeks?'"

I laughed aloud with happiness. "Oh, Harriet, it is good of you to come with me."

"Didn't I tell you, you have only just begun to live."

I felt it was true.

I was so happy as we rode through the night.

By great good luck we found the inn L'Ananas with the pineapple painted on its sign and there caught up with Edwin.

He, with his servant, was preparing to leave when we rode into the stables.

I did not think he was altogether surprised, though he pretended to be, and I was exultant because I had come to him and grateful to Harriet. I myself should never have thought of undertaking such an adventure.

We dismounted and stood before him. He caught us both up in his arms and hugged us.

"What . . . ?" he began. "Well . . ." Then as Harriet had predicted he started to laugh.

"I had to come, Edwin," I said. "I had to be with you."

He nodded and looked from me to Harriet.

"It seemed the best thing to do," she said.

He hesitated just for a second or so and then he said: "It calls for celebration. There's nothing but mine host's *vin ordinaire* . . . and very *ordinaire*, I warn you. Come let us go inside and we'll drink to our reunion."

He walked between us, an arm through each of ours.

"You must tell me all about it. What did my mother say?"

"She will know when she finds her note this morning," I said.

"Oh, notes, eh? Drama indeed! Bless you. I have never been more glad of anything in my life than the sight of you."

"Oh, it's all right, then, Edwin?" I cried. "You're not angry? We haven't been foolish?"

"Foolish, I dare say, but adorable."

What an enchanting hour we spent in that inn. The wine was brought and we sat, Harriet and I, one on either side of Edwin.

"Do you know," he said, "it's a strange thing but I was hoping you would come. That's why I hesitated about leaving here. I should have been on my way at dawn."

"It was Harriet who thought of it."

He put his hand over hers and held it for a moment. "Wonderful Harriet," he said.

"I must admit," I babbled, "when I first heard of it I thought it rather outrageous. I didn't really take it seriously. I wondered if you would be annoyed."

"Have you ever seen me annoyed?"

"No, but perhaps so far there has been nothing to be annoyed about."

"You are enchanting," he said. "I could never be anything but pleased to see you. We shall have to do something about clothes, however. You both look too splendid to be welcome in Puritan England. Are you good sailors?"

We declared we were excellent sailors, not that I could be sure of that—there was only one thing I could be sure of and that was that, when I was with Edwin, I was happier than I had ever dreamed possible.

"What Cousin Carleton will say when I arrive with two beautiful ladies, I do not know. He is expecting me and my one servant. Well, the more the merrier."

I was serious suddenly. "I hope we shan't make it dangerous for you, Edwin?"

"Indeed not. You will make it easier. A Puritan gentleman escorting two ladies . . . How natural. Whereas a man on his own with one who is obviously a servant . . . that could arouse suspicions."

"I can see," said Harriet, "that your husband is determined to make us feel welcome."

"Welcome," cried Edwin, "as the flowers in May."

I was so happy I wanted to burst into song. What particularly delighted me was his attitude towards Harriet. He was so charming with her and I could see that she felt as welcome as I.

We rode out in the pride of the morning, for we assured him we needed no rest although we had ridden through the night, and we sang as we went along—Edwin in the middle, Harriet and I riding on either side of him—on to the coast and England.

Stepping onto one's native shore from which one has been an exile for so many years must necessarily be an emotional occasion.

Wrapped in my sombre cloak, acquired before we set sail, I felt a strange exhilaration. This was home. Something we had talked of for years, certain that one day we would be there. And here I was.

I could not help my thoughts going back to that long-ago night when we had been accompanied to the coast by my grandparents; I remembered the smell of the sea and the way in which the boat had tossed, and our mother had held Lucas and me close to her while the waves rocked the boat and the wind caught at our hair. I remember our grandparents standing on the shore, watching and watching, and the strange, mingled feelings of sadness and exhilaration which I had felt then.

Now there was only exhilaration. Tom, Edwin's servant, jumped out of the boat and waded ashore. Then Edwin stepped out. He took first me in his arms and carried me to dry land, and then Harriet.

It was dark. He whispered to me: "Don't be afraid. I know every inch of this shore. Eversleigh is six miles from here. I used to ride down here to play on the beach. Come."

He took my hand in his left and Harriet's in his right and we walked over the shingle.

"Can you see anyone around, Tom?" he asked of his man.

"No, sir. Maybe if you stayed here with the ladies I'll scout around."

"I know where," Edwin said. "White Cliffs cave. We'll wait there. Don't tarry too long, Tom."

"No, sir. I'll be back at the cave in twenty minutes or so if I can't find what we need."

I listened to Tom's footsteps crunching on the shingle. Then Edwin said: "You ladies follow me."

Within a few minutes we were in the cave. "White Cliffs cave," he went on. "Why they called it that I don't know. It's all white cliffs here. I used to hide in here where I was a boy. I'd make a fire and spend hours here. It was my special hideaway."

"How lucky that we landed near it," said Harriet.

"It was due to my expert navigation."

"What is your cousin going to say when he finds us here?" I asked.

"That we shall discover," replied Edwin blithely.

"I am looking forward to playing the Puritan," said Harriet. "It'll be a testing role, because I have a particular dislike of Puritans."

"As we all have," replied Edwin.

"Edwin," I said, "what will be expected of Harriet and me at Eversleigh?"

"As we are not expected nothing will be expected of us," retorted Harriet, and she and Edwin laughed as though sharing a joke.

But I insisted. "This is an important mission and we have joined it . . . rather recklessly. Your cousin will be surprised to see us, I know, and as we are here, we could perhaps do something to help the enterprise."

"He will quickly make use of you if he feels a need to," said Edwin. "We have to wait to see what he has discovered. I shall make him agree that it is less conspicuous travelling with two ladies than alone with a manservant, and I am sure he will grant me that."

"Then we have been of some use," said Harriet. "It is good to be useful."

We lay against the hard rock and I felt I had never been so excited in my life. My quiet existence had suddenly become a thrilling adventure. How long ago it seemed since I had received a letter from my mother telling me that the Eversleighs would be inviting me. How could I have guessed what a sesame that would be to glorious living?

Edwin talked of his boyhood when he had camped in this cave. "My secret hiding place," he called it. "When the tide is high the water comes in. One could be trapped here. It's happened once in about fifty years. Don't be alarmed. It's low tide and at this time of the year we're safe enough. Besides, Tom will soon be back. You can be sure Cousin Carleton has not let us down. We are to have horses waiting to take us to Eversleigh."

"How many horses?"

"Two only, my darling."

"But we are four."

"Never fear, you will ride pillion. One with me, one with Tom."

"So it has worked out very satisfactorily," said Harriet.

I heard him chuckle in the darkness of the cave. "Couldn't be more so."

There was crunching on the shingle and Tom was at the mouth of the cave.

"The horses are waiting, sir," he said.

We emerged and climbed up the slight incline to a path.

"We're to be travellers in difficulties," said Edwin lightly. "Come." He looked from me to Harriet, and hesitated a moment. "I'll carry my wife," he said. "Tom, you take Mistress Main."

We mounted and were soon riding through the early morning.

The dawn was just breaking in the sky when we reached Eversleigh Court. A high wall surrounded it, and above this, one could glimpse the gables. The gates were open and we rode in. The austerity of the place hit me like a cold wind. Château Congrève and Villers Tourron had been shabby—second-rate dwellings of the rich offered by them to their needy friends who had become exiles—but this was different. Very clean, in good order, but on it was the stamp of that kind of Puritanism which sees sin in colour, beauty and charm.

I could imagine what this place had once been. I could picture lavish flower beds full of colour; the yews cut into quaint shapes, fountains and sequestered paths. The remains of these things were there, but everything proclaimed that this garden was not meant to be beautiful, only useful. There were herbs, fruit trees and vegetables. Everything for use and nothing ornamental.

"God!" whispered Edwin. "What a change. Eversleigh under the Puritans!"

My exultation was turning to apprehension. It was dangerous for Edwin to have come back to his own home, though it must be ten years ago that he had left it. He was now twenty-two, so he would have been twelve when he left. Would anyone recognize him? A boy of twelve could bear a resemblance to the young man of twenty-two whom he had become, but perhaps only those who knew who he was would look for it.

"Tom," he said, "go to the house and ask for shelter. You know your part. We'll stay here with the horses."

It was not long before Tom returned with a groom, who looked at us curiously. "If you will go into the house, my master will see you," he said.

"Ah," said Edwin, "I did not think we should be turned away. Tom, help with the horses."

Tom did so and we went across the path and into the hall. A serving girl was standing there waiting for us. I saw her eyes take in our appearance and come back to Harriet, who looked as beautiful as ever in her Puritan robes. It amazed me how she managed to convey a demureness which I knew was quite alien to her. She was a superb actress.

"Please to wait," the girl said. "Master will be down."

I studied the hall with its lofty vaulted roof and its panelled walls on which was displayed armour of all description. I supposed that was puritanical enough, as it was through force of arms that the Puritans had beaten the Royalists and driven them into exile. I could detect lightened patches where I presumed tapestry had hung. There was a long refectory table on which stood a few pewter utensils, and there were benches on either side of the table. I wondered whether they had been put there to create a lack of comfort while eating.

There was scarcely anything else in the hall, and although it was summer and promised to be a hot day, there was a chill in the air.

I shall never forget my first glimpse of Carleton Eversleigh.

He came down the stairs at one end of the hall. A fine, carved, wooden staircase of a kind which I remembered from before I had left England and which was typical of the Tudor era when this part of the house had clearly been built or reconstructed.

He was, as I remembered Edwin's telling me, tall and he was certainly impressive, perhaps more so in the plain black garments of a Puritan than he would have been in the silk and lace fripperies of the Royalist regime. His dark hair was short and fitted his head like a cap after the only acceptable fashion, and the touch of severity which I had noticed in people's dress since I had set foot in England was accentuated in his costume.

But he was an impressive man—his complexion pale, his eyes dark and luminous, his brows heavy, his features strong and large. What Edwin had said about his being larger than life was certainly true.

His footsteps rang out on the stone flags as he advanced towards us. I did not detect any expression of recognition for Edwin or surprise at seeing Harriet and me.

"God preserve you, friend," he said.

Edwin replied: "God preserve you, friend." He went on: "I am travelling to London with my wife and her sister. We stayed the night at an inn and during that time our purses were stolen by villains who left the inn before sunrise. We travelled with one servant and I propose now to send him off to my house in Chester to bring money for me. Until, then, we are in a sorry plight. Passing your house, sir, we called in the hope of finding a little shelter and perhaps a bite to eat."

"You will be fed and sheltered here, friend, until your servant rescues you."

"When, sir, you will be recompensed for all that you have given us."

"As the Good Book says, we must not turn away the stranger within our gates," replied Carleton Eversleigh, and I could not help feeling how incongruously this mode

121

of speech seemed coming from him. He had the face of an Elizabethan buccaneer rather than a godly Puritan.

He went to a bell rope and pulled it. Two maids came hurrying in from behind the screens. One was the girl we had already seen.

"We have visitors seeking shelter, Jane," said Carleton. "Pray have rooms made ready. A man and wife . . . did you say, friend? And sister-in-law and manservant. Two rooms then—one for the husband and wife, and another for his sister-in-law. The servant can be accommodated with our own."

"Yes, master," said the girl, bobbing a curtsy.

"Doubtless you are hungry," went on Carleton.

We were. We had not felt like eating much while we were on the boat and had had nothing since we arrived in England.

"Sit down at the table," he went on. "We abhor fleshly indulgence here and eat simply."

He was right about that. Rye bread was brought and cold bacon with mugs of cider.

We were about to eat when we received a stern look from our host. We had not thanked God for what we were about to receive.

The simple food, however, tasted like ambrosia and nectar to us, though I was too excited to want to eat a great deal.

Carleton sat at the table as we ate and plied us with questions about our house in Chester. Between them, he and Harriet did very well. Harriet described it in detail. She spoke of flower beds bordered with rosemary, lavender and marjoram and how she enjoyed cultivating her flowers.

She became fascinated by the idea and went on to describe the exquisite blooms she grew, and I was sure she had never pruned a tree or pulled up a weed in her lifetime.

Carleton looked at her sternly and asked in a cold voice whether she could devote her time to a more useful purpose than growing flowers which were no good for anything but to be looked at.

Harriet demurely lowered her eyes and murmured, "God made flowers beautiful," she reminded him, "but I see, my friend, that you have immediately probed my weakness. So much do I love flowers that they have become a vanity."

"Vanity should be suppressed," said Carleton, folding his hands together and raising his eyes to the vaulted roof, and I wondered whether he was immune from that sin— and even on such a short acquaintance I could well believe that he was not. "A sin," he went on, "a snare. Continually must we fight to avoid the pitfalls which gape at our feet."

"Amen," said Harriet, and I thought of how we should laugh about this when we were alone.

I must confess a certain curiosity to see the woman who had married this man. I knew she existed because Edwin had mentioned her, so I said I was wondering if we should be honoured by meeting the lady of the house.

"Mistress Eversleigh is away from home at this time," he told me.

"Then we shall not have the pleasure of thanking her for her hospitality."

"We are not put on earth to take pleasure, mistress," said Carleton, "so it is mercy that you are prevented from indulging in it." I fancied I saw a twist of his lips as though he might be enjoying the scene. "And your name is . . .?" he went on turning to Edwin.

"Edward Leeson," replied Edwin glibly. "My wife Bella and my sister-in-law, Harriet Groper."

Carleton bowed his head.

"When you have eaten you shall be taken to the rooms I have allotted to you. I doubt not the journey to Chester and back will take a few days. You are the guests of Eversleigh until the time your man returns."

"God will reward you in heaven for your goodness to these poor travellers," said Edwin piously.

"I seek no reward," retorted Carleton. "I only seek to do my duty to God."

I wondered whether they were carrying this a little too far, but my experience of the next few days taught me that this was a normal conversation in a Puritan home.

It would be small wonder if there was unrest throughout the country and people were looking to the new King to come back and set up a new set of customs and behaviour.

123

We were given rooms side by side, and what cold, dreary rooms they were! The only furniture the bed, a court cupboard and a chair. There was a chill about the place which suggested that no fires were ever lighted in these rooms even in the heart of winter. I was glad it was the height of summer.

Our bed was a large one with four posts. I was sure that once there had been elaborate hangings, but these were there no more and it looked starkly naked in some way. There was no rug on the floor . . . only the cold wooden boards. Harriet's room next to ours was similar, only slightly smaller.

"When you have washed you can come to my library," said Carleton. "I will explain the way to reach it."

Edwin was unable to suppress a smile. He knew every inch of this place. Wasn't it where he had spent so much of his childhood? Now he had to pretend he had never seen it before, and I was wondering how he was going to suppress that emotion which, returning from exile to a well-loved home, he must inevitably feel. It must be difficult for Carleton to act his part. He did it supremely well though.

When we were alone in our room Edwin took me in his arms and danced round the room with me. Then he drew me to the bed and sat down on it beside me.

"What do you think of my Puritan home and Puritan cousin?"

"They are both a little unreal," I said.

"They are. Where are all the tapestries, the bed hangings, the paintings, the best of the furniture? That's what I want to know. I can hardly believe it's the same place."

"Your cousin will doubtless explain."

"And him . . . what of him? I confess, I was hard put to it not to burst out laughing. He plays his part uncommonly well, don't you think?"

"Are you sure he has not *turned* Puritan?"

"Absolutely sure. Are you glad you came?"

"Edwin, I was so unhappy when you went and now . . ."

"You are here, in a Puritan land. You will sleep with me in a Puritan bed and we will make Puritan love . . ."

"How will that be?"

124

"You will see, my dearest."

There was a knock on our door. It was Harriet.

"Come in," cried Edwin.

She came looking about her, laughing.

"What an experience. Now, Arabella, would you rather be back in France?"

"I should be most wretched. It is wonderful to be here. It's home after all . . . and Edwin is here . . ."

"And I?"

"And you, Harriet."

"Yes, please don't leave me out. I should hate that."

"We would not dream of it," Edwin assured her.

"I should be hurt if you regretted coming, Arabella. I should think I ought to have come . . . alone."

She looked at Edwin and they burst out laughing.

"All this will be changed before long," said Edwin, waving a hand. "I'll wager in a year, perhaps less, all this drabness will be replaced by life, colour, gaiety . . . everything that our good King Charles will bring back to the land."

"Fine clothes," murmured Harriet. "Dashing gallants and . . . the theatre . . ."

"Come," said Edwin, "we are to go to the library where my cousin is awaiting us."

"Does he expect us to go with you?" I asked.

"I think the invitation was extended to us all. He will probably want to prime you on how you must behave. He will soon send you away if you are not wanted. He was always one to make his wishes clear. I could have died of laughing when I saw him. 'God preserve you, friend.' He is in complete control of the patter. I believe he is enjoying it."

"Should you take us to the library?" I said. "Shouldn't we wait to be conducted there? Won't it look odd if you know your way about the house?"

"He gave me instructions . . . for the sake of any servants who might be listening. Come, let us go."

He led us along a corridor to a staircase, not the one we had ascended. Our footsteps rang out on the wood because of the lack of rugs. I could see that the bare walls and bare floors were a shock to Edwin. I should have loved to see the house as it had been in the days before the King lost his throne.

We came to a door and Edwin opened it cautiously.

"Come in, friend," said Carleton.

We entered. He was standing with his back to a fireplace. He looked larger than ever, yet different.

Edwin took a quick look round.

"All religious works, friend," said Carleton. "You will find no sinful volumes here . . . nothing but godliness."

"What a comfort to rest in such a house," replied Edwin fervently.

"I want to tell you of the customs of the house so that you can conform to them during your stay here. I know it will be but brief, but it would distress members of the household if you did not fall in with our ways. We start the day with prayers . . . early morning prayers in the hall at six of the clock. Then we breakfast frugally, and there are prayers after. We all have our morning tasks and some will be found for you while you stay here, for idleness is an invitation to the Devil. There is service in the old chapel at noon, after which we dine. We do not linger at the table. We then work during the afternoon, sup at six of the clock and then there is another service in the chapel. Only the Bible and approved books on religion are read in the house."

"A godly house indeed," murmured Edwin.

"Pray shut the door, friend," replied Carleton.

Edwin did so, and when we were shut in a change came over Carleton's face.

"Who are the women?" he said in a different voice.

"Arabella is my wife, Harriet is her friend."

"You are a fool," snapped Carleton.

He went to the door, opened it and looked out. "One never knows when spies are about. I don't think we are plagued by them, but I take every precaution." He locked the door, then he went to the bookshelves and pressed himself against them; slowly the bookshelf moved inward and showed itself to be a door.

Carleton turned and looked at us. "To be used by any one of you in an emergency, but only in an emergency, and before the door is opened you must make certain you are

126

not observed." He lighted a candelabrum, picked it up and signed to us to follow him into the cavity, which we did.

We were inside what could have been called a room. It was in complete darkness, but as he shone the light around it I saw that it was full of goods. There were rolled tapestries, framed pictures stood up against the wall, chests, chairs, tables and other furniture.

"You didn't know about this concealed hiding place, did you, Edwin?" he said. "I almost told you once. Well, the fewer people who know of such places the better."

He looked with suspicion at me and at Harriet.

"What madness possessed you to bring the women?" he went on.

"He didn't bring us," I protested. "We came . . . after him."

He looked at me with mild distaste.

"You see," began Edwin, "we have been so recently married."

Carleton looked at me in a manner which I found most distasteful and burst out laughing.

"No one can hear outside," he said. "I tested it once with your father. We can come here to talk and be safe. But we must make sure that the library door is locked before we open the bookshelves. So . . . you are here and there is work to be done."

"I think that Arabella and Harriet make my story more plausible," said Edwin.

Carleton shrugged his shoulders. "That might be," he admitted. "They know, of course, the purpose of your mission?"

"Yes."

"Well, then, they will know how much depends on their caution and discretion."

"We understand well," said Harriet. She was looking at him earnestly, and knowing her well now, I realized that she was trying to claim his attention. I knew, too, that he was a man who would have had many experiences with women and would not be the easy victim of any. He might be aware that Harriet was trying to win his admiration, but if he did admire her he was not going to show it.

127

He was looking at me. I suppose as Edwin's wife I interested him.

Then he said: "You're General Tolworthy's daughter, I believe. Oh, don't look so surprised. I am kept informed of what is going on. I trust you will behave with the good sense he would expect of you while you are here."

"What is the position?" asked Edwin.

"Good. That is, hopeful. There is much we shall have to discuss." He looked at us and I knew he meant: When we are rid of the women. "There is a good support hereabouts. But a certain amount of probing to do. We have to be certain who are our friends." He was looking from Harriet to me with some amusement. "It may well be that you ladies can be useful. You can pick up a good deal from gossip. The great thing will be not to betray yourselves. Not too many airs and graces, please. Save those for the days when the King is safely back."

Harriet said: "You may trust me. I am an actress and know how to play a part. I will instruct Arabella."

"I think Arabella's best guide will be her regard for her husband," he retorted. "Know this! All might seem peaceful on the surface, but there is a torrent of unrest just beneath it. What we have been trying to do is find out how deep it goes. The ladies will have tasks to do in the kitchen and in the gardens. Everyone works. There is no idleness here. Listen to the servants. Be very careful in your own conversation. Don't forget your home is in Chester. I hope they are well versed in their parts, Edwin."

"They soon will be. I can assure you, Carleton, you need have no qualms on their account."

"Good. I brought you all here to show you how precariously we live. You must realize that if it were discovered that I had stored away some of our treasures which I had salvaged from their destructive hands, they would know me at once for the King's man. There would be no mercy. I should be strung up by the neck, I doubt not, and the fact that it would be done most piously with prayers said for my erring soul would give me little comfort. Our Puritan rulers are afraid. Perhaps they can hear the rumble of Royalist thunder in the distance. Fear breeds viciousness. So we must be wary. I have business to talk with Edwin. I shall leave him here to examine some of the treasures I have managed to salvage. Now I shall conduct you ladies to your rooms. There you may wait until one of the servants comes to you. She will take you to the kitchens where you will be expected to make yourselves useful. Is that understood?"

"Perfectly," I said.

He looked at Harriet. "Of course," she added softly.

We stepped into the library. The panel slid to, he unlocked the door and conducted us to our rooms.

"Remember," whispered Carleton and put his finger to his lips.

When he had gone, Harriet threw herself onto the double bed in the room which had been allotted to Edwin and me and, looking at me, started to laugh.

"What did you think of the worthy cousin?" she asked.

"Edwin had mentioned him to me so I was prepared."

"What a man," said Harriet softly.

"He certainly is somewhat forceful."

"I liked the double act," murmured Harriet smiling. "My God, what a Puritan he was. You could imagine him delighted in inflicting punishment on those who offended against the laws of God, which would be his own, of course. In his eyes I am sure he *is* God. And then, hey, presto . . . the doors slide and we see another. It was fantastic the way in which he changed. Did you notice it? The way he looked at us was different. You didn't notice that, of course. He was assessing us as . . . women. Whereas when he was a Puritan he was trying to probe how sinful we were."

"You seem obsessed by him."

"Aren't you?"

"What do you mean, Harriet?"

"Nothing. This is fun. Poor Arabella, but for me you would be sitting sadly at your spinning wheel waiting for the return of your husband."

"I don't spin."

"Just a figure of speech. I don't like that talk about working in the kitchens. I didn't come here to be a kitchen maid."

"What did you come here to be?"

"I only came because I knew you were pining to be with your husband."

"Sometimes, Harriet," I said, "I think you do not tell the truth."

"Dear Arabella, you are learning at last."

What a strange world we had dropped into. I found the situation enthralling. I was with my husband, adoring and adored; Harriet was close by; and we were all engaged in this thrilling adventure. For thrilling it was. Although in this household it was hard to believe that we were courting danger, this was, in fact, the case.

I disliked the cousin, as I knew I should. I found him overbearing, arrogant and excessively conceited, which was his true nature. As the Puritan he positively nauseated me. Moreover, he seemed to regard me with an inner, supercilious amusement. He referred to me when speaking to Edwin as "your good wife," and there was a hint of mockery in his voice and expression. To Harriet he maintained a cool, rather aloof attitude which I knew angered her. He was unusual certainly, for he did not offer her that ready admiration to which she was accustomed.

"I am not surprised," she said rather waspishly, "that his wife goes off in search of other gallants. Who wouldn't, married to him?"

She pretended to despise him, but for once she did not deceive me.

Tom had gone off, ostensibly to the fictitious Chester residence, but in fact to a place not far off from where he would be summoned when the business was completed.

Harriet and I did our tasks in the kitchens. We were not expected to wash floors or do the really dirty work, for Harriet had made it clear that we were the mistresses of our Chester household, and although like all good Puritans we did not believe in idleness, we were in the habit of doing more genteel work.

The head of the kitchen was Ellen, the wife of Jasper who worked on the Eversleigh land. They had a daughter, now six years old, who bore the name of Chastity. Like all good little Puritans, Chastity was set to do her stint in the kitchen under her mother's eye. There were Jane and Mary, two maids. More would have been considered an extravagance. I had to admire the way in which Carleton had adjusted to the times, which I realized that his ability to do so was an indication of his devious nature. How different from Edwin who was always so open and honest!

Edwin had his tasks. They were out-of-doors, and often he would ride out with Carleton about the estate. I knew, of course, that this was part of the sounding-out process and that Edwin would be explaining to those trusted Royalist adherents, who like Carleton and the rest of us were awaiting the day of the return of the Monarchy, how many troops could be mustered and brought into the country should this be necessary. The great hope was that it would not be, and that it would be possible for the King to be invited back to his kingdom.

Being fond of children and having had young brothers and a sister of my own with whom I had spent a great deal of time, I understood them, and Chastity and I were soon friends. I found some slate and drew on this for her with a piece of charcoal, much to her pleasure. But her mother was not sure that Chastity should enjoy anything, and so I said I would draw letters on it so that she could learn to read.

Ellen was puzzled. Was it good for Chastity to learn to read? If she had been meant to learn, wouldn't God have put her into that society where she would have done so? She would have to consult Jasper.

Jasper, in her eyes, was the omniscient one. Jasper had fought in Cromwell's army; he had been one of those who had always been against Royalty. He had been a serious man, a true Puritan and had not been afraid to admit it even in the days when it might have brought him into trouble with those who held opposing views and were in a position to enforce them. It was different at these times.

"We are the masters now," Jasper had proudly told Ellen, and she was fond of repeating it in the kitchen.

It was a difficult problem for Jasper to solve, because Ellen had obviously pointed out that there was not really enough work for Harriet and me to do in the kitchens, and we were not very good at it in any case, and it did prevent my being idle. After consulting with his Maker ("He were on his knees two hours last night instead of his usual one," Ellen told us), it was decided that Chastity and I might continue.

"Tell me a story," Chastity used to say, and I would think of something, but this was frowned on as lies, which could bring no good to anyone.

During those days I became a sort of nursemaid-governess to Chastity, which I quite enjoyed. Harriet would wander out, as she would say, to do some tasks out-of-doors.

Sometimes I wondered where Harriet went to, for she would disappear for some hours. Often she would return with a basket of plants or berries of some sort and tell us that she had a wonderful recipe for a cordial which she would make and which would bring great benefit to the household. The only point was the plants had to be left until they were ready for use, which would take some little time. She needed more plants, and she would invent names which had Ellen and her maids agog, for they had never heard of them. It did not occur to them that nobody else had either.

There was something unreal about those days. Every morning when I woke up I would, for a few seconds, wonder where I was, and it would be a few more seconds before I could bring myself to believe that I was really in England, in Edwin's home, playing a part. Sometimes Edwin was not with me when I awoke. Sometimes he went out at night. It was then I realized the danger of his mission. He would whisper to me: "Be very quiet. No one must know that I slip out at night. There are people it would be too dangerous to see by day."

Happy days! Strange days! Unreal days! I wished that Cousin Carleton was not there. I often found his eyes on me, as though he were faintly amused and at the same time a little sorry for me. I think he had decided that I was rather stupid which did not endear him to me.

There was an occasion when I was alone with him.

Edwin was out, so was Harriet, and I had gone to the library to see if I could find one of them, for the library was our meeting place. To my consternation I found Carleton there.

I flushed a little and murmured: "I am sorry. I thought I might find Edwin."

"Come in and close the door."

"I don't want to disturb you."

"If you were, do you think I should ask you?"

"No, I suppose not."

"I see you have made a true assessment of my character . . . in that respect."

"Did you want to speak to me?"

"Yes. You are teaching Chastity her letters, I hear."

"Do you object to that?"

"Indeed, no. It is an excellent project. I abhor ignorance and applaud the effort to eliminate it. Do you keep your ears open in the kitchen?"

"Yes. But I have discovered little. Ellen is a staunch supporter of her husband and he is an ardent follower of the Cromwells."

"Jasper is a fanatic. I am always wary of fanatics. A man who follows a cause because it is expedient to do so can be amenable. You only have to show him something which will be more advantageous and he could well become your man instead of the enemy's. But fanatics? God preserve me from them."

"Are you not a Royalist fanatic?"

"Bless your innocence, no! I support the King because the King's party will give me back what I have lost. It's true I believe that this killjoy rule can never profit a country and it's damned uncomfortable for the individuals. But you must not endow me with virtues I do not possess."

"I don't think I have endowed you with any virtues that I can think of."

He laughed. "So I guessed. And in that you show wisdom, for I possess so few that they are completely submerged by my sins."

"At least you are honest about yourself."

He shrugged his shoulders. "Only when it suits me. I tell you, dear cousin . . . I may call you that behind the protection of locked doors . . . that I am a wicked man. My wife prefers others and for good reason. We have one

133

taste in common, and although we cannot share our pleasure, we understand the other's need to pursue it. I am talking too bluntly. Forgive me. I was afraid you might form too good an opinion of me."

"As I have told you, you need have no anxieties on that point."

"I am relieved. I come of a lusty family, and since you are now a member of that family, you should have no illusion about it. Women have been the downfall of many of my ancestors. They have an irresistible fascination for us. My great-grandfather kept three mistresses all within a few miles of each other and not one of them knew of the existence of the others. It was quite a feat because there has always been a great deal of gossip about the family. There is . . . in such a place. We are the leading family, and our exploits used to be watched with interest. Great-grandfather was insatiable. No village girl was safe."

"How interesting," I said mildly, determined not to show that I was disturbed, because I felt he was leading to something.

"Now and then," he went on, "we throw up a paragon. My uncle—Edwin's father, who is now in Cologne with the King—is of a different calibre. Devoted to duty and faithful to his wife. Something of a phenomenon in the Eversleigh family."

"I am glad of that."

"I thought you would be, and I am glad to have an opportunity to talk to you. I daresay you will be leaving soon. It may well be within three or four days. We shall bring back Tom, who will then be thought to have the money from Chester, and then you'll ride away and we'll arrange to get you across to France again . . . your little adventure over. I admire your courage in coming and your devotion to your husband."

"It was Harriet who thought of it."

He smiled slowly and nodded. "Oh, yes. I guessed that."

Then he looked at me, and I could scarcely believe it but there was a hint of gentleness in his eyes. But I immediately told myself I must have imagined that.

I stood up, and this time he did not attempt to detain me.

I went to my room, for neither Edwin nor Harriet were in, and I thought for a long time about that encounter. I was sure it meant something, but I was far from sure what.

Chastity was becoming very fond of me. She followed me round and before I realized it we were playing games together. Poor little Chastity had never known what it meant to laugh and be merry before. I couldn't help it. I would take her some way from the house and play games with her. Alas, once we came too near the stables and Jasper heard our laughter. He came out, snatched up Chastity and carried her into the house, pausing only to dart a look of black suspicion at me.

When I next saw Ellen she told me that Jasper was very displeased. I replied that surely there was nothing sinful in a little childish high spirits.

"You should have been teaching her the word of God not to be making a mockery of godliness."

"I did nothing of the sort," I protested. "It was a simple game of hide-and-seek. She was enjoying herself for once and . . ."

"Jasper says we were not put on this earth to enjoy ourselves, mistress. Jasper says he don't know what sort of place you come from, but he reckons Chester must be a wicked place for you to carry on as you do."

I thought of poor little Chastity, who was no doubt being punished for enjoying a brief period of innocent pleasure, and I forgot caution in my anger.

"Oh, yes," I cried, "it's Sodom and Gomorrah all over again."

She stared at me, her hands lifted above the bowl dripping flour into it.

I flounced out of the room. I wondered what Jasper would make of that.

The next day Chastity came up to my room. I was there alone, mending one of my petticoats which I had caught on a bramble bush the day before.

Chastity crept in furtively. She was a bright-eyed, pretty little creature, and there was the faintest touch of defiance

135

in her eyes, and I imagined she had been told to keep away from me. She had learned that there was something else in life besides prayers that went on for so much of the day, and sewing garments that must not be pretty since beauty was sin, and learning the Scriptures off by heart and being shut in her room to commune with God on her sins.

For a brief while she had laughed and played games that did not have to improve the mind; she had acted just for the joy of being alive. And she had a will of her own.

"Chastity," I whispered, and I couldn't help sounding conspiratorial.

"Mistress Bella!" she cried and ran to me, burying her face in my lap and then looking up to smile—I must admit rather mischievously—at me.

"You're not supposed to be here, you know," I said.

She nodded laughing.

"I suppose I should tell you to go."

"You should take me down to my mother and tell her that I have been wicked," she said soberly. "But you won't, will you?" She looked at the closed door. "Nobody knows," she went on. "If anyone comes I'll hide." She ran to the cupboard, opened it and stood inside. Then she came out flushed with laughing.

She looked so pretty and so different from the poor little suppressed child I had seen when I arrived that I wanted to snap my fingers at the Puritans and let her be happy.

She came over to me and looked at the petticoat in my hand. It was a little too elaborate for a Puritan woman. It occurred to me then that we had not really been thorough enough. Of course we hadn't. Harriet and I had not been part of the plan. We had broken into it, disrupting it.

"Tell me a story," said Chastity. It was forbidden, of course, unless it was a homily on the wages of sin but I told her a story I had heard recently in France about a girl who had been forced by her stepmother to slave in the kitchens and whose fairy godmother had appeared and transformed her by conjuring up a ball dress so that she could go to the ball and meet the Prince who fell in love with her. Chastity was entranced and I couldn't help feeling gratified to see how much she enjoyed it. I thought: I'll be gone soon. What harm can it do for her to have a little pleasure?

While I was talking she was examining the petticoat I was mending, and putting her hand into the pocket, she brought out a shining button.

"Oh . . . pretty!" she cried.

She held it in the palm of her hand, her face transfixed with joy just to contemplate it.

"What is it?" she asked.

"It's a button. I remember the dress it was on. It was blue velvet and there were ten buttons like this. One of them must have come off. Yes, I remember now when I last wore it. I meant to sew it on and put it in the pocket of my petticoat and clearly forgot it."

Her fingers closed about it lovingly. She looked at me appealingly. What could I do? How foolish it was I realized later, but at the moment it seemed so trivial.

"Please . . . please, Mistress Bella, may I have it?"

How could I say no? What was it? Only a button. Poor Chastity, she was starved of pretty things.

I did say: "Your mother and father would perhaps not want you to have something so pretty."

She hunched her shoulders and looked at me slyly. I didn't say any more. I knew that she would be wise enough to keep it out of their sight.

I didn't see Chastity the next day. Ellen said she was in her room.

"Not sick, I hope," I said.

Ellen nodded gravely.

"Perhaps I could go and see her?"

"Indeed not," said Ellen fiercely.

Even then I was not suspicious.

I went out into the gardens to do my stint of weeding, and as I bent over the earth I was aware that a man was watching me.

I looked up sharply, uneasy as one always is when one feels one has been watched while unaware of it.

"Good day to you, friend," said the man.

137

I replied with the customary: "And good day to you, friend."

"I have travelled far and am in need of a bit to eat and a place to rest. Do you think I'll get it at the house there?"

"I am sure you will. People in need are never turned away."

"Can you be sure of it, mistress?"

"I can indeed."

I straightened up and surveyed him—black coat, broad-brimmed hat, cropped hair, the usual aspect of the Puritan. Indeed where did one see any other?

I went on: "I, with my husband and sister, have been given hospitality under that roof, so I can speak with knowledge."

"Ah," said the man, "you are not of the house, then?"

"No, but resting there while our servant brings us the means to continue our journey. It is for that reason that I cannot offer you hospitality myself but can assure you that it will not be denied you."

"Ah, tell me about the house. They are good Christian people?"

"As good Christians as you can find, I doubt not," I said.

"I am a proud man, I would not be turned away, mistress."

"Have no fear. If you are a good Puritan you will be given what you need."

"Oh, but we are all good Puritans now, mistress." He was looking at me oddly. "Needs must, eh?"

" 'Tis so," I said, not meeting his eyes.

"And you have come from afar?"

"From Chester."

"A long journey."

"Yes. Our money was stolen at an inn. We have thrown ourselves upon the kindness of these good people and we await the return of our servant with the means which will enable us to continue our journey."

"There are evil men about, mistress. One would have thought that with so much piety abroad we should not have to look to our purses."

"No, indeed."

"I was once in Chester," he went on. "Oh, many years . . . I knew it well."

I hoped I didn't show my uneasiness.

"A beautiful city, eh, friend? But cities are not meant to be beautiful. Where there is beauty there is corruption . . . so they tell us. And you travelled down from Chester, did you? A long journey. I once lived in Liverpool. Now you would have passed through it on your way."

"Oh, yes," I said quickly. "Let me take you to the house."

"Thank you, friend. I watched you at work. If you will allow me to say so, you did not seem as though you were experienced at it."

"No. I have done it only since I came here. It is fitting, of course, that we should all have our tasks . . ."

"Fitting, indeed." He came a little closer to me. "Perhaps the day will come when we have time for other matters, eh?"

My heart was beating fast. I was sure that he was not what he seemed. I believed he wanted to get to the house to talk to Carleton and Edwin. He was one of their friends.

"It may be," I said.

Slowly he closed one eye. It was meant to be a gesture of complicity. I started to walk towards the house.

Ellen was in the kitchen when we reached it. I said: "Here is a friend who seeks shelter."

"Come in," said Ellen. "That was never denied in this house."

I went to the room I shared with Edwin, feeling a little uneasy. I wanted to find my husband to tell him what had happened, but he was nowhere to be seen.

I couldn't find Harriet either. I supposed she was out gathering plants again. She had said she had to go far afield for them, and she was going to explain to Ellen how to use them when they were ready and to tell her what ills they would cure.

"I hope you won't poison them all," I had said, and she

retorted that they were all so virtuous that they should welcome a quick trip to Heaven.

Whilst I was pondering what to do, Carleton came into the room. He did not knock, he just walked in. I started up angrily but he silenced me immediately.

"Make your way to the library as soon as you can. Wait there until I come. Where are Edwin . . . and Harriet?"

I told him I did not know. He nodded and said: "Get down soon."

I knew that something was terribly wrong, and naturally I connected it with the man I had brought to the house.

I went down to the library. Carleton was soon there. He locked the door and opened the secret panel behind the books and we stepped into the storeroom.

"Trouble," he said. "Trouble and you are to blame."

"I!"

"You're a fool," he snapped. "Don't you realize the seriousness of our position? Clearly, you don't. You were the first to arouse suspicion. What a fool Edwin was to bring you."

"I don't understand . . ."

"Of course you won't understand. That's obvious. You gave the button to the child. Don't you know yet that no Puritan, whether she came from Chester or London or anywhere in Cromwell's land, would wear such a button, would have such a button, and to give it to a child . . ."

"I thought . . ."

"You never think. You are empty-headed. How could Edwin have been such a fool as to let you come? There is a man in the house. He has come to investigate. Jasper sent for him because he suspects you all. By the mercy of God he does not suspect me. I have played my part well all these years, and you come here and in a few days we are in acute danger. This man has come here to watch you, Edwin and Harriet. You are under suspicion . . . and our work not completed. You'll have to go as soon as we can arrange it."

"Oh, Carleton, I'm sorry . . ."

"Sorry. It's too late to be sorry. A little good sense

140

would have done us more good than sorrow. You must get out as soon as I can arrange it. The moment Edwin and Harriet return, you will have to leave. I don't know how much has been discovered yet. Apparently you said you had come through Liverpool which is north of Chester. They suspect you never came from Chester at all and they are beginning to see what happened. They suspect you are spies from France. The button betrayed you. In France they would wear such buttons, it seems. Well, there's no good to be served by telling you what a fool you are and how much better it would have been for us all if you had had the good sense to stay in France. Go to your room. Lock the door. Open to none but me, and if Edwin should return and you see him, make him lock himself in the room while you find me, but I shall be on the watch."

It was an hour or so later. I was waiting in my room for Harriet or Edwin to return. I was frantic with anxiety. I was afraid they would catch Edwin as he came back to the house.

Then Carleton burst into my room. His eyes were wild and I had never imagined he could be so distraught. Harriet was with him. Her cloak was bloodstained.

"What's happened?" I cried.

Carleton said: "Get out of your things—change at once. Into your riding habits. Be prepared. I have to get you out of here quickly."

He went out and I cried: "Harriet, what does it mean? . . . Where is Edwin?"

She looked at me steadily. Her eyes were burning blue lights in her pale, pale face, and I saw that there was blood on her hair.

"It was terrible," she said. "Terrible."

"What? For God's sake tell me."

"Edwin," she began, ". . . in the arbour. He was trying to save me. You know the arbour . . . on the edge of the gardens . . . that tumbled-down old place . . ."

"What about it? Tell me, Harriet, for Heaven's sake, tell me."

141

"I was near there with my basket of plants and I saw Edwin. I called to him and just then I saw a man with a gun . . ."

"Oh, no . . . no . . ."

She nodded. "He shouted something and Edwin tried to protect me. . . . He pushed me into the arbour, and stood in front of me. Then he was shot . . . The blood was terrible . . ."

"You . . . you've left him . . ."

I was ready to run from the room but she caught me.

"Don't go. Carleton said we must stay here. We must wait. He said I must keep you here. There's nothing you can do. He's gone to him. They'll bring him in . . ."

"Edwin . . . shot . . . dying . . . Of course I must be with him. . . ."

She clung to me. "No. No. They will kill both of us . . . as they've killed him. You can do no good. You must obey Carleton."

I stared at her. I could not believe it. But I knew it was true.

They brought him into the house. They had made a rough stretcher. I could not believe that was Edwin—my merry Edwin—lying there. Alive one moment, laughing at life, and then suddenly he was there no more.

Harriet was with me. She had taken off her cape and washed the bloodstains from her hair.

I kept moaning: "I must go to him."

But she wouldn't let me. There had been trouble enough. We must not make it worse.

I knew she was right, but it was cruel to keep me from him.

Carleton came in.

He looked at us steadily. "Are you prepared?" he asked.

It was Harriet who answered, "Yes."

"Ready. We're going down to the library at once."

We followed him down and there he locked the door and opened the bookshelves.

"You will stay here until tonight when I hope to get you away. I've sent word to Tom. He'll be waiting for you in the cave. The boat is there. You'll wait for the tide and pray for a smooth sea." He looked at me. "Edwin is dead," he said expressionlessly. "He was shot in the arbour. He died immediately and would have known little of what happened. There was no pain. Now this operation is over. I shall leave our findings with Tom and he can take them back."

I said: "I want to see Edwin."

"Impossible," he said. "He is dead. It would only distress you. I knew it would go wrong when he brought you with him. It's too late for regrets now. Fortunately, they trusted me."

He shut us in, and Harriet put her arm about me.

"You have to be strong, Arabella. We've got to get back. Think of your family and how much is at stake."

"Edwin is dead," I said. "I wasn't with him . . . This morning he was well and so alive and now . . ."

"He died instantly. He wouldn't have known anything. That must be a consolation."

"A consolation. What consolation can there be for me? He was my husband."

I could say no more. I sank down on one of the trunks and thought of Edwin . . . as I had first seen him; Edwin as Romeo; the occasion when we arrived at the inn and he saw us there. Oh, he was so much in love with life. He knew how to live it. How cruel that he should be taken.

Then I tried to look ahead to the rest of my life without him.

I could not talk to Harriet. I could talk to no one. I only wanted to be alone with my grief.

It was dusk when Carleton came to us. He smuggled us out of the house to where he had horses ready for us, then he rode with us to the coast where Tom was waiting.

The sea was calm but I didn't care. I wished there were a storm which would overturn our boat. I could not bear the thought of going back without Edwin.

And through my grief was the horrible suspicion. I kept thinking of myself playing with Chastity. I could see her holding the pretty button in the palm of her little hand.

143

Edwin is dead, I kept saying to myself, and your carelessness killed him.

What a burden I should suffer for the rest of my life. Not only had I lost Edwin, but I had only myself to blame.

Blithely I had entered into his adventure without fully grasping the seriousness of it. Instead of being the help-meet, I had been the encumbrance which was responsible for his death.

I knew that I was going to suffer acutely for as long as I lived. It was small wonder that I wished for a sea that would envelop the boat. It was ironical. How merrily we had arrived; how tragically we returned.

Last Days at Congrève

I suppose I should have been grateful to have made the crossing safely. But I could feel nothing but the numbness of my grief.

Harriet did her best to cheer me, but it was impossible for her to do so. She had been saddened even as I had, but at least she did not have to blame herself.

Tom looked after us well. He procured horses for us and we made our way to Château Congrève. He said he would leave us there and then make his way with the important papers he carried to the King, who was then in Brussels.

It was May, warm and sunny, and the gorse made golden clumps across the green landscape. There was bud and blossom on the hawthorn, and the birds seemed as though they wanted to tell the world how glad they were. How different was my mood, burdened as I was by the pain, the loss and the awful guilt.

Harriet tried to reason with me. "Forget that miserable button," she said. "They're so unnatural, Puritans. If one thing didn't offend them, something else would."

"We should never have gone. Don't you see, Harriet?" I insisted.

"Look," she said, "it didn't seem wrong at the time. Think how cheered he was when he saw us. He worked better for knowing we were there. It wasn't your fault. You've got to forget it."

"How can you understand—" I demanded. "He wasn't your husband."

"Perhaps I do understand, all the same," she said soberly.

How kind she was to me. How she tried to cheer me, but I set myself stubbornly against her cheering. I wanted to nurse my grief, to cherish it. I told myself my life was over. I had lost everything I cared for.

"Everything!" she cried angrily. "Your parents, your brothers and sister. My friendship. Do you value them so lightly?"

I was ashamed then.

"You have so much," she said. "Think of others who have no family . . . who are quite alone . . ."

I took her hand then and pressed it. Poor Harriet, it was rarely that she betrayed her needs.

We came to Château Congrève. It looked different from when we left it—gloomy, dreary—not amusing as it had used to look in the days when we played our games there.

Our coming was unheralded and the great excitement it aroused should have been gratifying. Lucas was there and he had told them how I had gone to England. The consternation had been great. Dick, Angie and Fenn squealed with delight when they saw us. Dick flung himself at me and the other two almost knocked me over with the exuberance of their welcome. It was impossible not to be moved.

I took them in my arms and kissed each one fervently.

And there was Lucas smiling tremulously before he too hugged me tightly.

"We've been so anxious . . ." said Lucas.

Dick cried: "We knew you'd be all right because Harriet was with you."

Then they were kissing her and dancing round us and

suddenly I did what I had not done at the height of my grief. I burst into tears.

I heard Harriet talking to Lucas, telling him the news.

Tom, who had left for Brussels, would stop at Villers Tourron on the way to tell the tragic news. I felt deeply for Matilda and for poor Charlotte. What a tragedy it would be for them—almost as great as mine!

Now there was a hush over the *château*. Jeanne, Marianne and Jacques walked about on tiptoe. Madame Lambard came and wept with me and insisted that I take a brew made from gentian and thyme which she said would help me to overcome my grief.

I would lie in my room without any desire to rise from my bed. I didn't care what happened, I could only think of Edwin.

The children kept away from me. I suppose I seemed like a stranger to them. Harriet was with me often. She would sit by my bed and try all manner of ways to rouse me. I would hear her voice without listening to what she was saying. She was very patient with me.

I only wanted to talk of Edwin. I made her tell me over and over again of his last minutes. She told it with drama and feeling, as I would expect her to.

"I had been going through that farce of gathering plants. Actually, I spent quite a bit of time in the arbour. . . . Do you remember that old arbour—relic of more splendid days? I would go over some of my parts and see how much I could remember. I had hoped to find something to read, but there was nothing but sermons and I wanted none of those. I took some satisfaction in just sitting there idling, thinking how that would have upset them if they had known. I was clever, Arabella. I had made them think I had some special knowledge and I believe Ellen was a little afraid of me. She thought I might be some sort of witch, that was why she let me get away with my plant hunting."

"Yes, yes, but tell me about Edwin."

"That day I was there in the old arbour . . . and I heard horses' hoofs in the distance. I peeped out and there he was coming towards the house. I called to him and he

147

stopped and dismounted. He said, 'Hello, idling away the hours God gave you, as usual.' He was laughing at me. . . . And then . . . suddenly there was the man with the gun. Edwin pushed me into the arbour, trying to cover me. There was an explosion and then . . . It was instant, Arabella. He didn't suffer. He was laughing at me one moment . . . and dead the next. . . ."

"I can't bear it, Harriet. It is so cruel."

"It's a cruel world. You didn't know how cruel till now."

"And now," I said, "the cruelest thing of all has happened to me."

"You must remember your blessings, Arabella."

"Blessings . . . with Edwin gone."

"I've told you so often. You know what I mean. Your family. They love you so much. Rouse yourself. Think of them all. The children are wretched . . . Lucas is unhappy. We all are."

I was silent. It was true, I knew. I was imposing my grief on them.

"I'll try," I promised.

"You are so young. You will grow away from it."

"I never shall."

"You think that now. But wait. A short time ago you did not know him."

"You can't judge what we had, by time."

"Oh, yes you can. You were a child when you met him. You are not fully grown yet."

"As you are, of course. Don't talk down to me, Harriet."

"That's better. A spark of anger. I do talk down to you because you have so much to learn."

"Before I become as knowledgeable as you, you mean?"

"Yes. Life doesn't go on all the time being one happy dream, you know. It wouldn't always have been so pleasing to you."

"What do you mean?"

"Your marriage was so brief. To you it was idyllic. It might not have gone on like that. You might have found Edwin wasn't quite what you thought. He might have been disappointed in you."

"What do you mean?"

148

"Just that you are a romantic and life is not as simple as you think it."

"Are you trying to say that Edwin did not love me?"

"Of course, he loved you. And you loved him. But you are so young, Arabella, and you don't understand these things fully."

"How can you understand my feelings for Edwin or his for me? Surely I am the best judge."

She laughed suddenly, throwing her arms round me and hugging me.

"That's better. You're hating me . . . now. That's good. It's taken the place of that overwhelming grief. Oh, Arabella, you'll grow away from it, I promise you, I promise you."

Then I returned her embrace, and she was right, I did feel better for my anger against her.

My mother came to Château Congrève. She must have set out as soon as she heard the news.

I was so glad to see her that my grief seemed less intense than it had since I had known of Edwin's death. The children were so overjoyed that it was impossible not to rejoice in their happiness. But I was the one she had come to see.

We were so close to each other. We always had been in the days when we could be together, and I found our enforced separation had made no difference to our feelings for each other.

We were alone together quite a lot, although she contrived to spend time with the others. But I was her chief concern.

She made me talk to her. She shared a room with me so that we could be together through the night, and if I could not sleep she would talk to me. It amazed me how, when I was sleepless, she would always wake up as though she knew at once that I was in need of comfort. She could not explain it. It was some bond between us.

She made me tell her everything. She wanted to hear in detail about the play and how I had been Juliet to Edwin's Romeo, how we had married so hastily and I had followed him to England.

149

"If I had not, this would never have happened," I cried. "But I wanted to be with him. You understand that."

She understood perfectly.

I told her about Chastity and the button. Who would have believed that such a trivial thing could be so important?

"It is often the trivial things in life that are," she answered.

Harriet came into the story. It was Harriet who had gone with us to the Eversleighs. It was Harriet who thought of the play, Harriet who had suggested we follow Edwin to England, and Harriet who had been with him when he had died.

I noticed that my mother often brought Harriet into our discussions. Harriet had come in the first place with some travellers, had she not?

Although I might deceive my mother by half-truths in a letter, I could not do so face to face. She had a way of probing, and soon the whole story had come out about the strolling players, but I did manage to hide the fact that the hurt ankle had been a ruse.

"How odd," said my mother. "So she was with this troupe of players. How did she join them?"

So I had to tell her then how Harriet's mother and stepfather had been drowned and how she had been saved and taken to a family where she had been governess. My mother wanted to know the name of the family. I said I would ask Harriet if she really wanted to know.

My mother said she would ask her.

I hastily said: "One of the sons of the household made advances to her and that was why she left. They might speak ill of her."

My mother nodded.

I had a feeling that she did not greatly like Harriet. That disturbed me, and I tried to make her understand how much we had all enjoyed her company and how good she was with the children.

"I can see they have a very high regard for her," she said.

How she comforted me I could not tell, but she did. She made me see that I had had great happiness and must be grateful for that. It was sad that it had been so brief, but at least I had something to remember.

She told me that she was going to call on Lady Eversleigh on her way back to Cologne to join my father, and she thought that I should come with her to the Château Tourron and be with Matilda for a few days. She was sure it would comfort her. Then when my mother left for Cologne I could return to Congrève.

This I arranged to do.

Poor Matilda. She was, as I had expected her to be, overcome with grief. She embraced me, called me her dear daughter and talked continually of Edwin.

She said: "He was the hope of our house. And he is gone. . . . Our only son. There is nothing left to us but to mourn."

My mother said to me later: "I'm afraid this does little to assuage your grief, my darling, but it comforts her to have you here. That I know. So for her sake . . . bear with it."

She was right. I found myself comforted by comforting Matilda Eversleigh.

Charlotte was like a sad, grey ghost. Poor Charlotte, who had lost her lover and her brother. She was like one who was wondering what blow could be dealt to her next.

I walked with her in the gardens and she asked me about Edwin's end. I told her as Harriet had told me.

"So she was the last one to see him alive. It would be so."

"She happened to be in an old arbour and heard him come towards the house. Someone must have been lying in ambush there."

She narrowed her eyes and said: "What could she have been doing in the arbour? Did you ask her that?"

I answered quickly: "We were all expected to do tasks. She went out gathering herbs and she used to rest there."

Charlotte's lips tightened. Of course she would never forgive Harriet for taking Charles Condey from her.

151

Then I poured out my feelings to her. I told her about the button and how foolish I had been and how it had aroused suspicions against me.

"You were not to know," she said. "It was all so innocent. You must not reproach yourself."

She was gentle and kind to me and I felt I had a friend in Charlotte.

What a house of mourning that was and how poignant I felt when Matilda thanked me for making Edwin's last weeks so happy.

She said: "We are a military family. He died for his King and that is something of which we must be proud. He died as bravely as his ancestors have died on the battlefields. Let us remember that."

My mother mentioned Harriet one day when we were sitting together—Matilda, she and I. Charlotte was not present. I guessed my mother knew that the subject of Harriet would be too painful for Charlotte to bear.

"A strange young woman," said my mother. "Arabella has been telling me how she came. What did you think of her, Matilda?"

Matilda Eversleigh hesitated. "She was very good with the play," she said. "We thought her a great asset . . . in the beginning . . ."

"And afterwards?" asked my mother.

"Well, there was Charles Condey."

I said: "It was scarcely Harriet's fault. He fell deeply in love with her."

"She is very attractive," admitted my mother.

"It was rather unfortunate. Poor Charlotte . . ."

"But a happy escape if he was so fickle," my mother pointed out.

"Ah, yes, perhaps," sighed Matilda.

"And that was all?" went on my mother. "Until that happened you were quite happy about her being here?"

"It was the best house party I have had since I left England."

"And it was all due to her," I said quickly.

"Oh, yes, yes," agreed my mother-in-law.

My mother appeared to be satisfied, but I who knew

152

her well realized that she was thinking deeply. I had a feeling that she was not completely happy about Harriet.

I said good-bye to my mother and the Eversleighs, and when I reached Château Congrève there was a great welcome awaiting me. Madame Lambard had baked a pie with "Welcome home, Arabella" worked on it with strips of paste, and the three young children sang a song of welcome which Harriet had taught them and which she whispered to me they had practised every day, so I must be pleased with it.

"No tears," she whispered. "They've worked so hard. You can't disappoint them."

Nor could I. I was surprised to find that the gloom which had till now enveloped me had lifted a little.

It was a revelation which came to me suddenly.

I had awakened to a bright morning, and as usual as soon as I opened my eyes and remembered that I was a widow, the terrible desolation swept over me. I lay for a while thinking of waking with Edwin beside me, and how I would watch him until he suddenly burst out laughing because he had only pretended to be asleep.

Then I would shut my eyes and wallow in my grief and assure myself that life was over for me. I would force myself to get up and remember that I had to be bright because of the children.

And as I lay there that morning it flashed into my mind. It was possible. Could it really be?

If it was, it would make all the difference in the world to me.

Of course I could not yet be sure. But if it were. Oh, God, I thought, I should begin to live again.

I lay there as though wrapped up in a cocoon of hopefulness.

The next weeks would tell me, and if it were true, I should have something to live for.

I could only keep saying to myself: I shall begin to live again.

They noticed the change in me.

"You're getting over it," said Harriet, and she looked so

happy that I knew she was truly fond of me. The children noticed it. They leaped about making strange contented noises as they used to. Lucas, dear Lucas—who seemed to have grown up so much in the last months—was quietly happy.

Oh, indeed, I owed it to them to shake myself out of my misery. And if this were true . . . oh, if only this were true . . . I should not have lost Edwin entirely.

By the end of July I was sure.

I was going to have a child.

Madame Lambard, who had acted as a midwife when she had had the opportunity, confirmed my condition.

She was so delighted that she burst into tears and became emotionally voluble.

The good God had answered her prayers, she told me. She had prayed to Him to give me this. He had made me suffer but He had His reasons. Now He was giving me this blessing.

They were going to take care of me—she and the good Lord together, and with such guardians I could rest assured I should come to no harm. I should have every care . . . every attention. I would be happy again.

Yes, I thought, I can be happy again. When I hold my child . . . mine and Edwin's . . . in my arms, I *shall* be happy again.

Of course I told Harriet.

She was amused and went into fits of laughter.

"What is funny about it?" I demanded.

"It just strikes me so," she answered. "I'm happy for you, Arabella. This is going to make all the difference to you, I know."

"It is, Harriet, it is."

I wrote immediately to my parents and then remembered Matilda Eversleigh. After all, this concerned her.

Her response was immediate. She wrote:

My dearest daughter,
    This news has filled me with such happiness as I feared never to feel again. Oh, blessed day when you came to us. Edwin will live on for us. Let us pray for a

154

boy. Though a little girl will be a comfort. But a boy will recompense us in so many ways. You see, my dearest child, I can talk to you like this because you are one of the family now. Edwin was the heir to a great name and a title, and it is a tragedy that we had no other son. His inheritance would have gone to my nephew Carleton whom you met in England. He is worthy enough, of course, but if your child is a boy, it will be kept in the direct line and that is important to us. My dearest grandson! Lord Eversleigh will be delighted. I am writing to him without delay. Oh, this is such a blessing. What a joy it is to have good news. You must take the greatest care of yourself. Perhaps you should come to me. I cannot convey what joy your letter has given me. . . .

Oh, yes, I was able to be happy again. Now I awoke in the mornings with a light heart. It was not the end of my marriage. I had something to live for.

I wrote to Matilda and assured her that Madame Lambard was the best midwife in the neighbourhood, and as she was determined to look after me, I thought I could do no better than place myself in her care. This child would be more precious than most because of the sad circumstances in which it would be born. I was determined to take no risks by travelling. I was going to rely absolutely on Madame Lambard. I was determined that there should be no danger to my child.

Messengers came back and forth to the *château*. My parents were overjoyed.

My father wrote that the entire situation was altering. There was hope everywhere.

The news from home is getting better and better. Edwin had sent back valuable information. More is coming from his cousin who has and is doing such good work.

My dear daughter, by the time your child is born it may well be that we have plans for the King's return to England. What a joy that will be to us all!

He sounded more confident than he ever had before, and he was not a man to conceal the truth.

I began to dream of the future.

My baby should make his appearance in January the coming year, sixteen hundred and sixty.

Now the days began to pass quickly. How differently I felt when I awoke each morning. I even welcomed the little discomforts which heralded the existence of the child. I began to count the days and months, so much was I longing for the day when I should hold the child in my arms.

Expectation pervaded the *château*. The main topic of conversation was "When the baby comes." I started to make garments under the tuition of Jeanne, who was good with her needle, and although I was scarcely the same, I did derive a great deal of satisfaction from the work.

The children were told that there was going to be a new baby and that they were going to be uncles and aunts, which made them hilarious with glee, particularly Fenn, who being the youngest had never felt so important before. Every day he asked if the baby had come and was he an uncle yet.

Harriet would sit with me while I sewed and sometimes read plays to me, enacting the parts as she did so—a pleasant pastime. The children liked to come in and listen. Even Harriet seemed to have changed. I could not quite say what it was; perhaps she had become more thoughtful; she moved less swiftly and I fancied she had put on a little weight.

She had been concerned because she thought my mother had not liked her and she wanted to know what questions she had asked about her. Had I mentioned the d'Ambervilles? "Not by name," I told her. "And I just told her you left because one of the sons made advances to you."

She was uneasy, I knew.

It was July, I remember, hot and sultry, and I felt listless in a contented kind of way because I knew my feelings were due to the child I carried. Letters came from my mother.

Dear Arabella,

What wonderful news this is. I trust you are taking good care of yourself. I feel that you are in good hands with Madame Lambard. She so prides herself on her skills and I believe with reason.

I long to be with you, but as I cannot I am happy to think of Madame Lambard. At the earliest opportunity I shall be with you. As you can imagine a great many things are happening here and it seems likely that by this time next year we may be home. What a joy that will be when we are all together. . . .

Oh, yes, I thought, there is a lot to live for. I went on reading and was slightly taken aback.

I have been wondering about Harriet. We need someone here to help us make our preparations. I have told your father about her and he thinks it would be a good idea if she joined us here. After all, if we shall soon be back in England, the children will not be so very old and they can resume their education in earnest then. We have heard of an excellent tutor . . .

The letter dropped from my hand. I knew her well. She did not want Harriet to stay here with us.

I said nothing to Harriet for a day or so. I meant to, but every time I attempted to, I found it difficult. She was clever enough to realize that my mother did not approve of her being here and wanted to get her away.

Of course I should have to write to my mother sooner or later, and one day when she was talking about going back to England, said: "Harriet, I have had a letter from my mother. She would like you to go to her."

She stared at me. "Go to her!"

The colour had left her face. For the first time I saw Harriet afraid.

"What do you mean?" she said sharply.

"That's what she says. They need someone there . . . to er . . . Well, you know, there are all these preparations. You write well . . . it might be that in some way . . ."

"She wants me to leave here, does she?"

157

"She did not say that."

"Oh, but she means it. I won't go, Arabella. I can't go."

"I shall write and tell her that we can't do without you here. Harriet, don't be angry. I never intended that you should."

She was silent for a few moments as though making up her mind.

Then she said slowly: "Arabella, there's something I have to tell you. I'm in the same condition as you are. I am going to have a child."

"Harriet!"

She looked at me ruefully. "It's true."

"How could that have happened?"

She made an effort to treat the matter flippantly. "Oh, in the usual way."

"But who . . . ? And when . . . ?"

"About the same time as you . . . perhaps a little earlier." She started to laugh—a little hysterically, for she was not nearly as calm as she pretended to be.

"Who . . . *who*?" I demanded. Then light dawned on me. "Charles Condey."

She buried her face in her hands.

I said: "Oh, Harriet, how could you! Then you must marry him. You must write to him at once. I wonder where he is?"

She raised her face and looked at me angrily. "I shall never marry Charles Condey."

"But he is the father of your child."

"Nothing would induce me to marry him."

"But what . . . ? How . . . ?"

"You will let me stay here to have the child? You'll not turn me away?"

"Harriet, as if I would! But it is going to be difficult."

"It's a difficult situation."

"What will everyone *say*?"

She shrugged her shoulders.

"Such things have happened before."

"Does anyone know?"

"The Lambard suspects."

"You haven't told her?"

"I have told no one but you. They will have to know

158

in due course. Madame Lambard will be overjoyed that her discerning eye did not deceive her."

"Oh . . . Harriet!"

"Don't look at me like that. I've always told you I was not what is called a good woman. I was bound to be caught sooner or later."

"Please don't talk like that."

"How else should I talk? You see now why I can't go to your parents."

"Yes, I see that, Harriet."

"They'll want to get me out of here when they know."

"Of course they won't. My mother will understand. She, herself . . ."

I hesitated and thought of my own birth which had been unorthodox. My mother would have to show sympathy for Harriet since I had been the daughter of her sister's husband and herself. But I knew she would. She had always been kind and helpful to any of the servants who had fallen into trouble.

I went on: "Don't be afraid, Harriet. We'll look after you. But I think Charles Condey should know."

"Please, please don't make any effort to find him or tell him."

"I wouldn't if you didn't want it."

"Oh, Arabella, what a wonderful day it was for me when we came to Château Congrève! I knew there was some special bond between us. You see we are together . . . like sisters . . . You have a child . . . and I am to have one too. In spite of everything, I can't help feeling excited."

I took her hand.

"Oh, Harriet," I said, "we must always help each other."

After the first shock of the news spread through the household, it ceased to be a nine days' wonder. It was accepted that Harriet was going to have a baby. I must say she carried the situation off with great aplomb, and somehow it seemed quite a glorious event rather than something to be ashamed about.

She had taken a lover whom she had met at Villers

159

Tourron, the servants said to each other. She had decided she did not want to marry him. It was not the first time it had happened to a girl, though in her case she had had the opportunity to marry and had declined.

There always had to be something special about Harriet.

Now the cozy period set in. We were together most of the time. She laughed at our increasing bulk. "The bulging ladies," she called us. She made a comedy of it. Whatever happened to Harriet must always seem like a play. But I was beginning to be happy again. For hours at a time I would cease to think of Edwin, and only a few weeks before I should not have believed that possible.

The babies were a great absorption. Madame Lambard discussed at length confinements she had attended. She declared herself satisfied with us both, and the idea of having two babies in the house at once was a double rejoicing, she told me, never mind if one of them was making a rather unconventional entrance into the world.

The summer was slipping away.

I had had to tell my mother that Harriet was pregnant. She wanted to know who was the father of the child, and I told her that it was a young man who had been at the house party at Villers Tourron. He had offered marriage to Harriet, but she had found she did not love him enough for marriage and had bravely decided that she would care for their child without him.

My mother did not criticize her and agreed with me that she must be cared for.

Lucas was a little bewildered, but his devotion to Harriet was complete. I believe he would have married her himself if she would have had him. As for the little ones they were not so surprised. Harriet was so clever, and they were sure that if I was going to have a baby, it was only natural that Harriet should have one too.

Fenn announced that he reckoned he would be a double uncle if Harriet would let him. She hugged him and said that he should be the uncle of all the children she would have. He confided to Angie that he thought Harriet would have ten children, and he wondered if they would

160

all cry at once, but he was confident of his avuncular abilities to keep them smiling, and he did wish they wouldn't wait so long before coming.

They were happy days—days of serenity. Christmas came and it was January.

Madame Lambard was in a state of preparedness. "It can't be long now," she kept murmuring.

It was typical of Harriet that she should be the first. On the fifteenth of January she gave birth to a healthy boy.

I sat by her bed, deeply aware of the child within me. She lay back, her lovely hair damp on her forehead, triumphant in a way and somehow rueful.

Madame Lambard brought the baby and showed him to me.

"If it had been a girl I should have called it Arabella," she said. "Now I'm going to call him Leigh. You see I want to call him after you in some way, and you are Arabella Eversleigh. Have you any objections?"

"Of course not. It's a lovely name and a lovely idea. How proud you must be of your little Leigh. If mine is a boy, you know what I shall call him."

"Edwin," she said.

And I nodded.

It was two weeks later when my son was born. I kept my word and he was christened Edwin.

Those were strange yet happy days; everywhere the excitement was intense. I had to admit that I could not take as great an interest in what was happening as most people did because I was so completely absorbed in motherhood.

I was exultant when I held my baby in my arms and he smiled at me; if he cried I would be filled with terror. I called Madame Lambard ten times a day for reassurance. She laughed at me. "Ah, madame, you suffer from First Baby Fears," she told me. "It is always so with a first baby. When the second comes, the third and the fourth . . . oh, it is a different matter then."

I said soberly, "I shall only have one, Madame Lambard, for I shall never marry again."

Then having raised a sad subject, she tried to cheer me by telling me that young Monsieur Edwin (whom she called Edween) was the most healthy and most happy baby it had ever been her joy to deliver.

It was a happy house, she said, that sheltered two young babies like Messieurs Edween and Leigh—though she had to admit that the last named gentleman's appearance was a little indiscreet.

Harriet imitated her perfectly, and I must confess we laughed a good deal during those months. Harriet loved her baby, I was sure, but differently from the way in which I loved mine. She was proud of him; I detected a smug satisfaction if he was better tempered or appeared to have grown more than Edwin. She wanted to be proud of him rather than to love him, I thought. I suppose because the circumstances of his birth were so different from those of my own child. I wondered whether Harriet often thought of Charles Condey. Matilda Eversleigh naturally was eager to see her grandson, and because I could not travel to her, she came to Congrève.

Harriet grimaced when she heard she was coming. "She'll hold up her hands in horror at the sight of Leigh," she said.

"Harriet, I really think you should marry the father. After all, you must have liked him to begin with."

"I never did, like Charles much," she admitted.

"And yet you did . . . that."

"Careless of me, wasn't it? Still I do love my little Leigh, and I can't help feeling pleased he's here."

"Harriet, you are incorrigible. But what can we say to Lady Eversleigh?"

"That I was secretly married."

"To whom?"

"Not Charles Condey. For Heaven's sake, keep him out of it. Someone who came here for a few days on his way to England. We fell in love, we married and this is the fruit of our union."

"You have so little regard for the truth."

"On the contrary, I have the greatest regard for it. But there are occasions when it is necessary to set it aside . . . for Lady Eversleigh's sake."

"And not your own?"

"My dear Arabella, you know me well enough to understand that I am outside convention. I only submit to it out of regard for those who hold it dear. So I will tell my little tale to Lady Eversleigh and you will not contradict me because to do so would make her most unhappy."

Lady Eversleigh came. She was entranced by her grandson. She held him in her arms and wept over him. He was very intrigued by her tears and crowed with delight. I am sure he thought they were some special game contrived for his pleasure.

It was touching to see her.

"Such tragedy, dear Arabella," she told me. "First Charlotte. Poor girl, she suffered. And then this terrible thing. Oh, how glad I am that you married before he went. Now we have our compensation, have we not?"

She made it clear that she found young Edwin immensely superior to any other child.

"The news is excellent," she said. "Very soon, dear Arabella, we shall be in England. Lord Eversleigh tells me that General Monck has been in touch with the King's most loyal supporters and that negotiations are already going ahead. What a happy day that will be when we may return to our country and build up our homes again. You and I will carry our great sorrow with us. But when we go, you will come to Eversleigh Court. We must try to subdue our sorrow, for we have our little Edwin now. We shall make such plans for his future. He will be my life from now on."

I had not thought of going to Eversleigh Court, but I could see that it would be expected of me.

I said: "What of Carleton Eversleigh? He must have looked upon himself as the heir when Edwin died."

"So he was . . . until our little one came. Carleton will be delighted. He was wonderful to Edwin when he was a boy. He used to alarm me a little. He was so rough with him, but my husband said it was good for the boy. Dear Edwin had rather a gentle nature. Though he was full of fun, he was not like Carleton. Carleton forced him to fence and box and ride. He tried to make him like himself." She shook her head. "Darling Edwin, he was so good-natured. He did his best. I daresay Carleton will want to take on this little Edwin."

"I will not have him at risk."

"Indeed, that shall never be. He is the most precious of children."

We talked at length of him. How he smiled; how he so rarely cried; how he was so much brighter than all other children. We became close through our love for the child.

To my surprise she accepted our story about Harriet. She was not really interested. She disliked her because of what had happened with Charlotte. I wondered what she would have said had she known that Charlotte had come near to taking her own life.

She showed very little interest in young Leigh at first, but he had such winning ways with him, that she could not but be charmed. She made it clear, though, that she had no desire for friendship with Harriet.

After she had left I had had letters from my parents who were now in Breda.

It was April. The babies were three months old and my parents were certain that departure for England was imminent. There were letters full of what was happening in the King's entourage. Negotiations were in progress. Envoys were going between Breda and London. Sir John Grenville had taken a letter from Charles to General Monck and the General had openly declared that he had ever been faithful to the King and that it was only now that he was in a position to be of service to him.

My mother wrote that there had been some, like our own dear General Tolworthy, who had shared the King's exile with him and given up all for his sake, but no matter. This was great news. "The King has been asked to return," she wrote, "and he has sent back his terms to Monck. It cannot now be long."

I read my mother's letter as we sat at the table. Lucas said we ought to start making our preparations, for we should be leaving. The children were excited at the prospect of change, but the servants were flatteringly subdued, and as for Madame Lambard, she demanded to know what she was going to do, having brought two darling children into the world and to have them snatched away from her.

"It is not yet arranged, Madame Lambard," I soothed her. "So many times there has been talk like this and nothing came of it."

The babies slept in a room next to mine. If they cried in the night I wanted to know. I would go and comfort them. Sometimes it was Leigh who needed to be picked up. Harriet never heard them, she said.

I scolded her. "You're an unnatural mother," I told her.

"Reluctant would perhaps be a more apt description," she answered.

I was disturbed when she talked like that, for I thought of poor Leigh who was really more aware of me and of Madame Lambard than he was of his mother.

One night Harriet came into my room just as I had retired to bed. That was in mid-April and there had been more news from my parents about the imminent return of the King to England, and this time it was indeed significant. The Parliament had voted that the government of the country should be by the King, the Lords and the Commons. That was good enough.

Preparations would now go on apace.

Harriet was in a pensive mood.

I was already in bed, so she took a chair and studied me.

"What a lot has happened in a short time," she said, "and now there will be more changes. Just think of it, Arabella. We really shall be going home."

"It's strange," I replied. "It's what we have been waiting for and yet at the same time I feel a little sadness. This old *château* has been home to me for a long time. I have been happy here. I loved it before I realized that it was shabby and life was rather dull here. It didn't seem so once."

"You have a contented soul, dear Arabella. In time I believe you would make a home wherever you went . . . and then start to enjoy it."

"I realize how little I knew of life before . . ."

"Before I came," suggested Harriet.

"Yes, I suppose that could be a starting point."

"Perhaps I shouldn't have stayed, Arabella."

"I wonder what would have happened if you had not?"

"To you . . . or to me? You would have met your Edwin and married him, for that was preordained . . . by your families. But you would never have followed him to England."

"Then he might be still alive. I should have had him and the baby."

"You see, I am a poor exchange."

"Oh, please, Harriet, don't talk like that. It's a mistake to say, if this had happened something else would. How can we know?"

"Yes, how can we know? But 'If' is a fascinating game and sometimes one can't resist playing it. If he had lived, perhaps it would not have been as you imagined. There might have been things you would have learned."

"What do you mean?"

"About each other. You parted when you both were ideals to each other. It is difficult to remain an idol for very long, you know. Unfortunately, every one of us has, if not a foot of clay . . . a heel . . . a toenail . . . You see what I mean?"

"I can't bear to think of what I did, Harriet. If I had stayed here . . ."

"Let's not speak of it, then. When you go to England it will be to the Eversleigh ancestral home."

"I don't know. There will be so much to be done. These homes were all but destroyed."

"Eversleigh Court wasn't. We know that by his good services to Cromwell, Carleton Eversleigh managed to keep the place intact, to say nothing of all those treasures stored in the secret compartment behind the books."

"Yes, they were fortunate in that."

"The treasures will be brought forth and there you will have a luxurious home. Yes, you will go there with your son, Edwin, the heir to a goodly estate, I don't doubt. For the Eversleighs will be one of those lucky families who will be high in royal favour. The same will apply to the Tolworthys. Little Edwin is well cushioned from either side. But from what I gather, Far Flamstead, the Tolworthy residence, was rather badly mauled by the Roundheads."

"I can't imagine what it will be like after all these years."

"Prayer meetings in the banqueting hall, I suspect, and hard pallet beds to replace the comfortable fourposters. One thing we know. It has not been kept cozy by a clever Carleton."

"You didn't like him, did you?"

"I know his kind. Arrogant, overpowering, wanting to be the master of us all. He didn't like me, and I have the common human failing of not liking people unless they like me."

"It is a new experience for you not to impress a man."

"Rare, I grant you."

"Doesn't that make him some sort of challenge?"

"Not for me in the case of such an overbearing, conceited creature as your cousin-in-law." Her voice changed suddenly. It was the first time I had ever heard her sound forlorn. "If you go to Eversleigh Court . . . which I am sure they will want . . . what of me?"

"You would come with me."

"Do you think I should be welcome? A woman of no consequence with a bastard boy?"

"Don't talk like that, Harriet. You know that I should always want you with me."

"Dear Arabella. But you see everyone does not feel so kindly towards me. Lady Eversleigh dislikes me . . . and makes no effort to hide her feelings."

"That is because of Charlotte."

"No matter what the cause, it exists. I should not be welcome there. Your parents? Would they invite me to Far Flamstead . . . or wherever they go? Be sensible, Arabella. Where shall I go?"

"Oh, Harriet, you have been with us so long. I can't imagine your not being there."

"You won't have to imagine it. It will be a fact."

I was silent, for what she said was true. I knew that Lady Eversleigh would not want her and my mother was suspicious of her. Lucas adored her and so did the children, but how much weight would they carry?

I was horrified by her plight and I said firmly: "No matter what the Eversleighs say, you shall come with me,

Harriet. You have done them no harm. Edwin was quite fond of you. They would be a little shocked by Leigh if they were to discover the truth. Ladies are not expected to have children unless they are married. Some servant girls do, and my mother was always kind when they did."

"Perhaps I shall be treated with the same leniency as a servant girl," she said with a laugh.

Then for some reason we were both laughing.

She came to the bed and implanted a light kiss on my brow. "Don't worry about me," she said. "I shall be able to look after myself when the time comes, never fear."

Then she went out and left me. She was right. I could feel confident that she would look after herself. And in my heart I believed that she would come with me. I could not imagine life without Harriet.

News came filtering in at speed.

The City of London and the Fleet declared for Charles.

This meant that as soon as the King was ready to sail, he might safely do so.

His statue had been set up in the Guildhall and the Commonwealth's arms had been reduced. That was not all. News immediately followed this that Charles had solemnly been proclaimed King in London and Westminster. There was to be a day of thanksgiving because the Commonwealth was ended and there was once more to be a king on the throne.

Then the greatest news of all. A committee of six lords and twelve commoners had arrived at The Hague with an invitation to the King. He was asked to return to his kingdom. His birthday by good fortune fell on the twenty-ninth of the month, and it seemed fitting that on that day he should make his triumphant entry into London.

So at last it had come. Our return was imminent.

It seemed as though friends emerged from all over France. They were making their way to the coast for the great day, and there were constant visitors at the *château*. The servants had always liked visitors but now they were saddened. They knew that soon we should be going. Sometimes I thought Madame Lambard might attempt to kidnap the babies and hide them away to prevent our taking them. The melancholy in the castle was an odd contrast to the high spirits of our visitors, but it was rather touching and very complimentary. We were sad too, for now that the promised land was in sight, we could spare a thought for those whom we should have to leave behind.

"We shall be back to see you, Madame Lambard," I said. "And you must come to see us. I shall bring Edwin over to show you."

She smiled at me and rather sadly shook her head.

There was always a great deal to do because of the constant stream of people who came—some staying for a day, others a night and a few much longer.

One of the latter was Sir James Gilley, a rather dashing gentleman in his late forties, I imagined—quite a dandy who admitted he had suffered a great deal from exile. He was a friend of the King and he used to say to us, "Charlie will change all that when he gets back," and, "Charlie would appreciate you ladies." I remarked to Harriet that he was on very familiar terms with His Majesty.

Harriet loved to listen to his tales of the Court, and although it had for the last years been a poor sort of Court, a travelling one looking for hospitality where it could find it, still the King was at the head of it; and as Sir James told us, "When he is back, Charlie is going to make up for all that." He had already confided to Sir James that, once back, he had made up his mind never to go wandering again.

May seemed a lovelier month than ever that year. I was sure there were more flowers than usual. The buttercups and dandelions made a sheen of gold in the fields and the slender bluebells a lovely mist in the woods. I used to awake early and get out of bed to make sure that the babies were happy. Then I would take Edwin back to my bed and lie there talking to him while I listened to the gay, abandoned singing of the birds.

Harriet seemed a little aloof. I guessed she was getting more and more anxious. There was such change in the air and she was thinking of her future.

No matter. I was going to take her with me. I was sure I could persuade Matilda Eversleigh that she was my friend and as such I wanted her to live with me.

Lucas was a little apprehensive. He was too old to be able to accept our return as the panacea of all our troubles. He had been too long at Château Congrève to be able to leave it blithely. Also he was wondering about Harriet, for he accepted the fact that I must go with my new family and it seemed likely that Harriet would come with me while he, of course, would go to our parents' home.

Dick was excited, and I heard him telling the others the wildest stories about an England he had never seen. But he had his own pictures of it, for he had heard much of it over the years.

Harriet seemed to enjoy the company of those who came to the *château*. She reminded me of the Harriet who had gone to Villers Tourron and had been the centre of attraction. She rode out with our guests, and I often heard their laughter when she amused them with her conversation and stories about herself which I knew were mainly fabrications. But they were always amusing and told with a wit which seemed to charm the listeners. She posed as the young widow, and it was assumed that her husband had lost his life in the same affray that Edwin had, and like me she was the widow of a hero who had given his life in the King's cause.

Sir James Gilley told me one bright morning that on the next day he would be moving on. He was making his way to the coast and there he would await the King's party. They would cross the Channel and a great welcome would be awaiting them on the other side, he doubted not.

"And, dear lady, it will not be long before you will follow us, I am sure of that. I trust we shall meet at the King's Court. Charlie will want to meet those who have been his good friends throughout the years."

I said that I doubted not my father would be coming to the *château* soon, for if the King were on his way, so would he be.

"Then we shall meet soon. Tomorrow morning early I shall depart and I shall say farewell to you this evening, for I shall be off, I doubt not, before you are astir."

"I will rise early."

"Nay, it would grieve me. You have been such a perfect hostess, I should not wish to cause you further trouble."

"It would be no trouble."

"Nay, dear lady," he said. "Let me slip away. Our next meeting will be in London, I promise myself."

That day he made preparations, and I saw very little of him, and after we had supped that night he thanked me formally for my hospitality and he vowed that when he saw my father he would tell him what a fine daughter he had.

He said he would retire early to be off at the first sign of dawn.

Harriet came to my room that night.

"He will be gone tomorrow," I told her. "You have been good friends. You will miss him."

She shrugged her shoulders. "In these days people come and go. Until we are living in a more stable society, one should not attach too much importance to passing acquaintance."

"James Gilley says we shall meet again ere long."

"That may be. I wonder if the King will remember all his friends. There will be so many around him to remind him of their loyalty."

"Perhaps he will remember those who do not need to remind him."

"Ah, there's wisdom there." She looked intently at me. "Change . . . everywhere," she went on. "You feel it all around you. It's in the air."

"Naturally. At least that for which we have waited all these years is about to come to pass."

"Do you think it will live up to expectations, Arabella?"

"It will be good to be home. We shall no longer be exiles living on the charity of our friends."

"Ah, that *will* be good. Oh, Arabella, we shall always be friends. I know it."

"I hope so."

"Whatever I've done you would forgive me, wouldn't you?"

"I suppose so."

"Always remember that."

"How solemn you are tonight."

"It's a solemn occasion."

"You are anxious about the future, I believe. You mustn't be. You're coming with me. I would not allow it to be otherwise."

She came over to the bed and kissed me.

"God bless you, Arabella."

I thought she looked unusually solemn. Then she laughed and said: "I'm tired. Good night."

And she was gone.

The next day stands out clearly in my memory.

I did not hear the departure. Sir James must have left early and quietly, as he had said he would.

I went in to the babies. They were sleeping peacefully. I picked up Edwin cautiously and sat for a while as I loved to do, rocking him in my arms.

He awoke and started to whimper. Then Leigh heard him and started too. So I took him up and sat for some time, holding one in the crook of each arm.

Madame Lambard came bustling in to attend to them and I went back to my room to dress.

When I was ready, I did not hear Harriet stirring, so I knocked at her door, and as there was no answer I went in.

Her bed was made. Either it had not been slept in or she had been up early and made it herself.

I went to the window and looked out. It was a peaceful scene; the countryside green and fresh, the budding trees, the birds still wild with joy because the morning had come.

I remembered that Sir James Gilley had left and we should have a quiet day free from guests. I should be getting my possessions together because I knew that any day now my parents would arrive and it would be our turn to travel to the coast.

I turned suddenly and saw the letter lying on a table. I went to it. It was addressed to me so I opened it and attempted to read it, but the words swam before my eyes and I had to go back and start again before I could believe what was written.

My dear Arabella,

This is good-bye. I am leaving this morning with James Gilley. He is devoted to me and will look after me. Believe me, when I tell you I hate to leave you, but I could see no other way. Your mother-in-law, with whom you will now live, dislikes me. She would never have tolerated me in your house. I fancy your mother is not overfond of me and would not have wanted me in hers. This seemed the answer. And when James asked me I said yes. He is rich and I like my comforts. I shall know how to handle him. I shall enjoy the Court, I am sure. I really have only one regret and that is leaving you, Arabella. We have been special friends, have we not? And we always shall be. For we shall meet again.

There is one other thing. I am leaving Leigh in your care. I know you will do the right thing by my baby. You will bring him up with your own dear Edwin, and there is no one else with whom I would rather leave him.

This is not good-bye, dear Arabella. It is au revoir.

God bless you

Your loving friend,
Harriet.

Again and again I read through what she had written. I didn't believe it. It couldn't be. She had gone as dramatically as she had come. But she had left something behind to remind us of her. Her own child! How could she leave him!

Of course she could. Harriet was capable of everything. I went into the room which we had made the nursery.

Madame Lambard was rocking Leigh up and down because, as she started to say, he had the wind.

I stared at the baby and Madame Lambard said: "Is anything wrong, Madame Arabella?"

I answered simply. "She has gone. She has left the baby and has gone."

During the third week of May my parents came to the *château* to take us back, and what wild rejoicing there was at our reunion. This, alas, did not extend to the kitchens and Marianne, Jeanne and Jacques were very subdued; as for Madame Lambard, she was desolate, though perhaps this was mainly due to the babies.

173

My mother was most disturbed when she heard that Harriet had gone, leaving her son behind.

"The unnatural creature!" she cried. "How could she do such a thing? And who is the father?"

I told her it was Charles Condey who had fallen passionately in love with Harriet during our visit to Villers Tourron.

"We know him well. He is such a sober young man. I find it hard to believe that he would not stand by a girl who was to have his child."

"He wanted to marry her but she wouldn't have him."

"He was, of course, meant for Charlotte."

"You do not know Harriet, Mother. She is so attractive. People find her irresistible . . . or most of them do."

"That is understandable . . . but to leave a child!"

"She knew I would always look after him."

"And what shall you do? Take him to Eversleigh?"

"Of course. He will grow up with Edwin."

My mother shook her head anxiously. Then she embraced me and said: "You are a good girl, Arabella. I can't tell you how often your father and I have thanked God for you. You know what you mean to your father?"

I nodded. "How wonderful it will be to be together again. I wish I were coming home with you to Far Flamstead."

"I know, my dearest. But you must comfort Matilda. Poor lady, she has lost her only son. She loves you dearly. She told me that as soon as she saw you she knew you were the wife she wanted for Edwin. And now when this terrible tragedy has come to her, it is you who are the greatest help to her because you have given her little Edwin. You've given her something to live for. A grandson is what she prayed for and, through you, she has him. So do not regret that you are not coming to Far Flamstead. We shall not be very far away. We will meet often and you will be happy because you have brought such joy to your new family."

Lord Eversleigh, Edwin's father, was a delightful man; he was considerably older than my own father, as Matilda was also. I remembered Edwin's telling me how they had been married for some time before they had any children and that was why Carleton had had his hopes.

Lord Eversleigh was deeply moved when he was presented to my son, and although at such a time I must miss my husband even more bitterly than at others, I was happy to have brought such joy to them by giving them a grandson.

We were all to cross the Channel together, and my parents would stay for a night at Eversleigh Court which was near the coast. Our emotions were at such a pitch that I felt part of the time that I was in a dream. After all, this was the fulfillment of our hopes of years. We had talked so much of going home that, now the time had come, we were uncertain of our happiness. In the first place we had to say good-bye to so much that we had known for so long; and the sad eyes of the servants at Congrève and the red ones of Madame Lambard could not do anything else but depress us.

How should I have felt had I been going back with Edwin? So different, I was sure.

The crossing was a smooth one, which was a blessing, and we made for an inn not much more than a hundred yards from the sea which had been well known to the Eversleighs in the old days.

Then it had been called the Jolly Waggoner but the Jolly had been painted out and it was now simply the Waggoner—a particular piece of Puritan folly which made us all laugh.

The landlord, Tom Ferret, was, like most people, I was to discover, eager to cast aside the gloomy piety he had been obliged to practice for a more convivial manner.

"Well, Tom," said Lord Eversleigh. "Times are changing."

Tom put his finger to his nose and said slyly: "And about time too, and good it is to see you back, milord."

"And how is your father?" asked Lord Eversleigh.

Tom pointed upwards, and I wasn't sure whether he meant his father was in the room above or in Heaven. I realized it was the latter, for he went on: "Sorry I am, milord, that he can't see this day. Now we'll look forward to the good times, we will."

"A return to prosperity," said Lord Eversleigh. "Puritanism is no good for business, eh, Tom?"

"It has been a struggle to keep going, milord, but praise God His Majesty is coming back. Do you know when the happy day will be, milord?"

"Soon, Tom. Soon. We want him back for his thirtieth birthday. And that will be the twenty-ninth of this month."

"God bless him. You'll drink his health, I hope, in my best malmsey wine." He winked. "Tucked away in the cellar these many years. No sense in giving good wine to them that thinks it's a sin to enjoy it."

"We will, we will, and will you have a message sent to the Court, Tom, to tell my nephew that we're home?"

"Master Carleton, he has been working for the King all this time it seems . . . and him playing the Puritan up there . . . one of the sternest of 'em, I heard, and all the big'uns coming to stay at Eversleigh to see him and talk about how they could make us even more miserable than we were."

"No Eversleigh would ever be disloyal to his King, Tom."

"No, milord, but Master Carleton fooled us all right."

"As was necessary."

"Yes, milord. Now for the message . . . I'll get a man off at once. Then for the malmsey."

Milk was brought for the babies, and we sat at the inn table sampling hot bread with cheese and malmsey wine, which tasted good to me.

An hour or so later Carleton Eversleigh was at the inn. Lord Eversleigh took his hand and shook it. Matilda embraced him. There were tears in her eyes.

"Oh, Carleton," she cried. "It is so long . . ."

He nodded. "But we knew it would come and here it is. So let us be joyful." I felt he was anxious to curtail the emotion, for I guessed he would hate any show of it.

He was looking at me, and I noticed the slow smile which I could not understand. "Ah," he said, "it is not so long since *we* met."

I nodded and introduced him to my parents.

He exchanged greetings with them and then he saw the

176

children. Of course he would not know. How could he? He was looking askance at my mother's two women holding them.

"My son," I said. "My son Edwin."

He was frankly amazed.

He looked down at the baby. "So . . . he left you a child, then."

"Yes."

"Twins?"

"No. This is Edwin. This is Leigh."

"And whose child is Leigh, I wonder?"

"You remember Harriet Main."

"Harriet Main." He gave a sudden, short laugh. He looked round him, obviously for Harriet.

"She is not with us," I said. "She went to London with Sir James Gilley. They are to be married. Then, I doubt not, she will come to claim the child."

I was romancing in the way Harriet herself might have done. It was foolish, but his sly smile angered me.

"Well, you can reckon that she will be long before she claims the child if she is waiting for Gilley to marry her. He is very much married to a lady I know well. A most respectable lady with two sons and four daughters, and as she is in a remarkably good state of health, it seems unlikely that James Gilley will be free for some time yet."

I hated him for exposing Harriet before them all. I could see that the Eversleighs were shocked, and my mother, although she told me afterwards that she had guessed this was how it was, was faintly annoyed.

Carleton had that effect, I discovered later. If there was a peaceful, happy atmosphere, he could be depended on to shatter it.

"So you are left with the baby, eh?" he went on laughing. "Well, the two of them will grow up together. Let me look at the little fellow. He's bonny." He held out a finger which Edwin, with what seemed to me superhuman intelligence, grasped. "I think he's taken a fancy to me." I wanted to snatch my baby away. I was sure Carleton was thinking that Edwin's existence robbed him of what he had been considering was his inheritance.

Carleton had brought a carriage and horses to take us to the house which was some three miles from the coast, and as we trundled along the lanes, everyone was exclaiming about the beauty of the countryside.

"Oh, those green, green fields," cried Matilda. "How I have missed them! Look at the blooms on that horse chestnut. Oh, Arabella, do look over there, my dear—apple trees! Rose-coloured blossom, and look there's white cherry."

We had, of course, seen green grass and fruit trees in blossom during our exile, but the fact that this was home endowed it all with a very special beauty.

It was indeed a lovely time of the year. The Restoration could not have come at a better time. We were all noticing the beauties of nature afresh—the bronze tufts of the sycamores and purple lilac and gold laburnum.

England. And we were no longer exiles.

And now we were at Eversleigh Court. Inevitably my mind went back to that day just over a year ago when I had arrived here with Edwin and Harriet. I could hear Carleton's voice oddly enough rather than Edwin's. "God preserve you, friend."

How well Carleton had done it. What an actor he was. He had not betrayed by a flicker of an eyebrow that he resented my baby, and yet he must do so, because merely by being born Edwin had deprived him of great estates and a noble title.

"We are gradually getting the place back to normal," said Carleton. "I had hoped, Uncle, that I should have done more by now. You will see how much I was able to save. It's really a remarkable achievement."

"You were always clever, Carleton," said Lord Eversleigh.

"By God, I've had need of my wits during the last year. I came near more than once to giving the whole show away. It wasn't the easiest role for me to play . . . that of the Puritan."

"I'll warrant it wasn't," Lord Eversleigh laughed. "But well done, nephew. It's good to be home. One deep regret . . ."

"I know," said Carleton. "It was a tragedy." He looked

178

at me quizzically, and I felt myself disliking him afresh.
"But you have the boy."

"God takes away with one hand and gives with the
other," said Matilda. "I have lost my dear son but I have
my new daughter. She has brought me great comfort and
I am filled with a gratitude I find hard to express."

She held out her hand and I took it.

"God bless you, Arabella," she said.

"Arabella has given you your grandson," put in Carleton. "I reckon that is a matter for rejoicing. Now come
along and see what you think of everything."

He walked beside me, and I fancied that he watched
me closely because he wanted to know what effect it had
on me, coming back to the scene of my tragedy.

I had never realized on my previous visit how beautiful
Eversleigh Court was. I remembered clearly the high wall
which surrounded the house and the gables which could
be glimpsed above it. The gates were wide open and we
rode in. The feeling of austerity was still there. It was too
early to have changed it. The erstwhile flower beds still
contained their herbs and vegetables. But a fountain was
playing and the yews had been cut into fancy shapes.
These stood out in the yards like an act of defiance to the
recent regime.

"A shock to you, Aunt Matilda," said Carleton. "But
never mind. You will soon have your flowers again. You
must remember that in my role of Puritan I had to get rid
of them. They were so beautiful. The herbs and the
vegetables were of use and therefore acceptable in the
eyes of our lords and masters. Some of them are not
without their charm, don't you think?"

"Oh, Carleton, how did you endure it!" cried Matilda.

"In a way I quite enjoyed it. It amused me to hunt
with the hounds while I was really running with the fox."

"So few could have done it," murmured his aunt.

We went into the hall. It had changed. The long table
was shining and laid with pewter utensils. Velvet curtains
had been hung at the minstrels gallery, which I had
scarcely noticed before. A tapestry, obviously freshly
brought from the secret store, hung on the walls.

"Home," said Lady Eversleigh. "What can I say?"

Her husband put his arm through hers and pressed it.

We went up the great staircase. Several pictures hung on the wall—portraits of long-dead Eversleighs.

"So you salvaged all this, Carleton!" said Lord Eversleigh.

"And more also," replied Carleton proudly. "You will see in due course. But now let me conduct you to your rooms. I am sure you are in need of rest. I was not aware that there would be babies. We have no nursery available. It is years since we had one here."

He grinned at me with what was meant to be an apology.

Charlotte said: "There's the old nursery."

"I daresay my Cousin Arabella will want the baby near her just at first."

"Indeed I do."

"And the nurseries are at the very top of the house. Nothing is prepared up there."

I said: "I'll take the room I occupied before. There was one right next to it . . ."

I stopped. There would be memories in that room of the nights I had spent there with Edwin, and the next room was that which had been occupied by Harriet.

I wished she were with me. She would laugh at Carleton. She would make me see everything differently. I knew she was an adventuress. Hadn't she told me often enough? She had taken Charlotte's lover; she had had a child and abandoned him; she had lied, with such facility that one never knew whether or not she was speaking the truth; but I was fond of her. And I missed her.

Of course it would have been impossible for her to have been here. Charlotte would never have endured that. In going away she had done the right thing, I supposed.

I would look after Leigh. He should be with Edwin in the nursery. But how I wished she were here!

There was the room I had shared with Edwin, but how different it was! There was a beautiful tapestry on the wall and it contained some elegant pieces of furniture. These things would have been hidden at the time I stayed here, but how they transformed the room! I could not look at the four-poster bed without emotion, but even that looked different with its silk curtains.

I went into Harriet's room where the babies were to be. My young brothers and sister were very silent, overcome with awe, I believed, by everything that was happening to them.

Charlotte seemed to have taken a fancy to them and I was glad, for they liked her and she said she would find a suitable room for them. She remembered so much of her old home, she said. It was all coming back to her.

I wondered how she would feel about the presence of Leigh. How did a woman feel about her lover's child by another woman? Charlotte, however, gave no sign of disliking him. I was sure she was much too sensible to blame the child. I was beginning to like my sister-in-law, and I hoped very much that we should be friends, but no one could, of course, take Harriet's place.

My parents would be leaving early the following morning, but as my mother told me more than once, we should all be in England now and we should see a great deal of each other.

Alone in my room, I washed the grime of the journey from my face and changed my travelling clothes for a gown of blue velvet which was somewhat the worse for wear. We had made our own clothes in Congrève and I wondered what they would look like now we were home. In Congrève it had not mattered what we wore, but I remembered vividly how bemused we were by the elaborate gowns which Harriet had worn and which looked so splendid by candlelight.

Nobody would want to dress like a Puritan now. Would it henceforth be as dangerous to do so as it was before to wear laces and ribbons?

My mother came into my room. She looked at me rather tremulously and said: "I keep thinking that you are my little girl, but of course you are grown up now."

"A widow and a mother," I reminded.

"Dearest Arabella, you are going to be happy here. I know it."

"I shall try, Mother."

"Matilda is a good woman. I know she talks a great

deal and seems superficial at times, but she really is not so. She loves you. Small wonder. You have eased her tragedy. She can be happy again in you and the boy. I know that Lord Eversleigh is grateful to you. They have said you are now their daughter and they will do anything for your happiness."

"I know, Mother."

"And Charlotte? She does not make friends easily but I think she likes you too."

"Yes, I think she does, Mother."

"There is the cousin."

"Carleton?" I said sharply.

"I don't quite know what to make of him. He was wonderful during the years. He was our most reliable agent in the country. Much of the success of all that is happening is due to him. He sent us information regularly. And yet . . ."

"You don't like him, Mother?"

"I can't say that. I don't know him. I fancy few do and that it would take a long time. Of course he has believed himself to be the heir to all this . . . which he would have been but for Edwin. I wonder how he feels about that? He gives no sign, does he?"

"Would you expect him to?"

"No, but I should expect to be able to judge what he is feeling from his conduct."

"Oh, Mother, you want to be a seer. I agree with you. I don't like him. But I shall not allow him to bother me."

She nodded. "You will be able to take care of yourself, I don't doubt. Never forget we shall not be far away. Both your father and I are happy to leave you in good hands. You have had some experience of life." She frowned slightly. "I am a little anxious about Harriet Main's child."

"Oh, Mother, he is but a baby . . . an adorable baby."

"Has it occurred to you that his presence here might be difficult for Charlotte to bear? He is the child of the man she was hoping to marry . . . How would she feel to find that child in her home?"

"She seems fond of him, Mother, as she does of Edwin. Charlotte is too sensible to blame an innocent child."

"Perhaps so," she said. "Well, my dearest, we shall say

au revoir. It is a comfort to know that you are not far off."

I stood between my parents-in-law watching the departure of my parents and brothers and sister. Charlotte was with us.

I went back in the house feeling that I had passed through one phase and a new one had begun.

THE
RESTORATION

Encounter at a Playhouse

The twenty-ninth of May of the year 1660— what an unforgettable day that was! We must all be in the capital for the King's ceremonial entry. How fitting it was that it should be His Majesty's thirtieth birthday.

We had travelled to London on the previous day and taken up residence in the Eversleighs' town house which, through his careful conduct, Carleton had managed to keep in the family in much the same manner as he had Eversleigh Court. Alas, he had not been able to put away treasures from this house, there being no secret hiding place, but he had, with great daring, carried a few of them from London to Eversleigh Court and it had been possible to bring a few back. So we found the house not so austere as it might have been.

What a happy scene that was! The city seemed to have gone mad with joy. It was clear that all believed that the evil days were over and that a new heaven had come on earth. As we rode out from our lodgings—myself and Charlotte with Carleton and Lord and Lady Eversleigh—

we had difficulty in getting through the crowded streets. Lord Eversleigh in his splendid uniform was cheered. Clearly he was one of the King's generals, and I knew that my father, who would be making his way through these streets, would be getting the same acclamation.

We were to go to London Bridge, where the grand procession was being organized. From there we would join the King, who would be journeying from Rochester through Dartford to Blackheath.

There were my father and mother with Lucas. I was so proud of my father who looked magnificent in his uniform. He was a very distinguished-looking man, and my heart warmed to him because I knew of the great love between him and my mother and that I was a living result of it. I felt very emotional in that moment and infinitely sad because my own husband had been taken from me.

The crowd was growing and the shouts were deafening. It was all "Long live the King." It seemed incredible that a few months before these people would not have dared mention his name.

A woman was beside Carleton—a tall woman who sat her horse most gracefully. She was what I would only call voluptuous, and there was a black patch on her temple to accentuate the beauty of her large brown eyes.

"I must present you to my wife," said Carleton.

I felt a shudder of revulsion which was inexplicable. I had heard that he had a wife. What was it Edwin had said? They go their own ways. It suits them.

"Madam," he said to his wife, "allow me to present my new cousin. Edwin's widow."

"I have heard of you," said Barbary Eversleigh. "You have a fine son, I believe."

I noticed that she threw a mischievous look at Carleton, as though she knew that the birth of my son had baulked his ambitions, and this gave her pleasure.

"I have heard of you, too," I said. "Are you often at Eversleigh Court?"

"Rarely," she answered. "Even though, I believe, my husband is frequently there."

She was studying me intently, as though taking in every

187

detail of my appearance. I felt uncomfortable, and I was glad that at that moment the trumpets announced that the King's arrival was imminent.

Barbary drew in her mount and brought it closer to Carleton's.

In the van of the procession were three hundred men of the Trainbands dressed in cloth-of-silver doublets; twelve hundred followed in velvet coats and then came the foot-men in purple livery. Brilliantly coloured uniforms were everywhere—buff-coated soldiers, with sleeves of cloth of silver, wearing rich green scarfs; there were men clad in blue, laced with silver, followed by the members of the City Companies in their black velvet coats and chains.

As this passed the great moment had arrived. There, between his two brothers, rode the slim, dark man, and as he appeared, shouts went up from thousands of throats: "God save the King." "A health unto His Majesty." These citizens were in love with him. He had a natural charm which it was impossible not to be aware of. His happiness in being back was obvious to all. There could scarcely have been a man or woman in the multitude who did not believe that this was the day he or she had been waiting for all through the dreary years of Puritan rule.

His thirtieth birthday! Not too young but still young enough. He was tall, very tall, so that he towered above his fellows; some might judge his dark, rather saturnine face ugly, but none could deny his charm. If any man in that press of people had dared raise his voice against good King Charles, he would have been hung by his neck on the nearest tree. From every church the bells were ringing; people had hung tapestries across the streets; from win-dows girls and women threw flowers at the King as he passed. There were trumpets and music and banners fluttering in the light breeze. Never had a people shown its monarch such loyalty; and because he had come home and not a drop of blood had been shed to bring him to his rightful kingdom, they loved him the more.

People danced. They scooped up the wine which flowed from the fountains. That night some would be drunk and perhaps quarrelsome, but for the moment it was all joy.

How exhilarating it was! I was caught up in the euphoric

joy, and I really felt, as I rode through the streets of London, that this was the start of a new life.

Then I saw her in the crowd. She was riding with Sir James Gilley and she was clearly the most attractive woman there. She was dressed in blue velvet and in her hat was a long curling feather. She looked pleased and happy, and I felt a pang of anger to think that she could as easily abandon her child.

I tried to push my horse through the crowd to reach her, when I felt a restraining hand on my reins.

It was Carleton's.

"You can't reach her," he said. "You should not try. The daughter-in-law of Lord Eversleigh should not openly consort with harlots."

I felt the colour flame into my cheeks.

"How . . . how dare you say that of . . ."

"Oh, good and loyal Arabella," he whispered. "Dear, sweet, simple Arabella! That woman is no friend to you. You should stop thinking of her as such."

"How can *you* know who is and who is not my friend?"

He brought his face close to mine. It looked mocking. "I know a great deal," he said. "*I* was not born yesterday."

"And nor was I."

"Who shall say how long ago was yesterday?"

I ignored him, still looking at Harriet.

"You should send her bastard back to her," he said. "Why should you be responsible for her mistakes?"

As I turned my horse away from him, I heard him laugh softly.

"Temper!" he whispered. "On such a day. Of course it may be that your good friend Harriet will soon be back, begging for admittance. It is well known that James Gilley doesn't keep his women long. He's a good husband, really, and does his duty by his wife. Now he is back he'll keep her pleasantly in Shropshire with a growing family, which well gives evidence that he visits her when he considers it necessary. If she had been in London today, he would have ridden with her. He never thinks of his women as anything but what they are."

189

"It seems," I said curtly, "that he is a most cynical man."

"You might say that of many of us. How, my dear, good Arabella, shall you adjust yourself to this wicked society?"

"I have no doubt that there are virtuous people even in . . ."

"Restoration London," he finished. "Perhaps so. Well, it will be interesting to see . . ."

"To see what?"

"How you like the new life. Come. You are scowling. People watch us. It is not in the mood of today to quarrel. You must smile. Everything has changed. You must believe that now the King is home, England has become a paradise."

"Is that what you believe?"

"No more than you do."

"What is he telling you?" asked Barbary. "Don't believe it. He's a deceiver, you know."

"There speaks my loyal wife," said Carleton, raising his eyes to heaven.

They made me feel very uneasy, those two. I couldn't stop thinking of what he had said about Harriet and her lover. And I wondered with an anticipation tinged with satisfaction when she would come seeking shelter from me.

I could see problems ahead. It would be different in Eversleigh Court from what it had been in Congrève. I was still thinking of this during the banquet in the King's honour, for belonging to two loyal families I was naturally entitled to be present at this.

I listened to the King, I was given his strangely appealing smile. He was a man whom women loved rather than men.

I heard him say in a musical voice which was not the least of his charms: "It must surely have been my fault that I did not come before. I have met no one today who did not protest that he always wished for my restoration."

This was murmured with a sardonic look, and I saw the cynical lips lifted in a smile. I thought then that he would be immune from all the flattery, and that, though he liked this outward manifestation of his country's approval, he suspected its depth. He could see below the glittering surface.

There in the banqueting hall I thought of Harriet, and I wondered what the future held for us all.

After the ceremonies were completed I went back to Eversleigh Court with Matilda, my father-in-law, Charlotte and Carleton. Barbary did not come with us. The days had been stimulating yet exhausting, and I hated to leave my son for longer than a few days. Even then he was in my thoughts all the time. Matilda laughed at me indulgently. "You don't really trust anyone else to look after him, do you?" she said.

It was more even than my anxieties about my son which made me want to return to the country. It may have had something to do with my glimpse of Harriet. She had sat there on her horse, magnificent, flamboyant, her complexion glowing. I knew that it owed something to artifice now, for I had learned some of her secrets, but that made the sight of her no less beautiful. It was not how beauty was achieved, it was merely a matter of its being there. That gaiety, the belief in the future, how long could it continue? I kept thinking of Carleton's cynical comment: "James Gilley doesn't keep his women long."

I hated to think of Harriet's being in that position. But I fancied too that both she and Barbary had been somewhat condescending in their attitude towards me. They took lovers wherever they fancied. Let them, but should they despise me because I had no wish to do so? Yet I was sure they did.

I decided I would put them from my mind, and the best way of doing this was to devote myself to domesticity in my new home. There was a great deal to do at Eversleigh. Many of the treasures had still to be brought out of hiding and put in their rightful place. Matilda wanted to set up her stillroom where in the past she had made wines and simples. She loved sweet scents and I had to admit I did too. She liked to fill pomanders and bowls with herbs of her own combining, and sometimes the smell of her concoctions would fill the house and we called that "Simple Time."

Charlotte shared my pleasure in the house, and there was no doubt that I was on happy terms with my husband's family.

Chief of all my pleasures was caring for my baby. I had a nurse, Sally Nullens, who had nursed Edwin and Charlotte and had just been waiting, she said, for another little one who would need her. She was old, but I thought it was right to have someone who was trusted by the family, and Edwin showed a partiality for her which settled the matter. She tried to make no difference in her treatment of the two boys, but I knew that Edwin was her favourite.

Ellen was still in the kitchens and Jasper worked in the stables. It was pleasant to see little Chastity again. She came and stood shyly before me, and when I knelt down and put my arms about her, she hugged me tightly. She was clearly one who was glad I was back. I took her to see the babies and she laughed with pleasure. She seemed very happy that we were there, and no wonder. From now on it was not going to be sinful to laugh and play. Chastity seemed to believe that I was responsible for the new state of affairs and regarded me as though I were some sort of benevolent goddess.

Ellen was a little shamefaced. As for Jasper he was inclined to be sullen. Puritanism had been so much a part of him that he would not abandon it lightly. It was clear to see that Ellen was not displeased to escape from the yoke, and although she was loyal to Jasper and if she found herself laughing would stop suddenly and look ashamed, she was glad not to have to suppress her natural inclination to enjoy life.

Ellen liked to talk to me, and I soon had the notion that she was trying to tell me something. Once when I went into the kitchen and we were alone there she said: "It were a terrible tragedy . . . what happened to the young master."

I nodded.

She went on: "We were not to blame. That's what I want you to know. 'Tweren't us. 'Twere nothing to do with us."

"Don't let's talk of it, Ellen," I said. "It distresses us all and nothing can bring him back."

"But I think, mistress, that you may blame us. I want you to know it was not through us . . ."

"Ellen," I interrupted, "it was my fault. I was careless. I did not consider that it would be thought irreligious to give a child a pretty button. It seemed such nonsense to me."

Ellen flushed with a certain shame. "It was thought to be, mistress. And Jasper, he was of the opinion that it was bad for Chastity."

"I understand, Ellen. And it was my carelessness that was to blame. Then that man came asking questions, and I betrayed us. We can talk of it now. There is no longer need for secrecy. Because of my carelessness my husband was killed."

" 'Twere not because of your talk, mistress. 'Twas not one of us that killed him. 'Twas something else."

"I don't understand you, Ellen."

"I shouldn't speak of it. But I know that you blame yourself. 'Twere known before. 'Twas not as you thought."

"You mean it was not one of your friends who killed my husband?"

"I mean, mistress, that it was not because of what you said. They were growing wise to why you were at Eversleigh and there would have been trouble in time. But it were not because of you that he was killed."

"Ellen, you are trying to comfort me."

"You should be comforted, mistress. 'Twere no fault of yours. I tell you that. I can say no more. But you should not fret. You had no hand in it."

I pressed her hand warmly. Ellen was a kindhearted, good woman now that she was at liberty to show her true nature.

"You must be happy, mistress," she went on looking searchingly into my face. "You have the dear baby. He will be your strength and comfort. And as for the rest, you must say it was as the good Lord meant it to be, and perhaps he was saving you sorrow in one way while giving it in another."

When I was in my room that night I thought, as I always did, of the nights Edwin and I had spent there. I remembered how he would often come in late at night and would sometimes leave early in the morning. I had not realized then the danger of his mission. I thought of Ellen's words. It was almost as though she knew something and was holding it back.

It was not they who had killed him, she implied. Not the band of Puritans who had grown suspicious of our presence in the house. Who then?

I dozed and fell into a half dream. Carleton was in that dream, with his wife beside him. She was laughing at me for my simplicity. They both were. Then Ellen was there. We did not kill your husband, mistress. 'Twere not us.

Barbary's voice, rather shrill and strident, broke into my dreams. "I have heard of you. You have a fine son, I believe." And she was laughing at Carleton, and suddenly he brought something he had been holding behind his back and placed it over his face. It was a mask, evil, horrible and frightening. I screamed and woke myself up.

"Edwin?" I cried. "Edwin . . ."

I was calling to my son and I had to get out of bed to assure myself that he was safe.

He was lying in his cot, smiling seraphically in his sleep. In the next cot was Leigh, one chubby hand clutching the coverlet.

All was well in the nursery. I had had a bad dream but the memory of it would not be dismissed. It stayed in my mind like a sleeping snake waiting to uncoil and strike.

A vague uneasiness had come to me.

I was very reluctant to leave my son, and for that reason I remained at Eversleigh Court and did not go to London and the King's Court, which I could so easily have done. If I went away even for a day, I would be uneasy, so that I could never have enjoyed any of the jaunts which had been arranged for me, in which case, as I explained to my mother-in-law and Charlotte, I was best at home. They agreed with me. Charlotte had no desire for society. She loved to be with the children and I was delighted that she seemed to have a special devotion for Leigh. In the begin-

194

ning she had not wished to see him, which was understandable; then her mood changed, and she really began to look on him as hers. This was good, because I was afraid that the little boy might begin to notice that Edwin was specially favoured, and I thought it might give rise to jealousy. Leigh had a strong personality, vociferous and demanding —taking after his mother, I thought. He had inherited her lovely eyes and was going to be very handsome, there was no doubt of that. He did not seem to notice that he was of any less importance in the nursery than Edwin and had a habit of pushing himself forward as though it was his right. This was amusing, while he was so young, and Edwin was of such a gentle nature that he loved everybody and seemed to be of the opinion that everyone loved him . . . which they did. But perhaps not everyone. . . . I often wondered what Carleton thought of him.

Not that Carleton ever came to the nursery, or showed the slightest interest in the children. He was at Eversleigh now and then, for there was much to be done on the estate and that was his main preoccupation. But he did spend a certain amount of time at Court. He was, Charlotte told me, on terms of intimacy with the King and they enjoyed each other's company immensely.

Nearly two years had passed since our return to England, and during that time my father had received lands and a title from the King for his services. He was now a baron, Lord Flamstead. This was gratifying and no more than he deserved. My mother was very happy. She had her family with her and I was not so very far off. We could meet now and then and she could have her brood almost completely under her wing. Cromwell's men had made almost a ruin of Far Flamstead and there was a great deal to do in the restoration of it. It was an exciting project to rebuild, and under my mother's direction, work was going on apace. She often accompanied my father to Court and she was, I knew, planning to get Lucas married. I doubt she had ever been so happy.

In spite of everything she did not forget me. I knew I had always been the very special favourite of my parents. I was their first child. They had suffered for me. I was a vindication to my father that he could beget healthy children and beneath that rather austere exterior, he was a sentimental man.

If only Edwin were alive, I used to think, I could be perfectly happy.

What celebrations there were when I visited Flamstead. My parents were determined to show me how much I meant to them. I took Edwin with me, and my father-in-law insisted that I travel in his carriage, a new acquisition of which he was very proud, and I set out accompanied by my father-in-law and about twenty men to guard me. I felt very moved that he showed such concern for me. He travelled all the way with us and stayed with us for two days before returning to Eversleigh.

When I arrived my parents said that now I was there with their grandson, their pleasure was complete. I was to stay for two weeks.

It was wonderful to be with my family. Dick, Angie and Fenn had grown up quite a bit. They remembered Congrève, though, and I think, in spite of everything, they looked back on those days with affection and perhaps a certain nostalgia.

They chattered a great deal about the play we had performed and they often mentioned Harriet, of course. Where was Harriet? they wanted to know. She had gone away, I told them. And did she take her baby with her? No, her baby had stayed behind with Edwin. Fenn informed the company that he was an uncle, which brought in a light note. I knew my parents did not want to talk about Harriet.

But my mother brought up the subject when we were alone.

"I am glad she has gone," she said. "I did not like her being there. She is an adventuress. She imposed on your kindness of heart."

"Perhaps," I said, "but we had such fun, Mother. The children loved her. There is something lovable about her. I hope she will be happy."

My mother shrugged her shoulders. "Gilley is notorious for his mistresses, apparently. She'll be passed on to some-

196

one else, I daresay. Of course she is outstandingly handsome and will not lack lovers now. But when she gets older . . ."

I felt depressed thinking of an ageing Harriet, poor, lonely, no longer able to appeal to men.

My mother touched my hand lightly. "Don't worry about her. You have done everything for her. You have even taken on the care of her son."

"He's an engaging little fellow."

"Most babies are," said my mother indulgently. "Arabella, perhaps before long you will marry again."

I stared at her in horror.

"My dear child, it would be natural. You are young. You should have someone to care for you."

"No one could care for me more than the Eversleighs. They are so good to me."

"I knew they would be and I rejoice. But if you should fall in love again?"

"I couldn't. You did not know Edwin, Mother. Nobody could be like him. If he had been less perfect . . . perhaps it would have been easy. But I should compare everyone with him . . ."

"Later on, perhaps?"

"Never," I said vehemently.

I rode with my father around the estate. He delighted in showing me his new lands and what he was doing to restore the old ones. On the ruins of the old castle folly my mother was making a beautiful garden. She spent a great deal of time there.

"It is a busy life," she told me. "I am in London with your father, and when I am weary of that we can come back here. I am hoping Lucas will have a place at Court. The King highly favours your father, although he is not one of his cronies. That could not be. Charles respects him as one of his great generals, but the men who surround him are more like Carleton Eversleigh. Amusing, witty, rather lax in morals . . . all that the King is himself. I believe Carleton Eversleigh is often in his company."

"He is frequently at the Court," I said. "He is very

197

good at managing the estate, I hear, but I believe he is restless and likes variety."

"Like many men, I daresay. I think God your father was never like that. That's the reason why he goes to Court only on business. The King is clever . . . cleverer than sometimes appears, and while he can be excessively lighthearted with some, your father is very impressed with his seriousness in other matters."

"Mother, I believe you are a very happy woman."

"You are right. I have suffered a great deal in my life, as you know. And even when your father and I were married, we were in exile and often separated. Now it seems we have come home to happiness."

"Is it all as you would want it to be, Mother?"

"Except one thing. I should like to see you happy."

"I am . . . as far as I can ever be without Edwin."

"One day," she said.

I smiled at her. I wanted to tell her that having known the perfect relationship I could not bring myself to accept something less.

Returning to Eversleigh Court I was given a welcome as warm as that I had had at Flamstead. I certainly had no reason to doubt that I was greatly loved.

Edwin was pounced upon by his grandmother, closely examined and declared more beautiful, more intelligent, than he had been when he went away and, of course, quiet perfect.

Sally Nullens told me that Master Leigh had enjoyed having the nursery to himself. He did not regard Edwin's return with a great deal of enthusiasm, so perhaps that was the explanation. Chastity came with a daisy chain she had made and insisted on putting it round my neck. Ellen had made a tansy cake which she knew I liked, and Charlotte came to my room and told me how relieved she was that I was back safely. Then she gave me an account of Leigh's doings during my absence and I was happy to think that she was beginning to love the child. Jasper examined the coach to see if any damage had been done to it, and muttered to himself so that I was not sure whether any had been. Poor Jasper, he was an uneasy man, as was to be expected. There were many like him in the neighbourhood, staunch supporters of the Roundheads who were not quite capable of making the easy turnabout as so many were.

It had been a happy visit and it was a gratifying homecoming.

Carleton joined us for dinner—a very happy occasion said my father-in-law because I was back with precious Edwin.

Carleton was fresh from Court with the news from there. We had always heard most of the Court news from him. We knew that the bodies of Oliver Cromwell and some of his supporters had been dug up and publicly hanged at Tyburn; that some people who had been buried in Henry VII's chapel and at Westminster were dug up and buried in an ordinary churchyard. We knew that there were many who sought revenge on those who had turned them out of their country and put them in exile.

"But," said Carleton, "the King is weary of these recriminations. He says, 'Enough.' What he wants to do is to be left in easy peace with his subjects. He'll love them if they love him; and if they will take him with all his faults, he'll take them. He is an easygoing man who finds quarrelling dull and witless, for it brings no good to any."

I said: "He sounds pleasant but perhaps a little weak."

"Treason," cried Carleton. "What if I report you to His Majesty?"

"As he wants me to accept his faults, he must accept mine," I retorted.

Carleton laughed and said: "How is my little cousin, the all important one?"

"You mean my son?"

"Who else?"

"He fares very well, thank you."

"Quite a man now. What is he? Two years old?"

"Yes, he is two."

"Old enough to show his character. I wonder if he will be like his father."

"I hope and pray so," I said fervently.

Carleton nodded. "Easygoing," he murmured. "Wanting all to love him and being ready to love everybody."

"That's what you said of the King."

"Some of us share these characteristics."

"And you?"

"Ah, I am an unknown quantity. There is only one thing you know of me and that is that you know nothing about me."

"That," said Matilda, "is a little example of Carleton's Court talk."

"Very subtle," I said.

"Ah, now you mock me. Let me say how glad I am that you are safely back. I trust you will go to Town for the wedding."

"Wedding?"

"That of our Sovereign Lord and the Infanta of Portugal. I heard she is a pretty little thing but homely, and she is to bring us Bombay and Tangiers with her dowry. Barbara Castlemaine is fuming. She'll brook no rival. What airs these women give themselves!"

"I'll dareswear we shall be expected to go for the wedding celebrations," said Lord Eversleigh.

"Yes," said Carleton. "I think it will be expected of you."

"I shall not want to leave Edwin," I said quickly.

Carleton was watching me intently. "I believe you think there are malicious influences at work against that child."

"They would have little chance if there were," retorted Matilda. "I never knew a child more cared for!"

I was deeply aware of Carleton's gaze and felt an alarm stirring within me again.

Time was passing quickly. Life had settled into a pattern. My mother still thought of finding a husband for me but I always eluded them. I could not forget Edwin. I looked back and saw the happiness I had shared with him, and I felt that if ever I married again it would be disloyal to his memory. I had decided that I would devote myself to my son, for Edwin lived again in him.

Edwin was now four years old. Bright, intelligent and getting so like his father that I sometimes felt like weeping when I saw him. He was quite different from Leigh, who

200

was noisy and always liked Edwin's toys better than his own. Edwin was of a mild nature, peaceable. He would smile seraphically even when Leigh snatched what was his. I used to remonstrate sometimes and tell him he must stand up for what he wanted. Edwin admired Leigh and was happy to play with him. Leigh was artful enough to realize this and used it as a form of blackmail. I could see his mother in Leigh just as I could see Edwin's father in him.

It was about this time that Lucas married. Her name was Maria and she was the daughter of Lord Cray, one of the members of the Court circle. Lucas had become debonair and as the son of my father very welcome at Court. He planned to go into politics and was already making his way in that direction.

It was silly of me not to want to stir from the country, but I didn't. I knew, of course, that I should have to go to London for the wedding which was to take place at the Crays' town residence. My mother visited us a month or so before and she said I must really bestir myself. It was foolish of me to bury myself in the country. I should meet interesting people, and now that Edwin was getting older and Sally Nullens had proved herself so reliable, she was going to insist on my emerging from my cocoon.

I knew what she was thinking of, a marriage for me. Lucas would be happily settled; it would be Dick's turn next. And there was I, her eldest daughter, shutting myself away in the country! It would not do.

I must admit that when she sent for the seamstress and showed me some of the latest fashions, which were becoming very extravagant and amusing, I felt a certain excitement bubbling up within me. She pulled my hair loose and demonstrated some of the new styles. We laughed together over the foretop—an odd loop of hair on the forehead and the loose curls on the brow which were called "favourites." We couldn't decide which suited me best—curls close to the cheeks which were known as "confidents," or drawn away from the face and looped over the ears which were "heartbreakers."

My mother said: "You see what fun it is to mingle with society."

"We entertain now and then at Eversleigh. Matilda enjoys it."

"I know. But this is not London, my child. You are behind the times here. You should visit Town more often. You should know what is going on. You should attend the theatre now and then. The changes that have been made there are astonishing. The King is devoted to the theatre and often goes. You are shutting yourself away with the past. I am going to stop it. This visit will be a start."

I shook my head. "I have come to love Eversleigh Court," I said. "The countryside is beautiful. I love to ride out. Charlotte and I are good friends.

"Ah, there is another! I cannot understand you young girls. How different I was. I wanted life . . . adventure . . . So much is changing now, Arabella. You would be amazed at what is happening. After the age of the Puritans we have swung in the other direction. Too far, some say. I expect they are right. Now for your gowns. You need them badly. What you wear here will not do for London, I do assure you."

To be with my mother was a stimulation. She seemed younger than Charlotte and younger than myself in my present mood. She radiated such happiness. She was so clearly delighted with her life that I caught something of her enthusiasm and I was excited by the prospect she was holding out to me.

I would laugh at her as she sat there while I was fitted. She insisted that the sleeves of my gowns leave my arms bare to the elbow.

"Such pretty arms," she crooned. "Then I had dresses with the sleeves slit all the way and caught here and there with ribbons."

"The height of fashion!" she exulted. She had brought with her silks, brocades and velvets. "You should see the shops in London. Every shopkeeper is determined to outdo all the others and so it goes on. I declare that the men are looking even prettier than the women. Lucas has Rhingrave breeches seamed with scarlet and silver lace. I can tell you, your brother is a sight to be seen!"

And while I was fitted and paraded I felt a change creeping over me. I felt young and gay again and suddenly I remembered that it was when Harriet had gone out of my life that I had found much of its savour gone.

I said to my mother: "Have you seen anything of Sir James Gilley lately?"

She hesitated for a moment. "Why, yes, he was at some Court function a few months ago. I saw him riding in the park. I hear his new mistress is a very notorious lady. She is very young, barely sixteen, and has the distinction of having pleased the King . . . briefly."

Oh, Harriet, I thought, what are you doing now?

It was strange to think of Lucas as a married man. His bride was a pretty girl and they were clearly in love, which delighted my parents. Although they wanted a suitable marriage for Lucas, they would not have been completely happy if the pair had not been in love.

He was no longer my little brother. I could not subdue him. I was the sister up from the country and he could patronize me as I used to him.

It was a turnabout I did not relish, and I knew then that my mother was right. I had shut myself away with no interest but in domestic matters when great events were going on in the world.

Lucas's wedding was celebrated with a banquet and a ball. I knew little of the new dancing but I had a natural rhythm and was able to make a reasonable showing.

My parents presented me with pride to people whom they thought would please me, and so I met several young men who I suppose would be called eligible. Many of them had known Edwin and the fact that I was his young widow made me a figure of interest. But having known and loved Edwin I found everyone of them suffered in comparison. Their wide breeches edged with lace, their flowing cravats, their enormous wigs, their brocade and satin coats, with ribbons everywhere, about their waists, in their shirt-sleeves, even tying their periwigs, made them seem like exquisite popinjays. It was hard to think of these delicate scented creatures as men. How different from my father and Lord Eversleigh in their uniforms which gave them such dignity. I felt nothing but the need to escape from these scented creatures with their swift repartee and a sort of spurious wit and constant innuendo.

I was a widow and therefore no inexperienced virgin. I was supposed to understand and to respond to their overtures.

I was rather relieved when Carleton Eversleigh took my hand and led me into the dance.

"I am not an expert performer," he warned me. "But at least I can rescue you from poor Jemmy Trimble. He's a foolish fellow and I could see how he wearied you."

I raised my eyebrows and he went on: "Mind you, you might consider the change one for the worst."

I replied: "It was good of you to give me a thought."

"It is not good at all to follow one's inclination. I saw you and thought how charming you look in fashionable garments. You should adorn the fashionable scene more often. You bring a freshness to it. You have a look of coming from another sphere."

"The country mouse, perhaps?"

"Mice can be such pretty things, especially when they come from the country."

"And what are all these exquisite creatures? Cats, I suppose, come to catch the mice?"

"Exactly. They are on the prowl. You see they have so recently been let out to roam freely. They can now adventure in the open. Their wickedness has become merely amusing. It earns them a laugh from their friends instead of eternal damnation as in the past."

"You are very flippant."

"It was ever a failing of mine. But without flippancy of any sort I will say how it delights me to see you here. You have at last decided to trust precious Edwin to his nurses. I'll warrant you are wondering even at this moment whether he is safe. Admit it."

"I do think about him."

"Old Sally Nullens looked after his father and his aunt. She is like an angel with a flaming sword. I can tell you I had one or two brushes with her when I was trying to make a man of Edwin. She was afraid a little rough treatment would kill her darling. I wonder if history is going to repeat itself?"

"What do you mean?"

"We can't have little Edwin growing up into an effeminate young gentleman afraid to venture out in case a drop of rain gives him a cold."

"I shall know how to bring him up."

"In some ways, yes. You will smother him with love and devotion. But even now he is aware that if he becomes too venturesome Mama is thrown into a panic. 'What would your dear mama say?' asks Sally Nullens. 'That's dangerous, that is.' And little Edwin thinks: 'I must be careful. I am so precious. I might get hurt if I did that.' That's no way to bring up a boy, Cousin Arabella."

"You exaggerate. He will be taught riding, fencing, everything that a boy ought to know."

"He lacks a father. Now a child needs both his parents. The mother's loving care and the father's guiding hand."

"It is good of you to be so concerned."

"Concerned. Of course I'm concerned. We are talking about the future Lord Eversleigh. Young Edwin will have a big responsibility and so will you."

"His grandfather is going to live a good many years yet."

"We hope that will be so, but when a grandson inherits he usually does so before he is mature. That is why Edwin will have to be rather especially reared for his role. I promise to help you. It is, after all, my affair. In a way I am his guardian. I know the Eversleigh affairs as well as my uncle does. You forget that before Edwin was born and after his father was dead, I was the heir to all that will now pass to your son."

I could not completely suppress the shiver which ran through me.

"Oh, yes," he went on. "Twice my expectations have been foiled. Once long ago before your husband was born—for I am some years older—I believed that on my uncle's death all would pass to me. Then Edwin appeared and I took a step back. Edwin died and I took one step forward. Then little Edwin arrives and I am back where I was."

"You are . . . resentful?"

"Wise men are not resentful of fate, dear Cousin. What is to be will be. That's a wise saying for how could it be otherwise, and to rail against what *is* is a waste of time. I speak thus to show you what an interest I have in the Eversleigh inheritance, and I want your son to be worthy of it when it comes to him."

"I believe his grandfather is fully aware of this. He will take Edwin in hand as soon as he is of an age to understand."

"And I will play my part. I hope you will not marry rashly."

"I have no intention of marrying rashly or otherwise."

"Sometimes these intentions come overnight. I believe you met and married Edwin within a short space of time, so perhaps you are a lady who makes up her mind quickly. I sympathize. It is a habit of my own. I know what I want and I go out to get it . . . as I am sure you do. But I want you to know that I am at hand to help you."

"I will remember that."

"I wish that I were free to help more."

I did not understand and I was silent. I heard him laugh quietly and there might have been a hint of mockery in that laugh. "I could think of a good solution to young Edwin's future. Alas, there are too many obstacles."

"I really don't know what you are talking about."

"Briefly, what a good thing it would be if you had the inclination to marry and I were free."

I drew away from him in horror.

"Oh, I am merely thinking of the convenience of the matter. Nothing more, I do assure you. Merely a supposition, you see. 'If' and 'if' and 'if' again."

"An insurmountable barrier of 'ifs,' " I said grimly. "I can see my father. He is looking this way. If you will take me to him."

"Your pleasure is mine. Oh, one thing more. You should visit the theatre while you are in Town. I am arranging a party for tomorrow. Charlotte will come and my uncle. I am asking your parents and I trust you will be of the party."

"Thank you," I said.

He disturbed me, that man. I did not like the manner in which he had pressed my hand as he had talked. If it had not been for the mockery in his eyes and the light and flippant talk to which I was becoming accustomed, I should have been more than a little alarmed. I could not believe that I heard aright. Could he really have meant that if circumstances were different we might have married! Of course it would be simply for Edwin's sake. He saw himself as the only one who could bring up my son in a suitable manner and that was because little Edwin had stepped in and taken what Carleton had hoped would be his. But in any case he was married. Thank God for that. What an extraordinary man! What an extraordinary conversation! But that was the changing society. It was growing more and more daring. People behaved as though they had been in prison for years and now that they were let out wanted to make up for the suppressions of the past.

There was something about Carleton Eversleigh which disturbed me. I would not admit it to myself, but somewhere at the back of my mind I accepted the fact that he had a powerful effect on me. My mother had said something which I couldn't forget. It was: "Women like us should marry. We are not meant to live alone." I knew then that she was thinking of her sister Angelet who had disliked physical contact and consequently had ruined her marriage. I did not fully understand myself in this respect. My relationship with Edwin had been completely satisfying. I had shared his passion and yet I could not feel desire for anyone else. I longed for Edwin. I was still in love with Edwin and I believed I should be for the rest of my life. I wanted Edwin, but I could not think of putting anyone in his place.

Perhaps I was not fully grown. Perhaps I was as Carleton had said, the country mouse. Certainly it seemed that in the few days I had spent here in this society which was so different from that of Eversleigh, my horizons were extending. I was beginning to wonder whether my view of life was too simple. Black had been black, and white, white. I had failed to see the shading in between.

These brought me back to Carleton. I believed him to

be a rake. He fitted into this licentious society. He had a wife and I was well aware that they went, as they said, "their own ways." I supposed that sort of life suited them both. They set great store on what they called "their freedom." But were they happy? I wondered. I was not sure. There was so much of which I was not sure and particularly regarding Carleton.

What disturbed me about Carleton was that as soon as he entered a room I was aware of him. He was taller than most men and he had an air of complete indifference to the effect he was having, which I suppose would be called poise. Certainly he gave the impression that nothing would ruffle him. Edwin had lacked that. Edwin was always eager to make everyone feel easy and happy. Carleton gave the impression that he was indifferent to them. He was so sure of himself. Arrogant! I thought. And something else besides. There was in him an essential masculinity which was apparent in spite of the fashionable garments he wore. No amount of velvet and brocade could make Carleton effeminate.

I wondered why he spent so much time at Court when I was sure that his heart was at Eversleigh. But of course having lost his inheritance he would need to make a career for himself and perhaps he would do that at Court. At the same time he was concerned for Eversleigh. He wanted to bring young Edwin up that he might be worthy to undertake his duties.

All sorts of thoughts were whirling round in my mind—I refused to catch them and examine them. I didn't want to. Some were wildly absurd . . . too ridiculous to consider for a moment.

But I wished I could stop thinking of Carleton Eversleigh.

My parents had another engagement and could not join us, so it was my father-in-law, Charlotte, Carleton and myself who rode to the playhouse in Lord Eversleigh's carriage. It was an adventure in itself to ride through the London streets to the King's House in Drury Lane. Those streets were full of noise and bustle. Carriages like our own were making their way to the playhouse and in them sat exquisitely clad gallants and patched and painted ladies. What a contrast they were to ragged beggars and those who lived by their wits. I saw them darting about among the passers-by, and I am sure many of the latter would be poorer by their purses before the night was out. The streets were ill-lit and mostly cobbled, dirty and unsavoury, and I should not have liked to be on foot and splashed by the filth which was thrown up by carriage wheels. I had never seen such a contrast of riches and poverty as there was on the streets of London.

"Never venture far on foot," Carleton warned me. "You would not be safe for a moment."

"I daresay," I retorted, "that I could give as good an account of myself as anyone."

"My dear," put in Lord Eversleigh, "these beggars are skilled at their craft. They have a hundred villainies at their fingertips. There are trained bands of thieves roaming the streets."

"The night watchmen, I hear, are of little use," added Charlotte.

"You are right. They have become something of a joke," replied Carleton. "Poor fellows, every night they take their lives in their hands."

"What a dangerous place London is!" I cried. "I wonder why people set such store by it."

"It is alive, Cousin," said Carleton, fixing his eyes on me. They glowed with some emotion. Amusement, contempt, indulgence? I wasn't sure. "I would rather face danger than stagnation. I am sure you would too."

"Is it stagnation to live in quiet dignity?"

"Ha, you see, my lord, your daughter-in-law loves a discourse. I do not complain. I do myself. One of these days, dear cousin, we will thrash out the matter, for now, if I mistake not, we are turning into Drury Lane and you will have your introduction to the King's theatre. This is His Majesty's favourite, I do believe, and the Duke's in Lincoln Inn does not enjoy the same patronage, for naturally fashion follows the King."

As we alighted from the carriage, beggars pressed round us. I wanted to give them something, but Carleton had his arm through mine and drew me away.

"Never open your purse in the streets," he whispered, "even though you have a protector."

I disliked the way in which he said the word "protector," but I could not protest as Lord Eversleigh and Charlotte would have heard and I thought might have wondered why I always wanted to take up Carleton's words and contradict them.

I shall never forget my first sight of the interior of the playhouse. There was a magic about it and I guessed I was not the only one who felt this. We were in a box close to the stage, which gave me an opportunity to study the rest of the audience. There was a great deal of noise as patrons came in. There was the pit, which I should have felt not the best place to sit, for the roof above it was open and I imagined what would happen if the rain came in. The occupants of that part of the playhouse would have to scatter or be drenched. The middle gallery was slightly more expensive than the gallery above, which was now filling rapidly.

In the box opposite was a very fine lady in a mask, and with her an overdressed gentleman. The gentleman bowed as we entered and Carleton and Lord Eversleigh bowed back. The gentleman—if he deserved such a name—fixed his gaze on first me and then Charlotte and then came back to me.

"I hate these insolent men," muttered Charlotte.

"Dear Cousin, that is Lord Weldon," explained Carleton. "He thinks he does you an honour by gazing on you."

"An insult more likely," retorted Charlotte.

"His lady does not like it."

"And who is she?" I asked.

"Don't ask me. He changes mistresses every night."

"Perhaps one day he'll find his Scheherazade," I suggested.

"She'll need more than exciting tales to keep him, I do assure you."

"At least she does not want us to see her face, since she is masked."

"A fashion, Cousin."

"Should we not have worn them?"

"You have no need to hide behind them. You are in respectable company. Weldon has his eye on you though. It would not surprise me if he seeks me out tomorrow with eager enquiries."

"I hope you will reply to him in a suitable manner, and let him know that you consider his impertinence an insult to your family."

"Dear Cousin, I will challenge him to a duel if that pleases you."

"Duelling should be stopped," said Lord Eversleigh. "It's against the law in any case."

"Agreed, Uncle, but although we ourselves might be guilty of insulting certain ladies, we must become incensed when insults are directed against our own."

Carleton was smiling cynically and I turned away from him, and looked below to where the orange girls with their baskets were trying to tempt the members of the audience to buy, and exchanging badinage with the men. There were scuffles as the girls were seized and some of the men tried to kiss them. Oranges rolled on the floor, and people trying to retrieve them scrambled about shrieking with laughter.

The place was filled with noise and the smell of none too clean humanity; yet it excited me. I was all eagerness for the play.

It was to be *The Merry Wives of Windsor*. Carleton told us that it had to be comedy. Nobody wanted tragedy anymore. They wanted laughter not tears. "Tears went out with the Roundheads." They wanted frolics on the stage, not falling bodies. And what they wanted most was women on the stage. For so long men had taken women's parts and although some like Edward Kynaston took women's parts still, and looked so pretty on the stage that it was said many women fell in love with him and used to wait for him after the play and take him out in their carriages, it was the women who were now appearing on the stage who were largely responsible for its growing popularity.

Carleton told us how the King had gone to see *Hamlet*

in which Kynaston was playing the Queen, and when the play was late in starting Charles demanded to know why. The manager, beside himself with anxiety, went to the royal box and explained: "May it please Your Majesty, the Queen is not yet shaved."

His Majesty was highly delighted with the explanation and was in a particularly good mood which reflected throughout the playhouse and made a success of the play.

"His Majesty, of course, has already shown himself somewhat partial to the ladies," said Carleton. "And his loyal subjects like to follow him in all his ways."

Lord Eversleigh shook his head. "I say this out of no lack of loyalty," he said, "but I think it would make his loyal subjects happier if he were more devoted to his Queen—and less to those harpies who surround him."

"The Castlemaine's hold is as strong as ever," Carleton put in. "But that does not prevent the royal eye roving and the playhouse has much to offer . . . as you will see when the play begins."

He seemed to be amused by some secret joke. I wondered what. I was soon to discover, for candles set along the front of the stage were lighted and the play was about to begin.

Shallow and Slender had emerged, but for a few moments nothing could be heard because of the noise in the audience. Shallow came to the front of the stage and some shouted: "Look out. You'll catch your breeches in the flame."

Shallow held up a hand. "My lords and ladies, one and all. I beg silence that we may play before you."

The manner in which he spoke took me back to a snowy night in Congrève when the strolling players had come. The dramatic cadences and gestures reminded me of the strolling players.

The audience grew quieter and some shouted: "Come on, then, man."

"With your permission," said Shallow making a deep bow.

The play had begun.

Never having been in a playhouse before I was in a state of great excitement. I had always loved to playact and now I was seeing it done in a professional manner. I knew the play and I settled to enjoy myself.

It was scene one of act two when Mistress Page came onto the stage.

"What! have I 'scaped love-letters in the holiday-time of my beauty, and am now a subject for them?"

She was holding the paper in her hand and my heart leaped as I watched her. There was no mistaking her. Harriet!

I turned and saw Carleton's eyes on me. He was smiling sardonically. He had known. He had brought us here for this purpose.

I turned my attention to the stage. She had changed little. Perhaps she was less slim. Perhaps she was a little older. But she was as beautiful as ever.

I was aware that Charlotte had grown tense. She had recognized her too.

I turned my attention back to the stage. I could not stop looking at Harriet. She had that magnetism of which I had always been aware and the audience was, too, for they had ceased to fidget and cough and there was a deep silence in the playhouse.

I was deeply moved. I could not follow the play, I could only think of Harriet. What had happened to her? How had she come to this? Had James Gilley discarded her or had she left him of her own free will? Was she happy? Was she doing what she wanted? I would speak to her tonight.

I was aware of Charlotte tense beside me.

"Are you all right?" I asked.

"Did you see?" she whispered.

I nodded.

"He must have left her. She has come to this. . . ."

Carleton whispered, "Silence, ladies. This audience oddly seems intent upon the stage."

I kept thinking of her, wondering about her. I felt exhilarated because I had seen her again.

"I must go to her," I said. "I cannot leave without seeing her."

Charlotte cried: "No, Arabella! It is wrong. We do not want to see her again."

"I can't ignore her," I said. "I want to see her."

Carleton said: "I'll take you to their green-room. She'll be there, I doubt not."

"Thank you," I answered.

"Always at your service," he whispered.

I could see that he knew his way about the playhouse. The management knew him too. We met a man and told him that we were friends of Mistress Page and would like a word with her.

It could be arranged, was the answer and I saw money pass between them.

For the first time I was grateful to Carleton.

We were shown into a small room and very soon Harriet came in.

"Harriet!" I cried, and I could not stop myself rushing towards her and putting my arms about her.

She embraced me. "I saw you in the box," she said, "and I knew you would come to see me."

Carleton bowed. "Your performance was superb," he said.

She bowed her head. "Thank you, good sir."

"I will leave you to talk and come and collect you in ten minutes, Cousin."

Harriet grimaced as the door shut. "I never liked him," she said.

"Harriet, what are you doing here?"

"I should have thought that was obvious."

"Are you . . . do you . . ."

"I am one of Thomas Killigrew's players and, believe me, that is something of an achievement."

"But Sir James . . ."

"Him! Oh he was just a stepping-stone. I had to get away. He was there . . . providing the means."

"So you weren't in love with him."

"In love! Oh, my dear romantic Arabella, always thinking of love. What's the good of love to a girl who has to keep a roof over her head and has a fancy for the luxuries of life."

214

"You are so beautiful. You could have married Charles Condey."

"I see you had sour-faced Charlotte in the box tonight. I'll warrant she won't be here to see me."

"You treated her rather badly, Harriet."

"Badly? By being kind to a young man who clearly didn't want Charlotte? But we waste time. Tell me, what are you doing? How do you like England now? How are the boys?"

"Very well and happy."

"And young Leigh?"

"He's handsome and knows how to stand up for himself."

"He gets that from me, and you're a good mother to him, are you?"

"Harriet, how could you leave him?"

"How could I take him with me? Oh, it was a wrench but what could I do? I could see I wouldn't have been very welcome with you. Madame Charlotte would hardly want me there. Your mother was not prepared to issue an invitation. It was poor Harriet all alone again. So I said: James Gilley will get me there and I'll be with him until I'm tired. I always wanted to get onto the stage and here I am."

"Is it a good life, Harriet?"

She burst out laughing. "Dear Arabella, you always amused me. For me it's good enough. Full of ups and downs . . . always exciting. I was made for it. And you? Still brooding for Edwin?"

"There was never anyone like him."

"What of Carleton?"

"What of him?"

"He has a reputation for being irresistible. I've heard he can pick and choose. Castlemaine herself has her eyes on him. He's a bit too wily for that. He doesn't want to get in the Black Boy's bad books."

"I don't understand all this talk."

"Castlemaine's the King's mistress and the Black Boy is H.M. himself. Carleton's quite a character. He sets the town wagging with gossip and then he slips off to Eversleigh and stays there for a while. I hear he is furious

215

because there is now a baby heir. Your own sweet child, Arabella. Oh, there's quite a bit of gossip about Carleton Eversleigh and I lap it up . . . having once been a connection of sorts."

"Harriet, I want to know that you're happy."

"I want to know that you are."

"As happy as I can be without Edwin. Reassure me, Harriet."

"As happy as I can be without a grand mansion of my own and a fortune so that I can live in luxury until the end of my days."

"Oh, Harriet," I said, "it's been wonderful seeing you."

"Perhaps we'll meet again. I intend to be the toast of the London playhouses. Carleton will be coming to take you back now. I'm glad you came, Arabella. There'll always be something, won't there, between us two?"

She smiled at me somewhat enigmatically. I couldn't make out whether she was really happy or not. I felt frustrated and uneasy. I wanted to persuade her to give up the stage and come back with me to Eversleigh.

I knew I couldn't. For one thing she would refuse, and for another my new family would never agree to it.

I said good-bye to her, and as she kissed me she said: "We'll meet again. Our lives, as they say in plays, are interwoven while we are on earth together."

It was the most exciting experience of my trip to London.

Plague

Eversleigh seemed dull after London, but I was glad to be back with Edwin and to reassure myself that he had not suffered from my temporary desertion.

Charlotte and I went first to the nursery where we were greeted vociferously by the boys, and when they saw what we had brought for them their welcome became even warmer. We had been careful that what one had so should the other, so they each had a popgun with clay pellets, a trumpet apiece made from cows' horn, and kites—a blue one for Edwin, a red one for Leigh. With these and the peppermint drops in boxes with pictures of Whitehall Palace on them, the boys were enchanted. It was typical that Leigh's favourite should be the popgun which he proceeded to fire at everyone and everything while Edwin loved his trumpet. The kites were almost equally favoured, I think, and they wanted to go out immediately to fly them.

Charlotte said: "Which do you love best, us or the presents?"

Both little boys looked puzzled. Leigh kept his eyes on his popgun, Edwin fingered his trumpet. Then with a gesture which moved me deeply because it reminded me of his father, Edwin put down his trumpet and ran to me and flung his arms about me.

Leigh thoughtfully did the same to Charlotte.

We laughed a great deal and then Edwin said: "If you hadn't come back you couldn't have brought the presents, could you?"

Leigh nodded solemnly.

Even though this did suggest that the presents might be more desirable than our company, we were amused and delighted with the sagacity of the children.

They were happy days—flying the kites, listening to the sound of the trumpets and escaping from clay pellets. We were so glad to be back. But all the time I was haunted by my memories of Harriet. I could not get her out of my mind.

I thought of Carleton who had obviously arranged our visit to the playhouse knowing she was there. There was undoubtedly a streak of mischief in him, but what disturbed me most was his undoubted interest in me and his reference to the fact that Edwin had come between him and his inheritance.

That he loved Eversleigh I had no doubt. Its concerns were of the utmost importance to him. He was very often there, and I noticed that the visits to London were becoming more rare.

It was towards the end of the summer when Carleton's wife, Barbary, came to Eversleigh Court. Carleton treated her with an indifference which I found ungallant.

I realized during the day after her arrival that she was far from well. When I enquired of the servants—not having seen her throughout the day—I heard that she was in her bed, feeling too unwell to arise.

I went to see her.

She looked ill and I asked if there was anything she needed.

She shook her head. "I have come to the quiet of the country for a rest," she said. "I do now and then . . . when I feel tired. I don't think her ladyship likes it very much, but, after all, this is my husband's home and I have a right to be here, don't you think?"

"Yes, of course."

"Well that's nice to hear since you are a kind of deputy *châtelaine*. Don't you feel lonely living here?" She waved her hand disparagingly.

"I find it peaceful," I said, "as you obviously do since you come for a rest. Do you often feel that need?"

She nodded. "Quiet . . . one day very like another, cows mooing, sheep bleating, and the birds are nice in the spring."

"I had no idea you had a taste for such things."

"You must know, Cousin Arabella, that things are not always what they seem."

"That's true. Shall I get something sent up to you?"

"Sally Nullens makes a good posset. I believe the children have it when they're irritable."

"I'll ask her."

I went down to Sally who was in the nursery sewing Leigh's jacket where he had torn it.

Yes, she had the very thing. She had given it to Mistress Barbary before. "Poor Mistress Barbary," she commented, "I don't think she is a very happy woman."

"I should think not . . . married to . . ."

"Well, it takes two to make a marriage work . . . or go wrong, I've always heard. They're wrong, these arranged marriages. Young people should be left to themselves."

"So theirs was arranged?"

"Yes, ten years ago. Master Carleton was pretending to be a Roundhead. Hers was one of the families who had always been on Cromwell's side. I reckon he married her to show what a good Roundhead he was. He played the part well, considering. The marriage never worked. They went their own ways. Wild, both of them—she perhaps because she'd been brought up so strict, and he because that was his way. Now she comes here to be made well. My possets do her a world of good, she always says. But I think the rest has a lot to do with it. I think sometimes something comes over her and she would like to be different."

I took to going to see how she was and a kind of friendship grew up between us. That she was not averse to my

219

visits was obvious and after a while she began to talk to me.

She normally visited Eversleigh, she told me, when Carleton was away. "We don't like to meet, of course."

"That seems strange since he is your husband."

"He didn't want the marriage. He only entered into it because he had to create a good impression at that time. People were suspicious of his motives. There was a danger of his being found out. Marriage with a family like ours gave him standing . . . if you know what I mean. My father was a dedicated Roundhead. Marriage into such a family was a guarantee for a man who might have aroused suspicions because he belonged to a family most of whom were in exile with the King."

"I see . . . a marriage of convenience."

"Exactly."

"And you didn't love each other at all?"

She was silent. Then she said: "You know a little of him."

"Y . . . yes."

"He is unique. I have never known anyone like him. There's a strength about him . . . a power. He's the sort of man who, when he makes up his mind that he wants something, won't rest until it is his."

"Is that so unique?"

"No. But he is a man who goes out to get it with more vigour than anyone I know. I was very young when we were married. Seventeen, in fact. Young, romantic, and heartily sick of the way of life in my parents' house. If you smiled during the week, that was sin, and if you happened to on a Sunday you were set for hellfire."

"I saw some of it when I came here."

"Yes, but that was pretence, wasn't it? You could escape from it. I had scarcely known anything else. And then to be with him. For three weeks he treated me like a wife. I believed he meant it. It was a new way of life—exciting, intriguing. It was all pretence on his part, of course. But he never had difficulty in convincing a woman that he was fond of her. He's practised so long that it's second nature to him. Then I found he was unfaithful. As a pious Roundhead he was living dangerously, but that was what he liked.

I think as much as women he likes danger. I was young and angry."

I said: "You were in love with him."

"It was easy to fall in love with him. He had those strong good looks. He suggested power. He had all the tricks at his fingertips. He knew exactly how to treat me. When I remonstrated with him, the truth came out. He had married me because it was necessary. He liked me well enough but I must not expect his exclusive devotion. I should do what I wished and he would do what he wished. There was no reason why we should not go our separate ways. You can imagine how hurt I was . . . how angry. You've guessed I was in love with him. I was a romantic girl. I was ready to believe that I had made the perfect marriage. And now I was told we would go our own ways. I am impulsive. I am not a good character. I was so hurt and bewildered I went to bed that night with one of the grooms who had been watching me as much as he dared with a certain look in his eyes. Now you are shocked."

"No. I think I understand."

"You. With your dead husband to whom you remain faithful forever! You couldn't begin to understand. I am no prude. I will not pretend. I like men . . . as Carleton likes women. He taught me to cast aside all scruples so I did. He knew, of course. I think it pleased him. He rather encouraged me in my affairs, although he was a little shocked by the groom. He took me to London and introduced me to people of what was considered a more worthy station of life to share my bed. I have had scores of lovers since. Why am I telling you this?"

"Tell me by all means if you find some relief in doing so."

"Yes, I do find relief. I want to talk to you . . . you of all people. For several reasons. One because at the moment you have set up a shrine to your dead husband and are going to spend the rest of your days worshipping that shrine like a vestal virgin. Not quite a vestal though . . . since you are the mother of young Edwin. And this is what makes the situation what it is." She laughed suddenly. "It won't last, you know. You'll break out one day and then . . . and then . . ."

I said: "I have decided that I have no wish to marry again, if that is what you mean."

"Don't be too sure. I know there are eyes watching you." She lowered her voice and involuntarily I looked over my shoulder.

"Yes," she said, "You are chosen for a destiny. I know it. Someone has his eyes on you . . . but there are obstacles . . . living obstacles."

"You are talking in riddles."

"Easy ones to solve. Do you know what Eversleigh means to Carleton?"

"A great deal I am sure."

"A great deal! That's putting it mildly. It means everything to him. Poor Carleton, he has been cheated twice. Once as a ten-year-old when his uncle, the present Lord, most inconsiderately sired a son—your own beloved husband. In a confiding mood Carleton once told me what that had meant to him. 'I was only ten,' he said, 'but I can remember my baffled fury now. *I* had been brought up at this house. My uncle taught me everything. He was always saying . . . or if he didn't say it he implied it: "One day this will be yours." I learned about the estate. When I rode out it was as though trumpets sounded and voices were singing, "It's yours. It's yours." ' "

"Did he really feel as strongly as that? He was only ten years old!"

"Carleton was never childish. He always knew what he wanted, and he had been led to believe Eversleigh was his. Well, he suppressed his anger and, loving Eversleigh, tried to make his cousin worthy of his inheritance. He told me how he made him sit his horse, hold his arrow, shoot his guns. Making a man of him, he called it. He said Edwin was too soft to manage Eversleigh. He would never have made a good job of it."

"That was nonsense. Sheer jealousy."

"As his loyal widow it would seem so to you. Carleton was determined to hold Eversleigh after the King was beheaded. As you know he stayed behind when so many were fleeing the country. He risked his life for Eversleigh. Then Edwin came and was killed and he was the heir again. I

222

remember him then—the quiet confidence . . . the assurance."

"It sounds as though he rejoiced in his cousin's death."

"He had never had a high opinion of him. I think it seemed to him that fate had decided to watch over Eversleigh by giving it a strong master."

"This does not endear me to him."

"I think he has plans for you."

"Plans?"

"He is attracted to you in some way. He is easily attracted to women."

"He had better begin to look elsewhere."

"You would seem different to him."

"The simple girl up from the country—" I said. She was talking to me as Harriet had done, patronizingly, faintly amused by my unworldliness. Well, if I was unworldly at least I had found more happiness than either she or Harriet. I had lost my husband, it was true, but I had my dear little son to comfort me.

"Oh, more than that," she went on seriously. "You have a strong will. He would like that. You have turned against him. He would like that too. He never wanted easy conquests."

"You had better tell him that this is one citadel which will remain unconquered."

"That would only increase his ardour."

"Ardour! An odd word to use."

"He would like to offer you marriage. He sees that as the perfect solution. If you married him he would be your son's guardian and the care and management of Eversleigh would remain in his hands, as it does now. At this time Lord Eversleigh leaves everything in his hands. He managed the estate during the difficult years, so it is only natural that he should go on doing so now. There is one impediment. He is already married to me."

"I am thankful to say it is an unsurmountable one."

"If I were to die . . ."

"You . . . die. You are young."

"Look at me."

"You are at the moment suffering from a minor indisposition. You will soon recover from that."

She lay back and said nothing.

I went on: "This is a strange conversation. Tell me what you fancy to eat and I will have it sent to you."

"Yes," she said, "a strange conversation, but I am glad we have had it. I think you ought to know . . ."

There was a dreamy look in her eyes and I wondered whether she was in a fever. Fevers filled the mind with odd fancies.

I went to the bed and touched her hand. It was quite cold.

"Perhaps a little soup and a capon to follow. I will go and see about it."

Her eyes followed me to the door. I heard her whisper: "Take care, Arabella. Take care of yourself . . . and your son."

I went downstairs feeling very uneasy.

The next day Barbary was very much better, and seemed to revert to her old character, which was one of cynical sophistication. I wondered whether she regretted her confidence, for she seemed to avoid me and a few days after that she left for London.

Sally Nullens shook her head over her and was unaccustomedly confidential.

"I've always felt rather sorry for Mistress Barbary," she said. "She was flung into this when she was nothing more than a child, and I don't think Master Carleton did anything much to help her."

I felt my lips tighten. I couldn't forget what Barbary had suggested about his thinking of marrying me if he could find some way of removing her. The second marriage of convenience, I thought. Not for me, Master Carleton. I couldn't help feeling a satisfaction that he was for the second time cheated of what he wanted "more than anything."

At the same time I found the prospect a little sinister. "He is a man who won't rest until he's got what he wants."

"She never took care of herself," went on Sally. "Master Carleton always said so. A serious illness, he said, and she'd snuff out like a candle."

"He said that?"

"Oh, yes, more than once."

"But she is young and strong and I believe leads a very active life in London."

"You could call it that," said Sally Nullens. "Master Carleton's right though. She's not strong and ought to take more care of herself. A silly girl . . . the life she leads. Like a moth fluttering round the candle."

"You seem to have candles on your mind, Sally. I hope you keep them away from the children."

"Now, Mistress Arabella, do you think I'd be so foolish as not to?"

"I know you are wonderful with the children, Sally. I'm grateful."

"Oh, you're nothing but a girl yourself. As for the boys, I couldn't get them in to their dinner today. They didn't want to leave the kites you brought them. Master Leigh's must go higher than Master Edwin's and then Master Edwin's higher than Master Leigh's. Always got to go one better. I don't know."

She was good, Sally was, and devoted to the children. At that moment I thought: I wish they needn't grow up. I wish Carleton would go to London and stay there. I didn't want to think of him or what might be in his devious mind.

But my encounter with Barbary had started up uneasy trains of thought in my mind because of the dreams I was having.

Silly dreams about kites and popguns. I remember one in which Edwin was flying his kite, and as it went up into the sky, I could see that painted on it was a picture of Eversleigh Court. As I watched, it grew bigger and bigger and there were people on the lawns so that it was no longer a picture. Then I saw Carleton running towards Edwin and trying to snatch the kite away from him. Edwin would not release it and started to shout: "Be careful, Mama. Be careful!" Then I saw the clay pellets from the popgun scattered everywhere . . . and I was frightened.

Silly, stupid dreams but an indication of an uneasy mind. I wished Barbary had not put such thoughts into my head, but if they were in hers it was as well for me to know.

It was round about Christmas time of that year 1664. The boys were thinking of their fifth birthdays which closely followed Christmas. It was a cold snowy afternoon, with the flakes fluttering down and great fires roaring in every room.

The boys were kneeling on the schoolroom window seat, looking out at the snow, when Leigh shouted: "Someone's coming."

Edwin cried: "I can see a man. He's riding into the courtyard."

"Some travellers," I said to Sally. "Someone who finds the weather too bad to go on. We shall doubtless have a visitor today. I will go down and see who it is."

The children came with me.

Charlotte was already in the hall. When the bell started to clang, she opened the door and a man stepped in.

"Good day!" he cried. "A merry good day. What weather. Still I'm glad to be home!"

He looked at me with astonishment and then grinned at Charlotte.

"Now which one of you would be my niece, Charlotte?" he asked.

Charlotte stepped forward.

He seized her and kissed her.

"Is your father at home?"

Charlotte said: "Yes. I'll send for him. You must be . . ."

"Your Uncle Tobias, Niece. Uncle Toby that is. Home from Virginia. Looking for a welcome warmer than the weather."

Matilda Eversleigh was standing at the top of the staircase. He went towards her. "Matilda, my dear sister. Where's John?"

"Why," cried Matilda. "You must be . . ."

"Don't you know me? Well, it's been some years. A lot has happened since I went away, eh?" Lord Eversleigh had appeared behind his wife.

"Why—Tobias!" he cried. "Welcome home, Toby. I thought you were dead these many years."

"Not me, brother. Alive and kicking as they say. Well,

226

I thought I'd give you all a surprise. I want to hear all the news and I want to give you mine."

"First," said Matilda, "you must eat and drink and we'll have a room made ready. Charlotte . . ."

"I'll see to that, Mama."

"My dear Toby . . . After all these years. We thought . . ."

"That I was dead. Yes, I know, John has just told me. No, there's life in the old dog yet, Sister. Well, it's good to be home. Eversleigh has not changed much. Been through hard times, I hear. But all's well with the world now, I believe. The King's come back, so I thought it was time Toby Eversleigh did the same."

"It's a wonderful surprise," said Lord Eversleigh. "We have new additions to the family. This is Edwin's wife."

"What, young Edwin with a wife! And where is he . . .?"

There was a short silence and then Lord Eversleigh said: "I should have said Edwin's widow."

"Oh!"

The children had run down into the hall and were gazing with bewilderment at the newcomer.

"My grandson," said Lord Eversleigh proudly. "Come Edwin and say good day to your Great-Uncle Toby."

"*Great*-uncle," said Edwin, looking upwards with awe.

"Yes, boy, I'm your great-uncle. I hope you're going to be my friend."

"I will," said Edwin.

"So will I," cried Leigh pushing forward.

"Another nephew for me?" asked Tobias.

"No . . . Leigh is an adopted child."

"There's much I have to hear, I doubt not," said Tobias.

"First something to eat and drink," said Matilda.

"It's good to be home," replied Tobias warmly.

So that was Edwin's Uncle Toby. The family had been so convinced that he was dead that they had never mentioned him to me. I gathered that he came between Edwin's and Carleton's fathers and could only have been Lord Eversleigh's junior by about two years, but his

227

bronzed complexion and his rather plentiful hair made him look much the younger.

He was a colourful addition to the household, and it was soon clear that he intended to settle there. Being very convivial he was extremely popular. His weakness was a love of wine and he would sit at the table after dinner and consume quantities of it while his mood grew more and more mellow and he more and more talkative.

He was rich and had made a fortune in Virginia from tobacco. He had wanted to come home for years but feeling no affinity with the Puritan state, had waited until he heard the King was back.

"Mind you," he said, wagging a finger at me as though I was about to contradict him, "there was much to be done. I couldn't just up and off . . . not with my business activities . . . oh, dear me, no. I had to find managers . . . people I could trust. I didn't want to give up my interest out there. Why, if the Roundheads came back, I'd be off again. Wouldn't live under them, I promise you that."

"They will never come back," Lord Eversleigh assured him. "The people have had their fill of them."

"Then I'll rest me here . . . as long as you'll have me."

'My dear Toby," said his brother, "this is your home as much as mine."

Toby nodded, his eyes slightly misty. "What is it about old places like this?" he asked. "They get under your skin . . . they get in your blood. You never forget them, however far you roam. And if you're in line for them . . . well, then, there's something special." He looked at me steadily. "Why, do you know if it wasn't for young Master Edwin I'd be the heir to this place, that's so, eh, Brother?"

Lord Eversleigh said it was indeed the case.

"Mind you," replied Toby with his booming laugh, "you're going to outlive me by the look of it. I'm more fond of the bottle, Brother, than you, and they say that while a little of it is good, for your stomach's sake, too much is likely to rot the gut. There, I'm shocking the ladies. Forgive. I've got a bit rough on my travels. And what about Harry's boy?"

"Carleton," said Matilda. "Oh, he is still here. I daresay he will be coming back soon. He moves between here and London."

"I remember Carleton. He must have been about two when I went away. What an upstanding little fellow, eh! I can see him strutting around. He owned the place already. Of course then we thought you'd not get a son and I was off to the wilds and that meant everyone had decided I'd be eaten by sharks or Indians. Young Carleton was very sure of himself. I've just thought of it. He'll take a step back, won't he? . . . Not that it matters. We have our young Edwin. What a fine little man, eh? Madam, I congratulate you on giving us such a grand little heir."

And so he talked, and I have to admit to slight and unworthy elation because Carleton had had to take another step backwards.

The children were fascinated by Uncle Toby. Being a great talker—fond, Charlotte commented, of his own voice—there was nothing he liked more than an appreciative audience. In the morning his talk was fascinating; in the evenings it was likely to get a little slurred; but of course it was in the mornings when the children heard him. They would desert their kites and their popguns and trumpets to sit at his feet and listen to his tales. I would join them too. He was always talking about Captain Smith who was his hero and whom he called the founder of Virginia.

"Named, my hearties, after the Virgin Queen by a man named Walter Raleigh." Then he would tell them about Walter Raleigh and how he became the queen's favorite by spreading his cloak over the mud when she stepped from her carriage, thus preventing her from getting her pretty shoes dirty.

Raleigh brought tobacco to England, and tobacco was what grew in Virginia and it was tobacco that had made him a rich man.

I can see them now, their little faces alight with interest, and every now and then if the adventures grew horrific they would squeal with delight. Chastity came to join them. She was as fervent an admirer of Uncle Toby as the boys were.

What tales he had to tell of Captain John Smith who knew when he was a boy that he was going to be a great adventurer.

"I'm going to be a great adventurer," cried Leigh jumping up, his eyes shining so that he looked remarkably like his mother. I remembered what she had said about having to adventure for the good things of life if they did not fall naturally into one's lap.

Edwin said that he was, too, but he would have to stay at home most of the time to look after Eversleigh.

So he knew already. He must have listened to talk.

Uncle Toby patted his head. "Ah, yes, boy," he said. "You'll keep this place as it should be, and that's another kind of adventure."

"I shall go out to Virginia," boasted Leigh. "Then I'll come back and . . . and . . . I'll tell you all about it."

"In the meantime," I said, "let's listen to Uncle Toby."

That was what everyone wanted to do, so we heard how Captain Smith joined the Christian army and went out to fight the Turks and defeated three of them in single combat and how later he became the prisoner of a wicked Timor and had a heavy iron yoke about his neck; how he slew the Timor and escaped, overcoming every difficulty, and how finally he landed up in Virginia where his life was saved by the beautiful Indian Princess Pocahontas.

So many stories he had to tell that the children were completely entranced. They played new games now. Leigh wanted to be John Smith but so did Edwin. Edwin, I noticed, almost always gave way and played the Timor. Then in the Pocahontas story Chastity was Pocahontas, Leigh, John Smith and Edwin, the Indian chief who was going to kill John.

I said to Edwin: "You should not let Leigh always play the best parts."

Edwin looked at me with his serene and beautiful smile and explained: "But, Mama, he wouldn't play unless he could have them and I like to play."

I kissed him, but I did think Leigh was growing more and more like his mother.

It was not to be expected that Toby, who had lived so adventurously, would stay all the time at Eversleigh Court. He wanted to know what was happening in the country, and therefore he must go to Court. There were many people there who would be interested to hear his accounts of his travels and his brother said he must be presented to the King and Queen.

Carleton came to Eversleigh. I wished I had been present when he was confronted by Uncle Toby. I wondered what his immediate reactions were. When I saw them together he had had time to overcome his surprise and, I imagine, chagrin.

Once when we were riding Carleton was beside me and I asked him how he felt about his uncle's return.

"It is always interesting to discover members of the family."

"It's odd that I never heard him mentioned."

"We thought he was dead. The ship we presumed he had sailed in floundered. Uncle Toby has always had amazing luck. He took another ship right at the last moment so his doting family were under the impression that he was gone forever."

"So all those years, until you reached your tenth birthday, you were strutting around imagining yourself to be the heir of Eversleigh, when the real heir was making his fortune in Virginia!"

"In absolute innocence! But what did it matter? Edwin was soon there to step in front of Tobias, and now you have provided us with another Edwin to do the same."

"Uncle Toby comes before you though."

"Neither of us comes anywhere while we have precious Edwin."

"Toby is very fond of him."

"Who would not be fond of that perfect child?"

"And you?"

He looked at me sardonically.

"Fond of Edwin? What a question. You know I dote on him. Mind you, I think at the moment he is inclined to cower behind Mama's skirts and those of his nurse, while he allows young Master Leigh to be lord of the nursery. That should be changed."

"How?"

He leaned towards me. "Very soon, dear Cousin, I am going to help you make a man of Edwin."

"I will have no interference," I said sharply.

He laughed. "For the good of Eversleigh," he cried and then he galloped off.

When Uncle Toby went to London with Carleton and Lord Eversleigh, we missed him very much and the children were constantly asking when he was coming back. The two boys were very much absorbed at this time with their ponies, and Jasper used to take them out each day. I insisted that they should be on the leading rein except in the home fields. Even then I used to suffer agonies when I saw Edwin galloping round.

Jasper said: "Master Carleton be right, mistress. You're too careful of the boy. You're putting him in a glass case."

"He is very young yet, Jasper," I retorted.

Jasper grunted. He was a most surly man and I never could like him. I knew he would like to take us back to the days when it was considered a sin to smile. One thing I was sure of, his daughter Chastity was happier now than she had been before the Restoration.

I couldn't forget that Jasper had been suspicious of me and had informed against us. I was rather surprised that he remained at Eversleigh, but Lord Eversleigh was a very just man. He said that Jasper had a right to his opinions. He made no secret of them. He was a Puritan at heart and there would always be people like him. He was a good groom and had never failed in his duties in that respect.

To my surprise Carleton agreed with him. His comment was: "Jasper couldn't inform against us now. To whom could he carry his tales? He has a right to his opinions. After all, that was really what the war was all about. The King would be the first to agree."

So Jasper stayed and gave us good though surly service. I think he was grateful in a way. Although he deplored our love of what he would call sinful luxury, he accepted us as we did him.

I had reason to be grateful to him at this time.

The boys had new riding jackets made of brown velvet

232

with gold-coloured buttons and velvet caps to match. They were very proud of them. Leigh strutted in his. He was an arrogant little boy, but there was something about his delight in everything which made him appealing.

They were eager to ride out in their new clothes and they took their ponies into the field close to the house where they were accustomed to ride round and round. Jasper was always in attendance and I liked to watch them.

How smart they looked in their new jackets and how excited they were as always to mount their ponies. I watched them trotting round the field and then breaking into a canter.

Jasper was never very far away. He was teaching them to jump. He sat straightbacked on old Brewster, who was grey and had a dour look to match Jasper's own.

How glad I was of Jasper that morning because for some reason Edwin's pony decided to bolt. I felt my heart stop and then start to pound away at such a rate that it seemed as though it would choke me.

Time slowed down and minutes seemed to pass, though it could only be seconds while I saw the pony bolting for the hedge and Edwin, who had somehow slipped off his back, managing to cling round his neck. I expected him to fall at any moment.

Oh, God, I thought. He is going to be killed. I am going to lose my son as I lost my husband.

I ran, ineffectually, I knew, for the child would be thrown before I could possibly reach him.

But Jasper was there. He had halted the pony, had leaped to the ground and was disengaging Edwin from the pony's neck and had him in his arms.

I was panting, feeling lighthearted with relief, wanting to promise Jasper anything he asked, for nothing could repay him for what he did.

" 'Tis all right, mistress," he said.

Edwin was laughing. I thanked God for the sound of that laughter. Then he was concerned, for he had seen my face. What it looked like I could not imagine. I was clearly white and shaken.

Edwin said: "It's all right, Mama. I haven't hurt my coat. My cap though . . ."

It was on the ground where it had dropped off his head. Jasper put him down and he immediately retrieved it.

He looked a little distressed. "It's a bit dirty, Mama. Never mind. Sally will clean it."

I felt I wanted to burst into tears . . . with relief . . . with thankfulness. I felt a wave of hysteria. My darling was safe. I felt as though I had died a thousand deaths while I watched him and he thought I was worried about his cap!

I wanted to pick him up and hug him, to tell him he must never risk his life again.

Jasper was scolding: "You should never have let him go like that. He's got to know you're the master. After all I taught you!"

"I know, Jasper, but I couldn't hold him."

"No such word as couldn't, Master Edwin. Up on his back."

I started to protest but Jasper pretended not to hear me.

"Now off you go. Let him out. Full gallop now."

Jasper looked at me.

"Only way, mistress. Do you want him so he'll never mount a horse again?" He looked at me pityingly, for he could see how shaken I was. "They know no fear, mistress. That's why they have to learn when they're young. He didn't know what happened then. Just as well."

"Jasper, take care of him."

"Aye, mistress. I'll make a horseman of him yet."

That incident made us friends in some odd way. I noticed Jasper looking at me now and then. Of course he despised my fancy gowns, the trappings of the Devil, he would call them. But he respected my love for my child and he knew that I had made him the guardian of Edwin and he liked that.

One day when I was in the stables there alone with him, he came and stood before me rather awkwardly.

"Mistress," he said, "I'd like a word. Have wanted it these many days."

"What is it, Jasper?" I asked.

" 'Tis about your husband, mistress. He were shot over here . . . not far from this spot."

I nodded.

"I want you to know it were none of my doing."

"Jasper," I said, "he came here into danger. He was posing as a stranger. I should never have come with him. It was through me that he was betrayed."

"That were so, mistress. You showed your true nature and it were not that of a woman who serves God as she should, and I told those who should know and one came to see. But nothing had been done then. 'Twere not because of that that he were shot. Mistress, I want you to know that nor I nor any of my friends fired the shot that killed Master Edwin."

"Do you know who?"

He turned away. "I want only to say it were not my doing."

"So it was nothing to do with his being . . . the enemy."

"It were not done by us, mistress. That's all I can say. 'Twouldn't have been for us to kill him. We'd have took him for questioning but not to kill."

"You know who did it, Jasper?"

" 'Tis not for me to say, mistress. But I don't want you to think I was the one who had anything to do with the killing of that boy's father."

"I believe you, Jasper," I said, and I did.

News was coming in from the neighbouring towns. It appeared that a very virulent form of bubonic plague had broken out in the slums of St. Giles's and so fierce was it that it was fast spreading through the capital and beyond. People were collapsing in the streets and were left there to die because none dared go near them.

We were very worried because Lord Eversleigh was there with Carleton and Uncle Toby and we had had no news from them.

Each day we heard horrific tales. No one who could get out of the capital stayed. The Court had left and an order of council had been issued that stringent measures must be taken to deal with it.

Lady Eversleigh was frantic with anxiety.

"Why don't they come back?" she demanded. "They would never be so foolish as to stay there. What can it mean . . .?"

"Not all of them," she went on frantically. "It couldn't happen to all of them. Have we gone through those years of exile just to come back to this?"

Charlotte and I shared her anxiety. I realized how fond I was of my father-in-law and his brother, but somewhat to my surprise it was Carleton who kept coming into my mind. I kept picturing him, writhing on a bed of pain, his face and body disfigured by hideous sores, and fervently I wished that he were here and I could nurse him. That seemed crazy, but I told myself I felt this because I should have enjoyed having him in a position which I was sure he would find humiliating—shorn of his dignity, at my mercy. What a strange thought to have at such a time, but Carleton did arouse emotions in me which I had not suspected I possessed. And with them came a certain elation, because however mysterious their absence might be, something within me told me that Carleton would be all right. Nothing would ever get the better of him—not even the plague.

Then when I was with my mother-in-law and Charlotte I wondered how I could have thought so much of Carleton to the exclusion of my father-in-law and Uncle Toby who had both become dear to me.

Each day we waited for news of them. There was none, but we did hear how the plague was spreading, and that, even as far from London as we were, we must take precautions and be very careful of strangers travelling from afar.

Everyone was talking of the plague. There were such epidemics two or three times in every century, but there had been nothing to compare with this since the Black Death. I thought of what I had seen of London—those evil-smelling gutters in the back streets where rats foraged among the rubbish left on the cobbles, and all the time I was thinking of Carleton lying on his bed, needing care.

And what of Lord Eversleigh and Uncle Toby? They

were not so young. They would be less able to fight the terrible disease.

The weather was hotter than usual. Even in the country it was stifling. I imagined what it must be like in plague-ridden London. So far the towns and villages around us were free. Canterbury, Dover and Sandwich, it seemed, had no cases, but the people were watchful. We had fearsome stories of what it was like in London. If a member of a household was afflicted, a red cross must be painted on the door and beneath it the words "Lord Have Mercy on Us," so that everyone could be warned there was danger by entering that dwelling. Even when someone died, that person would have to be lowered from the windows and dropped into one of the death carts which prowled the city at night led by men, masks over their mouths, bells in their hands which mournfully tolled while they cried out: "Bring out your dead." Pits were dug on the outskirts of the city and the bodies thrown in one on top of the other. There were too many for proper burial and it was the only way.

We prayed for the terrible affliction to pass and still it went on. The servants talked of it continually. The names of Lord Eversleigh, Uncle Toby and Carleton were mentioned in hushed whispers as the dead were spoken of. Lady Eversleigh went about looking like a grey ghost, her face a tragic mask. Charlotte was resentful against life. "Are we never going to know?" she cried. I had rarely seen her so emotional and I was surprised that she cared so much about her family, for she generally gave an impression of indifference to people—even in their presence.

I heard the servants discussing it. "You know you've got it when you're sick and you get headaches and a fever so that you ramble on. That's how it starts. Then you have to watch out for the next phase. It's horrible sores like carbuncles—'buboes' they call them. They cover you all over."

There were prayers in the churches. The nation was in mourning. We did not know whether we were personally bereaved or not. Lady Eversleigh grew more depressed each day, Charlotte more angry. As for myself, I could not possibly believe that anything could subdue Carleton Eversleigh. Then I thought: But if he were well, why does he not come to tell us what has been happening to the others? I began to feel that I was being foolish, that I had endowed him with some superhuman power. When I doubted his ability to overcome just everything, I too fell into the general depression.

Jasper said it was God's answer to the lawlessness which was spreading across the land. Had the country suffered from plague when Oliver Cromwell kept it godly? It had not. But when the King returned with his licentious friends, look what happened.

"The King and the Court have left London. They are safe," I pointed out. "Why should God punish others for their sins?"

"We have become a sinful nation," retorted Jasper. "Who can say where He will strike next?"

"Lord Eversleigh was a good man," I cried. "Why should he . . ." I stopped. Before that I had consistently refused to believe that he was dead.

It was early afternoon when they came back. I was in the nursery with the children when I heard Carleton's voice.

"Where is everybody? We're back. Come and greet us."

I ran down to the hall. There they were. Carleton, my father-in-law and Uncle Toby. There was someone else with them but I could pay no attention to him just then.

I threw myself into my father-in-law's arms. I felt the tears on my cheeks.

"My dear, dear child," he kept saying. Uncle Toby was beside me.

He embraced me as though he would never let me go.

Carleton was standing by, watching with an amused look in his eyes. Then when Uncle Toby released me he picked me up and held me against him. Our faces were level; he looked at me, holding my eyes for some seconds. Then he kissed me hard on the mouth.

I broke away.

"Where have you been?" I cried, almost hysterical between joy and relief at their return and anger for what

238

they had made us suffer. "We have been frantic with anxiety."

Lady Eversleigh was on the stairs with Charlotte behind her.

She gave a cry of joy and ran towards her husband.

So they were back, and with them was Sir Geoffrey Gillingham, a friend of long standing who had been with them for the last few weeks.

"It seemed the best thing," said Carleton.

"We knew," added Lord Eversleigh, his arm through that of his wife, "that you would be anxious. We knew that you would fear the worst, but even that seemed better than putting you in danger. Only those who have seen something of this terrible scourge can understand its horrors."

The explanation was that the men had been dining with Sir Geoffrey when one of his servants had collapsed and it quickly became obvious that he had the plague. In a short time every servant had left the house with the exception of the wife of the stricken man, who immediately pointed out to Sir Geoffrey that he must go quickly for fear of infection.

Carleton had reminded them that the man must have been suffering for a few days and therefore they could all be infected. The reason why the plague was spreading was because people were not careful enough in isolating themselves when they came within range of it. One would have to wait several weeks to be sure that one was free from infection, and this is what he suggested they do. They could not communicate, for how did they know in what ways the disease could be carried? They would go to a hunting lodge on the edge of the Eversleigh estate. There were no servants there. It was only a small place and rarely used. If they all went there for a few weeks and they were unafflicted, then they could, with a good conscience, join their families.

"Was there no way you could have let us know?" I demanded.

"Carleton was insistent that it was the only way," said Uncle Toby. "He took charge of us."

"I can well believe that," I said.

"Carleton was right," insisted Lord Eversleigh. "It was better for you to suffer a little anxiety for a while than to have this dreadful thing brought into the house. Think of the boys."

"Children are particularly susceptible," said Carleton and that suppressed my complaints.

Sir Geoffrey Gillingham stayed on with us. He was gentle and charming and in a way reminded me of Edwin. He had lost a young wife three years before in childbed and there was something rather sad about him.

I found I could talk to him about Edwin and how happy we had been. I felt he understood.

He had a great admiration for Carleton. "He is the sort of man who would take over in an emergency. I must say that when we realized we were in close proximity with the plague and had actually eaten food which the man had touched, we really thought we were all doomed. It was Carleton who said it was not necessarily so but that we must regard ourselves as potential victims and hide ourselves away."

"He is a very forceful character, I know," I said.

"It's a pity there are not more like him."

"Perhaps," I said. "But I suppose wars are made by forceful characters."

"And sometimes prevented by them."

Sir Geoffrey was quickly very popular with the family. Lady Eversleigh said he must not think of returning to London. He had had news that both the servant and his wife had died of the plague and that, as they had died in his house, it would be unwise for him to return to it just yet. The children liked him—rather to my surprize, for they were usually fascinated by more colourful people— great romancers like Uncle Toby, for instance. Edwin particularly liked him, and Sir Geoffrey used to ride out with my son, and since he was there to look after him, I allowed Edwin to venture out beyond the field. I had a confident feeling that no harm could come to him while he was with Sir Geoffrey.

Carleton said: "You should be grateful to me. Look what a pleasant friend I have found for you."

I flushed slightly and that annoyed me, because I was

finding that Carleton's remarks often discountenanced me. He knew this and revelled in it.

"Don't get too friendly, will you?" he said and moved off. It was an irritating habit of his that he would make some remark like that and before I had time to challenge it be gone.

It was he who told me that the theatres had been closed. I thought at once of Harriet and so did he. She was, of course, the reason he mentioned it.

He came close to me—he had made a habit of doing that and it angered me—and he gripped my arm tightly. "Don't worry about that woman," he said. "She will always find some way out of a difficult situation, no matter where and when."

"Like you," I replied.

"Yes, there is a similarity. I'll wager that whatever happens to anyone else, she'll come through safely."

But I was not sure of that and I worried about her.

That was an eventful time. While the plague was raging in the cities, England was at war with the Dutch and there was great rejoicing over a victory at sea off Harwich when the King's brother, the Duke of York, became the hero of the day, having blown up Admiral Opdam, all his crew and fourteen of his ships, and capturing eighteen more.

In London there was a thanksgiving service to commemorate the victory and immediately afterwards a fast was ordered because of the plague for the first Wednesday in every month. Money was raised to help young children who had lost their parents, to set up centres where the infected could be cared for and to make every effort to stop the spread of the scourge. All those who could retire to the country were advised to do so, and the holding of fairs or any such gatherings where disease could spread was prohibited.

The heat was great that summer and people saw in this a reason for the spread of the plague. In the gutters the filth stank and rotted and the rats multiplied. The city was the scene of desolation; the shops closed, the streets emptied except for the pest carts and those who were dying on the cobbles. Orders were given that fires should

241

be lighted in the streets for three days and nights in succession in the hope of destroying the rotting rubbish and purifying the air. The deaths, which in the beginning had been one thousand a week, were reaching ten thousand. The King and the Court had moved to Salisbury, but when the plague reached that town they adjourned to Oxford.

At Eversleigh we were ever on the alert. I was terrified that some harm would come to my son. Every morning, as soon as I arose, I would hurry to the nursery to assure myself that he was in perfect health.

Sir Geoffrey stayed on. We impressed on him that it would be folly to return to London just yet. He seemed very willing to agree to this and interested himself in the estate and made himself useful in several ways. He himself had estates much closer to London and he told me that he really should be there. However, it was pleasant to linger and his affairs were in the best of hands.

"It has been so pleasant here," he went on. "I have grown so fond of the little boys. I always wanted a boy of my own and I would have liked him to be just like Edwin."

Nothing he said could have pleased me more. He had made me see too how fortunate I was. I had lost my husband, but fate had been kind in giving me my son.

What a relief it was when September came and the weather turned cold. The good news came that the number of deaths in the capital had dropped considerably. There was no doubt that the excessively hot weather had been in some respects responsible. Rain came and that was a further help and gradually parishes began to be declared free of the plague.

There was great rejoicing throughout the country and those who had left London were now eager to return.

Geoffrey went, declaring he would soon be back. We must visit him, he said. He would enjoy riding round his land and showing it to young Edwin. We missed him when he had gone, and this applied particularly to my son. We all said we must meet again soon. The kind of experience we had had was a firm foundation for friendship.

It was disconcerting to hear that ninety-seven thousand people were known to have died from the plague but, as Carleton pointed out, many deaths would not have been recorded. One hundred and thirty thousand was more like the number.

It was a sobering thought.

"There is too much filth in the streets of big cities," he said. "They are saying that the rats carry the plague and where they are this will be. We could clean up our streets and then perhaps we should not be cursed with this periodic plague."

We were all greatly relieved to have come through safely. Uncle Toby said what a delight it would be to visit London and the Court again. He was fascinated by the theatres which had improved considerably since the King had come home.

"The King loves the play," said Carleton, "and since the fashionable world will follow its king, we have improved playhouses."

"Very different from what they were when I went away," agreed Uncle Toby. "Though we had the apron stage then."

"Ah," said Carleton, "but not the proscenium arch with the window opening onto a music room and the shutters which can be open and shut, thus making a change of scene."

"A great improvement!" agreed Toby enthusiastically. "But I'll tell you what is best on the stage today, Carl, my boy."

"Don't tell me, I know," said Carleton. And they said simultaneously: "The women players."

"Think of it!" went on Uncle Toby. "We used to see a delicious creature on the stage and just as we were getting interested we'd remind ourselves that it was a boy, not the pretty lady it seemed."

"There is nothing to compare with the real thing," said Carleton. "The King is all for the playhouses. He thinks they make his capital gay. The people need to laugh, he says. Odds fish, they've been solemn enough for too long. He won't have them taxed, although some of our ministers have tried to make it difficult for them. The answer was that the players were the King's servants and part of his pleasure."

"Was it right," asked Uncle Toby, "that Sir John

Coventry asked whether the King's pleasure lay with the men or the women?"

"He did, the fool," replied Carleton, "and for once His Majesty did not appreciate the joke. Nor did others, for Coventry was set on in Suffolk Street and ever after bears the mark of a slit nose for that bit of foolery."

"It seems a harsh punishment for a remark which might be considered reasonable," I put in.

"Dear Cousin, have a care," said Carleton lightly. "What a tragedy if that charming little nose of yours should suffer the same treatment."

I put my hand to my nose protectively and Carleton was at my side. "Have no fear. I would never permit it. But it is a fact that even the most good-natured kings can now and then give sharp rejoinders."

"I'll swear the theatres will soon be full again," said Uncle Toby.

"You can be sure that Killigrew and Davenant are rubbing their hands with glee at the prospect," said Carleton. "When we are absolutely sure that it is safe, you must visit a theatre again, Cousin. I wonder if the handsome Mistress Harriet Main is still about. You would be interested to see her, Uncle Toby, I don't doubt."

"Always like to see a handsome woman, my boy."

"You shall, Uncle. You shall."

By the following February the King had returned to Whitehall with the Duke of York, and the courts of justice were once more sitting in Westminster. Carleton went to London and was away some weeks and it was while he was away that Tamsy Tyler came to Eversleigh.

I knew Tamsy before, because when Barbary had come to Eversleigh, she had brought Tamsy with her as her personal maid. Tamsy had been adept at hairdressing and adding the right touch of colour to cheeks and knew exactly where to apply a patch or a black spot to enhance a particular feature. She had been a plump and rather pretty creature and I had had no doubt that she shared her mistress's pleasure in the opposite sex.

The Tamsy who returned to us was quite different and alone.

She arrived at the gates footsore, weary and almost

starving. I was in the garden when she came and it was some time before I recognized her.

I thought she was a beggar and I went to her in some concern because her state was pitiful. As I approached she cried out: "Mistress Arabella. Oh . . . Mistress Arabella . . . help me."

Then she sank half fainting to the ground.

I didn't believe then it could be the coquettish Tamsy, and it was only the timbre of her voice, which was rather high pitched, that gave me a clue to her identity.

"Tamsy," I cried. "What has happened? You poor girl. Come along into the house. Where is your mistress?"

She could scarcely walk. I said: "I'll call Ellen." I laid my hand on her arm. Its thinness shocked me.

"I thought I could not get here . . ." she stammered.

Charlotte came out. "What is it, Arabella?" she asked. I said: "It's Tamsy."

"Is Barbary with her?"

Tamsy shook her head. "Mistress . . ." She looked from me to Charlotte. "Mistress Barbary is dead, mistress. 'Twas some months ago. Right at the end of it all too. I nursed her through it and took ill myself."

"Tamsy!" I cried in horror, my thoughts immediately going to Edwin.

"I am well enough, mistress. I was one of those who came through. Once you've had it you're free of it, they say, forever. I've been free these two months or more. I wouldn't come here till I was sure."

"Let's get her into the kitchen," said Charlotte. "Oh, Ellen, look who this is. She's ill. She needs looking after."

"Tamsy," cried Ellen. "Well, then, where is Mistress Barbary?"

"She's dead," said Charlotte. "She died of the plague."

* * *

Tamsy recovered quickly under Ellen's care. In a day she looked less like a skeleton and could tell us what had happened without breaking into hysterical tears. She and her mistress had been in Salisbury when the Court was there, and when it left they went to Basingstoke because

245

of a gentleman friend whom Mistress Barbary was meeting there. She did not know that he had come from London.

They had dallied there for three days and nights until he was taken sick. It was soon clear what ailed him.

Barbary had been frantic. She had been sharing a bed with the plague.

"Before we could leave the gentleman was dead and we were there in his house, all the servants gone and only the two of us. Then my mistress was taken ill and there was no one there to nurse but me, and I nursed her, and there she lay on her bed shivering and sick and not being sure whether she was there or not.

"She kept calling out for Carleton. It was pitiful to see her. She kept calling out about starting again and how she'd give anything to do that. How she'd accept him . . . and do what he wanted and how she'd be a good wife to him and how wrong it had been to take all those lovers . . . to pay him out for what he had done to her. Pardon me saying this, mistress, but 'tis gospel truth."

"It was good of you to stay with her, Tamsy," I said.

"Oh, I reckoned I couldn't have escaped. You see there was his manservant who had been my friend, and he too was stricken."

Poor Tamsy! Poor Barbary! Jasper would say it was God's punishment for their sins.

"Oh, it were terrible, terrible," cried Tamsy. "To see her horror . . . her fear when the horrible sores started to come. She screamed out to God to take them away, that she'd do anything to be rid of them. . . . And there they were . . . horrible to behold, and they would not break open either . . . great sores, they were, like carbuncles. If they break there's a chance you can live but not if they don't. . . . Then one day I saw it on her breast. . . . She saw it too . . . the macula they call it. They say when it shows on the breast that's the end. She saw it and she thanked God for it because she wanted to die by then. And she did . . . she died within an hour. And there was I . . . alone . . . in the house with her. The cart had come to take him. So it would come to take her. I had been out in the dead of night and painted the red cross of death on the door. Now I waited at the window for the cart to come and I wrapped her in a sheet and I dropped her through the window. And there I was alone in the house behind the red cross of death."

"My poor, poor Tamsy," I cried. "You were a brave woman."

"Brave, mistress? 'Tweren't nothing else to do. I knew then, for the faintness and the sickness was getting me and there was I alone. I dunno. Perhaps because I *was* alone . . . I had to look after myself and funny like I said, 'If I die, how'll they know at Eversleigh? Master Carleton will never know he is a widower. So I mustn't die.' It seems funny now to live for such a reason. But I was half dazed with fever and I just had this feeling that I had to live. I saw the horrible sores taking over my body but I knew I'd never see the macula on my breast. Then they started to open . . . those sores did, and the plague came out of me and I knew I'd live. And gradually, they faded away and the sickness and the fever left me. And there was I alone in the plague house . . .

"I sat at the window and the pest cart came and I shouted: 'I'm here. I've had the plague and I'm well again.'

"They wouldn't come near me for two days and then they shouted to me. I had to burn everything in the house. I had to light fires everywhere. Burn all my clothes and everything on the beds. They passed food in to me and they sent me clothes and I came out.

"People came to look at me. It wasn't many who had come through the plague.

"Then I set out for Eversleigh because I knew what I must do. I had to come and tell Master Carleton that he hadn't got a wife anymore."

The Seduction

Geoffrey insisted that we keep our promise, and we had met several times during the year. He would ride out to Eversleigh on the slightest pretext, and it seemed as though some business constantly brought him our way. Both Edwin and Leigh delighted in his visits and used to vie with each other to ride on his shoulders. He would carry them through the house and allow them to make crosses on the beams with a piece of chalk which meant that we should have good luck.

Carleton had accepted the news of Barbary's death without emotion. I supposed it would have been quite false for him to have pretended grief considering the nature of the relationship between them. He merely shrugged his shoulders and said: "Poor Barbary. She had a talent for getting herself into awkward situations." He looked at me quizzically and went on: "I know you are thinking that the most unfortunate of these was her marriage to me and you're right."

He went back to London but it was not long before he

was back and he made a point of spending time in my company.

I was not really displeased about this although I pretended to myself that I was, which was foolish of me, of course, but I'm afraid I was rather foolish at this time. It was becoming clear to me that Geoffrey's visits were not without some meaning. We liked each other very much. We had both been widowed. We had loved and lost and perhaps were both looking for someone who could give us companionship and fill that void which I was sure he felt in his life as I did in mine.

Geoffrey was a cautious man. I should admire that in him. He would not be the sort to rush into a relationship without having given it considerable thought beforehand. I believed that now he was weighing up the situation. He wanted to know so much about me; he wanted to make sure that we should be happy together.

It was wise, I told myself, and if not as romantic as my love for Edwin and his presumably for his dead wife, it was sensible.

I would never love anyone as I loved Edwin. I kept telling myself that. But should I deny myself the pleasures of marriage because I could no longer share them with Edwin?

There was my son, too. Perhaps he needed a father. He was surrounded by love. He lacked nothing really, and yet I had noticed how he loved to be with Geoffrey who could give him a certain kind of companionship which I couldn't.

These were the thoughts which were in my mind on a lovely, sunny June day in that year 1666.

I was in the garden gathering roses, which I loved to arrange in containers and set about the house. I liked their scent to fill my rooms. I had always had a fancy for the damask rose, perhaps because my great-great-great-grandmother had been born at the time Thomas Linacre brought it to England and had been named after it.

I heard the sounds of arrival, and I immediately thought of Geoffrey, and as always when he called on us I would ask myself: I wonder if it will be today?

I always hoped not, because I was unsure. I could see so many reasons for saying yes and so many for refusing. Such a good father for Edwin, I thought. And I was fond of him. He was pleasant, charming, kindly. The sort of man one could rely on always . . . very different from . . .

Why should I want to think of Carleton at such a moment?

"Carleton!" He was there grinning at me and I felt that foolish flush rising to my cheeks.

"A charming picture," he said. "The lady of the roses." He took the basket from me and smelled the blooms. "Delicious," he said looking at me.

"Oh, thank you, Carleton."

"You look as if you were expecting someone else. Geoffrey Gillingham has become a very frequent visitor. Do you know, I begin to regret bringing him here."

"Why should you? We all like him very much."

"And he likes us . . . or some of us . . . and some of us probably like him better than others. Give me the basket. We'll sit by the willows. I want to talk to you."

"I have not finished gathering the roses yet. I want more of them."

"You have enough here."

"Pray, let me be the best judge of that."

"Dear Cousin Arabella, you can trust my judgement in this matter. What I have to say to you is of far greater moment than a basket of roses."

"Say on, then."

"Not here. I want you to sit down and give me your undivided attention."

"As serious as that?"

He nodded and looked grave.

"Edwin," I began.

"Yes, it concerns Edwin."

"Carleton, is something wrong?"

"By no means. It could be right . . . very right . . ."

"Then pray tell me. Why do you beat about the bush?"

"It is you who are beating about bushes . . . rosebushes. Come and sit down and I'll tell you at once."

250

He had alarmed me, and I allowed myself to be led to the stone seat sheltered by the weeping willow trees.

"Well?" I said.

"I want you to marry me."

"Marry *you*!"

"Why not? I'm free now and so are you. It would be the best possible answer to everything."

"*Everything*! I'm afraid I don't . . ."

He had seized me suddenly so that I was taken off my guard. He was kissing my face and caressing me in a way in which no one but Edwin ever had.

I tried to hold him back, but his strength was greater than mine and clearly he meant to remain in charge of the situation.

I whipped up my anger.

"How dare you!"

"I would dare everything for you," he said. "Don't be prudish, Arabella. You know you want me as I want you. Why make a secret of something so obvious?"

"Obvious?" I cried. "To whom?"

"To me, and that's the one it should be obvious to. I sense it every time we meet. You're crying out for me. You want me."

"You have the most extraordinarily high opinion of your charms. I can assure you I want nothing so much at this moment as to be out of your sight."

He looked at me, his mouth turned down in mock dismay and his eyes alight with mischief.

"Not true," he said.

"Absolutely true. How dare you take me away from my . . ."

"Roses," he supplied.

"From what I want to do to bring me here under false pretences."

"What false pretences?"

"That something was wrong with Edwin."

"Something *is* wrong with Edwin. He's rapidly become a spoilt child tied to Mama's apron strings."

"How dare you . . . !"

"Speak the truth? The boy needs a guiding hand. Mine.

251

And he's going to get it. He has to learn that there is something more in the world than love and kisses."

"From what I've heard these things play quite a part in your life."

"You are speaking of my reputation, which interests you. There is never smoke without fire, so they say, and it is true that I am a man of experience. . . ."

"Not in bringing up a child."

"But I am. But for me, your late husband would not have been the man he was. I was the one who brought him up. I was the one who made a man of him."

"I wonder what his father would say to that."

"He would confirm my story. He was away from home and Edwin's mother doted on him just as you do on his namesake."

"In any case Edwin left England when he was ten years old, I believe, and your shining influence must then have been removed from his life."

"It is the formative years that are important . . . from five until ten."

"How is it that you are so knowledgeable on these matters?"

"It can't have escaped you that I am knowledgeable on many matters."

"It has not escaped me that that is your opinion of yourself."

"It is always better to believe the best of oneself. After all, there are so many people to believe the worst. But enough of this. I want to marry you. You are too young to live as you do. You need a husband. You need me. I have wanted this for a long time, but now that I am free to make the proposal there is no need for further delay."

"No delay is necessary. Your proposal is declined."

"Arabella, I am going to marry you."

"You have forgotten that it takes two to agree to marry."

"You will agree. I promise you."

"Don't be so lavish with your promises. This one is certainly going to be broken."

He caught my chin in his hand and forced me to look

at him. "I can make yet another promise. Once you are mine you will never want to leave me."

I laughed. A wild excitement had taken possession of me. If I were honest, I would admit that I hadn't enjoyed anything so much for a long time. It was so wonderful to be able to deflate his pride, to let him know that I had no intention of letting him tell me what I should do.

"Then . . . I shall never be yours, as you put it."

"Don't be too sure of that."

"I am completely sure of it."

"You are making a mistake, Arabella."

"In refusing your offer?"

"No, in thinking that I shall not take you."

"You talk as though I'm a pawn on a chess board."

"More important than that. A very important piece, in fact. My queen."

"Still to be used at your will."

"Yes," he said, "at my will."

"I've had enough of this." I rose.

"I have not," he said, and rising with me placed both his hands on my shoulders and forced me down on the seat.

"I see that you would make a rough-mannered husband," I said.

"When the occasion demands it, but on every occasion you will find me just the right husband for you."

I said seriously: "There has only been one who can be that and I thank God that he was, even briefly."

He raised his eyes to the sky. "The sainted Edwin," he said.

"Pray do not mock him."

"You are like everyone else, Arabella. You disappoint me. I always thought you were different. As soon as a man's heart ceases to beat he becomes a saint."

"I did not say Edwin was a saint. I said he was the most wonderful man I ever knew or ever shall know and no one else can take his place with me."

"It's a mistake to deify human beings, Arabella."

"I loved Edwin," I said seriously. "I still love Edwin.

253

Can't you understand? No one . . . *no one* . . . can take his place with me."

"You're wrong. Someone will supplant him. That is what you are going to discover when you marry me."

"I want to hear no more."

"You shall hear more. I am going to talk to you . . ."

He was silent suddenly and I looked at him in amazement. His mood had changed. He said: "Do you think I am afraid of the dead? I am afraid of no one, Arabella. Certainly not saints with feet of clay. They can topple so easily."

"Stop sneering at Edwin. You are unworthy to unlatch his boots."

"Boots are no longer unlatched and that remark would be considered highly irreverent by Jasper."

"I am not concerned with Jasper."

"But you should be concerned with truth."

"I am going back to my roses," I said. "Your wife is so recently dead . . ."

"Barbary would laugh at that if she heard you. You know what our marriage was like."

"All the more reason why I should refuse you. She has set an example of what not to do."

"But you are not Barbary."

"You would never be faithful to any woman."

"A challenge, my dearest Arabella. Just think how exciting it would be for her to make me."

"She might not think it worth the trouble. Barbary didn't."

"Poor Barbary. She knew it would be hopeless. But why do we constantly talk of the dead? I'm alive. You're alive. We're two vital people. You've been only half alive for many years, it's true. Come out of your shell and live."

"My life has been full and interesting. I have had my child."

"Oh, come. You have shut yourself in with the dead. You have built a shrine and worshipped at it. It's a false shrine. Edwin is dead. You are alive. You have a child. You need me. I can make you happy. I can help bring up your son. We'll have our own . . . sons and daughters. I want you, Arabella. From the moment I saw you,

I wanted you. All this time I have been patient. But I can stand aside no longer. I'm going to wake you up . . . show you what you have been missing. You're a woman, Arabella, not a romantic girl."

"I know exactly what I am, Carleton. I know what I want and that it is not to marry you. Now . . . good afternoon."

I stood up and started to stalk away, but as I did so I tripped over the rose basket. He caught me and his arms were round me. I felt him tilt back my head and kiss my throat. I was overcome by horror because I wanted him to go on. He had aroused memories of lovemaking with Edwin and I felt ashamed of my feelings.

I forced myself back from him and he looked at me mockingly, still holding me.

"Pride goeth before a fall," he said. "If I had not been here to rescue you, you would have slipped. You see, it's symbolic. You need me to protect you."

"I never needed anything less."

"One thing I insist on in my wife is truthfulness."

"And I hope when you find one you will give her the same in return."

"Why fight the inevitable?"

"I think you are the most arrogant man I have ever met."

"I confess you are not the first to have told me this."

I wrenched myself free and turned away. I broke into a run, but he was beside me, the rose basket on one arm, the other he thrust through mine and held it tightly against him.

"Now, dearest Arabella, you will go into the house and think over what I have said. Remember again how delightful it was when I held you in my arms. Brood on the pleasures that await us both. Then you can think of Edwin . . . the living one, I mean. Let us forget that other. He is dead and gone and best not brought back to live in your thoughts. You are better without him. Forget the past, Arabella. Perhaps it wasn't quite what you thought. Pictures are different when seen from afar. It is wise not to look too closely at them. So look ahead. Just think what this would mean. This our home for the rest of our lives. So many problems are solved."

"I begin to see your motives."

"It is very agreeable when so many things are in our favour."

"You have always wanted Eversleigh, haven't you?"

"Who wouldn't?"

"And it will come to Edwin. You want to control it . . ."

"I control Eversleigh now, Arabella. I have since I was of an age to do so. My uncle being in the King's army cannot give his estates the attention they need. We have always realized that."

"But there will come a time when Edwin is of age . . ."

"We have much to enjoy before that day. Let us make the best of life."

I wrenched myself free from him. "I shall certainly not do that with you," I said.

I ran into the house, leaving him standing there holding the rose basket.

I did not miss it until much later, which showed to what a state he had reduced me. I could not stop thinking of him, and I tried hard to think of Edwin and how much I had loved him and how wonderful our life would have been. As if anything could ever be like that again, even with a kind and gentle man like Geoffrey.

I avoided Carleton. This seemed to amuse him. When we were together in the company of others, I would find his eyes on me, mocking. What arrogance, I thought. He really believes I shall find him irresistible.

There was a great deal of anxiety over the Dutch war and we were constantly hearing disturbing news. Everyone was talking about the chain shot which the Dutch had invented and which was doing such harm to our ships, and orders were given that cattle must be driven off Romney Marsh in case the Dutch should come in and steal them. In July we won a victory over them, but there were great losses on both sides.

However it was decided in August that there should be

a thanksgiving service and Lord Eversleigh thought we should go to London to take part in it.

Geoffrey came down to Eversleigh to tell us about the service and what was going on in London. The weather had been much cooler and there was great relief that there had been no return of the plague that summer. There was a serenity about Geoffrey as though he had come to some conclusion. I guessed what it was, and I was right, because during that visit he asked me to marry him.

It seemed strange that I should have had two proposals of marriage within a few weeks of each other, but perhaps not so strange. I was sure Carleton had suspected Geoffrey would ask me soon and wanted to get in first. That amused me. At the same time I did not want Geoffrey to ask me . . . yet. I had been considering marriage with him for some time, and there had been occasions when I had almost convinced myself that it would have been perhaps the best thing. Now I was very uncertain.

He had brought new kites for the boys, and they were very eager to try them so we took them out-of-doors and I watched Geoffrey with the children and noticed how they shouted to him and treated him as though he were an elder brother—young enough to play with them and yet older to have special knowledge and give them help when needed.

I sat in the sunshine on the stone bench near the willow with flowering shrubs on either side. It was a delightful afternoon, warm and sunny. I felt a certain contentment sitting there watching my son and marvelling at his beauty and giving grateful thanks for his good health, listening contentedly to the buzzing of the bees as they hovered about the lavender. There would be good honey this year, I thought.

Geoffrey came and sat down beside me.

I said: "It was good of you to bring them kites."

"I know how they like them. Look. Edwin's is flying higher than Leigh's."

"Leigh won't like that."

"No, he's a boy who will have to be curbed more than Edwin, I think."

"Yes, he has a more arrogant nature. Edwin reminds me so much of his father."

"He was gentle was he . . . good-natured?"

"He hated trouble. He wanted everybody to be happy. Sometimes I think he would have done anything rather than cause trouble."

Geoffrey nodded slowly. "Do you still think of him?"

"All the time . . ." I said.

"It is some years now."

"Before Edwin was born. In fact I didn't know I was to have a child when I heard that Edwin was dead."

"You can't mourn forever, Arabella."

"Do you think one ever gets over such a loss?"

"I think one should try to."

I sighed. "Edwin often asks about his father."

"I know. He has told me about him. Edwin thinks he was one of the saints."

I smiled. "He would be pleased if he knew. I want my son to live up to him. I tell him he must never do anything of which his father would be ashamed. He must try to be like him."

Geoffrey nodded. "But he needs a father here on earth, Arabella. All children do."

I was silent, and he went on: "I have thought a great deal about this. I have almost spoken to you so many times. Would you marry me, Arabella?"

Again I was silent. I didn't want to say no, I could never marry anyone, because I wasn't sure, and he was right when he said one should not mourn forever. Edwin would have been the last person to wish that. For a moment I gave myself up to the pleasure of seeing myself announcing my intention to marry Geoffrey and watching the effect on Carleton. I should enjoy that. But that was not a good enough reason for marrying.

Geoffrey had seen the slow smile on my lips and misconstrued it.

"Oh, Arabella, we'll be happy. I know we shall."

I drew away from him. I said: "I'm sorry, Geoffrey, but I'm not sure. I sometimes think I shall never marry. I will confess I have thought of it, and when I have seen how much you love Edwin and he, you, I have felt it would be good for us all. But I am not sure. I still think of my husband and as yet I cannot say."

"I understand," he said. "I have spoken too soon. But I want you to think about it. I am a lonely man and I think sometimes you would be happier with someone who was close to you as only a husband can be. I would be a father to the boy. I love him already. I take a great interest in him."

I said: "He would be expected to live here. You know that he is the heir to all this."

"I would come here for a great deal of the time and we could go now and then to my own estates. I have my bailiffs there who look after things while I am away much as it is managed here. Edwin would be my concern."

I followed the flight of the kites and on the surface of Edwin's I seemed to see the house take shape. Eversleigh Court and all it entailed which would one day be Edwin's. In my imagination I saw Edwin lifted off the ground, caught up with his kite. I saw his terrified face, heard his screams and I realized that I was remembering a dream I had had long ago.

"Are you all right?" asked Geoffrey.

"Oh, yes . . . quite all right, thank you. You'll think me ungrateful but I do appreciate what you are offering me. It is just that I am unsure . . ."

He put a hand over mine.

"I understand," he said. "You must realize this, Arabella. I should always understand."

I believed he would and I wished that I could have said yes.

A horrible suspicion had come to me that I might have done so but for that scene not so long ago with Carleton in this very garden.

Lord Eversleigh thought that we should all go to London for the thanksgiving service. Uncle Toby was delighted. He was always eager to get to London and he spent a great deal of time there. Lord Eversleigh said that the town house was more often occupied since Toby had been home than it ever was before. My mother-in-law told me that she was a little disturbed about Toby. He was inclined to drink too much and to gamble. He greatly enjoyed the conversation in the coffeehouses and he was devoted to the theatre. He had a fondness for the pretty actresses and was very interested in Moll Davies, who was said to be favoured by the King.

"That was always Toby's trouble," said Matilda. "Your father tells me that in his youth he gave his parents much anxiety and they were not altogether displeased when he decided to go to seek his fortune in Virginia. I doubt he saw much of playhouses and pretty women actresses there."

But we were all indulgent with Toby. Whatever his excesses he could always charm us.

So he, at least, was anxious to go up for the thanksgiving service.

There was a letter from Far Flamstead. My mother hoped that we should be going and perhaps would spend a night there on the way, for naturally they would be present. It would make the family very happy for us all to be together again.

So it was arranged that we went.

I always enjoyed being with my family, although the children no longer gave way to wild expressions of joy to see me. Even Fenn no longer leaped round me and gave those great war whoops of pleasure. He was twelve years old now and beyond such childish matters. As for Dick, he was all but sixteen, fast growing in dignity, and Angie at thirteen was quite a young lady.

My father embraced me warmly and I saw the anxious look in his eyes which was reflected in my mother's. They both wanted to see me married and they would have approved of Geoffrey, I was sure. I toyed with the idea of confiding in her that I had had two proposals of marriage but decided against that. She would want to know how I felt about my two suitors and I couldn't bear any probing at that time, even from her.

It was a merry party. Carleton was already in London, staying at the Eversleigh house in fashionable Clement's Lane where we would join him. My parents would go to my father's house, the gardens of which ran down to the river and which had been in his family's possession since the days of Henry VIII.

In London we should be joined by Lucas and his new wife. I never saw my mother in such good spirits as she was when she could gather her family together.

But I was never completely happy when my son was not with me, though Charlotte kept assuring me that in the care of Sally Nullens the boys were as safe as if we were there, and I had to accept this.

In due course we went to the service and there I had the pleasure of being presented to the King and Queen. I was fully aware of his charm, as indeed who could help being, and I liked his gentle Queen with the great, brooding, dark eyes. Poor woman, I was sorry for her if all the tales I heard of his infidelities were true, and I was inclined to believe that they were.

When we came out from the service Carleton was beside me and he pointed out Barbara Villiers, Lady Castlemaine—a woman I instinctively disliked.

Carleton laughed at me. "She is reckoned to be irresistible."

"If I were a man I should find it the easiest thing in the world to resist her."

"Ah, but then you are not a man and you are noted for your powers of resistance. Look how you resist me."

I left him and joined my father.

We all returned to Clement's Lane, and later that day my family left for their own residence. That night at supper Uncle Toby suggested that we all go to the play on the following day.

It was declared a good idea and I was excited at the possibility of seeing Harriet again, although I had heard no mention of her name. I think Carleton knew this, for he was watching me closely.

So to the King's House we went, and I was thrilled to be once more in the playhouse and sit in the box and watch the life that went on below me. The gallants, the orange girls, the ladies in their masks and patches, and the exquisite gowns. There was much more order than there had been on the previous occasion, and when I commented on this, Carleton told me that playgoers had at last realized that they had come to the playhouse to see and hear a play and were becoming more and more interested in what was going on on the stage than the trouble they could stir up among the audience.

So it seemed, for there was a hushed silence when the play began and no need this time for one of the players to step forward and ask for silence.

The play was called *The English Monsieur* and it had been written by the Hon. James Howard, one of the Earl of Berkshire's sons. His brothers also wrote for the stage, Carleton had told me as we rode to the theatre, and so did his brother-in-law John Dryden.

Uncle Toby said he had seen Dryden's *The Rival Ladies* and found it very good. "And the fellow worked with Robert Howard on *The Indian Queen*. That was a fine play about Montezuma and most splendidly was it put on the stage. But give me a comedy. I look forward to tonight. There is one little actress who gives me great pleasure to watch."

"I am sure Arabella will enjoy her acting too," said Carleton smiling, and I wondered what innuendo there was behind that remark. For it was a fact that I always suspected that there was some hidden intent behind everything he did or said.

"There will be a crowd at the playhouse tonight," said Lord Eversleigh. "After having been closed for so long, people cannot wait to get back to them."

"It was very necessary for them to be closed during the time of the plague," I pointed out.

"Indeed, yes, but what a loss. So much to make up for."

The play began. I waited for Harriet to appear, but it was not Harriet who took the part of Lady Wealthy, the chief character in the play, but a small woman, very pretty with great vitality and a gamine charm. She took the part of a rich widow who was courted by fortune-hunters and played with the idea of marrying, as they said, "well" and in the end cast aside such nonsense and married her true love.

The plot was slight, the dialogue scarcely sparkling, but the amazing personality of this delightful actress carried it along, and the audience was with her every moment she was on the stage.

I should always remember her dainty looks, her jaunty charm, her constant laugh and the way her eyes almost disappeared when she gave way to it. She was dark and sparkling and the entire audience loved her.

As we rode back to the house Carleton said: "What did you think of Nelly?"

"I thought she was enchanting."

"So it seems to others—including His Majesty."

"I thought he was enamoured of an actress called Moll Davies."

"Alas, poor Moll, she is by way of being superseded by Nelly."

"I doubt not Nelly's reign will be as brief," I said.

"He is faithful to the Castlemaine, so perhaps he is capable of fidelity to others."

"I would not agree with your definition of fidelity."

"What a glorious day that would be when we could agree about something."

We went on to discuss the play and it was a most stimulating hour.

The days that followed had a quality of unreality about them, and even now I cannot really believe in them. A very strong east wind had sprung up. I heard it during the night, blowing through the narrow streets, and I sat up in bed listening to it and wondering how strong it would be in the open country round Eversleigh, where it was always so much more fierce than in London, for coming in from the east it had spent a little of its energy before it reached the capital.

Just before dawn I was aware of an unusual light in the sky, and going to my window I saw that it was a glow from what must be a large fire.

By the time I arose the glow had deepened. I remarked to the maid that it must be a very big fire indeed. She replied that one of the tradesmen had just come in and said that it started in a baker's shop in Pudding Lane. The house was in flames in no time and the strong east wind had spread the fire to the neighbouring buildings.

During that day there was no talk of anything but the

263

fire which was rapidly spreading and had already consumed a number of buildings, and at night our rooms were as light as day from the glow of the flames. A pall of smoke hung over the city and it was getting worse.

"If it continues like this," said my father-in-law, "there will be nothing of London left."

Carleton suggested that Charlotte and I return to Eversleigh, and my mother wanted us to go to Far Flamstead which was a safe distance from the city.

I said firmly that I should not go until the danger was over. There was a great deal for us to do on the spot, for the refugees from the fires were put into certain empty houses and Charlotte and I had joined the band of helpers who were arranging to look after them.

People were bewildered. Many of them were bent on running away, and the river was full of craft containing families with what posessions they had salvaged. Some were escaping to the country, others were going to the houses which had been set up to receive them, and others to camp in the fields about Islington and Highgate.

Three days had passed while the fire was still blazing. It was useless to try to put it out by ordinary means. The whole of the Thames would not douse this fire, it was said.

Alarm was spreading. We kept getting scraps of news. We heard that the roof of St. Paul's Cathedral was ablaze and the glow in the sky could be seen for ten miles around the city. Melting lead was running into the streets and the stones of St. Paul's were flying like grenades through the streets, the cobbles of which were too hot for people to walk on. The great bells of the churches were melting. The wind caught the ashes and spread them for miles around. I heard that some of these were blown as far as Eton.

The Church of St. Faith was collapsing. Its roof was gone and its walls had fallen in. In Paternoster Row, the home of the booksellers, the contents of the shops had been burning for several days.

Something must be done.

The King hastened to London with his brother and members of the nobility to find a means of stopping the fire. Carleton was with him; so were my father, Geoffrey, Lord Eversleigh and Uncle Toby. They believed they had a solution. It was desperate, but they must try it, for two-thirds of the city was already in ruins, and from the Tower along the Thames to the Temple Church and along the city wall to Holborn Bridge, there was scarcely a building standing, and if it was it must be an empty shell.

The drastic plan was to blow up those buildings towards which the fire was racing so that, when it reached them, there would be only an empty space and the flames would have nothing to consume and therefore would necessarily become less fierce and perhaps be able to be brought under control.

We awaited the outcome with trepidation. All day long we heard the explosions. The men came home, their garments and even their faces blackened with their exertions. But there was an air of triumph about them. They had halted the great fire of London, and now, they prophesied, it would only be a matter of time before they had put it out.

The nightmare was over, but the damage was enormous. Four hundred streets had been completely destroyed with about thirteen thousand houses. An area of four hundred and thirty-six acres had been devastated. We had suffered four days of calamity and during that time eighty-eight churches had been destroyed, including St. Paul's Cathedral. The City gates and Guildhall, the Exchange and the Customs House had also gone, and the value of the lost property was over seven million pounds. There was only one matter for rejoicing. In spite of this colossal destruction, only six people had lost their lives.

The fire was discussed interminably around dinner tables.

"The King," said Carleton, "surprised his people . . . though I guessed he would behave as he did. People are inclined to think that because he has a keen wit and likes to use it, because he has an appreciation of beauty and a love of pleasure, he is incapable of being serious. Now they realize their mistake. None worked as hard as he did."

"It was an inspiration to us all," agreed Geoffrey, "to see him, sleeves rolled up, his face blackened by smoke, giving orders as to where the gunpowder should be laid."

"And he was merry with it," said my father-in-law.

"A man," put in Uncle Toby, "who would meet any disaster with a merry quip which puts heart into us all." He raised his goblet. "A health unto His Majesty."

And we all drank it and someone started the ballad which was being sung throughout the country:

> "Here's a health unto his Majesty
> With a fal, la, la, la, la, la, la
> Confusion to his enemies
> With a fal, la, la, la, la, la, la
> And who will not drink his health
> I wish him neither wit nor wealth
> Nor yet a rope to hang himself
> With a fal, la, la, la, la, la, la."

And we all joined in, thanking God that, in spite of the plague and the fire which He had seen fit to bring upon us, there was not one of us who would have gone back to the Puritan way of life. All of us were with the King in spite of his growing reputation for profligacy.

There was rejoicing in the streets. The fire was over, and if many had lost the homes they had known for years, there were now promises to rebuild London, a different city, with wider streets where the sun and air could reach the lower rooms of houses, proper gutters where the drainage could run away and not harbour rats and give out noisome smells.

Carleton said: "This fire could well be a blessing in disguise. Christopher Wren is going to build a fine cathedral in place of old St. Paul's. He has designs for other buildings. The King is excited by them. He showed me some of them today."

And in spite of the terrible problems created first by the plague and then by the fire which had followed so closely, there was optimism in the air. Then this was tinged with suspicions and doubts.

Someone had caused the fire. Who? That was the question everyone was asking.

It was not long before a scapegoat was found.

There was whispering in the streets that it was the

Papists. Of course it was. Had they not destroyed eighty-eight churches—the great cathedral among them? They wanted to destroy the Protestants just as they had on St. Bartholomew's Eve in France nearly a hundred years ago. The method was different. That was all.

People were marching through the streets, demanding the arrest and execution of Papists.

"The King will not allow that," was the comment in our house. "He's all for tolerance."

"And some say," said Uncle Toby, "that he flirts with the Catholic faith."

"Flirting with the ladies is more to his choice, I'd say," said Carleton quickly. "And if I were you, Uncle Toby, I would not repeat such comments. They might be ill construed."

The King did set up an enquiry for the Privy Council and House of Commons to undertake, and it was relief to have it proved that there was no foundation in the accusations.

Those days of terror had their effect on us, at least that was what I tell myself, but perhaps I am trying to make some excuse for what happened almost immediately afterwards.

We had not yet returned to Eversleigh but planned to do so within a few days. My parents had gone to Far Flamstead and Geoffrey to his estate. Lord and Lady Eversleigh, with Uncle Toby and Charlotte, had gone in the carriage to visit some old friends of theirs on the other side of Islington. Carleton had ridden over. As I had never met their friends and wished to make my preparations for our departure, I said that I would stay in the house.

It proved to be a fatal decision. I often thought how such a small incident, seemingly insignificant at the time, can affect the course of our lives.

No sooner had they set out than it started to rain. Within an hour it was torrential. The wind had come up again and I wondered how they were faring.

I busied myself with getting my things together and laying out the little gifts I had bought for the boys. I had drums and a hobbyhorse apiece and battledores and shuttlecocks, and I had bought them new jackets and complete riding outfits apiece.

I gloated over these things, packed them and unpacked them while I anticipated the pleasure they would give.

The afternoon grew darker. The rain was still falling, the wind still howling. It was going to be a rough night.

At six o'clock I ordered that the candles be lighted, for it was very dark, and Matilda had said they would be back not later than six. She had no fancy for being out when the light was failing. The roads were thick with thieves and no one was safe. These men carried blunderbusses and did not hesitate to use them if their victims did not surrender their possessions with speed.

So I was sure Matilda would insist on their returning early, as it was such a dark day. In fact I had expected them to be in before this.

The minutes ticked away. It was seven o'clock. Something must be wrong. I was now beginning to be anxious.

It was just after seven when I heard someone come in. I hurried down the stairs and, to my surprise, there was Carleton. He was soaked to the skin, the water dripped from his clothes and was even running from his hat down his face.

"What a plight!" he cried seeing me. Then he laughed. "I rode back because I thought you'd be anxious. The carriage was stuck in the mud close to the Crispins' place. They are all staying the night there. It would be folly to come back on a night like this."

"Oh . . . they are all right then?"

"Perfectly all right. No doubt feasting on roast beef and warming themselves with malmsey wine at this moment, and I should not at all object to following their example. Have you supped?"

"Not yet . . . I was waiting . . ."

"We'll sup together."

"First you must get some dry clothes. I will have hot water sent to your room immediately. Get those things off without delay. Take a bath and get into dry things . . ."

"I am delighted to obey you."

"Then pray do not stand there. Get to your room and I will have the water sent up at once."

I felt excited. I pretended not to know why. I had not realized how anxious I had been. It was wonderful to know that they were all well, and I was glad that I was not going to be alone for the evening. Even Carleton, I told myself, was better than no one.

I went to the kitchen. "Master Carleton is wet through," I told them. "He has ridden through this terrible weather from beyond Islington. He needs hot water . . . plenty of it. And have some soup made hot. We will sup as soon as he is ready."

I went to my room. It was rather silly, I told myself, to be so elated, but I was looking forward to one of those verbal battles which were always inevitable when we were together.

I looked at myself in my mirror. It was a pity I was wearing this dark blue gown. The material was velvet and quite pleasant but it was not my most becoming gown. My eyes went to the cherry red silk.

What was I thinking of? If I changed I could be sure he would notice and he would imagine it had been done for him.

No, I must stay in my blue gown.

He was quicker than I had believed possible. He came into the winter parlour, which was used when there were only a few to eat together and where I had ordered that a fire be lighted, and I thought the room with the small tapestry on one wall and candles flickering in their sockets while the log fire threw a glow over the room was very attractive. The table had been laid for two and the dish of soup was already on the table, hot, steaming and smelling delicious.

He came in, fresh from his bath, ruffles at his neck and the sleeves of his shirt. He wore no jacket but a brocade vest. I thought: I suppose he looks handsome if one cares for that kind of saturnine looks.

"What a pleasure!" he cried. "Supper *à deux*. I could not have wished for anything more delightful. I enjoyed your solicitude . . . hustling me into my bath, making me take off my wet garments, making sure that I put on clean dry ones."

I shrugged my shoulders. "I merely suggested what would seem good sense to anyone. There is nothing to be grateful for in that."

"You really did seem concerned. This soup tastes good."

"Hunger seasons all dishes, they say."

"Now that is a very profound statement." He lifted one eyebrow and I was reminded poignantly of Edwin. "One which," he went on, "I would expect from you. This wine is good. I have always had a fondness for malmsey. Come, you must drink with me."

He poured more into my goblet.

"To the King," he said. "May he reign many years."

I could not refuse a loyal toast so I drank a little wine.

"Let me give you more soup."

"I have had enough, thank you."

"Then you will allow me to partake. Oh, this is pleasant. To sit here opposite you, dear Arabella. It is something I have always dreamed of doing."

"We have sat opposite each other at table many times, I am sure."

"You miss the point . . . deliberately, I think. But never alone. That was my meaning."

"Tell me, were they much put out?"

"At first. It will be easy to get the carriage moving when the rain subsides. They were fortunate to be so near their destination. I rode on and had a carriage brought to them and we took them there safely. They will now be sitting round a table like this, talking of their adventures, wondering what will happen next. First the fire of London, and then my Lord Eversleigh and his family get stuck in a coach!"

"It was an ordeal for them."

"Amusing, really. I said I shall ride back in good time so that I can let Arabella know what happened. You see, I was thinking of you. What good roast beef this is. Excellent!"

Silently the servants moved in and out carrying the food. He ate very heartily and drank equally so, I thought.

270

When he had eaten of the roast beef and taken some capon besides and then apples and nuts, he said to the servants: "Leave us now. You can clear this away in the morning. Mistress Eversleigh and I have much to discuss."

I could not protest before them, but as soon as they had gone, I said: "I cannot imagine what we have to discuss which is so very private."

"You know there is our Great Matter."

"What is this Great Matter?"

"Our future. Our marriage. When is it going to be, Arabella?"

"Never, I should say."

"That is cruel. And untrue. I'll wager you . . ."

"I rarely wager and never would on such a matter."

"Wise lady. You would be sure to lose. I believe you are one of those clever one who only wagers when she is certain of winning."

"It's a good principle."

"Ah, if only more of us had the wit to carry it out. Now, Arabella, we decided when last we talked that it would be an excellent solution for us to marry. Edwin would have a father, which he sorely needs, and you a husband for whom you need is as great."

"I happen to think differently. If Edwin is in such sore need as you imply, there might be another alternative."

"If you married Geoffrey you would be regretting it in a week."

"Why should you come to that conclusion?"

"Because I know him and I know you. You want someone who is a man."

"So Geoffrey is not?"

"He is a good sort. I have nothing against him."

"I can see you are determined to be fair-minded."

He rose suddenly and was round the table. He had put his arms about me and began kissing my lips and my throat.

"Please go away. If the servants come in . . ."

"They won't. They daren't disobey me. That's what I mean about being a man."

"Well, subduer of servants, I am not one of them, remember."

271

"I did not forget that for one moment. If you were one of them, I should not have put up with your nonsense so long."

"You would have commanded me to submit to you, I daresay. And you being such a man and I in a humble capacity, I would not have dared refuse."

"You quiver a little, Arabella. When I hold you like this, I can feel you trembling in my arms."

"With rage."

"You would be a passionate woman if you would be yourself."

"Who am I . . . if not myself? I am myself and I know this: I want you to go to your room and stay there and I shall go to mine."

"What a cruel waste of time! Listen, Arabella, I want you. I love you. I am going to marry you and show you it is the best thing in the world for us both."

"I think I will say good night and go to my room."

I rose and went to the door, but he was there before me, barring my way. I shrugged my shoulders, trying hard to quell a rising excitement. He is capable of anything, I thought with a shudder, which if I were honest I must say was not entirely unpleasant.

"I insist on talking to you. I rarely have such an opportunity."

"Really, Carleton, I do assure you there is nothing more to be said. Now let me pass."

Slowly he shook his head. "I insist that you listen to me."

With a weary shrug I went to the table and sat down. "Well?"

"You are not as indifferent to me as you pretend. When I hold you I sense that. You are fighting your impulses . . . all the time you are doing that. You are living a pretence. Pretending you have finished with love . . . pretending that you don't want me . . . pretending to think all the time of your dead husband . . ."

"That is not pretence," I said.

"Give me a chance to prove it."

"*You* prove to me what I think! I know without proof from you."

272

"You are wasting your life."

"That is surely for me to decide."

"If only you were concerned, perhaps. But there is someone else."

"You?" I said with a laugh.

"Yes . . . me."

"It is you who should face up to the truth. You would like to marry me. Yes, I can see that. It would be very convenient. You want Eversleigh. You believed you would have it one day. Then Edwin was born and he stood in your way. He died, but he had a son and now he stands between you and what you hoped for. And there is one other who comes before you, Uncle Toby. Even if my Edwin did not exist, Toby would inherit before you did. However, you want to be in command. If I married someone else he would be Edwin's stepfather. He would guide Edwin. He would teach him what he has to learn. That does not appeal to you. You might lose your hold on Eversleigh. Therefore, being most conveniently free to marry, you would marry me. Now is that not the whole of it?"

"Not the whole truth," he said.

"So you admit to part of it."

"Unlike you, I face facts."

"And I do not?"

"Certainly, you do not. You want to marry me, and you pretend you don't. Perhaps you don't even realize that you want to. You are caught up in such a web of deceit."

"You talk nonsense. What you don't know is that I was once married to the only man I could love. He was noble, honourable . . . He died for the cause he believed in. Do you think anyone could ever replace him in my heart?"

Carleton burst out laughing. His eyes suddenly blazed with anger. "Are you telling me that you have never guessed the truth?"

"The truth? What truth?"

"About your saintly husband."

"I hate to hear you mention his name. You are unworthy . . ."

"I know . . . to unlatch his shoes, I believe. Edwin

was no worse than the rest of us, perhaps . . . but no better."

"Stop it, I say, stop it."

He took me by the shoulders and shook me.

"It's time you knew the truth. It's time you stopped living in a dream. Edwin married you for the same reason that you accuse me of wanting to marry you. His parents wanted it . . . and so did your parents. He would have preferred . . . Surely you know?"

I felt myself go limp with rage and horror. I could not believe I was hearing correctly.

"I am tired of remaining silent," went on Carleton, speaking tensely and rapidly. "I'm tired of standing by and joining in the pretence. Edwin had great charm, didn't he? Everyone liked him. He tried to be everything to everyone . . . just the very man each one wanted him to be. He was always liked and he was very good at it. You wanted the young romantic lover, and it seems he played the part to perfection. He had you believing him."

"What do you mean? Whom . . . would he have preferred?"

"That great friend of yours, of course. Harriet Main. Were you completely blind? She hoped he would marry her, but that would be asking too much of him. His parents would have objected. Edwin never upset anyone if he could help it. Besides, he knew at once that you were the suitable partner. That didn't stop those two though. I can assure you of that."

"Harriet . . . and Edwin?"

"Wasn't it clear? Where do you think he was on those nights when you were alone in the big bed, eh? Out on his secret mission? Oh, it was secret all right. He was with her. Sleeping with her. Forgetting his dear, little, trusting wife. Why do you think she brought you to England? Because she wanted to be with him. That's why. She was out collecting her plants! He was on his secret mission! How odd that both should take them to the old arbour. They spent a good deal of time there together. Too much. Do you know why he was shot? I would take you to the man who shot him, but he is dead now. It was Old Jethro, the hermit-Puritan. He shot his dog for coupling with a bitch, and what he did to a dog he was clearly ready to do to a man and woman. . . if these things were done outside the lawful marriage bed. In an arbour, for instance."

"I . . . don't believe it."

"You know it's true. Come, Arabella, you are a sensible young woman. You know the way of the world."

"I don't believe it of Edwin."

"Shall I have to prove it to you?"

"You can't. The man who killed him is dead, you say . . . a likely story. When did he so conveniently die?"

"Soon after he killed Edwin. He told me himself. He had watched them when they met. He had put himself into a place where he could see. Then he brought the gun and he shot them . . . in the act."

I covered my face with my hands, trying in vain to shut out the vivid pictures which forced themselves into my mind.

I could only repeat: "I don't believe it. I will never believe it."

"I can prove it to you."

"If it's true, why have you kept quiet so long?"

"Out of my regard for you. I thought you might come to realize it gradually. But when you keep flinging him at me . . . the sainted husband . . . it was more than I could bear. I am not a saint. I have been involved, doubtless, in more amorous adventuring than Edwin ever was . . . but I could never be as deceitful as he was. I could never have lied to you as blatantly, nor would I have brought a mistress and a wife on such an errand . . . unless of course they knew the circumstances and agreed to come."

"Harriet . . . and Edwin," I murmured. "It just is not true."

"I am going to show you something," he said.

"What?" I demanded.

"I found it on his body. Harriet came in in a state of distraction. She was safe, though I think the intention was to kill them both and leave them there . . . exposed . . . a lesson to sinners. That would have been typical of Jethro. But she escaped and came to me. She told me what

275

had happened and I had him brought into the house. It seemed best then to let you think he had been killed because of his work and to hurry you and Harriet Main out of the country."

"I don't trust you."

"No, you trusted Edwin. You trust the wrong people, as I am showing you."

"It is merely your word . . . and I don't trust you."

"Then I will prove it to you. Wait there a moment."

He had gone but I could not wait. I followed him up the stairs to his room. I stood in the doorway watching him as he lighted the candles and opened a drawer.

He brought out a piece of paper and, coming towards me, put an arm about me and drew me gently into the room.

The paper was bloodstained, and I recognized Harriet's writing.

"I kept it," he said. "I suppose I knew that one day I might have to show it to you. Sit down."

I let him put me into a chair and he held me close while I read.

I do not want to record those words. They were too intimate, too revealing, and they had been written by Harriet. I knew her writing too well to doubt it. There could be no doubt of their intimacy . . . an intimacy such as I had never dreamed of. She reproached him a little for marrying me. Poor Arabella! That was how she wrote of me, how they must have spoken of me. It was clear that they had been lovers from the beginning, before he had asked me to marry him, that when he had married me, he had gone on wanting her.

Of course. Of course. It was so easy to understand now. She was sublimely beautiful. No one could compare with her. It was understandable. Charles Condey had been a blind. She had never had any feeling for him. My mother-in-law had seen more than I had. That was why she had insisted that I play Juliet. But how innocent she was . . . as innocent as I. As though that could have made any difference.

So they had met when they could. They had deceived me, told me lies. "Alas, my love, I must go out tonight

276

. . . this secret mission." And he was going to Harriet. Harriet! I could see her laughing with him. "You managed to get away from her, then? Poor Arabella! Always so easy to deceive." It was true . . . right from the beginning. I had believed she had hurt her ankle and was staying for that reason. I had believed she wanted to help me stay with Edwin and she had wanted him himself. I had believed . . .

Leigh, I thought. It was so. It must be so. Leigh was *Edwin's* son.

My lips formed the boy's name. "Leigh . . ." I said.

"Of course. There is a likeness in the boy. It'll be more noticeable when he gets older."

"Why . . . ?" I began.

He knelt down by my chair and, taking my hand, kissed it. I let it lie in his.

"Because you had to know. It's always best to know. I told you in a fit of passion. Perhaps it was wrong. But it's best to know, Arabella."

I was silent. He went on: "When you saw her again on the stage, I was afraid you were going to ask her to come here. You must never do that, Arabella. You must never trust that woman again."

"I thought she was . . ."

"I know you thought she was your friend. She could never be a friend to anyone but herself. Forget her now. You know the truth. It's over, Arabella. It was over years ago. Seven years have passed. Let them both pass out of your life as well."

I said nothing. I sat there in a daze. I kept thinking of scenes from the past. They were going round and round in my head. Their faces gazed at me, laughed at me, sneered at me. I thought I could bear no more.

I wanted to run away and yet I wanted to stay. I could not bear to be alone now.

Carleton said: "It has been a shock. Here. Give me the letter. I am going to destroy it. It is better that it is lost forever."

"No," I said, "don't."

"What would you do with it?" he asked. "Read it again and again? Torture yourself with it?" He held it in the flame of the candle. I watched the edge of the paper scorch and shrivel before it burst into flame. "There, it is gone. Forget now that it was ever written." Carleton dropped it in the grate, and I watched it until there was nothing left but the charred remains.

He went to a cupboard and, taking out a bottle, poured liquid into a glass and held it to my lips.

"It will soothe you," he said. "It will make you feel better."

He had his arms about me and I drank. The draught was like fire in my throat.

He was murmuring soothingly: "Now you are going to feel better. You are going to see that it happened a long time ago. It is over now. You have your beautiful son . . . and if it had never happened you would not have had him, would you? It is your legitimate Edwin who is heir to Eversleigh, not the bastard Leigh . . . not her child. And does she care? No, she went off and let you bring up the boy. Doesn't that tell you the kind of woman she is?"

I felt dazed, as though I were floating in midair. He picked me up and carried me as though I were a baby. He was sitting in the chair holding me, rocking me tenderly, and I felt comforted.

So we sat thus and I heard him telling me that he loved me. That there had never been anyone he wanted as he wanted me, that everything was going to be wonderful for us both. I had not lost anything. Instead I had found that which would compensate me for everything I now thought I had lost.

I felt him gently unbuttoning my dress. I felt his hands on my body. He lifted me and, kissing me with the utmost tenderness, lay me on his bed.

Then he was with me and I felt dazed and yet somehow happy. It was as though I was escaping from bonds which had been restraining me for a long time. I heard him laugh in the darkness. His voice came from a long way off. And he kept calling me "His love, his Arabella."

The Return of the Prodigal

When I awoke, for a few seconds I felt dazed and bewildered. I looked about the unfamiliar surroundings. Memory came back. I was in his room. I sat up in bed. He was not there. I saw my clothes lying on the floor where they had been dropped last night.

I closed my eyes, childishly trying to shut out memories with the sight of that room. Last night . . . I thought of Carleton holding that piece of paper in his hand . . . that revealing paper which was positive proof of the deception which had been carried out against me. The desolation . . . how could I describe it? My dreams, my ideals on which I had lived for seven years had been demolished by one single stroke.

And afterwards . . . I could not fully remember how it had happened. He had comforted me. He had soothed my wounded vanity, perhaps. He had given me something to drink which had warmed me and at the same time dulled my resistance.

I had been like a wax doll in his hands—no will to

resist, I just gave myself up to him. How could I! How *could* I!

And yet I had been unable to do otherwise.

Where had he gone? What time was it?

I got out of bed, and horrified by my nakedness I slipped my gown over my head. I went to the window. The rain was still falling. It was probably later than I had realized because it was a dark morning. I thought of the maid arriving at my room with hot water, finding my bed unslept in. Strange that at such a time I should be thinking of the proprieties.

I snatched my things from the floor and opened the door. I looked out. The house seemed quiet and I sped along to my room.

To my relief I saw from my clock that there were a good fifteen minutes before they would bring my hot water. I took off my dress and threw it into a cupboard with the rest of my things, then putting on a nightgown I got into bed.

Now I gave myself up to contemplation of what had happened. I wished I could stop thinking of that piece of paper writhing in Carleton's hands. The words on it were indelibly written in my mind. How could they have deceived me so! How could I ever trust anyone again? But my overwhelming preoccupation was with my surrender. He had arranged it purposely. He had come to me when he knew that I was weak with misery. My conception of my marriage had crashed about my head, and he was there seizing the opportunity to offer me tender comfort, to daze me with his beverage, whatever that was, to weaken my resistance to him, to remind me that I had to turn to someone, to seek comfort somewhere, and he was there. Opportunity. No. He had contrived it. The idea must have come to him when the family coach was stuck in the mud and he knew they would be away for the night. He was cunning, he was devious, and I had given way to him.

I was trying to ignore those memories which came back to me. A wild and searing joy to be with him . . . Ecstasy there had been with Edwin, but different somehow. . . . Perhaps because with Carleton there was more than love and passion. There was a kind of mingling of love and hate which was surely wrong and yet . . . and yet . . .

I was a little afraid of myself. I was thankful that he had not been there when I awoke and realized how my life had changed overnight.

I thought then of my mother and my father in the days when he had been married to my Aunt Angelet. The passion which had flared up between them, of which she had written so vividly that even before I had experienced such emotions I had understood.

I was like her. I needed that which was called fulfillment. During the last years since Edwin's death I had been only half alive. I had been living in a false world. I saw that now, and how inevitable it was that sooner or later I was going to let Carleton become my lover.

Why Carleton? Why did I not accept Geoffrey's honourable offer of marriage? Because instinctively I had known that Carleton was the man for me. His virility could call forth a response in me. That I disliked him seemed to be no deterrent. Physically we were a perfect match. That I had discovered, and it was something he—with his knowledge of women and the world—had known immediately. He might feel that marriage with me was good for his ambitions, but at the same time it suited his physical needs.

I had grown up overnight.

Perhaps that was something I should be grateful for.

There was a knock on the door. The maid came in with hot water.

She said "Good morning, mistress," and drew back the curtains.

I expected her to show by some way that she noticed the change in me. Surely I must seem different after my experiences? But she set down the water and brought me a note.

"Master Carleton went off early this morning, mistress. He left this note for you."

I wanted to tear it open but had no wish to appear over-eager.

I yawned, I hoped convincingly.

"Not a very good morning, Em," I said.

"Still raining, mistress. I believe it's been raining all through the night."

Yes, I thought, the patter of rain against the windows . . . lying there with him . . . just not wanting to move away . . . forgetting everything but the need to be there.

" 'Tis to be hoped milord and milady and the others will get the coach set to rights."

"I daresay they will, Em."

She went out and I opened the note.

It was brief. "I have had to go out on Court business. I shall return during the day. C."

No indication that anything unusual had happened. I felt a rush of disappointment. How could he go like that after what had happened? Was he implying that there was nothing extraordinary? It was all very natural that he and I should become lovers? It was what he had always suggested. Was he laughing in triumph now?

I felt angry with him and with myself. How could I have been so weak, so foolish!

It was the impulse of a moment, I told myself. I had had a shock and he was there. He had dulled my resistance with his strong wines. What was that he had given me? It had acted like some witch's love potion. Perhaps it was. I could hardly imagine his trafficking with witches. But he was capable of anything.

I washed and dressed. I was thankful that I did not have to face him yet.

I was very pale. I found a little rouge and rubbed it into my cheeks. That was better. I thought how I had loved Harriet. She had been as a sister to me. I had been really upset when she had gone away. If I had known . . .

But what a stupid innocent I had been!

How long and dreary was that day. Nothing happened. I stood at the window watching the raindrops. The grass was sodden. The last of the leaves were rapidly being tossed to the ground and there was a wet bronze carpet on the grass.

Why didn't he come in? How like him to go off on business. I didn't believe it. Where was he? I wondered if he were with a woman. A feeling of intense rage possessed me. I should hate her . . . and him. I could never trust anyone again. Oh, Edwin . . . Harriet . . . how could you? How could I ever bear to look at Leigh again?

In the early afternoon a messenger came to the house. I ran down to greet him, sure that he came from Carleton.

He did not. He was from my mother-in-law. They had had greater difficulties with the coach than had seemed likely yesterday. A spoke in one of the wheels had been damaged and was being repaired. This meant that they would be away for one more night. If the rain would stop it would be easier. They would be with me tomorrow without fail.

The evening came and Carleton had not returned.

I was angry with him. He had succeeded as he always said he would. Was that what he wanted? One single victory.

I ate alone—or made a pretence of eating. How different from last night. I found myself longing to see his dark, clever, wicked face opposite me. I wanted to hear his voice mocking me. I wanted to respond.

I retired early. I went to bed. I tried to sleep but I could not. I could not read because I kept going over the events of last night.

It must have been nearly midnight when my door opened and he was there. He wore a loose night robe.

I felt faint with baffling emotions as he looked at me.

"I did not know you had returned," I stammered.

"Did you think I could stay away? There was much business, but I was determined to be with you." He blew out the candle he was carrying. "We shall not need it," he said.

I struggled up, but he was beside me, pinning me down. "There is so much to say."

"We shall have the rest of our lives in which to say it, Arabella. I have been thinking of you all through the day. At last. At last . . . My heart's desire . . ."

I heard myself laugh. "To hear you talk so . . . it is unlike you. Sentimental . . ."

"I can be sentimental, romantic . . . foolish . . . with one woman in the world. You are that woman, Arabella. At last you know it."

"You should not be here," I said.

"There is no other place where I should be."

I suppose everyone wonders at himself or herself at some time. I wondered then.

Afterwards I could tell myself that I was so unhappy, so wretched that I had to stop myself thinking. I had to be shocked into forgetfulness.

In any case that night, without the aid of spirits or love potions, I was submissive . . . no, not that . . . responsive . . . and I knew that in the morning I should despise myself for giving way so blatantly to the sensuous demands of my nature.

When I awoke I was alone in my bed, and as before with the coming of daylight, I was surprised at my behaviour on the previous night. It seemed that I had two natures—one daytime and one my nighttime other self. Carleton filled my thoughts so that I even forgot to brood on Edwin's deceit. What was the outcome to be? There seemed an inevitable solution. Marriage.

Marriage with Carleton, who clearly wanted it so that as Edwin's stepfather he could have a stronger control over the Eversleigh estates. I had been married once for convenience. Should I do so again? Oh, but with Edwin . . . I thought of those delightful interludes which had seemed to me the expression of pure romantic love. I shivered. I would never again allow myself to be so used.

When I went to breakfast Carleton was already there. He smiled at me. "Good morning, dear Arabella." One of the servants was hovering and he went on with a lift of his eyebrows: "I trust you slept well?"

"Thank you, yes," I replied.

"The rain has stopped at last," he added. "Let us take a turn in the garden after breakfast, shall we?"

"I should like that," I replied.

When we were a little way from the house he said: "The question now, Arabella, is not will you but when will you marry me?"

"I . . . am not sure about marrying."

"What! You do not want to remain my mistress, surely?"

I was angry with him just as I used to be. He had the power to make me so. In place of the passionate lover who could be sentimental and romantic just for me, here was the cynic, the Court wit, the man I always wanted to do battle with.

"Let us forget what has happened."

"Forget the most wonderful nights of my life! Oh, come, Arabella, that is asking too much."

"You are mocking me as you ever do."

"No, I am serious. When my uncle returns I shall tell him the good news. He will be delighted. I know he has long decided that a marriage between us would be an ideal solution for Eversleigh."

"I am tired of being a pawn in this Eversleigh game."

"Not a pawn, my darling. I told you once before, you are a queen."

"A piece then . . . to be moved about this way and that. I am not at all sure that I want to marry you."

"Arabella, you shock me. Remembering what I shall never, never forget . . ."

"You tricked me. You shocked me . . . and then you gave me something to drink. What was it?"

He laughed at me and lifted his eyebrows again.

"My secret," he said.

I turned away. "I am undecided," I retorted.

"At least there is some hope."

"After what happened . . ."

"And it will happen again."

"I don't want it to."

"Oh, Arabella, still deceiving yourself! There was no magic in a glass last night and yet, and yet . . ."

"Oh, you . . . you . . . !"

He took my hand and kissed it. "Tonight when they return we shall tell them?"

"No," I said.

"You are surely not thinking of my rival Geoffrey *now,* are you?"

I was not, but I could not resist the impulse to let him think I might be.

"Because," he said, "there would be trouble. Don't think that what has happened between us is an isolated incident. When we are alone together it will happen again. We're drawn together like the moon and the sun . . ."

"You are the sun in this partnership, I presume?"

"What does it matter which is which? It's the drawing power of which I speak. Our being lovers is inevitable. It was from the first. I knew it. I wanted you. I wondered I didn't take you down to the arbour and show you how your husband died. Taken in adultery."

"Stop it!"

"I'm sorry. You arouse the worst in me . . . and the best, because you are the most maddening woman on earth . . . and yet I adore you."

I softened as I always did when he showed me affection. I wanted to say: "Yes, I will marry you. After what has happened I must marry you." On the other hand it would be for the convenience of them all, and after having been so cruelly deceived by Edwin, how could I be sure that Carleton was not deceiving me in the same way?

"I want time," I said. "Time to think."

"You need that . . . *now*?"

"Yes, I do, and I shall have it."

I turned away from him and went into the house.

In the afternoon the party returned in the carriage. They were full of their adventures and could talk of nothing else. I listened, I must admit, with divided attention, for I could not but be amazed by all that had happened since I had last seen them.

Charlotte came to my room in the early evening and said: "Something's happened. You seem different."

"Do I?" I tried to sound surprised. I glanced round my bedroom and the bed which last night I had shared with Carleton as though I thought there must be something there to betray me. "In what way?" I asked.

She shook her head. "I don't know . . . but you seem . . . excited and at the same time . . ."

"Yes?" I prompted, playing for time and wondering what she had noticed.

"I don't know. I can only say . . . different."

"I was very anxious on the first day when you didn't come back. It was late before I heard what had happened."

"Yes, Carleton said you would be worried and he would ride back to tell you."

286

"It was a relief," I said. "Well, we shall be going back to Eversleigh soon. I must confess I am longing to see the boys."

Charlotte said no more of the difference in me, but I did catch her looking at me rather intently as the day wore on.

It was just before suppertime when the messenger came. There was some consternation, for his livery proclaimed that he was from the King.

During the digging after the fire, workmen had discovered Roman walls and tessellated pavements beneath the streets, and the King was greatly excited. He knew that Carleton had some knowledge of these matters and he wanted him to come to Court without delay. He wanted to talk with him and the next day they would pay a visit to the site.

Carleton, of course, had no alternative but to leave at once.

We returned to Eversleigh. We had been away much longer than we had intended and the children were delighted to see us. I had to tell them about the great fire and they listened round-eyed to the details of falling masonry, blazing roofs and molten lead running through the streets.

"Shall we have a fire here?" asked Leigh wistfully.

"Pray God not," I replied sharply.

I was not sorry that Carleton had been called away. I wanted to think about the future and I found it easier to do that when he was not near.

I wondered what Edwin would feel about the change in our relationship. He did not dislike Carleton. Of course he had not the same feeling for him that he had for Geoffrey. Was that because Geoffrey had gone out of his way to interest and amuse? Both boys loved Uncle Toby who attracted them to him effortlessly.

I could not ask Edwin outright how he felt about Carleton. In any case I didn't want to talk about Carleton. I really wanted to put him out of my mind. I was still stunned by my easy surrender, and in a way—perhaps unfairly—I blamed Carleton for it.

I made a habit of going to the arbour where Edwin's body had been found. It was a gloomy place, hidden from the house by a shrubbery. As a place where murder had been committed it was neglected. No one cared to go near it, particularly after dark. I knew the servants avoided it, and so did the gardeners. The foliage round it was overgrown and rarely tended. It was a wooden structure and must once have been a very pretty retreat, secluded enough for privacy. The window through which the shot had been fired was now boarded up. No one had ever suggested that it should be replaced. I looked inside. It smelt damp and musty. There was a bench, a wooden chair and a small table with iron legs. I forced myself to step inside, and I stood there, imagining them together. A good place for an assignation. I saw the key hanging on a nail near the door. They could lock themselves in. They had forgotten that someone could have looked in from outside. Old Jethro . . . the avenging prophet!

Why did I come here, to exacerbate my wounds, I asked myself? I let myself picture the self-righteous Jethro, watching the lovers' meeting, peering through that now boarded-up window at their abandoned lovemaking. I wondered if he had watched salaciously. That would not have surprised me. And then he brought out his gun and killed Edwin, taking him in the very act, which was scarcely what a Christian should do, since according to Jethro's beliefs, Edwin would go to eternal damnation without hope of remission of his sins. Surely Jethro's would be the greater crime in the face of heaven?

I often sat in the kitchen and talked with Ellen.

"Did you know Old Jethro?" I asked.

"Indeed, yes, mistress. Everybody hereabouts knew Old Jethro. Some said he was mad. His religion turned his brain. He used to beat himself with whips and wear a hair shirt just to make himself suffer. He thought it made him holy."

"What did people hereabouts think of him?"

"Well before the King came back they reckoned he was a good man. He was all for the Parliament, but I think even they would not be stern enough for him. He once killed his dog for going with a bitch."

"I had heard that."

"He was all against maidens who forestalled their marriage vows. He'd be there in church when they was called to atone. He wanted 'em beaten and their bastards killed at birth."

"A good Christian!" I said with sarcasm.

"It depends on what you see as Christianity."

I thought I must go carefully, for Jasper had remained a stern Puritan and I would never forget how he had thought a pretty button was an object of the Devil.

"They say Young Jethro be as bad as his father and growing more like him every day."

"Young Jethro?"

"Oh, he'd not be so young. I reckon he must be nearly forty now."

"So he had a son. I am surprised, since he disapproved of dogs propagating their kind."

"Old Jethro were married once. Oh, he was a bit of a rake in them days, so I heard. Then suddenly he saw the light. That's what he says. God came to him in a vision and said, 'Jethro, what you're doing here is sinful like, You get out and preach my Word.' So then he was reformed. His wife left him. Young Jethro was about five then. He kept the boy and, as I said, he's made him another such as himself. Used to keep him chained up on his knees praying four hours a day."

"Old Jethro died, then?"

"Yes, some time ago. Some said he starved himself to death and all them whippings didn't help."

"Where does Young Jethro live? Is it near here?"

"Not far. On the edge of the estate. In a sort of barn. Very rough it is and Young Jethro be his father all over again. He's got a nose for sin. If there's a bit of sin hereabouts he'd sniff it out. Polly, one of our kitchen girls, was in a bit of trouble. Jethro knew it before the rest of us . . . almost before Polly knew herself. Took her in his barn and told her she was damned and how the Devil was laughing his head off and getting his imps to stoke up the fires for her. Poor Polly: she went to her grandmother's place and hanged herself. 'Wages of sin,' said Young Jethro. Poor Polly, 'twas only a little frolic in the stables. If she hadn't got caught, she'd have been no worse than the rest."

"This Young Jethro sounds a very uncomfortable sort of person to have about."

"Them that's over good is often uncomfortable, mistress."

I agreed.

By an odd chance a few days later when I was riding with the boys, we tethered the horses and went down to the beach near that cave where I had sheltered with Harriet and Edwin when we had come back to England. I had a morbid fancy for returning to such places and conjuring up visions of the past.

There on the shingle the boys took off their boots and dabbled their feet in the sea while I sat watching them.

The waves were a little rough on that day and every time one came in they would shriek with laughter, run forward daringly and then run back. Then they amused themselves by sending pebbles skimming over the water.

The noise of the sea, the odour of seaweed, the happy shrieks of the boys were a background to my thoughts. I remembered the boat's coming in. I pictured Edwin and Harriet exchanging looks. I tried to remember what they had said, and how they had said it. It was there for me to see and I had been blind.

I was aware suddenly of a crunching of boots on the shingle and looking up I saw a man coming along. He carried a basket in which he had some pieces of driftwood and perhaps other things he had picked up during his beachcombing.

He was muttering to himself. "Sinful. Should be beaten."

I knew instinctively that I was face to face with Young Jethro whose father had murdered my husband.

I could not let him pass. "Sinful?" I cried. "Who is sinful?"

He pulled up and looked at me with fierce, fanatical eyes shaded by brownish yellow brows so untidy that they sprouted in all directions and threatened to cover his eyes themselves. His great pupils stood out, for the whites of his eyes showed all round them so he had a look of fierce surprize and horror. His mouth was tight and drawn in, turning down at each side.

"Them bits of sin," he said pointing to the boys.

"I can assure you that they do not know the meaning of sin."

"You go against God's Word, woman. We be all born in sin."

"Even you?"

"God help me, yes."

"Well since you share in the sin, why are you so eager to point it out in others?"

"Laughing, shrieking . . . two days off the Sabbath!"

I felt angry with him. His father had killed Edwin. But for his father Edwin would not have died. I might never have discovered his infidelities. But could he have gone on through his life pretending . . .

"Nonsense," I said, "people are meant to be happy."

He moved away from me as though he feared to be contaminated by such wickedness.

"You're a sinful woman," he said. "God will not be mocked."

Edwin had seen the man. He thought I needed protecting and came running up.

"Mama, Mama, did you want me?"

I was so proud of him. He looked up boldly into that repulsive face and said: "Don't you dare hurt my mama."

I had risen to my feet and placed my hand protectively on my son's head.

Recognition dawned on Young Jethro's face. "I knew your father," he said.

"My father was the best man in the world," said Edwin.

"Ananias," cried Young Jethro. "Ananias."

"What does he mean, Mama?" asked Edwin.

I did not speak. I was very shaken by this man who knew so much about my husband.

"The wages of sin . . ." muttered Young Jethro, his eyes on Edwin.

Leigh came running up. He was breathless. "I've thrown a pebble over and over the water. It's gone all the way to France."

"It couldn't have," said Edwin.

291

"It did. It did. I saw it go."

Young Jethro had gone off muttering, "And the wages of sin is death."

"Who's that old man?" asked Leigh.

But Edwin was thinking of the pebble which had gone skimming across the water to France and was determined to throw one himself.

"Show me," he said. "I'll send one farther than you."

They raced back to the water while I watched the retreating figure of Young Jethro.

I think I knew it was going to happen, and when I was sure, I felt a sense of relief because fate had made up my mind for me.

I knew I must act quickly and I did.

When I was alone with Carleton, I said: "I am pregnant."

His eyes lighted up. His face seemed to shine with the enormity of his satisfaction.

"My dearest Arabella. I knew it." He had lifted me in his arms. He held me tightly. He kissed me again and again. We were in the garden and I said: "We could be seen."

"Does it matter? A man is allowed to embrace his future wife. Oh, my dear girl, this is the happiest moment of my life."

"It is what you wanted. You will be Edwin's stepfather and Eversleigh will be yours in all but name."

"As if I was thinking of Eversleigh."

"You know you always are thinking of it."

"I am thinking of everything. My wife and already carrying our child. That is wonderful. I am an impatient man, you will find, my darling. This suits my mood. I am to acquire a wife and a child in the shortest possible space of time."

"I see no alternative but marriage," I said, trying to sound doleful.

"There *is* no alternative. I shall go straight in and tell my uncle. I know he'll be delighted. It was what he wanted. Or shall we marry secretly? Then we might have another ceremony and festivities later. That would account for the early arrival of our child."

"I did not think you were one to set such store by the proprieties."

"I like to observe them when they fit in with my needs. Oh, Arabella, I am a happy man this day. That which I have so long desired has come to pass. Yes, let us marry in secret. I will arrange for a priest to do this. Then we will tell my uncle, and I know they will probably want another ceremony and celebrations here."

"There seems no point in such subterfuge."

"Yes. Because the sort of wedding they will wish us to have might take a little time to arrange. There is our child to consider. We want him to make a respectable entrance into the world."

"Please do not think I am duty bound to provide you with a boy."

"Believe me, it is Arabella I want. I shall be grateful for whatever she deigns to give me. Leave this to me, Arabella. Arabella, how I adore you."

"At least," I said, "I should be grateful that you are ready to make an honest woman of me."

"Never change." He smiled at me gently. "I could not bear you to change. There was always something of the polygamist in me, so I need my two Arabellas. Arabella of the sharp tongue by day and Arabella adorable, loving me as I love her in the dark of the night."

"There is only one of me, you know. Do you think I can really supply all your needs?"

"You already have the answer to that. Proof positive."

He went off that day and did not come back until the morning of the following one. I was to meet him at the stables that afternoon. We rode off some five miles together and there in a small church we were married. Two of his Court friends were witnesses.

I said: "It is exactly like what I hear of a mock marriage. I believe that is a practice some of your profligate friends indulge in now and then."

"Alas, they do. But this is no mockery. This is true and binding. We shall go straight back to Eversleigh and I will tell my uncle that we are married, but I shall not tell him

293

when the ceremony took place. I'll promise you he will insist on our being married in the Eversleigh church with many spectators and a feast to follow. Then you will not be able to say it is like a mock marriage."

I felt an odd elation, a desire not to look beyond the moment. I was too excited to be unhappy.

By a stream we paused to rest awhile. We tethered the horses and sat on the grass.

Carleton took my hand and said: "So at last it has happened."

"You always knew it would, didn't you?" I said. "You made up your mind and what you decide you want you get eventually."

"It seems to work that way," he admitted with unaccustomed modesty.

I looked at the ring he had put on my finger. I had taken off that which Edwin had given me and had left it in a drawer in my court cupboard.

He took my hand and kissed the ring. Then he put his arms about me and drew me down beside him.

I said uneasily: "We should be going."

He answered that we should celebrate our marriage.

I knew what he meant and I tried to rise. "Someone could come past," I said.

"This is a very isolated spot. Besides, I want you now. Do you realize this stupendous fact? You and I have just been married."

Then he held me to him and laughed and the leaves fluttered down on us as he made love to me.

The notion came to me that it would always be what he wanted unless I firmly resisted which, I promised myself, I should do if the inclination so moved me.

But I would be honest. I was elated. I didn't know whether this was happiness. It was not what I had found with Edwin, but I wanted no more of that.

Excitement, passion, satisfaction. How much more appealing than romantic love!

I never intend to be hurt again, I told myself.

Carleton was right. There was great rejoicing when my father- and mother-in-law were told the news.

"You sly dog," cried Lord Eversleigh, gripping Carleton's hand. "Marrying in secret, eh? Keeping it from us."

Matilda embraced me warmly. "My dearest daughter," she said, "for that is what you are to me. Nothing could have pleased me more." She whispered: "You will be so good for Carleton . . . after that unfortunate marriage. It makes everything so *right*."

"Why did you keep it secret?" asked Charlotte; her voice was cool but there was a strange edge to it.

Carleton was ready for her. "We decided on the spur of the moment. We knew that if we announced a formal betrothal, you would have wanted us to wait and do everything in style. I know you, Aunt Matilda."

"Yes," said her husband, "that would have been just like you, Matilda."

"Naturally I should have wanted to have had a beautiful wedding. In fact . . ."

"It's coming," said Carleton. "What did I tell you, Arabella?"

Then Matilda said that of course it would be pleasant to have another celebration. That could be done. "Everyone will be so disappointed if we don't. We owe it to everyone on the estate . . ."

Carleton looked at me and smiled.

"We'll consider it, eh, Arabella?"

I said we would, for I could see that Matilda was already making her plans.

She thought that we should have a ceremony in the church—people never really liked those secret ceremonies—and there would be a reception afterwards at the house. The servants should have theirs in the hall beyond the screens. It was traditional.

"We must let everyone know that it is a repeat performance," said Carleton.

"Oh . . ." said Matilda, a slow smile spreading across her face.

Then she turned to me and embraced me. "You have brought great happiness to Eversleigh, Arabella . . . as always."

Charlotte sought an opportunity to speak to me. I was passing her bedroom and she called me in to show me, she said, how she was progressing with a piece of tapestry she was working. That was just a pretext, I quickly realized.

"I am thinking of working in a new shade of red, so you think it would be the right thing to do?"

I said I thought it would be very good.

"So you are already married to Carleton?" she went on.

"Yes."

"It seems so strange. I thought you didn't like him. Were you pretending?"

"Of course not. It was just . . . our way."

"You always seemed to be sparring together . . . trying to score over each other."

"I suppose we were."

"Then how could you be . . .?"

"Relationships are complicated, Charlotte."

"I see that they are. You were different with Edwin." My lips tightened. "Yes," I said.

"You loved Edwin dearly. It was a terrible tragedy. People suffer when they fall in love. Perhaps it would be better not to."

"That's certainly a point of view."

"Was Carleton implying that you are already . . .?"

"I am going to have a child," I said.

"Is that why . . . I'm sorry. I shouldn't have said that. It was just that it was such a surprise. You and Carleton, when I thought you disliked him. Of course I knew he was interested in you . . . but then, if all accounts are true, he is interested in lots of women."

"From now on," I said lightly, "he will have to be interested in one only."

"Do you think that you can make a man interested in you only?"

"I believe that is what a wife must find out for herself by trying, of course."

"You are attractive, Arabella. I've always seen that. It was only when that woman came . . ."

"You mean Harriet," I said firmly.

"Harriet Main," she repeated softly. And I guessed she was thinking of how Harriet had wantonly taken Charles Condey from her and then refused him.

"I am going to change things at Eversleigh, Charlotte," I said. "We shall have balls and banquets. I think we should. And then you will . . ."

"Yes—" she said.

"Perhaps you'll find out that there are other men in the world besides Charles Condey."

"Oh, I always knew that," she replied, smiling at me.

I'll do it, I told myself. I'll bring her out. I'll find a husband for her. I'll stop her brooding on the past.

I had freed myself from it. So should she.

Yes, that was how I felt during the months that followed. I was free from the ghost of the past. Edwin had never really loved me. A bitter revelation, but it was proving helpful. I could not let my resentment against him smoulder. I was someone else's wife now.

And Carleton. What can I say except that he carried me along on the waves of passion like a frail craft on hitherto uncharted seas? I began to wait to be alone with him, to long for him, to give myself up to him entirely.

I understood so much of what my mother had told me. I knew how she had fought against such a passion. I understood her story as I had never been able to before. She came to Eversleigh for the wedding celebration with my father and the rest of the family. Lucas could not come because his wife was having a baby.

My parents were delighted. I could see they liked Carleton. My mother told me confidentially that she could clearly understand the attraction, and she was sure I should be even happier in my second marriage than I had been in my first. I realized then that, although she had considered Edwin a suitable husband, she had felt he was so young and not quite as serious as she would like the husband of her darling daughter to be.

Carleton talked a great deal with my father. They discussed the state of the country—my father from the military angle, Carleton from that of politics. They were clearly interested in each other.

After they had returned to Far Flamstead, my mother wrote frequently and they were all delighted at the prospect of the birth of my child.

Happy days they were. Uncle Toby was beside himself with delight.

"There is nothing pleases me so much as to see young people happily married. There is nothing like marriage. Married bliss—ah, it should be the dream of us all." He became maudlin when he had drunk too much wine, talking of all he had missed. And now he was forced to go and watch pretty women on the stage and try to live vicariously the adventures they portrayed there. If he had married he might have had sons and daughters by now. Ah, it was sad. Life had passed him by.

He was constantly going to London. Carleton said there was not a play in London that he had not seen. He was either at the King's House or the Duke of York's. He was an honoured patron there and well known in the green rooms.

"Poor Uncle Toby," said Carleton. "He's trying to catch up with youth."

Christmas came and went, and with the New Year I began to be more and more aware of my child. Sally Nullens was joyous. Nothing could delight her more than the prospect of having a baby in the house. "The boys are growing out of babyhood," she said. "My word, they're a handful. It will be pleasant to have a little one."

Carleton was the devoted husband. He was beside himself with joy, and I realized how frustrated he must have felt during all the years when he was married to Barbary. I knew he was thinking of a son. I kept reminding him that our child might well be a girl.

He said it wouldn't matter. We should have boys in time.

"Pray allow me to deliver this one first," I retorted.

Indeed, they were happy days. We bantered our way through them, always taunting each other, and there were nights tender more than passionate now that my pregnancy was advancing.

I was no longer mourning for Edwin. I realized that I had kept that grief alive. Someone had said that the wise drown their sorrows, and it is only the foolish who teach them to swim. I thought that was apt. I had nourished my grief, I had brooded on it; I had built a shrine to Edwin in my heart—and I had worshipped a false god. Feet of clay indeed!

I was longing for my baby to be born.

She was born on the seventh of July, and I called her Priscilla.

Carleton tried to pretend that he was not disappointed by the sex of the child, but he was; but to me she was perfect, and from the moment I saw her I would not have exchanged her for any other.

Priscilla. My Priscilla. I was taken right back to the days when I had first held Edwin in my arms. How dearly I had loved him; he had been more than my own child; he had been the consolation for the loss of his father. Priscilla I loved none the less. I loved her because she *was* a girl. She would be more completely mine. If Carleton was disappointed in her sex, I was not.

Great events might be happening away from Eversleigh. I could not think seriously about them; my life was centred round my child. When I heard that the Dutch fleet had sailed up the Medway as far as Chatham and had made themselves masters of Sheerness, I said how dreadful it was, but I was not thinking much about it. The *Loyal London,* the *Great James* and the *Royal Oak* were burned by the enemy and fortifications were blown up. I shuddered, but my thoughts were all for my child.

"We had never been so disgraced," cried Lord Eversleigh, and I knew how deeply shocked my parents would be by the news.

But I could only think that Priscilla was gaining weight, that already she knew me and would stop whimpering if I took her. Already she would smile at me. I delighted in her.

The boys came to see her, and were amazed at her little hands and feet.

"She'll never be able to run fast with little feet like that," declared Leigh.

"Silly," said Edwin. "She'll grow big, won't she, Mama? We were little like that once."

"I was never as little," boasted Leigh.

"Oh, yes, you were, I saw you," I told him. I could

never look at him without thinking of Edwin and Harriet together. I wondered when he had been conceived. It was before Edwin had been, because he was the elder.

I had to stop thinking of that because it was affecting my attitude to Leigh. It was not his fault that his parents had both deceived me so blatantly.

Uncle Toby was always making excuses to come to the nursery. He was enchanted by Priscilla.

"You lucky man," he said to Carleton. "I'd give a lot to have a child like that." Then he would talk sadly of his misspent youth and how different everything would have been if he had settled down and become a family man.

"It's never too late," said Carleton. "Shall we find a bride for him, Arabella?"

"We'll have a house party," I said. "We'll invite as many eligible ladies as we can muster . . ."

And I thought: Someone for Charlotte. Poor Charlotte, she seemed to have grown even more unhapy of late. It was almost as though she had been affected by my marriage. I suppose it was seeing me with the children.

There was great jubilation when peace was declared with the French, the Danes and the Dutch, but Carleton told me that people were beginning to murmur against the King for concluding a peace which it was said was dishonourable.

"The country's honeymoon with Charles is long over," he said. "They are now murmuring . . . not so much against him as against his mistresses."

"Which is somewhat unfair of them."

"Alas, dear Arabella, the world often is unfair."

I agreed it was, and we talked about Uncle Toby and the possibility of his finding a wife.

"We really must bestir ourselves," I said.

At it happened there was no need for us to do that.

That September Uncle Toby went to London for a brief visit and it became a long one.

He wrote back to us that he was enjoying life in London. He was at the playhouse most days. He had seen Nell Gwyn as Alice Piers in *The Black Prince,* and better still in Dryden's comedy *An Evening's Love* as Donna Jacintha. He wrote lyrically of the charms of Nelly and how the rumours were that the King's attentions were now fixed on her and poor Moll Davies was nowhere in the running.

"It appears he is enjoying the London scene," said Carleton. "That will compensate him for all he has missed as a family man."

Then quite suddenly came a letter which was addressed to Lord Eversleigh. We were all shown it and read it again and again. Carleton laughed immoderately.

"I never thought he would have gone as far as that," he declared.

"What will happen now?" demanded Lord Eversleigh.

"What is natural!" said Carleton. "He will return here with the lady."

The fact was that Uncle Toby had married a wife. According to him she was the most beautiful of women; she was attractive, amusing; everything he had wanted in a wife. He was the happiest man alive and he was going to share that happiness with his family.

The day after we received this letter he would be with us, for he was following close on the heels of his messenger.

The whole household waited eagerly.

True to his word Uncle Toby arrived with his bride. As they came through the gates we were all there waiting.

I stared. I thought I was dreaming. It could not possibly be so. But it was. Uncle Toby's bride was Harriet Main.

The Shadow of Death

Matilda's immediate reaction had been alarm.
For a few moments she could only stare at her unbe-
lievingly when Toby presented her. I was sure she felt as
I did that she was dreaming.

"Oh, I know you've already met Harriet," Uncle Toby
announced. "She has told me all about it, have you not,
my love?"

"I said we should have no secrets," she answered softly.

"And the devil of a job I had getting her to accept
me," went on Uncle Toby. "I thought I never should get
her to agree."

I felt my lips turning up at the corners cynically. I had
no doubt that it had been her idea from the first and that
her reluctance would have been as false as she was.

She lowered her eyes and succeeded in looking modest,
but I knew, of course, what a good actress she was.

"Oh, Arabella," she said. "How happy I am to see you
again. I have thought of you so much. And you are
married again . . . to Carleton. Dear Toby has been
telling me."

"It was their married bliss that made me see what I was missing," said the doting old man. Poor Uncle Toby! He had no idea of the kind of woman he had married.

Matilda had recovered her composure. She could never for long fail in her duties as the perfect hostess.

"Well, Toby, I have had the blue room made ready for you."

"Thank you, Matilda. It's what I was hoping."

"Shall I take Harriet up?" I asked.

Matilda looked relieved. "That would be very pleasant," said Harriet.

I was very much aware of her eyes on me as she followed me up the stairs. I threw open the door of the blue room. It was pleasant, as all the rooms at Eversleigh nowadays, and so called because of the colour of its furnishing. Harriet studied the four-poster with blue hanging, the blue curtains, and blue carpets.

"Very nice," she said. She sat on the bed and looked up at me smiling. "This is fun," she said.

As I did not smile with her, her expression changed to one of concern.

"Oh, Arabella, you are not still holding out against me, are you? I had to leave Leigh with you. How could I take him with me?" I knew you would be the perfect mother to him . . . far better than I ever could."

"I know who his father was."

She was wrinkling her brows and preparing to look innocent.

"Charles . . ." she began.

"No," I said, "not Charles Condey. You contented yourself merely with taking him away from Charlotte. I know his father was Edwin."

She turned a shade paler. Then her lips curled. "He told you, of course. Your new husband."

"Yes, he told me."

"Just what I should expect of him."

"It was right that I should know after having been deceived by you for so long."

"I can explain . . ."

"No, you can't. There was a letter of yours on Edwin when he was killed. It was bloodstained, but not too

303

much so to prevent my being able to read what you had written to him. It explained everything. I know about the meetings in the arbour and how you were caught there and shot by the Puritan fanatic."

"Oh," she said blankly. Then she shrugged her shoulders and reminded me so much of the occasions when I had discovered her prancing into the room—the first discovery of deceit which should have warned me. "Well," she went on. "It's the way of the world."

"Your way, I know. I hope such behaviour is not general."

"So now you hate me. Why should you? You have another husband now." She smiled. "Let us forget the past, Arabella. I hated deceiving you. It made me so unhappy. It was just that I fell so madly in love that I couldn't help it. But it's over now."

"Yes," I said, "it's over and now you have caught Uncle Toby."

"Caught him! He was the angler. I was the little fish."

"A fish who would only be caught if she wanted to be, I'm sure."

"I've changed, Arabella. I'll admit I let myself be caught." She got off the bed and, going to the mirror, looked at her reflection. "I'm no longer quite so young, Arabella."

"No," I said bluntly.

"Nor are you," she retorted sharply. Then she laughed. "Oh, Arabella, it is good to be with you. More than anything I have missed you. I'm so excited to be here. No one can turn me out now, can they? I'm a legitimate member of the household. I have the marriage bond to prove it. Harriet Eversleigh, of Eversleigh Court. There are only two people standing in the way of my becoming Lady Eversleigh. Lord Eversleigh himself and your son Edwin."

"As my son is but seven years old I am inclined to think your chances are slight."

"Of course. But it is nice to feel near, you know. Particularly when you have been a hardworking actress—and I'll admit that times have been hard sometimes. To be able to say it's quite unlikely *but* . . ."

304

"Stop it!" I cried angrily. "You are saying that if Edwin were to die . . ."

"I was only teasing you. How could Toby inherit? What made me feel a little jubilant was that he has made Carleton step aside."

"I think this is a rather unpleasant conversation."

"We are rather outspoken in the theatre, I'm afraid."

"Then you will have to change now you are at Eversleigh Court."

"I will, Arabella. I promise you. Dear Arabella, don't be angry with me. Let us be friends. I want that so much. I have missed you. When anything unusual or comical happened, I always used to say to myself: 'I should love to tell that to Arabella.' I can't bear that you should be cold to me."

"In the circumstances how can you expect anything else?"

"You've changed, Arabella."

"In the light of my discoveries, wouldn't you expect that?"

She sighed. "I suppose so."

"Now I will leave you. If you need anything, pull the bell rope and the maid will bring it."

I turned and shut the door. My heart was beating fast. Something dramatic was certain to happen now that Harriet was in the house.

I went back to the drawing room where Matilda was sitting in the window, looking out.

"Oh, Arabella," she said. "I don't like it. How could Toby have done this?"

"He's so enamoured of her. She is very attractive."

"I suppose so. I shall never forget her coming to Villers Tourron, and how she suggested the play. It seemed such a good idea at the time and I was so pleased. But how it turned out! She took Charlotte's lover. You can see how Charlotte feels about her being here. The poor girl was quite put out. I do wish she would be more amenable."

"I have been intending for a long time to arrange some

305

parties for her. I want her to meet people. I am sure it would be good for her."

"You are a dear soul, Arabella. Such a comfort. I never cease to be grateful that you have become one of us. But this Harriet. Oh, how could Toby have done this to us!"

"It was I who brought her in the first place so I am to blame rather than he."

"And having a child and going and leaving him with us as she did."

I slipped my arm through hers. I was thankful that she did not know the real story. I wondered what her reaction would have been had she learned that Leigh was her own grandson.

"We have to accept it," I said. "I daresay we shall grow accustomed to her being here."

"You're such a comfort," said Matilda fondly.

Carleton and I discussed Harriet's arrival when we were alone in our bedroom that night.

"You must be watchful of your old friend, my darling," he said. "I wonder what she is planning now."

"I think she must have fallen on lean times. So perhaps she is revelling in the comfortable position she has brought herself to."

"Just at first perhaps. Then she will be looking around for mischief."

"Perhaps she has grown out of that by now."

"I'll wager she never will."

"How *could* she come here!"

"She didn't know that you were aware of the part she had played with Edwin."

"But she knew you did."

"She wouldn't care about me. She would regard me as a fellow sinner."

"I told her I knew. It came out. I had to."

He nodded. "I would have expected you to. You could never hide your feelings. My dear, honest Arabella." He came over to me and put his arms about me.

"We will be on our guard," he said. "And now . . . let us forget her."

So Harriet was once more with us and this time she was in her rightful place. She had become an Eversleigh—one of us.

Uncle Toby's pride in her was touching. His eyes followed her; he was bemused as though asking himself how such a glorious creature could possibly have married him. She had aged a little, although she concealed this with artifice and it was only occasionally that it was noticeable. Then I saw that there were light shadows under her eyes and fine lines about her mouth. But she would always be outstandingly beautiful and everyone must admit that.

It was amazing how she settled in. That Matilda was cool to her did not affect her. Nor did the fact that she had been my late husband's mistress. Her manner of shrugging these facts aside was disarming.

She was very eager to see Leigh, and when I took her to the nursery he was with Edwin. She looked from one to the other, not knowing which was her son.

Both boys regarded her with some sort of awe.

"You're a stage actress," said Leigh. I suppose he had heard the servants talking.

"You're Uncle Toby's new wife," added Edwin.

She told them they were both right, and very soon she was telling them about the stage and the plays she had acted in and they were clearly fascinated.

She had lost none of her charm. Uncle Toby was her adoring slave and that was easy to understand, but when I saw her exert it over the boys, I knew that she had lost none of her gifts and I remembered how little Fenn had adored her.

What was almost incredible was that I found myself being caught up in the old spell. My resentment was gradually weakening. Although I still thought of her and Edwin together now and then, it no longer angered me. She made a great effort to win back my friendship and she was gradually succeeding.

She had a gift of narrative and it was not long before I was hearing about her adventures.

"I knew it wouldn't last with James Gilley," she told me. "But I had to go. What else could I do? What life could I have given Leigh? I had to think of my baby. I knew that you would look after him and that with you he would have a good life. So I forced myself to part with him. It was a wrench. You don't know how I suffered . . ."

I narrowed my eyes and smiled at her.

"You don't believe me. I understand. I don't deserve your trust. I can see how you feel. But Edwin was so persuasive and I was half in love with him. He wasn't good enough for you, Arabella. I used to tell myself that and it would salve my conscience. I used to say if I was not the one, there'd be someone else. Better for Arabella's sake that I should be the one."

"That's an odd way of looking at it."

"I thought at first he would marry me, Arabella. I think he would have if he'd not been so weak. But he had always done what he was told and what the family expected. Then when I realized that he was going to marry you, it had gone too far to stop."

"You were so deceitful, Harriet."

"I know. It was forced on me. You know how I have had to battle. Nothing came easily for me. I used to tell myself: Once you are married to a man who can keep you in comfort then you can repent your sins and start to be a good woman."

"So you are now embarked in that path of virtue?"

"I am. Arabella, I assure you I am. It can happen you know. Look at Carleton."

"What about Carleton?"

"What a rake he was and now he's reformed. He is a model husband now, I am sure. He glances neither to left nor to right. His eyes are firmly fixed on his Arabella."

I looked at her sharply. Was she laughing at me? Was she hinting at something?

She read my thoughts. "No, I mean it. He's turned into the devoted husband. Well, now I shall turn into the devoted wife."

"I am glad to hear it. I should hate Uncle Toby to be hurt. He's such a darling."

"I agree with both those sentiments. You must admit I have made him a happy man. I shall keep him so to the end of his days. Oh, he was so good to me. He used to

308

come to the playhouse whenever I was playing, and when I heard who he was, naturally I pricked up my ears. I was Roxalana in *The Siege of Rhodes* when he first saw me. He came backstage afterwards, and you can guess how excited I was when I heard he was Toby Eversleigh. I asked him a good many questions about his family when we supped together, and over the wine of which he partook more freely than I did, I heard of you and what was happening here at Eversleigh Court."

"And decided to join us."

"Not just then. I had to wait until I was asked. It was after I was Carolina in *Epsom Wells* that he was so deep in love with me that he had reached the pestering stage. He was different from others. He spoke of marriage right from the first. Of course I was reluctant. What a situation! And I told him, No I could not think of it, and the more I said No the more determined he became. Then I made my little confession . . ."

"When you were sure of him, of course."

"Of course, and I had to forestall Carleton whom I wouldn't have trusted to keep quiet. And he said no matter what I had done, he loved me. I was the most beautiful woman in the world. He wanted me to marry him and so on. And I thought: To go back there . . . to live under the same roof as Arabella . . . You may not believe it but those were some of the happiest days of my life at Congrève. I enjoyed them. I loved little Fenn and Angie and Dick. You remember the play we did? And those Lambards. Wasn't it fun? I wanted to recapture all that. Besides, I wanted the standing of a married woman. I could have gone higher. Oh, yes, I've had lovers. The King noticed me one night. He would have sent for me but the plague came and the theatres were shut. Then there was the fire and after that there was Moll Davies and now Nell Gwyn. Young girls really. When I was their age . . ."

"You would have outshone them all."

"Youth! How wonderful it is! I never did like things that didn't last, and there's nothing more perishable than youth."

"You were still young enough to capture Toby."

"Toby's an old man. I was wise to choose an old man. It's one way of keeping perennially young. When he is sixty I shall be . . ." She smiled at me mischievously. "Still in my thirties. Quite a girl in his eyes, you see."

Yes, she was winning me over. I was already forgiving her.

But I should always be wary.

The autumn came in wet and blustery. One day Lord Eversleigh, who had been to London, returned with a shivering fever. He was wet through to the skin and had come from the inn where he had spent the night, riding throughout the day in the heavy rain.

Matilda was most distressed to see him. She set the maids scurrying for warming pans and got him to his bed. He would be all right in a few days, she insisted, and he should have known better than to get wet through and stay wet all those hours. He knew very well it was bad for his chest.

I had rarely seen her so anxious—and not without cause. Lord Eversleigh developed a cold and in a short time his lungs were congested and there was a hushed pall of anxiety hanging over the house.

Carleton had been in London with the King, who was still interested in the Roman finds, but he hurried back to Eversleigh. He was too late to see his uncle alive.

It was a very sad, dark day when we buried him in the family vault in the Eversleigh churchyard. He had been a quiet, unassuming man for all his position, and he had been generally respected. Matilda was beside herself with grief. She told me she could not imagine life without him.

"My dear Arabella," she said, "you suffered a similar loss. My dearest Edwin, taken in the prime of his youth. I cannot imagine which is worse, to lose a young husband or one who was become part of one over so many long and happy years."

I did my best to comfort her, and we were together a great deal. I listened to her accounts of the pleasant life she had had since her marriage and how wonderful her dear husband had been at the time of Edwin's death. "I could not have lived through that but for him," she de-

clared. "Dear Edwin, he was such another as his father."
I thought, if she knew! But she must never know. "Thank God there is young Edwin. He is Lord Eversleigh now."

I had been thinking of that. We must be careful. I was not sure that it would be good for a boy of eight to know that he had such a title.

I heard Sally Nullens refer to him as "my little lord," and I discussed the matter with her.

"It's better for him to get used to the idea gradually," she said. "He'll discover it sooner or later. Servants talk, you know, and you can't stop them short of sealing up their lips. Boys will listen and there's nothing will stop them short of plugging up *their* ears."

Sally was wise with children, so I told Edwin what had happened. His grandfather, Lord Eversleigh, was dead and as his father, Lord Eversleigh's son, was also dead, that meant that he, young Edwin, was now Lord Eversleigh.

"What shall I have to *do?*" he asked.

"Nothing that you didn't do before," I said. "Though you will have to be a little more thoughtful of others, a little more kind to people."

"Why?"

"*Noblesse oblige,*" I replied, "which means that the nobly born must act nobly and that rank carries with it special obligations."

"Well, I haven't been born different, have I? Why should I have to change now?"

"It really shouldn't be a change. You should have been kind and thoughtful before."

Leigh, who had been listening, spoke. "Then I will have to be the same," he supposed.

"You're not a lord," Edwin pointed out.

"I will be," was Leigh's retort. "I'll be a bigger, better lord than you. You'll see."

Yes, I thought, he was indeed Harriet's son.

We did not celebrate Christmas with any great festivities because we were in mourning. On the other hand we could not ignore it altogether because of the children. The carol singers came, and so did the mummers who did a morality

311

play and another about Robin Hood, Friar Tuck, Little John and Maid Marian, which the boys loved. The Dollan family, who lived some ten miles away, rode over and joined us for Christmas Day. They had recently taken the Priory, the nearest big house, and they had come to offer condolences at the time of Lord Eversleigh's death.

They were delightful people—Sir Henry and Lady Dollan, their three daughters and a son, Matthew. Matthew was a lively young man interested in politics and this meant that he and Carleton got on well together. They met in London occasionally and Matthew had taken to calling quite frequently on us.

I was particularly interested in Matthew because, although he was very good company, there was in him a gentle streak. I encouraged him to come often.

So passed Christmas Day. I fancied that we had managed rather cleverly in making a celebration for the children and at the same time not failing in our memory of Lord Eversleigh.

Before we retired that night, I looked in at the nursery as I always did. The boys were fast asleep, smiles of contentment on their faces. Priscilla in her cot was sleeping too. This was my darling's first Christmas, but she had been unaware of it, naturally, at six months old. Next year, I thought, it will be different. Then she will be of an age to begin to take notice.

Sally Nullens came tiptoeing in from where she slept in the next room.

"Don't wake them, mistress," she said. "They've been up to tricks. Overmuch Christmas excitement . . . too much for Master Leigh and for his lordship too."

I said good night and went to our bedroom where Carleton was waiting. He was in bed propped up with pillows.

He said: "Where have you been? Don't tell me, I know. Drooling over your daughter, I have no doubt."

"Your daughter too, sir," I said.

"You will spoil that child."

"I don't think so."

"It will be good for her when she has a few brothers."

"She has Edwin and Leigh now."

"I'll swear they take little notice of her."

"Oh, but they do. They love her."

"Perhaps this time next year we'll have a boy."

"Why are men so set on sons? Is it because they so admire themselves that they are hoping to see themselves repeated?"

"That could be a very good reason."

I was sitting at the mirror, brushing my hair. Carleton was silent watching me. I said: "It was a good Christmas Day considering the circumstances."

"You found it so."

"Didn't you?"

"No. I thought you were far too interested in Matthew Dollan."

"Of course I'm interested. He's a very attractive young man."

Carleton sprang and, picking me up, carried me over to the bed.

"I'd not tolerate any infidelities."

"Carleton, you're mad. Infidelities. With Matthew Dollan!"

"I'm warning you. And you're laughing."

"Of course, I'm laughing. I am not interested in Matthew Dollan other than as a friend."

He bent over me, his lips on mine.

"You have been warned," he said.

"Of what?" I asked.

"The dire fate which would befall you if ever you played me false."

I laughed. He really loved me, I knew. Harriet had said he was reformed since he married. I had heard it said somewhere that reformed rakes make the best husbands.

That was a pleasant thought to go to sleep on on that Christmas Day. It meant that my marriage was turning out a great deal more satisfactorily than I thought it possibly could. Our relationship was changing. We still sparred and bantered, but our lovemaking was becoming more and more satisfying.

I believe, I thought, I am going to be happy.

In the New Year Carleton went to Whitehall. The King had sent for him. They were still excited about the Roman remains which the excavations following on the fire had disclosed. Carleton talked of them with great enthusiasm and I was becoming as interested as he was.

He wanted me to go with him and I was torn between going and leaving the children.

"What nonsense," said Carleton impatiently. "As if old Nullens isn't as good as any watchdog."

"I know. But I hate to leave Priscilla."

"What about me? You have no objection to leaving me!"

"It's just that I should be worrying about them all the time."

"And you don't worry about what might be happening to me?"

I lifted my shoulders in exasperation.

"Husbands need to be looked after if they are going to be kept in good order," he reminded me.

I was tempted to go and I should have gone if Edwin had not caught a chill the day before we were due to depart.

When I went to say good night to the children, Leigh and Priscilla were sleeping but Edwin was not in his bed. Sally came in and said: "I've moved his bed into my room. His coughing might disturb the others and I want to keep my eye on him."

I was immediately concerned.

"Just a chill," said Sally. "I've got a flannel on his chest and hot bricks wrapped in more flannel for his feet. I've also got some good cordial for him."

I went and looked at my son. His face was flushed and his forehead far too hot.

"Hello, Mama," he said. "You're going to London to see the King."

I knelt by his bed. "It won't be for long."

"How long?" he asked.

"A week perhaps."

"Tuesday Wednesday Thursday Friday Saturday Sunday Monday," he said.

Then he started to cough.

"You shouldn't talk," said Sally sharply. "I told you not to."

"It was my fault," I said. "Now try to sleep, my darling."

"Will you come and see me before you go?" asked Edwin.

"Of course I will." I bent and kissed him. He took my hand and clung to it. His fingers were burning.

I covered him up and when I went out Sally followed me.

"Now don't you fret," she said. "I'll look after him. It's just one of his colds."

I nodded and went back to our room. While I prepared for bed Carleton talked excitedly about London and the Roman remains. He noticed my inattention and complained of it.

"I'm worried about Edwin," I said.

"You are like an old hen with her chicks."

"I am a mother," I said.

"You are also a wife. Never neglect your husband for your children. That's an old adage isn't it, or it ought to be. Come to bed. Thank God tomorrow I shall lure you away from your domesticity."

But in the morning Edwin was worse. Sally was anxious, I could see.

"Sally," I said, "I'm going to stay."

I could see her relief.

"It's not just a cold, is it?"

"The fever still stays and he's been talking excitedly and thinking he was riding his horse. I've sent one of the men for the doctor."

I went back to Carleton. "You should be ready," he said.

"I'm not going."

He stared at me incredulously.

"What nonsense. Of course you are. The King expects you."

"Edwin is very ill."

"He has a slight chill."

"It's not slight. I'm staying here."

For a few seconds we faced each other. He was angry. He didn't believe Edwin was ill. I told myself that in his heart he had never liked Edwin. He resented him, I knew it. He had several reasons for resenting him. For a long time, before Toby had returned, he had stood between him and Eversleigh. Moreover he was my son, and he suspected that the boy reminded me of Edwin and that whatever ill I heard of him I would still harbour romantic thoughts about him. Carleton was a man who had to be first; he had to be the centre of everything, and that included my life. He wouldn't even stand aside for his own daughter, but to do so for another man's son infuriated him.

I knew Carleton. I was fully aware of his faults. I was not going to make the mistake of turning him into a model of virtue. That would be scarcely possible with a man like Carleton. He was virile, arrogant, essentially male and I enjoyed my marriage, which was because I was a woman who needed marriage. Physically we were well matched. I liked our encounters, even our verbal battles, which still persisted. We loved to score over each other. Perhaps that was not the way a wife should feel about her husband, but it was how I felt about Carleton.

My marriage was exciting rather than tender. I was sure he felt the same about me.

Now he was angry. He could not bear me to prefer anyone else, even my own children . . . particularly Edwin. He desperately wanted a son of his own. He was making that more and more clear.

Life with him was far from tranquil and now we were moving into a new storm.

"You are coming with me," he said.

"No, Carleton, I am not coming. I will not leave Edwin. I have told Sally Nullens I am staying. She is relieved. That means Edwin is worse than he appears to be."

For a moment I thought he was going to pick me up forcibly and ride off with me.

I was sure that was in his mind. Then he said abruptly: "Very well. Do as you please."

And he went off.

He did not say good-bye.

I could not think much about Carleton because my concern was all for my son. The doctor had come and had found him suffering from a fever. He was to be kept warm and fed with broth. He would come again the next day.

In the afternoon Edwin went into a deep sleep and Sally said he should be left alone. We would look in on him from time to time and she had put a little bell under his pillow in case he should wake and need something.

After about fifteen minutes I crept into his room. Someone was standing at the foot of his bed, looking at him.

"Harriet," I whispered.

She turned.

"He must not be disturbed while he sleeps," I said and we tiptoed out.

"Poor Edwin," she said. "He looks very sick."

I said: "He will recover. The doctor says that we must keep him quiet. Sally is wonderful with children. She nursed his father through several illnesses. Matilda says she is the perfect nurse and doctor combined."

She followed me to my room.

"Poor Arabella," she said, "you look exhausted."

"Naturally I'm worried. I didn't sleep well all night. I was so anxious . . . wondering whether to go or stay."

"So you let Carleton go without you!" She shook her head. "Was that wise?"

"I could not have gone with him while Edwin was in this state. Why, I would never forgive myself if . . ."

"If?" She was looking at me, her eyes alight with speculation. I could see the thoughts chasing themselves in her head. She was trying to draw a veil over her eyes but she was not quite clever enough to do that. I knew what she was thinking. If Edwin died, Toby would be Lord Eversleigh. She would be Lady Eversleigh, she, the strolling player's daughter!

"Edwin is going to recover," I said fiercely.

"Of course he will. He's a most healthy little boy. This

317

is nothing. A childish ailment. Children have these things. They come close to death . . . and then and then . . ."

I turned away. I wanted to shout at her: Don't stand there lying, pretending you want him to get well. You want him to die!

"You must take care of yourself, Arabella," she said. "You'll be ill yourself if you worry like this."

I said: "I want to rest. Just for a short while. Sally will watch over him while I rest."

I lay on my bed and she put the coverlet over me. Her face was close to mine, so beautiful, so compassionate, and yet there was a certain glitter in her eyes.

The door closed on her but I could not rest. I thought of her and Edwin together . . . I had had not an inkling. How clever they were! She had hoped to marry him herself.

Then I thought of the coldness in Carleton's eyes when he turned away from me. He was very angry. He could not bear that anyone should come before himself.

But what did any of these things matter while my son was ill? I could not rest here. I rose and went back to Sally's sick room. Edwin was still sleeping. My entrance awakened Sally, and the two of us sat there listening for any sound from the sick child.

Through the night Sally and I sat beside him. He was quietly lying on his bed and every now and then we would hear his heavy breathing. I sat listening in terror that it might stop.

Sally rocked herself silently to and fro.

I whispered: "Sally, I smell something. Is it garlic?"

She nodded. "There by the fire, mistress."

"You put it there?"

She nodded again. "It keeps evil away. We always have used it."

"Evil?"

"Witches and the like."

"You think . . ."

"Mistress, I don't know what I think. 'Cept that 'tis as well to be safe."

I was silent for a while. Then I said: "He's breathing better now."

"I noticed he were better when I brought the garlic in."

"Oh, Sally, tell me what's in your mind. Is there anything in this house that could harm him?"

"I'm not saying it is so, mistress, and then again I'm not saying 'tis not. 'Tis only that I would be on the side of safety."

"Oh, God," I whispered. "Could it really be so?"

"The garlic keeps evil away. They don't like it. There's something in it that upsets 'em. I don't like what's in this house, mistress."

"Sally, tell me everything. If there is something threatening my son, I must know."

"There's some I wouldn't trust, mistress."

No, I thought. Nor I.

"This little one," she went on, "to be a lord . . . to own all this, for that is how it is. He lost his father who would have had it first, and then by the time our little one came into it, he would have been a man. That would have been natural and easy. But when a little child has all this . . . It has been so with kings, I believe. I'm not clever and know nothing of these matters, but 'tis human nature, that's all, and I reckon I know a bit about that."

"Has something happened?"

"There was one I found in here . . . looking at him as he lay in his bed."

"I saw someone too."

"I reckon it was the same one."

"What did she come for?"

"She said she was anxious about you. She knew how worried you were and she was sure the child had only a cold. She went out soon when I came in, and I thought what benefit it could be to her if . . ."

"You suspect . . . witchcraft?"

"It's always been in the world and I reckon should be watched for. But we'll guard him. We'll save him from whatever be threatening him. We'll do it, mistress, together. Witchcraft can't stand against good pure love. That I do know."

At any other time I should have laughed her to scorn. But it is different when a loved one is concerned. By daylight I could be bold and laugh at stories of ghosts and evil influences, but by night I could fear them. Thus it was. My child in possible danger and I could not turn sceptically away from that.

Sally believed in witchcraft. Morever, she was suggesting there might be a witch in our house.

Harriet. Standing at the bed, the glitter in her eyes seeing a title within her reach but my son standing in her way.

I remembered what I had read in the diaries of my great-grandmother Linnet Casvellyn who had let a strange woman into her house—a witch from the sea.

It could happen. I would not leave Edwin again until he was well. I would not allow Harriet to step across the threshold of this room.

All through that night Sally and I sat in her room and at Edwin's slightest whimper we were at his bedside. Halfway through the night his breathing was easier. And in the morning his fever had gone.

I could smell the garlic in the grate. I looked at Sally's simple, loving face and I embraced her.

"He is going to get well," I said. "Oh, Sally, Sally, what can I say to you?"

"We pulled him through, mistress. Together we pulled him through. No harm shall come to our little lord while we are close."

Edwin was well on the way to recovery by the time Carleton returned, angry still because of what he called my defection.

"I told you so," he said. "There's nothing wrong with that boy except too much pampering. I'm going to get to work on him as soon as he's completely fit."

I was so happy in my son's recovery that I wanted to celebrate it and Carleton's return together. Harriet said she would sing and dance for the company and perhaps we could get everyone to join in the dance. The boys would enjoy that.

Carleton was amused, but I noticed that his attitude

had changed since his return. He had not forgiven me for staying behind, and our relationship was more as it had been before our marriage. He seemed critical of me and tried to make me so with him—which did not need a great deal of effort on his behalf. I missed a certain tenderness in his lovemaking. He was as fiercely passionate and demanding as ever and talked even more frequently of his desire for another child—a boy this time—and I accused him of a lack of interest in Priscilla.

"For the child's sake," he retorted. "If she had two parents treating her as if she is the only creature of any importance in the world, she'd grow up to be insufferable."

"A little too like her father perhaps," was my retort.

So we sparred during the day and made love at night. It was exciting but vaguely disturbing. I knew that he really was angry. He is the most arrogant, self-centred man in the world, I thought. And I was a little angry with myself for caring for him in the way I did. But I could not help my nature, I supposed, any more than he could his.

At supper one night soon after his return, he talked about his stay in London.

"It's like a breath of life to get up there," he said. "One gets stultified in the country. I must go more often." He was looking at me, implying: And you should come with me, and if your children are more important than your husband, take the consequences! He went on to talk of the new plans for rebuilding the city in which the King was greatly interested. Carleton had met Christopher Wren, who had brought out a plan for rebuilding the city which would make people see the great fire of London almost as a blessing.

Of course, it would be very costly and great sums of money would be needed, he explained. "It seems unlikely that these will be raised, but the building must start at once so it will doubtless be done piecemeal." Carleton was eulogistic about Christopher Wren.

"A genius," he said. "And a happy man. He knows he won't be able to build what he wants, but he'll settle for second best. He has plans for a cathedral and about fifty parish churches. We shan't recognize the old city but what a grand place it will be when he has finished it. Moreover it'll be healthier. Those wooden buildings huddled together, those filthy gutters . . . With our new London we shan't have epidemics every few years, I promise you."

He was quite clearly exhilarated by his visit to London and that seemed to make him all the more angry with me for refusing to share it with him.

As we sat round the table he discussed the prevailing scandals. Everyone was now talking about the Duke of Buckingham's affair with Lady Shrewsbury and his duel with her husband.

"Buckingham may well be accused of murder," said Carleton.

"Serve him right," said Matilda. "People should not fight duels. It's a stupid way of settling a quarrel."

"They say it was a great love affair between Buckingham and Shrewsbury's wife," said Charlotte.

"She has been his mistress," Carleton put in. "That has been common knowledge for a long time and Shrewsbury, like a self-respecting husband, challenged Buckingham to a duel."

Harriet smiled at Uncle Toby. "Would you do that, my darling, if I took a lover?"

Uncle Toby almost choked with laughter. "I would indeed, my love."

"Just like my Lord Shrewsbury," cried Harriet, raising her eyes to the ceiling.

"I hope," went on Carleton looking steadily at her, "that *you* would not behave like Lady Shrewsbury. That lady dressed herself as a page and held Buckingham's horse while the duel took place, and as soon as it was over and Shrewsbury mortally wounded, the lovers went to an inn and Buckingham made love to her dressed as he was in his bloodstained clothes."

"An act of defiance against morality," I said.

"Trust you to discover that," said Carleton half mocking, half admiring.

"And what is going to happen to these wicked people?" asked Matilda.

"Shrewsbury is dying, and Buckingham is living openly

with Lady Shrewsbury. The King has expressed his displeasure but has forgiven Buckingham. He is such an amusing fellow, and in any case Charles is too much of a realist to condemn others for what he practises so assiduously himself."

"Not duelling," said Charlotte.

"No, adultery," added Carleton. "Charles hates killing. He thinks Shrewsbury was a fool. He should have accepted the fact that his wife preferred Buckingham and left it at that."

"Kings set the fashion at courts," said Charlotte. "How different from Cromwell."

"One extreme will always follow another," pointed out Carleton. "If the Puritans had not been so severe, those who followed might not have been so lax."

"Oh, dear," sighed Matilda, "what a pity things can't be as they were before the war and all these troubles arose."

"It's the perpetual sighing for the old days, I fear," said Carleton. "They seem so good looking back. It's a disease called nostalgia. It affects quite a lot of us."

He was looking at me, resenting the happiness I had had with Edwin, believing that in spite of what I had discovered I still remembered it.

The celebration took place shortly after that conversation. It began as a happy occasion and almost ended in disaster. For several days they had been preparing for it in the kitchens and our table was a credit to the servants. We had the family and the Dollans and the Cleavers and another family who came from a few miles away. The two boys were with us and everyone was complimenting me on Edwin's healthy looks and saying that there could be little wrong with a boy who could recover so quickly from a virulent fever.

Harriet somehow managed to make herself the centre of attraction just as she had in the old days. She sang for us, and as she sat there strumming her lute with her lovely hair falling over her shoulders, my mind went right back to the days in Congrève when she had seemed to me like a goddess from another world.

That she seemed just that to Uncle Toby was obvious.

He was so proud of her, so much in love, and it occurred to me that even if she had contrived to marry him for what she could get, at least she had made him happy.

I was pleased too that Matthew Dollan was there, and Charlotte, too. Charlotte seemed to be quite happy, although she could not rid herself of that suspicious attitude which seemed to say, I know you're only being pleasant to me because it's polite to be so.

When the children had gone to bed we went to the ballroom which had been made ready for dancing, and there the musicians played and we were very merry.

As Carleton led me into the dance, he asked if I felt it was an occasion worthy of the reason for having it.

"I think it goes well," I said.

"A thanksgiving because our young Edwin was snatched from the gates of death?"

I shivered.

"What a fond and foolish mother you are, Arabella! The boy is completely healthy. You should be thanking the fates for my return to you, not his from the afore-mentioned gates."

"It is to celebrate two happy events."

"So you are glad to have me back?"

"Have I not made that clear?"

"On occasions," he said. "I say, look at Toby."

I looked. He was dancing with Harriet. His face was overred I thought and his breathing a little short.

"He drank too much wine," I said.

"Not unusual, I'm afraid."

"Harriet shouldn't let him exert himself like that. Will you speak to her?"

"I will. When the dance is over."

But that was to prove too late, for there was a sudden cry, and a hushed silence. I looked around. Toby was on the floor and Harriet was kneeling beside him.

Carleton rushed over and examined his uncle. "He is breathing," he said. "We must get him to his room. Arabella, send them for the doctor."

That was the end of the dance. Toby was carried up to his room and in due course the doctor came and told us that Toby had had a heart attack. It was due, it seemed, to overexerting himself. I sat with Harriet at his bedside. She was very subdued. There was anxiety in her face and I knew that she was thinking of what her position would be if Uncle Toby died.

He did not die. In a few days it was clear that he would recover. The doctor said that he had had a warning. He had overexerted himself and must, in future, remember his age. He must go very carefully now.

"I shall insist," said Harriet. "I am going to look after you, my darling."

It was pathetic to see the way in which he relied on her, and I have to say that she nursed him well.

Carleton said: "It's probably a good thing that it happened. It's brought home to him the fact that he's not the young man he has been thinking he was."

Spring came. Edwin was himself again and Sally's theories about witchcraft seemed ridiculous. The boys were very fond of Harriet and she seemed to be a model wife to Toby. She was soon exerting the old fascination over Edwin and Leigh as she had over my brothers and sister. She was always singing and acting for them and they enjoyed being in her company.

Uncle Toby's eyes followed her wherever she was. "What a mother she would make," he said.

Although I suspected her motives for marrying him, I must say that she made him happy. She was never irritable or bad tempered with him. She always called him "my darling husband" and to him she was always "my love." He put such a wealth of feeling into the endearment that it was never used lightly, as in some cases.

Carleton had turned his attention to Edwin. He accused me of pampering him and said it was time someone took him in hand. I was a little afraid at first. I thought that he was going to wreak his resentment on my son. It occurred to me that I didn't really know about Carleton everything a wife should know of her husband. I knew that he was strongly drawn to me; I knew that he desired me and that desire had not yet abated with familiarity. But sometimes I felt he wanted to be revenged on me. He had a strange, wild nature.

However I could not stop his supervising the outdoor education of my son, and as Leigh was with him, I supposed that it really was good for Edwin to have a man to teach him. I myself was giving them lessons and Harriet insisted on helping me. It reminded me so much of the old days at Congrève. There was a great deal of acting in the schoolroom and of course the boys loved that.

It was Carleton who said that we should have a tutor for the boys. They could not be taught forever by two women. "Besides," he said, "I can see you making excuses that you have your schoolroom duties when I want you to come with me to London."

It was like Carleton to act immediately, and within a few weeks of his announcing that the boys should have a tutor, Gregory Stevens arrived.

Gregory was an extremely good-looking young man, the second son of a titled family and therefore without great means but with some expectations. He was an excellent sportsman and as he was something of a scholar and interested in young people, he had decided to become a tutor for a while until those expectations were realized. Carleton said he possessed all the necessary qualifications for teaching the boys, and he was right. Gregory was strict, but he won the boys' respect and it seemed a very good arrangement.

Harriet still insisted on going to the schoolroom to tell the boys about plays and act for them. Although Gregory Stevens had thought this unnecessary at first, he was soon agreeing that Harriet's special knowledge and her ability to interest the boys in the literature of the day and of the past was beneficial.

Carleton was teaching them riding, shooting, falconry and fencing. Gregory Stevens helped in this and my misgivings faded when I heard the shouts of triumph when one of them scored and listened to their excited chatter. I knew that Carleton was right and I must not be so afraid of Edwin's hurting himself that I might curb his mastery of these manly activities.

I spent a great deal of time with my daughter who was now developing a personality of her own and was a little wilful I must admit, which I said must be expected with such a father. I was angry with Carleton because he expressed so little interest in her and I determined to shower her with extra love in case she should notice her father's neglect.

In the early spring I became pregnant again. Carleton was beside himself with joy. He was so certain that this time I was going to provide a child of the right sex. It worried me—this obsession for a boy.

He could scarcely talk of anything else. He was so tender and careful of me that I could not help enjoying that, but sometimes I was filled with misgivings.

I said to him: "What if this child should be a girl?"

"It won't be," he said firmly, as though he could arrange these matters. "I know I'm going to have a son this time."

"It's absurd," I said. "You have a beautiful daughter and you hardly notice her."

"You're going to give me my son, Arabella. I knew you would from the moment I saw you."

I began to feel apprehensive. Sally Nullens noticed it. "It's bad for you," she said. "Give over. Just sit back in peace and wait."

I wished I could.

Harriet came to the bedroom often when I was alone. She liked to sit and watch me sewing a baby garment. I took a great pleasure in doing this although I was no needlewoman.

"Carleton is beside himself with joy," said Harriet. She watched me anxiously. "You're worried, Arabella."

"I just want this to be over. I want to be lying in that bed with my son in his cradle beside me."

"He is going to put Madame Priscilla's nose out of joint."

"No one could change my feelings for her," I said.

"Of course not. You're the perfect mother. Oh, Arabella, what a lot has happened to use since the old days. We are both mothers . . . both Eversleighs. Don't you think that's strange?"

"That we are both Eversleighs? It did not come about without a certain contrivance."

"That old theme! Why should it not have been contrived? Was Toby ever as happy as he is now?"

"That's true. But being married to you must put a certain strain on him. It obviously has."

"You mean his heart attack. I'm very careful of him, Arabella. I'm fond of him. Oh, yes, I am. Besides, what would my position be if he were to die?"

"Your home would still be here."

"I suppose so. But the old lady doesn't like me. Charlotte hates me. Carleton . . ." She laughed. "See I only have you, and you are sometimes suspicious of me. Now if *I* was the one who was pregnant . . . If *I* was the one who was going to have a son. Has it occurred to you that if I did, my son would be next in line to your Edwin? He'd come before this son you may . . . or may not have."

There was a silence in the room. I had the sudden uneasy feeling that we were not alone.

I turned and looked over my shoulder.

Sally Nullens was standing there. She was holding a cup in her hand.

"I've brought you this," she said to me. "Good, strengthening broth. Just what you need."

It was later that night, after midnight I saw later when I was able to take note of the time. Carleton and I were asleep when we were awakened by a shout. We started up, and by the wavering candlelight I made out the figure of Harriet.

"Arabella. Carleton. Come quickly," she cried. "It's Toby."

We jumped out of bed, threw wraps around us and ran to the room which Toby and Harriet shared. Toby was lying in bed, his face ashen, his eyes wild.

Carleton went to him and took his wrist. Then he put his ear to his chest.

I knew as he turned that Toby was very ill.

"Shall I send for the doctor?" asked Harriet.

"Yes," said Carleton.

She ran out of the room.

"Carleton," I said, "is there anything we can do?"

"Get some brandy. But I'm afraid . . ."

I went to a sideboard and poured out some brandy. It had been kept in the room since Toby had had his first attack. Carleton lifted him and tried to pour the brandy into his mouth. It fell over his chin.

"It's too late," murmured Carleton. "I feared it."

Harriet came back into the room.

"I've sent one of the men," she said. "Oh, God, he looks . . . awful."

"It may be too late," said Carleton.

"No . . ." she whispered.

She went to stand on the other side of the bed. Carleton had gently lowered Toby down onto the pillows. We stood in silence looking at him.

Then Harriet spoke: "If only that doctor would come. How long he is!"

"The man has only just left," Carleton reminded her. "He will be an hour at least."

Then the silence fell again. I stood at the head of the bed—Harriet on one side of it, Carleton on the other.

Then there was a sudden gasp from behind us. Charlotte had come into the room.

"I heard running about. What's happened?"

"He's had an attack," said Carleton.

"Is it . . . bad?"

"Very bad, I'm afraid."

"Oh, poor, poor Uncle Toby."

Silence again. I could hear the clock on the mantelpiece ticking. It sounded ominous.

We stood like statues round that bed. I was deeply aware of Charlotte. There was a kind of knowing look in her eyes.

Nonsense, I said. You're overwrought. It's your condition.

It struck me that we were like a tableau . . . full of meaning which I could only vaguely realize.

They were somber days that followed. "Two deaths coming so suddenly one on another," mourned Matilda. "Oh, how I hate death. He was so content. So much in love."

"Perhaps that was why," said Charlotte.

I saw a shiver run through Matilda. Then she said:

"He forgot he was an old man. It happens like that some-times."

"At least," I reminded them, "he was happy. For the last year or so he was living in a kind of paradise."

"What kind?" asked Charlotte. "A fool's paradise."

Of course she hated Harriet and had always resented the way in which she had been brought into the family.

There was another one who hated Harriet and that was Sally Nullens. But perhaps she feared rather than hated her. She mourned Toby sincerely. She had remembered him before he went away. "He always believed the best of everyone," she said with meaning.

Poison in the Marriage Cup

I began to feel unwell. The months of waiting seemed longer than they had when I was awaiting the birth of Priscilla. I think I was obsessed by the fear that I might not have a son.

That made me resentful towards Carleton. It was so stupid to blame a woman because the sex of her child was not what her husband hoped for. Kings had done it in the past. I thought of Anne Boleyn and all that had happened through her failing to get a son and how she must have felt during the long waiting months, the outcome of which would decide her future. The reverberations of that affair had affected my ancestress Damask Farland and her family. It was unfair, so arrogant, so typical of a certain kind of man. Henry VIII's kind. Carleton's kind.

Our own King Charles could not get a legitimate son, although he had several boy bastards. I wondered how his gentle Queen felt about her inadequacy. Perhaps she was not so anxious as I was. Charles might be a blatantly unfaithful husband but by all accounts he was a kindly one.

It was a hot summer's day when it happened. I had four

more months to go before the expected birth of my child and I was in the garden with Priscilla. I could hear the boys at the shooting butts just behind the lawn. Every now and then I would hear a shot, then a whoop of delight or perhaps a groan. They were happy. That much was certain. Edwin was really enjoying the discipline imposed by Carleton and I was rather gratified to notice that he had a great respect for him. He did not love him; he was too much in awe of him for that, but he certainly looked up to him with a kind of reverence. I was pleased at this, and I knew Carleton relished it. I hoped it would make them feel closer together.

I was thinking of this and had not noticed that Priscilla had toddled away. She had an exploring nature and was constantly attempting to evade supervision. Looking up suddenly I saw to my horror that she was making towards the shooting butts.

Horrified, I sprang up and ran towards her, calling her name. She seemed to think it was some sort of game, for she increased her speed. I could hear her chuckling to herself. Then I caught the heel of my shoe in a gnarled root and fell.

I was panic-stricken and in sudden pain. I called, "Priscilla, Priscilla," and tried hard to rise. "Come back. Come back."

I stood up and fell again.

Then I saw Carleton coming towards me. He was carrying Priscilla.

When he saw me, he put her down and ran towards me. "What happened?"

"I was afraid . . . She was running towards the butts. I . . . I fell."

He lifted me in his arms and carried me into the house. I heard him shout to one of the servants: "Send for the doctor . . . at once."

I lay on my bed. The room was darkened, for they had drawn the curtains across them to shut out the light. I was tired and dispirited though the pain had passed.

I believe I had been very ill.

Sally Nullens came into the room.

"Ah, awake then." She was standing over me with the inevitable bowl of broth.

"Oh, Sally," I said.

"You'll be all right, mistress," she said. "My word, Master Edwin has been in a fine state. I've not been able to quieten him. I can tell him now, though, that you're on the mend."

"I've lost the baby," I said.

"There'll be other babies," she answered. "Praise God, we didn't lose you."

"Was I so bad, then?"

"Don't do you much good talking. Take this. It'll put life into you."

So I took it. She watched me. She said: "I'll bring them in to see you before they go to bed. The three of them. I've promised them, you see."

She brought them in. Edwin flew at me and hugged me so tightly that Sally protested.

"Do you want to strangle your mama, young man?"

Leigh tried to push him aside. "Me too," he said.

Priscilla was crying because she was being left out.

I smiled happily at them.

Whatever happened I had them.

Carleton came and sat by my bed. Poor Carleton, how disappointed he was!

"I'm sorry," I said stretching out a hand. He took it and kissed it.

"Never mind, Arabella. There'll be another time."

"There must be. I shall not rest until you have your son."

"There has to be a rest after this . . . a year at least, they tell me. Perhaps two."

"You mean before we have a child?"

He nodded.

"At least," he said, "you've come through. You've been very ill, you know. If only you hadn't . . . But what's the good?"

"I was terrified."

"I know. Priscilla!" He said the name almost angrily.

333

"I thought she would get into the shooting range and . . ."

"Don't fret about it. She didn't. In any case I should have seen her and stopped the firing."

"Oh, Carleton, I'm sorry."

"Don't say it like that. As though I'm some . . . monster. . ."

"You are," I said with a return of my old spirit.

He bent down and kissed me. "Get well, quickly, Arabella," he murmured.

Matilda came.

"Oh, my dear, dear child, how wonderful that you can now have visitors. I have been beside myself with fear. It was so dreadful . . . my dear husband, Toby . . . and then you. It was as though there was some evil spell on the house. . . ."

She stopped. I noticed that Sally was in the room.

"It was just an unfortunate chain of circumstances," I said. "Let's hope this is the end of our troubles."

"It must be because you are well again. Sally tells me that you are picking up very quickly. That's so, eh, Sally?"

"I know how to treat her, milady. I'm going to have her on her feet before the week's out. You'll see. . . ."

"I've always trusted you, Sally. Ah, Charlotte."

Charlotte had come into the room.

"Charlotte, see how well Arabella is looking," went on Matilda. "Almost her old self, don't you think?"

"You look much better," said Charlotte. "I am so glad and very sorry that it happened."

"It was an unfortunate accident," I said. "I should have been more careful."

"Yes," said Charlotte quietly.

"Do sit down, Charlotte," said her mother. "You look so awkward standing there."

Charlotte meekly sat and we talked for a while of the children. Poor Edwin had been heartbroken. Having been introduced to death through his grandfather and Uncle Toby, he had feared that I was going to die.

"It was hard to comfort him," said Charlotte. "Leigh

334

could do it better than anyone. How close those two boys have become."

We talked of Priscilla and how bright she was. She too had missed me and kept saying my name and crying for me.

"So you see how glad *everyone* is that you are getting well," said Matilda.

Then Sally came and said that I ought not to tire myself and she thought I had talked enough for a while.

So they went out and left me alone with my thoughts. I could not stop thinking of Carleton's disappointment, and I wondered how deeply he blamed me . . . and perhaps Priscilla . . . for what had happened.

It was two days later when Harriet came to see me. I was much stronger then, sitting up and even taking an occasional walk round the room.

"We must not go too fast," Sally ordered, and she was undoubtedly mistress of the sickroom.

I had insisted that she take a rest that afternoon, for I knew how tired nursing me made her, for she insisted on keeping her eye on the children as well, and she was lying down. I guess that that was why Harriet had chosen this time to come.

She tiptoed into the room, her lovely eyes alight with a kind of mischief.

"The dragon is sleeping," she said in a dramatic voice. "Do you know she has been breathing fire at me every time I approached."

"So you came before?"

"Of course I came. You don't think I would stay away when you were ill, do you?"

Her presence made me feel alive again. She exuded vitality. I was pleased to see her.

"You don't look as though you're dying," she said.

"I am not," I answered.

"You had us all very worried, I can tell you."

"I feel so angry with myself. After all that waiting . . . it is gone."

"You mustn't fret. That's bad for you. You must be

335

thankful that you were not taken away from your beloved family. Edwin was distrait."

"I know, they told me. He is a dear boy."

"So devoted to his mama and so he should be. So should we all. Arabella . . . I haven't told anyone yet. I want you to be the first to know. It's wonderful really. It's made me feel happy again. I did love Toby. I know you doubted my feelings. You've never really forgiven me for Edwin, have you?"

"Oh, that . . . It's so long ago."

"I know your nature. You forgive but can't forget. You'll never quite trust me again, will you?"

"Perhaps not."

"I'm going to make you. I'm so fond of you, Arabella. That makes you smile. You think I couldn't do what I did and be fond of you. I could. What happened between me and Edwin was outside friendship. Those things always are. The attraction arises quite suddenly sometimes and it's irresistible. One forgets everything but the need to satisfy it. When it's over, the rest of one's life slips back into shape and it's just as it was before. . . ."

I shook my head. "Let's not discuss it. We shall never agree."

"I was brought up so differently from you, Arabella. I always had to fight. It's become natural with me. I fight for what I want and take it and then consider the cost. But I didn't come to say all this. It's just that when I'm with you, I feel I have to justify myself. Arabella, I am going to have a child."

"Harriet! Is that possible?"

"Obviously. Toby wasn't all that old, you know."

"I can see you're happy."

"It's what I need. Don't you see? You, of all people. Didn't it happen to you? Think back. Your husband died suddenly and afterwards you found you were going to have a child. That is how it is with me. Come, rejoice with me. I feel like singing the Magnificat."

"When . . .?"

"Six months from now."

She came to me and put her arms round me. "It makes all the difference. I shall stay here. I have a right to now.

I had before, but a double right now. Old Matilda was hoping I'd go. So was Charlotte, and as for your Sally, she looks at me as though I'm the Devil incarnate. But I don't care. I'm going to have a child. A little Eversleigh. Think of that. My own child."

"You won't go away and leave this one, I hope," I said coolly, but I was beginning to succumb to the old charm.

She laughed. "Your tongue's getting sharp again, Arabella. You get so much practice with Carleton."

"Is it so noticeable?"

"Perhaps. But no doubt he enjoys it. Now about this baby . . ."

"You say you haven't told anyone?"

"I was determined that you should be the first."

"If only Uncle Toby had known, how delighted he would have been."

Her eyes were a trifle misty. "Dear Toby," she said. I was moved, and then I wondered if she was still playing a part.

The news of Harriet's expectations astounded the household, and for a few days it was whispered that she must have imagined this was so. But as the weeks passed it became obvious that she was not mistaken.

She was quite smug, and clearly enjoying her position. She behaved as though it was a great joke and in some way she had scored over us all.

Carleton was shaken. I could see that.

"If this is a boy," he said, "he will be next in line to Edwin."

"Not when Edwin marries and has a son of his own."

"A good many years will have to pass before that."

"I wish you would stop talking of Edwin as though his days are numbered."

"Sorry. I was merely thinking . . ."

"Of the line of succession. Really one would think Eversleigh was the throne."

He brooded on it, I know. I often saw him watch Harriet with an odd speculation in his eyes.

There was a good deal of friction between us. Life had not been smooth since my miscarriage. He seemed resentful of my love for Priscilla and of course Edwin. Although I could understand a certain jealousy of Edwin, it seemed incredible that a man could blame his own daughter because of the loss of a possible son.

Carleton was unnatural, I told him. He was obsessed by his desire for a son. I knew, I said, that this was a common desire among a certain type of man but Carleton carried it to extreme. He was away a good deal. He went to Whitehall and I knew was prominent in Court circles. I often wondered about his life there. I used to worry about the weakening of our feelings for each other and I told myself it was inevitable. I knew I was in some ways to blame, and yet I longed for him to come back and to be to me what he had been in the beginning. But had he really been as I imagined him? There had been a violent passion between us, but was that the foundation on which to build a lifetime's happiness? Perhaps I was wrong. I had always harked back to that glorious time with Edwin—which had been entirely false. Because of it I had been determined not be duped again. Had that made me hard, suspicious?

Life seemed to have become unreal during the months that followed. Harriet was the only one who was content. She went about hugging her secret joy, and in the way I remembered so well she began to dominate the household.

She would get us all together to sing ballads in the evening—myself, Charlotte, Gregory Stevens and often Matthew Dollan, who was constantly riding over. Charlotte was aloof with him, as though she knew that I hoped they might be attracted and was determined to foil me.

Harriet would tell stories of her life as a player and her audience would be tense with excitement. She certainly was a true Scheherazade, for she had a trick of stopping at an exciting point and saying: "No more now. My voice is going. I have to protect it, you know."

Edwin and Leigh would creep in and listen. They thought her enchanting and she made a special point of charming them. Even Priscilla would toddle up and watch her wonderingly while she sang or talked.

Anxious as I was about my relationship with Carleton, saddened by the fact that I was not the one who was expecting a child, I allowed myself to be drawn into her spell and I would find myself excited by her as the others were.

Through the winter months she grew larger but nonetheless beautiful. There was a wonderful serenity about her which added to her beauty.

Even Sally Nullens was excited by the prospect of a new baby in the nursery.

I said to her one day: "Sally, you're longing for this baby, I know."

"Oh I can never resist them," she admitted. "There's nothing as beautiful as a helpless little baby to my mind."

"Even Harriet's?" I said.

"Whatever else she is," answered Sally, "she's a mother."

I had not noticed that Charlotte had come into the room. She was so self-effacing. She seemed to want not to be noticed.

"Do you think she will have an easy confinement?" I asked.

"Her!" cried Sally, her eyes flashing suddenly. "With her it will be like shelling peas. It is with her sort. . . ."

"Her sort . . ." I said.

"There's something about her," said Sally quietly. "I've always known it. They say witches have special powers."

"Sally, you're not suggesting Harriet is a witch?" murmured Charlotte.

Sally said: "I'm saying nothing."

"You just have," I reminded her.

"I can only say what I feel. There's something . . . some special powers . . . I don't know what it is. Some call it witchcraft. I don't like it and I never will."

"Oh, Sally, what nonsense. She's just a healthy and attractive woman . . ."

"Who knows how to get what she wants."

Charlotte and I exchanged glances which implied that we shouldn't take old Sally too seriously.

It was February when Harriet gave birth to her child, and as Sally had predicted it was an easy birth. She had a son and I must admit I felt a twinge of envy.

It was a week or so after the birth of the child, whom

she had christened Benjamin, when Carleton came home.

He embraced me warmly and I felt a sudden thrill of happiness. I determined that in time, when I had recovered from this lassitude which had been with me since my miscarriage, I also would have a son.

Carleton noticed at once. "You're better," he said. And swung me up and held me against him.

"I'm glad you are home," I said.

We walked into the house arm in arm. I said to him: "We have an addition to the household. Harriet's child has arrived.

He was silent for a moment and I went on: "It's a son. Trust Harriet to have a son."

"Yes," he said slowly, "trust Harriet."

I went with him to her room to see him. She was in bed; her Benjie was in his cradle and Sally hovered.

Harriet held out her hand to Carleton. He took it and it seemed to me that he held it for a long time.

She withdrew it and said: "Sally, give me Benjie. I want to show him off. I tell you this, Carleton, he is the most beautiful baby in the world. Sally will bear me out."

She sat there. How beautiful she was, with her magnificent hair falling about her shoulders, her face serenely happy, her lovely eyes soft as I had rarely seen them.

I was deeply aware of Carleton. He was watching her intently. I thought again it was like one of those tableaux, full of meaning.

Benjie thrived. Sally said she had never seen a baby with a finer pair of lungs. When he bellowed, Priscilla watched him in wonder. He showed a determination to get what he wanted from his earliest days. He was beautiful with big blue eyes and dark tufts of hair. Priscilla liked to stand and watch Sally bathe him and to hand her the towels.

I had never seen Harriet so contented before. Her maternal instincts surprized me, but I told myself cynically that she loved her baby partly because he consolidated her position here. Of course as Toby's widow she had a right to be in the house, but the fact that she had borne

340

one of the heirs to lands and title made her position doubly assured.

But even so I was aware of growing tension all about me. I fancied that Harriet was alert, that she was engaged in some secret adventures. Perhaps it was my imagination, I told myself. Perhaps I could never really forget.

I sometimes wandered to the edge of the gardens to the arbour in which Edwin had died. It was such a gloomy place, and the shrubs about it were becoming more overgrown than ever. It looked eerie, ghostly, as the scene of a tragedy can become when people hate to go there and build up legends about it.

Chastity had let out that the servants said it was haunted. Haunted, I thought, by Edwin. Edwin who had been cut off suddenly with his sins upon him, caught in the act by Old Jethro the reformer. I wondered what Harriet felt when she went past it. She had participated in that death scene and must remember, but she never said anything when the arbour was mentioned. Harriet, I believed, was the sort of woman who in an adventuring life put unpleasant events right out of her memory.

For the last few months there had been complaints about the pigeons and the damage they were doing to the fabric of Eversleigh Court, and the grooms and menservants were constantly taking potshots at them. Ellen said that everyone in the neighbourhood was getting tired of pigeon pie and pigeon stews, or roast pigeon and pigeon cooked in pots.

"I tell them," she said, "they should be glad of good food whatever it is."

Carleton had said the boys might shoot at them. A moving target would give them good practice. I often heard them boasting together of the number they had shot. Then they would take them along to the cottage people.

It was one summer day. I was in the garden picking roses and I thought suddenly of another occasion when I had been similarly engaged and when Carleton had come upon me there and how we had talked and bantered and he had asked me to marry him.

The scene of the roses brought back memories of that day vividly and the excitement I felt even though I had pretended not to want him. Then I went on to think of our marriage and the sudden awakening of what was new and exciting in our relationship. What had happened to that now? Perhaps it was impossible to keep passion at such fever heat. Perhaps there had been nothing deeper than that. I kept comparing my relationship with Carleton to that which I had shared with Edwin. How romantic my first marriage had seemed, how perfect! And how foolish of me to think it was so! It has been a sham from the beginning. And yet I could not forget it. It had done something to me. People were affected by experiences, naturally. They became warped and suspicious. That was how I had become with Carleton.

The scent of roses, the heat of the sun on my hands, the buzzing of bees, and memories carried on the warm summer air . . . and then suddenly . . . it happened. I was not sure what it was. Except that I fell towards the rosebush and the sky began to recede further and further away. I had put my hand to my sleeve and touched something warm and sticky . . . I was aware of looking at my hands . . . They were as red as the roses in my basket. I was lying against the rosebush, slipping silently into the grass. It seemed to take a long time and then there was nothing.

I was in someone's arms being carried. Carleton. I heard a child's voice screaming: "I didn't do it. I didn't. I didn't." Vaguely I thought: That is Leigh. Then a voice —Jasper's. "You godless imp. You've killed the mistress."

After that the darkness was complete.

I was aware of Carleton all the time. Carleton talking, Carleton bending over me, Carleton angry. "How could this have happened? By God, I'm going to find out . . ." Carleton tender. "Arabella, my darling, darling Arabella . . ."

And awakening suddenly, a small figure at my bedside. "I didn't do it. I didn't. I didn't. It came right over my head. It did. It did."

The light was dim. I opened my eyes.

"Leigh," I said. "Little Leigh?"

A hot hand seeking my free one. I seemed to have lost the other.

"I didn't do it. I didn't. I didn't."

Then: "Come away, Leigh." That was Sally's voice, gentle, understanding. "She knows you didn't."

"Leigh," I said. "I know."

Sally said softly: "Poor mite. Brokenhearted he is. They think it was him taking potshots at the pigeons."

I knew then that I had been shot. As I had put up my hand to pluck the red roses the pellets had entered my arm.

The doctor had removed the pellets. They had been deeply imbedded it seemed, and that was why I had been so ill.

It was a blessing, they said, that they had struck me in the arm.

Carleton was often at my bedside and I felt a great comfort to see him there.

It was three days before he told me. Then I had recovered from the fever which the operation of taking the pellets away had caused.

"I shall never forget it," he said. "Leigh screaming and running and seeing you there on the grass. I was ready to kill the stupid boy . . . but I have my doubts now. Do you remember what happened?"

"No. I was picking roses. It was warm and sunny and now and then I heard the sound of shooting. There is nothing exceptional about that. Then it happened. . . . I didn't know what it was at first. I heard the shouting and I realized there was blood . . ."

"So you saw no one?"

"No one at all."

"Not before you started picking the roses?"

"No. I don't remember."

Carleton was silent. "I've been very worried, Arabella."

"Oh, Carleton. I'm glad. I'm so glad you care enough to be worried."

"Care enough! What are you talking about? Aren't you my wife? Aren't I your loving husband?"

"My husband, yes. Loving . . . I'm not sure . . ."

"Things have been difficult lately, I know. I expect it's my fault. All that fuss about the child we lost . . . as though it was your fault."

"I understand your disappointment, Carleton. I've been touchy, anxious, I suppose, disappointed in myself for having disappointed you."

"Foolish pair! We have so much. It makes one realize it when one comes near to losing it."

He bent over me and kissed me. "Get well quickly, Arabella. Be your old self. Flash your eyes, scorn me, lash me with your tongue. . . . Make it like it used to be. That's what I want."

"Have I been too gentle?"

"Aloof," he said, "as though there is something keeping us apart. There isn't, is there?"

"Nothing that I have put there."

"Then there is nothing."

I was content while he sat by my bed. I was longing to be well again and I was determined to bring about that happy state.

He said: "I was so worried about that shot. I have to find out where it came from. The boy was so insistent. I don't think he could be lying. He's a brave little fellow. Not afraid to own up when he's done wrong. He was so insistent. He was there alone. He is a good shot and I had given my permission for them to shoot the pigeons. He was doing nothing wrong. He said he wasn't shooting in your direction at all. There weren't any pigeons there. They were fluttering down from the roof. He said the shot went right over his head, to you, and it occurred to me that someone might have been hiding there in the bushes at the side of the house."

"Someone hiding to shoot me. Why?"

"That's what I wanted to find out. That's what bothers me. I had an idea, and I went to see Young Jethro."

"You think that he . . .?"

"It was an idea, and if it was possible to get to the bottom of this I'd made up my mind to. I went to the old barn where his father used to live and I said, 'I want a word with

you, Young Jethro.' He was a little puzzled and I said,
'Your father shot my cousin. Now my wife has been shot
in the arm—but that may have been a lucky chance—and
I wondered whether your family made a habit of shooting
at mine.' "

"Carleton! Do you really think . . .?"

"Not now. He swore to God that he had done no such
thing and I am sure a man with his beliefs would never
swear to God unless he was telling the truth. 'Master,' he
said, 'I've never killed none. If I was to, I'd be unworthy to
enter the Kingdom of Heaven. 'Tis wrong to kill. It says
so in the Bible. "Thou shalt not kill." Should I kill another soul I could suffer torment for it.' Then he fell down
on his knees and swore to me that he had not been near
the house that day. That he knew nothing of the accident.
He had no gun. I could search the barn. He never killed
. . . not even pigeons. He didn't think it was right and fitting to kill God's creatures . . . And so he went on and
on . . . and I was convinced that he was telling me the
truth."

"Perhaps it was Leigh, after all."

"It seems likely. He was there. He had the gun. He was
shooting pigeons. Yes, it seems very likely. And yet . . .
He was so insistent. He cried and cried. Sally couldn't
comfort him. He kept saying he didn't do it. The shot had
come right over his head . . . which points to the
bushes behind the house. Never mind. Perhaps he did.
Perhaps he didn't realize which way he was shooting. He's
not usually an untruthful boy."

"If he did, it was an accident."

"But of course. As if Leigh would want to hurt you. He
adores you. But I'm going to find out . . . if I can."

"Who else could it be? If it be? If it wasn't Leigh or
Young Jethro . . ."

"It could have been one of the servants who is afraid to
own up."

"Perhaps we should forget it."

"You're getting too excited. Yes, perhaps we should
forget it."

But I knew he went on thinking of it, and I lay back in bed feeling cherished and greatly comforted.

But not for long. As my arm began to heal and first it came out of its bandages and then out of its sling and I saw that there was only the faintest scar to remind me of it, I began to sense a tension in the house, a lurking fear, the awareness that all was not as it outwardly seemed.

"You've had a proper shock," Sally Nullens told me, and Ellen confirmed this. "First that miss," went on Sally, "then this. It's too much for one body to stand. It begins to have its effect on the nerves, that's what."

Ellen said: "It's funny how shocks come . . . never one at a time. It's often in twos and threes."

"Am I to look out for number three?" I asked.

Sally said: "It's always well to be on the lookout. But just at first we've got to get you well. I've got a very special cordial and it takes a lot of beating, don't it, Ellen?"

"Are you talking of your buttermilk one?"

"That's the one," said Sally. "You shall drink it every night, Mistress Arabella. You'll drop into a nice peaceful sleep and we all know there's nothing like that for putting you to rights."

So they talked to me, but although I drank Sally's buttermilk cordial, I did not sleep well. My anxieties, it seemed, went too deep to be lightly thrust aside.

My suspicions had returned. Did Carleton really love me? Did he really want me now that I had failed to give him a son? What a magnificent delusion he had created with the Roundheads when he had pretended he was one of them. He was as good an actor as Harriet was.

And Harriet? There was something about her. She was sleekly happy, although she was no longer so much with her son, and I did not believe this contentment came from motherhood. I remembered when she had come to England with Edwin and me. Was it the same satisfaction I had glimpsed on her face then?

What did it mean?

When I walked out in the gardens, my footsteps invariably took me towards the arbour. It was beginning to exert a fascination over me. Now that the trees were losing their leaves I could see it from my bedroom window and I made a habit of looking at it.

Once when I found my footsteps leading me that way, I heard my name being called and turning saw Chastity running after me.

"Don't go there, mistress," she said. "Don't go nowhere near that place. 'Tis haunted."

"Oh, nonsense, Chastity," I said. "There's no such thing as hauntings. Come with me and we'll go together."

She hesitated. She had always been particularly fond of me since the day when I had given her a pretty button.

"Come on. We'll go and look. I'll prove to you that there's nothing to fear. It's just four walls overgrown by shrubs because no one has cut them back for a long time."

She put her hand in mine, but I was aware that she was trying to drag me back as we went along.

I opened the door and stepped inside. The place smelt a little musty. The dampness of the wet wood and the smell of leaves permeated it.

They were together here . . . Harriet and Edwin . . . My eyes went to the window where the fanatical eyes of Old Jethro had looked in. I could almost hear the shattering of the glass, the firing of the fatal shot . . . at closer range than the one which had been fired at me. I could picture Harriet, stunned, and yet collecting her wits quickly enough to run to tell Carleton what had happened.

Chastity was looking up at me, her eyes round with horror.

"Mistress, it *is* haunted. Come away . . . now. . . ."

Yes, I thought. It is haunted . . . haunted by memories. I never want to come here again.

Chastity was tugging on my hands and we went outside.

"Well, you see," I said, "there was nothing to fear."

She looked at me curiously and said nothing. I noticed how hard she gripped my hand until we were well away from the arbour.

That night looking from my bedroom window I saw a light flickering close to the arbour. I stared, fascinated, watching it moving among the bushes like a will-o'-the-wisp.

Now the light had disappeared. A lantern, I guessed, and

I wondered who carried it and whether he—or she—had gone inside and for what purpose?

I watched for a long time, but I did not see the lantern again. I began to think that I had imagined it.

I was still feeling weak.

Sally said: "Women can take a year or two to recover from a miss. Some says it's worse than a birth. It's unnatural, like, you see. And then of course that other affair . . ."

She seemed to be right. I was not like the Arabella I had been. Sometimes I thought I would like to go to Far Flamstead and try to tell my mother something about the doubts and suspicions which seemed constantly to be chasing themselves round and round in my mind.

And yet I wanted to stay here. I felt there was something going on in the house, something which deeply concerned me. I wished I could shake off this uneasiness, this feeling of foreboding.

Was it really that someone had shot at me, had hoped to kill me? It had been said that I was lucky. The pellets had hit my arm. Had they gone into my head or some other vital part of my body, they could have been fatal.

If Leigh had not accidentally shot me, who had? Was it someone aiming at a pigeon . . . or at me?

Carleton had been summoned once more to Whitehall. He looked a little sad sometimes, as though he wondered what was going wrong with our marriage, for after that display of tenderness when I had had my accident, we seemed to be on edge, both of us. I was unable to express what I felt for him; indeed I was not sure. I wanted him to love me, to be with me, to act as a husband. It seemed sometimes that I was trying to make him a different person from what he was. I was suspicious, uncertain of him, asking myself whether it was possible for a man who had lived as he had to reform and become a faithful husband. I could not forget Edwin and the manner in which he deceived me; and I could see—while I was unable to prevent it—that I was allowing this to colour my life.

I continued to be fascinated by the arbour. One after-

348

noon when the household was quiet, I went out into the garden and almost involuntarily my footsteps led me there.

It was November now—a dankness everywhere; almost all the leaves had fallen and only the conifers gleamed a shiny green. Cobwebs were draped over them, for it was the season of spiders.

And as I came near to the arbour I heard a voice which seemed to be singing a mournful dirge. I went closer and to my amazement there against the wall of the arbour knelt a man. I recognized him at once as Young Jethro.

I approached and studied him. He was on his knees and his hands were clasped together as in prayer. Then I realized that he *was* praying.

He stopped suddenly. He must have been aware of my presence. He turned sharply and looked at me out of those wild eyes which were almost hidden by the unkempt eyebrows.

"What are you doing?" I asked.

"Praying," he said. "Praying to God. There have been murder done here. 'Tis an unhallowed place. I'm praying to God for the soul of my father."

"I understand," I said.

"Oh, God, save his soul from eternal torment," he said. "What he done, he done for the glory of God but the Book says, 'Thou shalt not kill' and that means even in His name. My father killed a man here. He were Satan's own, caught in Satan's work . . . but, the Lord says, 'Thou shalt not kill.' "

I said gently: "It was all long ago, Young Jethro. It is best to forget."

"He burns in hell. A good life and one false step and for it . . . he burns in hell."

I kept seeing it again. Should I ever forget it? The scene in the arbour and the madman with the gun. The lovers . . . caught there. Illicit love and Edwin dying instantly, and Harriet running into the house and the self-righteous man of God going back to his barn, the task he had set himself to do, done. And afterwards? Had he suffered remorse? He was a murderer no matter in which cause he had murdered. And he had disobeyed the law of God.

I felt stirred with pity for this strange, near-mad man. I

wanted to comfort him. To tell him that I who had suffered the loss of my husband through his father's action forgave. And he must forget.

But there would be no reasoning with him. I could see that reason and Young Jethro were strangers. There was only the law of God as he saw it, and he believed that his father, in spite of all his piety, had committed a mortal sin.

I turned, and as I walked away I heard him muttering his prayers.

There was one thing I was sure of now. Young Jethro had not been the one who fired the shot at me, and Carleton's theory that the Jethros harboured enmity towards our family because we were Royalist and Young Jethro thought we were responsible for the licentious state of the country had no foundation in truth.

Then it was someone else.

It was Leigh, I told myself. It must be so. Poor child, he had fired in the wrong direction and then was so terrified of what he had done that he had convinced himself that he hadn't done it.

I was all right now. All I had to do was regain my inner health, to muster my spirits, to throw off my misgivings and feel life was good again.

Carleton was still away. I was in the nursery with Sally and she was going through the children's clothes and trying to decide what was needed. Later we should go to London and buy what was required.

Both Benjie and Priscilla were having that afternoon nap which Sally insisted they have, and the boys were out riding.

I was on the point of telling Sally about Young Jethro's prayers at the arbour when Charlotte came in.

She went to the cots and looked at the sleeping children.

"How peaceful they look!" she murmured.

"Not much peace about them half an hour ago," said Sally. "Benjie was screaming his head off and Mistress Priscilla had fallen down and dirtied her clean dress."

"It's all forgotten now," commented Charlotte. "How

soon *their* troubles are over. I was thinking we ought to do something about the arbour. It's getting so overgrown."

"Yes," I said, alert suddenly.

"That old place should be pulled down, I reckon," put in Sally. "What do you think of this muslin, mistress? Priscilla is getting too big for it. It's in good order though. I'll wash it and put it away. Who knows when it might come in handy?"

I knew she was referring to the fact that in due course I should have another child. It was a habit of hers, done, I believe, to reassure me. Dear Sally!

"I went inside the old arbour. I couldn't resist it," said Charlotte. "What a musty old place it is! Yes, I do think it should be pulled down. The paving must have been quite pretty at one time."

I thought of the paving—a mosaic in pale blue and white, stained red with Edwin's blood and Harriet watching him, panic seizing her, wondering what she must do.

I had to stop these pictures coming into my mind every time anyone mentioned the arbour.

"I tripped over one of the paving-stones which was loose," went on Charlotte. "I stopped to fit it in place and I found these funny things . . . like little dolls. . . . They seemed to have been put under the loose stone. What are they?"

She drew two little figures from the pocket of her dress.

"What would you say they are meant to be?" she went on.

Sally had come to look. She turned pale, then I saw that they were wax models. One had a look of someone. The set of the eyes, the shape of the moulded nose. Myself!

I looked at Sally and saw the hot colour flame into her face which a moment before had been so pale.

"That's a witch's work," she said.

"What do you mean, Sally?" asked Charlotte. "They're children's toys, I think. But what were they doing under the paving stone in the arbour?"

Sally picked up the figure which resembled me. "You see where the pins have been. There . . . where you would have been carrying the child." She picked up the

351

other figure. "Oh, my God. I see what it's meant to be. It's the wax image of an unborn child."

We all looked at each other.

"How long have they been there, I wonder?" I said.

"I . . . I have only just found them," stammered Charlotte.

"It looks as if . . . " began Sally. "No, I can't say it." She turned to me and laid her hand on my shoulder. "Oh, my poor Mistress Arabella, now we know . . ."

"Know what?" I demanded. "What are you talking about?"

"It's witchcraft," she said. "It's killed the child . . . and it's meant to harm you."

Sally had kept the wax dolls. "I'll destroy these," she had said. "That's the best thing that can be done with them. The mischief they've done is over. It's a good thing you found them, Mistress Charlotte. Now we've got to keep our eyes open. At least we know what's going on."

When we had left her Charlotte said to me: "I wish I hadn't shown them to her. I'm sure they mean nothing. They must be dolls children have had at some time. They might have been there years and become misshapen."

"One of them had a look of me, Sally seemed to think."

"Well, she would because of the accident. I wish I hadn't been so thoughtless." She looked at me anxiously. "All this hasn't upset you, Arabella, has it?"

I assured her it hadn't, but of course it had.

I was very uneasy. Carleton was in London. I wished he were here. I told myself that if he had been I should have gone to him and told him of Charlotte's find and Sally's comment. I could imagine his laughter. But I wanted to hear his laughter. I wanted to hear him pour scorn on what he would call "old goodies' tales."

I went to bed early. I could not sleep. I lay listening to every sound, and how the boards creaked! I would start to doze and then start up suddenly because something had roused me. Probably my own uneasy thoughts.

I heard midnight strike and lay listening to the timbre of the tower clock chime. I lay wondering about Carleton and what he was doing at Whitehall. I thought of all the stories one heard of the life that was lived there. The King was surrounded by favourites like Lady Castlemaine, Moll Davies—although I believe her reign was over—and Nell Gwyn. They lived lightheartedly, promiscuously, and Carleton was a member of that Court. I had heard it said that the King enjoyed his company. How could I help wondering who else did?

A sound in the corridor. Yes, footsteps. Silently creeping.

I leaped out of bed. I was shaking. I kept thinking of a doll made in my image with pinholes showing in the wax. It had not lain under the flagstone so very long. Those holes were too fresh for that. And what was the use of pretending it had? And it had been made to look like me!

The light sound of a footfall. Someone was creeping slowly along . . .

Cautiously, silently, I opened the door and peeped out. A light was moving along. It came from a candle which was being carried.

She was going carefully, her lovely long hair flowing about her shoulders, her feet in soft slippers, a robe flowing open to show the edges of a silken bedgown.

Harriet!

If she turned now she would see me. But she did not turn. She went on along the corridor.

I closed my door and leaned against it. What was Harriet doing creeping along the corridor when the household was alseep?

In the morning, I thought, I will tell her I saw her and ask her where she was going.

But I did not ask, for when I left my room and went downstairs the first person I met was Carleton.

"Carleton!" I cried. "When did you come home?"

"Last night," he said. "Rather late."

"Where did you sleep?"

"In the grey room. I thought I wouldn't disturb you. Sally tells me you haven't been sleeping well of late."

"That . . . was thoughtful of you," I said coolly, thinking of Harriet creeping silently along the corridor.

Carleton had gone off for the day; he had some estate business to attend to. So much time spent at Court was not good for the estate, he said. It meant that when he did return he found arrears of work.

"Will you be back tonight?" I asked.

He kissed me tenderly. "I shall," he answered. "And however late I am I'll disturb you."

He kissed me with passion and my response was immediate. If only, I thought, all could be well between us, how much happier I should be.

I did not see Harriet during the morning. She seemed to have disappeared. Then I heard that the boys had gone riding with Gregory Stevens and Harriet had decided to accompany them. They would be away for most of the day, as Gregory had promised to take the boys to an inn where they could have a mug of ale and some hot bread and bacon. Chastity told me that they had gone off in high spirits.

It was a dark and misty afternoon. I was in my room when there was a knock on the door. It was Charlotte.

She looked strange, I thought, uneasy. But then she often did.

"Oh, Arabella," she said, "I'm glad I found you alone. There's something I wanted to say to you."

"Yes."

"Something is going on in this house. Oh, I don't mean witchcraft, as old Sally says. But something nevertheless."

"What?" I asked.

She was silent for a moment, then she said, "Oh, I know you think that I'm rather stupid . . ."

"Of course I don't."

"You don't have to pretend. Most people do. Well, perhaps not stupid, but not very bright and not attractive . . . not like you and Harriet, for instance."

"You're imagining this."

"I don't think I am. But I'm *not* stupid. There are things I see which some people miss. You, for instance . . ."

"Why don't you tell me what you came to say, Charlotte?"

"I'm trying to. It's not easy. I don't forget how you saved me once . . ."

"Oh, that's long ago."

"I've always remembered. Sometimes I wonder whether I should have done it. People think they will leave this world and then at the last minute they're afraid. I just thought there wasn't anything to live for. They had made so much fuss about Charles Condey . . . having that house party, talking of making the announcement . . . I just didn't think I could face it."

"I understand that."

"Harriet is evil, Arabella. Do you know that? Oh, I'm not sure about witchcraft. But I do know she is evil. She wantonly broke up my life . . . now she will do the same to you. She already did it once, didn't she? I knew how it was with her and Edwin. I knew right at the start. I daresay you'll despise me, but I listen at doors. I pry and peep and find out things. It's mean and underhand but it compensates me in a way. I don't have much life of my own so I live other people's. I know more than they do, because I listen and peep and that justifies me in a way because I'm not bright and attractive. Do you understand?"

"Of course I do. But, Charlotte . . ."

She waved her hand. "Listen. She married Uncle Toby, didn't she, because she wanted to come here and she wanted his name and title because she was determined he should get it. You don't think Benjie is Uncle Toby's son, do you?"

"Whose?" I asked.

"Are you so innocent, Arabella?"

I felt myself flushing hotly. "Charlotte, you are talking nonsense."

"No. She wanted a son who was a claimant. Benjie to follow on Edwin."

"Are you suggesting that she would dare hurt Edwin? That's nonsense."

"Perhaps I have said too much. You would rather not hear." She shrugged her shoulders. "Forgive me, Arabella. I wanted to repay you . . . for saving my life once, but

355

if you would be happier not knowing . . . if you would rather wait until doom overtakes you . . ."

"Tell me what you know," I said tersely.

"I know this. Edwin was her lover. He was shot when they were in the arbour. At that time she was already carrying his child. Leigh is not Charles Condey's son."

"I know," I said.

"So she deceived you with Edwin. Then she ran away, leaving you to look after your husband's bastard, and you did. Arabella, you are a good woman. It grieves me to see you treated thus. But you are blind . . . sometimes I think wilfully blind. You really thought Benjie was Uncle Toby's son. That was rather naive. Poor Uncle Toby, he had to die when she was pregnant."

"Are you suggesting she . . . killed him?"

"In a comfortable, natural sort of way which could hardly be brought against her. It wasn't difficult to excite the old gentleman. She knew he had already had his heart attack. Child's play. She knew she would do it sooner or later. So natural, they said, didn't they, an ageing husband, a young exciting wife."

"Oh, don't, Charlotte."

"I know you hate it. I wouldn't say anymore, but *you're* in danger, Arabella. Don't you see what they want?"

"They? Who?"

"Harriet and . . . Carleton."

"Carleton!"

"Surely you know. Why is he away so much? Is he in London, do you think? Edwin was away on secret business, wasn't he? Secret business with Harriet. She has their son. Benjie. Have you noticed that Carleton is rather fond of him? She has proved *she* can have sons. They want to marry. They want to take Eversleigh and rule it between them."

"Carleton already does that for Edwin. You've forgotten Edwin. Eversleigh is Edwin's."

"What do you think they plan for Edwin? A little pigeon shooting? No, perhaps that wouldn't do. The last one was not a success."

"Charlotte, this is madness."

"There's madness in this house, Arabella. The madness

of greed and illicit passion and hatred and murder. Open your eyes and look. Who was the first on the scene when you were shot? He hadn't far to come from the bushes, had he? Don't you see? Death's hovering over your head. Like a great black bird. Can't you hear his wings? You first, then Edwin . . ."

"Oh, no . . . no . . ."

"They are together. I've seen them."

I closed my eyes. I pictured Harriet moving stealthily along the corridor, a candle in her hand. I could hear Carleton's voice: ". . . Rather late. I thought I wouldn't disturb you . . ." I cried: "No. No!" But it could fit so easily.

"They have a meeting place. They leave notes there. In the arbour. I have seen some of them. That was how I came to find the wax dolls. It's a sort of bravado that makes them go there. It's like snapping their fingers at fate. Then, of course, not many people would want to go there after dark, would they? It satisfies their sense of the macabre . . . and at the same time it's safe. That's a good point. They don't want to be discovered before they've completed their plans . . . their devious, hideous plans. Oh, Arabella, you look at me so strangely. I think you don't believe me." She shrugged her shoulders. "Perhaps I shouldn't have told you. But how could I keep silent? I tell you death is right overhead. It's come very near to you and you've escaped by the luck of the moment. It frightens me, Arabella. I don't know what to do . . . to save you . . . to save Edwin. I know what is in their black hearts. I have seen them together, I have listened to them. But you doubt me. I tell you what. Let us go to the arbour . . . now. They leave notes there for each other. Perhaps she is there now . . . with him. Who can say? She said she was going riding, but is she, I wonder?"

"As soon as Carleton comes in I shall talk to him," I said. "I shall talk to Harriet."

"You cannot mean that. What would they say? Charlotte is lying. Charlotte is mad, and they might even convince you. They would be shocked to think they had not been careful enough to escape detection. But I know it would only postpone your fate. You are doomed, Arabella—you

357

and your son Edwin. No matter what I reminded them of they would stand together against me . . . and you would believe them because you wanted to. You won't give yourself a chance to see the proof . . . even now."

"Show me this proof," I said.

Her eyes lit up suddenly. "Oh, Arabella, I'm so glad you're ready to look at the truth. Let us go to the arbour now. I saw her go in there before she went off. I know where they hide their messages. If he has not already been in to take it we shall find it. Come now."

She put her arm through mine and together we went out of the house.

The arbour looked dismal in the dim light of a November afternoon, and I felt sick with fear as we went across the grass.

"It's a horrible place," said Charlotte. "I always hated it. Come on . . . quickly, Arabella."

She pushed open the door and we went in. I was relieved that no one was there. She stopped and lifted the broken paving-stone.

"There's nothing there," I said.

"There's another one over there. Look."

I went to the spot where she pointed. She was right. I lifted the stone. There was a piece of paper there. I felt sick with horror. Something was written on it but I could not see what.

"It looks just like childish scribble," I said.

I turned. I was alone, and the door was shut.

"Charlotte," I called. I went towards the door.

I heard her voice: "It's jammed. I can't open it." She was right. It would not budge. Then I noticed that the key which usually hung on a nail there was missing.

"I'll go and get someone," she called.

So I was alone in the arbour. I looked at the paper in my hand. Just a scrawl across it. What did it mean? A code of some sort, perhaps. What a foolish notion. It was like something Priscilla might have done.

I sat down on the bench. How I hated the place. Edwin . . . Harriet . . . and now Carleton and Harriet. History grimly repeating itself.

"I don't believe it," I said aloud. "I can't believe it."

I heard a sound. I was alert, listening. They must have come to release me. I called out. Then I heard a sound which made me cold with terror. It was the unmistakable crackle of wood and I saw that smoke was seeping into the arbour. The place was on fire.

I ran to the door and threw myself against it. It did not budge. I understood. It was locked from the outside.

"Oh, God," I prayed. "What is happening to me? Charlotte. Charlotte . . . is it you, then, who are trying to kill me?"

"Let me out!" I cried. "Let me out!"

I hammered on the door. How firm the old wood was. The heat was getting intolerable. It could not be long before this wooden structure was ablaze.

I felt myself fainting, for the heat was becoming intense. This is the end, I thought. I should die without knowing why Charlotte hated me so.

I felt a rush of air suddenly. Then the flames roared up.

I was seized, picked up and carried into oblivion.

Old Jethro had killed Edwin, and Young Jethro had saved my life.

Regaining my consciousness I was vaguely aware of him as he knelt beside me, giving thanks to God. "A miracle," he was shouting. "God has seen fit to show me a miracle."

I was carried into the house. He put me into Sally's charge.

To have faced death once more and this time being saved only by Jethro's miracle gave me a strangely exalted feeling. I suppose my mind was wandering and I was unaware that I was lying on my bed. Sally had sent for the doctor. I had suffered no burns, only a scorching of the skin of one hand. It was the smoke which had come near to suffocating me. Not more than a few minutes could have lapsed between the time Charlotte set the arbour alight and Jethro got me out. He had been watching us. It seemed that he had spent many hours of his days watching and praying at the arbour. He had seen Charlotte lock me in; he had seen her throw inflammable oil on the bracken about the arbour and on its walls and ignite the place. Then he had come straight in and got me out.

He was like a man possessed. He had prayed for a sign that his father was forgiven and taken into Heaven, and this he was sure was it. His father had taken a life and he had been given the chance to save one.

"Praise God in His Heaven," he cried.

I was deeply shocked, said the doctor. I must lie quietly. I must take care.

And indeed I had every reason to be shocked. Within a short time murder had been twice attempted and I its victim. No one—except Sally—could say that my miscarriage was due to anything but natural misfortune, but that there had been two attempts on my life was obvious.

When Carleton returned to the house he came at once to my room.

When I saw his face I asked myself how I could ever have been so foolish as to have doubted him. If ever I needed proof that he loved me, it was there in his eyes for me to read.

He knelt by my bed. He took my hand, the one which was not bandaged, and kissed it.

"My dearest, what is going on? Is this a madhouse?"

"I think there is madness in it," I said.

He knew that I had been shut in the arbour but when he heard that Charlotte had locked me in, he was astounded.

"Where in God's name is she?" he asked. "We must find her. She will do someone an injury. She must have gone completely mad."

But Charlotte had disappeared.

They searched for her but they could not find her. Carleton stayed by my bedside. He made me tell him everything that had happened. I could hold nothing back now. It all came tumbling out, my doubts, my suspicions, my fears, and as I talked and he listened there came to us a revelation and that was that we had been brought face to face with ourselves. We loved each other; no one had ever or could ever mean the same to us. Edwin had not really died in the arbour; he had lived on to stand between us. We had both of us built up our own image of Edwin and his importance in our life. I had convinced myself that I had truly loved him and that because he had deceived me I would never trust anyone again. Carleton had believed that I would never let him take that place which had been Edwin's. I think we saw then how foolish we had been. How we had allowed a false conception to corrode our marriage.

Lying there in my bed with Carleton sitting beside me while we talked to each other in low, intense voices, laying bare our innermost thoughts, the revelation came to us. It was a chance to begin again, free from our shackles, to live again to find our happiness together.

One of the servants going into the library early next morning found a letter which was addressed to me.

My hands shook as I opened it, for I saw that it was in Charlotte's handwriting.

"How did you get this?" I demanded.

"It was in the library, mistress," was the answer, "propped up against the books on one of the shelves."

I opened it and read:

Dear Arabella,

I owe you an explanation. When I had set fire to the arbour I came into the house and watched from one of the windows. When I saw Young Jethro carry you out I knew that was the end for me. Do you remember when you came with Edwin and Harriet you hid in that secret cavity in the library? Few people knew about it. It has been kept like that for family emergencies. . . . I went and hid myself there. I took paper and pen there and I am writing this to you now. I hate anything to be unfinished. So I don't just want to disappear. If I did it would create one of those mysteries about which people speculate and make up all sorts of legends.

You know how it has always been with me. I am the outsider . . . the disappointment. Even my parents couldn't hide their exasperation with me sometimes. I never shone at parties. I remember hearing my mother say once, "How are we ever going to find a husband for Charlotte?" I was fifteen at the time. I was so desperately unhappy I decided to take my life. Cut my veins as the Romans die. So you see when you found me at the

361

parapet there it was not the first time I had contemplated taking my life. It was a sort of balm to my anger. They'll be sorry then, I would say, and would be comforted contemplating their sorrow. People who constantly threaten a suicide for the discomfiture of others rarely do it. But there can come a time when there is no turning back.

I'm giving myself the luxury of writing to you now and I must resist the temptation to go on and on. I have to be brief.

I thought I was going to marry Charles Condey but Harriet spoilt that. If I had married him I might have settled down and become an ordinary wife—not very exciting, of course, but then Charles was not exciting. He was the one for me. How I hated her. I could have killed her. When I found out Edwin was her lover I was comforted in a way. I had not been the only one who had suffered. It shows you my nature, which is not at all admirable, I fear.

Then we came home and when I saw Carleton I admired him so much. He seemed to be in command of his life as I never could be. He is the sort of person I should have liked to be. My parents were always saying what a pity it was he was married to Barbary, and when she died I heard them say, "Now if Carleton married Charlotte, what a marvellous solution that would be." I don't think I should have thought of it as a possibility but for that. Then I started to think about it. Why not? It would be convenient. Married to Carleton. I thought that would be wonderful. I almost loved Harriet for preventing my marriage to Charles Condey.

Then you married Carleton so suddenly and unexpectedly because you'd always seemed to dislike each other. I hadn't thought of *you* as a rival. It wasn't that I hated *you*. I could never do that. I just hated life and fate or whatever you call it which had been against me from the start. I watched Harriet. I saw how she used people and I said to myself, why shouldn't I use people too? Of course I know she is very handsome and amusing and people are attracted by her, but if you have none of these gifts you can be subtle and clever and work in the dark. So that was what I did. I thought that if you died Carleton would be so distressed he would turn to me. I believe my mother would have done everything she could to bring about a marriage between us. I knew how Carleton felt about you. I'd seen him watching you.

362

I know him well. I know all people well. When you don't have much life of your own, you watch other people . . . you *live* other people's lives. The sound of his voice when he spoke of you . . . the look in his eyes. I knew that if you died he would not care very much, and if it was convenient, which it would have been, and if there was a little gentle persuasion from the family . . . someone to look after the children . . . it could well be. That was what I worked for. As for Harriet, he disliked her. I don't know what it is about people like those two. They are both experienced with the other sex . . . both very attractive to people . . . and yet with each other there is an instant dislike. He hated Harriet being in this house. He hated her influence with you. I knew that he would never marry her—nor she, him, unless it was to get control of Eversleigh. And that was Edwin's. She was proud to have her Benjie next in line, but she was leaving that to fate. She would never hurt Edwin. All she wanted was a place of comfort. That was what she had worked for all her life.

So it was you I wanted out of the way. I wanted Carleton. He saw how I liked the children. He once said to me: "You should have had children, Cousin Charlotte." That seemed to me a signpost. I started to plan. I knew how things were between you. I understood you both well. He was angry because he thought you cared for Edwin as you never could for him, and you couldn't forget how Edwin had deceived you and you thought Carleton was doing the same. You were both of you pouring poison into the marriage cup. You deserved to lose each other.

I used to dream of the years ahead, Carleton and I married, children of our own. That was what I wanted. Then I would be able to forget everything that led up to it. I'm telling you this because I hate loose ends. I want you to understand why I did what I did. I don't want you to say: "Oh, Charlotte was mad." Charlotte was not mad. Charlotte was clever. She knew what she wanted and she was only trying to get it. But things went wrong. I shot at you from the bushes, but you moved at the wrong moment and you were only wounded in the arm and that put you on guard which was not helpful to me.

Then I decided that I must act quickly because you were going to be very watchful after the shooting. I put the wax dolls in the arbour. I was going to make Sally suspicious of Harriet. I was going to make it believed that she was a witch. After all, people were only too ready to accept that. They would say it was witchcraft which made you lose the child . . . though I had no hand in that. Of course it wasn't witchcraft that wounded you. But it could be said that the Devil guided Leigh's hand. That was what people *were* saying. Then I thought of the arbour. That would have worked but for Young Jethro. Who could have believed that a mad man could have spoilt all my plans?

It's over for me now. I am caught. What can I do? I have to put into practice what I had often thought of doing and failed to do before. This time there is no turning back.

As soon as it is dark I am going to creep out of this house. I shall walk to the sea. Look in the cave . . . you remember the cave? You hid there while you waited for horses to bring you to the house. There you will find my cloak . . . high on a rock where the tide cannot reach it. I shall have disappeared from your life forever. I am going to walk into the sea . . . and walk, and walk . . .

Good-bye, Arabella. You can be happy now. Learn to understand Carleton, as he will learn to understand you.

Charlotte.

We found her cloak where she had said it would be. We went to the hidden cavity behind the library books. There she had left paper and pen, so we knew it was all as she had said.

Poor Charlotte, I think of her often. Where the arbour was we have made a flower garden. The roses flourish there, and we have cleared away the charred bracken and it has become part of the garden. No one says it's haunted now. Few remember that once an arbour stood there.

Harriet left us only a few weeks after Charlotte's death.

The elder brother of Gregory Stevens was killed when his horse threw him and Gregory inherited lands and title. Harriet married him. They had long been lovers. They went, taking Benjie with them. Harriet told me that he was Gregory's son.

I see them about twice a year. Harriet has lost her slim

364

and willowy figure. She is in truth a little plump but I don't think that detracts from her charm. She still retains that, and now that she is contented with life, having achieved her goal, seems to live very happily.

And I too. Carleton and I have our son, Carl. It is a good life. Not without its conflicts, of course. We rage against each other now and then, but our love deepens as time passes and we know that we belong to each other and nothing can alter that.

This morning I was at the arbour cutting roses to fill my basket, and I realized suddenly that I saw only the beautiful flowers now.

I had learned to bury the past, and when I did remember it, to see it as an experience which would show me the way to preserve the contentment which life was offering me.

I said something of this to Carleton. He was inclined to be flippant—but then he often is, I have discovered, when he is most serious.

I am content. Life is good. It is for us to keep it so.

A-3

Romantic Fiction

If you like novels of passion and daring adventure that take you to the very heart of human drama, these are the books for you.

☐	AFTER—Anderson	Q2279	1.50
☐	THE DANCE OF LOVE—Dodson	23110-0	1.75
☐	A GIFT OF ONYX—Kettle	23206-9	1.50
☐	TARA'S HEALING—Giles	23012-0	1.50
☐	THE DEFIANT DESIRE—Klem	13741-4	1.75
☐	LOVE'S TRIUMPHANT HEART—Ashton	13771-6	1.75
☐	MAJORCA—Dodson	13740-6	1.75

Buy them at your local bookstores or use this handy coupon for ordering:

HELEN MacINNES

Helen MacInnes's bestselling suspense novels continue to delight her readers and many have been made into major motion pictures. Here is your chance to enjoy all of her exciting novels, by simply filling out the coupon below.

☐	ABOVE SUSPICION	23101-1	1.75
☐	AGENT IN PLACE	23127-5	1.95
☐	ASSIGNMENT IN BRITTANY	22958-0	1.95
☐	DECISION AT DELPHI	C2790	1.95
☐	THE DOUBLE IMAGE	23512-2	1.95
☐	FRIENDS AND LOVERS	23538-6	1.95
☐	HORIZON	23434-7	1.75
☐	I AND MY TRUE LOVE	23303-0	1.75
☐	MESSAGE FROM MALAGA	X2820	1.75
☐	NEITHER FIVE NOR THREE	23566-1	1.95
☐	NORTH FROM ROME	23285-9	1.75
☐	PRAY FOR A BRAVE HEART	22907-6	1.75
☐	REST AND BE THANKFUL	23621-8	1.95
☐	THE SALZBURG CONNECTION	23611-0	1.95
☐	THE SNARE OF THE HUNTER	23502-5	1.95
☐	THE VENETIAN AFFAIR	23667-6	1.95
☐	WHILE STILL WE LIVE	23099-6	1.95

Buy them at your local bookstores or use this handy coupon for ordering:

A-8